To The Board of St[...]

At the time of t[...] my great-grandson [...] a detective agency has been continuing to search for my sole heir, Fitz Connely of Ireland. In the event of my death I wish the hunt to go on until he is either found or it is established that he is dead. Halsey De Vilbiss, my representative on the board, shall have the responsibility of seeing that my wishes in this matter are carried out.

Sarah Stockwell Tyler

After the letter was read, a silence descended upon the boardroom. The time-darkened oil portraits of the various Stockwells and Tylers who had built the family fortune stared down with stiff neutrality as if they, like the board members present, were mulling over the ramifications of what they'd just heard.

It was obvious to Patrice, as it must have been to the others, that it was to Halsey's advantage if Fitz Connely was *not* found. Sarah's estate would be in limbo and Halsey would continue to administer it and to exercise control on the Stockwell board.

Fitz was also a threat to Max Tyler, who represented all the Tylers' interests on the board. If Fitz was as much a Tyler as the rest of Max's clan, he might be able to claim his rightful share of all that they had inherited. Indeed, if Fitz could make such a claim stick, his combined shares would come perilously close to giving Fitz, the illegitimate Irish heir, control of the Stockwell board. That, Patrice realized, would threaten not only Max, but all of the Stockwell board members—including herself. . . .

Other books in the RIVERVIEW series:

RIVERVIEW

PRIDE OF PLACE

KATHLEEN FULLER

IVY BOOKS • NEW YORK

The author of this work is a member of the
National Writers Union.

Ivy Books
Published by Ballantine Books

Produced by Butterfield Press, Inc.
133 Fifth Avenue
New York, New York 10003

Library of Congress Catalog Card Number: 88-91152

ISBN 0-8041-0032-2

Manufactured in the United States of America

First Edition: September 1988

With Peace and Love for my daughter,
Kathy Gutierrez of Cottonwood, Arizona.

THE STOCKWELLS

Governor Matthew Adams Stockwell: Patriarach of the family, deceased
Mary Linstone Stockwell: His first wife, and mother of his children, deceased
Brenda "Buffy" Cabot Stockwell: His second wife
Jack Houston: Buffy Stockwell's present husband

James Linstone Stockwell: Governor's eldest son, widowed
Patrice Stockwell O'Keefe: His eldest child, divorced
Matthew Sykes Stockwell: His eldest son
Michael Stockwell: His youngest son
Lisa Stockwell: His youngest child

Alice Stockwell Lewis: Governor's eldest daughter
David Lewis: Alice's husband

Jonathan Charles Stockwell: Governor's youngest son
Ellen Smith Stockwell: His wife
Peter Stockwell: Jonathan and Ellen's only child

Terry Stockwell: Governor's daughter, deceased
Holly Stockwell Meyerling: Her daughter, divorced from first husband, Christopher Millwood, married to Zelig Meyerling
Nicholas Millwood: Holly's only child

Susan Stockwell Wells Gray: Governor's youngest child, widowed
Decatur "Deke" Wells: Susan's child

THE TYLERS
Sarah Stockwell Tyler: Governor Stockwell's eldest sister
Max Tyler: Sarah Tyler's grandson
Diana Tyler: Sarah Tyler's granddaughter, Max's younger sister
Beth and Carrie Tyler: Sarah Tyler's great-granddaughters
Tyrone Fitzwilliam Connely: Sarah Tyler's illegitimate great-grandson

PRIDE OF PLACE

BOOK ONE

1

T HE ROLLS-ROYCE limousine glided along the banked curves of the mountainside highway. Seated beside the liveried chauffeur on the front seat, a redheaded young woman attired in an expensive cocktail dress peered nervously outside the window at the riverbank scenery. "There it is!" she exclaimed as they eased around a bend. A crest of hill emerged, crowned by a palatial manor house, its facade of white Ossining marble gleaming in the starlight. "Riverview."

"Still a fair distance," the driver replied. "Twenty minutes or more. Don't be twistin' like that now to see what you've seen before," he added. "You'll be wrinklin' your fancy gown."

"Sorry, Pa. I keep forgetting it's a week's wages I've got on my back." Unconsciously she mimicked his brogue, a habit Kathleen O'Lunney fell into when she was in her father's presence.

Kathleen had been a small child when her parents had split. After living with her mother, she hadn't seen much of her father for years. Then her mother died, but Kevin O'Lunney's job as chauffeur at the Riverview estate had precluded having his daughter with him, so he'd sent Kathleen to a Catholic boarding school. When she'd started attending college at SUNY Purchase—about an hour's distance from Riverview—Kathleen and her father had at last begun seeing each other with real frequency. The reemergence of her childhood brogue now helped Kathleen through some of the awkwardness of their relationship.

"And well worth the cost." Responding, Kevin turned from the road to smile at his daughter. "Lovely as you are, and looking the proper lady for sure."

"Ladies don't have freckles." Kathleen wrinkled her nose. "Nor hair the color of tomatoes, perm or no perm."

"You're the bonny Irish lass you are, and what beauty can compare with that? So stop denyin' yourself. There's no lady at Riverview can compare."

"You wouldn't be prejudiced now? Bein' my pa and all?"

"Not a bit of it."

"Well, thanks, Pa." Kathleen leaned over to kiss him on the cheek. "I need all the reassurance I can get." Still, the prospect of a family dinner at Riverview with Matt Stockwell was making her apprehensive. Matt might be a renegade Stockwell, but he was a Stockwell of Riverview nonetheless. "Why does this road wind so instead of going straight to the top?" she asked, her tone edgy. "We're not even on the estate yet."

"No, indeed. We've been running alongside the border for the last five minutes, though. And another five to come before we turn in at the main gate."

"All Riverview. All fenced in and patrolled," Kathleen remarked. "What do they need it all for, the Stockwells? Most of them are never here anyway."

"Ah, well it's only three thousand acres now. And most of that wild forest land. There's estates twice the size in Ireland, and owned by the bloody Brits, too." The latter reference was delivered in a tone of bitterness.

2

"If the Stockwells can afford to keep up three thousand acres, you'd think they'd build a straight road instead of all this circling around the mountain."

"Sure and you can blame your darlin' Matthew's great-granddad, the governor's father, for that. A far-seein' man with an eye for his privacy he was. Bought his first automobile, it's said, and then realized there was no road to take it to Riverview. Along about the time he decided to build one, he heard about this fellow Henry Ford in Detroit starting to turn automobiles out on assembly lines at a price for farmers and other poor folk. 'Noise buggies,' old Mr. Stockwell called them, and he announced his intention not to have their fumes corruptin' the fresh air of Riverview, nor their ugliness spoilin' his view. So he decided to build a road because it was needed for his family's personal use, but one which would give him no bother from future motorists. He was wealthy enough, you see, to be havin' his cake and the eatin' of it, too."

"But how could he do that?" asked Kathleen. "Aren't highways built by the federal government, or by the state with federal aid?"

"Now how is it you're so smart about such things?" her father asked.

"Courtesy of Government One oh one." Kathleen told him.

"Well, I've no wish to be cynical, me darlin', but the fact is that a college education likely doesn't teach the half of it when it comes to the gentry of the Hudson River Valley. New York State and the federal government as well have always done pretty much what the Stockwells want in local matters such as highway construction. After consultation with the Rockefellers, the Harrimans, and the Vanderbilts, of course. But it's not likely they'd stand in the way of Stockwell comfort any more than a Stockwell would be standin' in the way of theirs."

"Noblesse noblige." Kathleen nodded. "Believe it or not, Pa, college is where I learned about that."

"And did they teach you how far an almighty Stockwell might go to insure his privacy?"

"No."

"Then I'll tell you. The governor's father, he bought up all the surrounding property within sight of the Riverview manor house on a clear day. All the land he didn't already own, that is. This included a small village name of Pleasant Haven."

"Pleasant Haven?" Kathleen's brow furrowed. "I've never heard of a town by that name around here."

"Nor will you. It doesn't exist anymore, you see. Courtesy of Mr. Stockwell. He bought the land under the buildings and stores and shut them down. Then with the homeowners havin' no place to go for food, nor clothes, he picked up the houses and small farms for a song. Five years, more or less, it took, and Pleasant Haven was gone."

"But what happened to the people who lived there?"

"Sure now, didn't many of them resettle in the new place we call Riverview Heights? It stands today with a depot for those who want to visit the Stockwells by train. But out of eye from Riverview manor, behind the mountain, to be sure. The land is owned by the family, and the stores are financed by the bank that's owned by the family."

"But that's awful!"

"Ah, but you see, there's only two kinds of people in the world, Kathleen—landlords and tenants. The lord of the manor proposes, the landlord's agent disposes, and the tenant-folk make the necessary adjustments. It's always the way."

"But why was the original village disposed of that way? What did it have to do with the highway?"

"Sure and Mr. Stockwell, he wanted the highway off-routed from Riverview. Pleasant Haven was in the path of the detour he desired."

"But that's heartless."

"Oh, he wouldn't have seen it that way a-tall, a-tall. It was only his comfort concerned him. Some twenty years later he saw to it that the interstate was looped seventeen miles so as not to come too close to his property. And

4

didn't the railroad accommodate him by detouring its tracks off the straight-and-narrow so that the soot and smoke from the steam engines wouldn't discolor the fairway of the Stockwell estate golf course. But no malice in any of it, Kathleen. Just their due so far as the almighty Stockwells of Riverview were concerned.''

''The almighty Stockwells of Riverview,'' Kathleen echoed, and then asked with some distress, ''Pa, whatever have I gotten myself into?''

2

''OUR CHAUFFEUR'S DAUGHTER?'' Jonathan Charles Stockwell had just been told that his nephew Matthew Sykes Stockwell had invited a guest to share the Stockwells' traditional Sunday evening family dinner. ''I don't understand.'' Jonathan raised eyebrows accustomed from birth to riding herd on the proprieties. ''What can you two possibly have in common?''

''Love,'' Matt replied, his usually serious coffee-colored eyes dancing with joy. ''We're in love, Uncle Jonathan. We're talking about getting married. And so I thought it was time the rest of the family got to know Kathleen.''

The family was gathered for cocktails in the Riverview sitting room, one of the mansion's more comfortable chambers. A homey, comfortable atmosphere was created with Early American overstuffed sofas and chairs and small antique maple tables with hand-braided throw rugs, which although among the finest examples of American folk art were not hung on the walls but scattered on the parquet floors.

A Hepplewhite table in one corner displayed a valuable assortment of colonial sewing boxes and thimbles, and canvasses by painters of the Hudson River school, Thomas Cole and Frederick Church, hung on the nearby walls.

Above the knotty pine mantel sat a stirrup cup crafted by Paul Revere. Over it hung a likeness in oils done in the twentieth-century traditionalist style by top-flight society portrait artist Aaron Shikler. The painting depicted the late Matthew Adams Stockwell, two-term governor of New York State and a leading contender for the Republican presidential nomination in the 1960s.

Despite all its precious artifacts, the sitting room had been designed for informal intimacy rather than show. By contrast, the assorted Stockwell family relatives had dressed for Sunday dinner, as was the custom at Riverview. The men were attired in formal jackets, and the women—except for Diana Tyler, whose causal dress was an off-the-rack slip-on from a SoHo boutique—wore one-of-a-kind designer gowns.

Matt's sister, Patrice, wore a particularly stylish, ankle-length, asymmetrical spiral twist in emerald wool crepe fashioned exclusively by haut-monde designer Emanuel Ungaro. Baring one shoulder with a golden bow gathering the material at the other, the evening gown flattered Patrice's svelte, petite figure, contrasting beautifully with her auburn hair. In the wake of Matt's declaration, Patrice automatically smoothed the bow.

Such bows were something of a trademark with her. Whether wearing bikini or evening gown, shirtwaist or cocktail dress, culotte top or business-jacketed blouse, Patrice was rarely without the frill of a bow. Her wardrobe included satin bows and string bows, floppy silk and crinkly taffeta, bows that were stiff and bows that were droopy.

At thirty-two Patrice was a businesswoman known for playing hardball in both the advertising and financial worlds. But even when her shrewd brown eyes were regarding some male adversary through her tortoiseshell glasses, her small, slender hands would drift over one of

6

her bows and find confirmation of her femininity. Patrice could be hard as nails; her bows indicated that she could be soft as well. Growing up surrounded by men in a family that still looked at its male members for direction and leadership, Patrice had always equated feminine softness with vulnerability. The bows were her one concession to her feminine side. And divorced—although still going by her married name of O'Keefe rather than her maiden name of Stockwell—Patrice had reason to feel vulnerable. The happiness of a satisfying relationship with a man had eluded her since her marriage had ended. More than the other family members present, she had reason to greet her brother's declaration with cynicism. Nevertheless, Patrice was the first to cross over to Matt and congratulate him with a kiss.

"I think Kathleen is terrific," she said. "I know you're going to be very happy."

Matt grinned down at her gratefully. A long-muscled, tousle-haired man of thirty who thrived outdoors, Matt was as tall and lanky as Patrice was petite. Reaching down with a curled finger, he flipped the small golden bow at the shoulder of her gown. "Thanks, sis."

Patrice's gesture paved the way for the others to react to Matt's news. The first to follow her lead was their cousin Holly—Mrs. Zelig Meyerling. Patrice stood aside as sleek, golden Holly, tall, poised, and with an aristocratic air that had always characterized her, kissed Matt on the cheek and wished him well.

"We haven't set the date yet," Matt said anxiously, wearing the look of a man who feared he might have spoken precipitously and was wondering how the woman in his life would react to the foot in his mouth. "I mean, nothing's definite."

"Male-female relationships are like diplomacy," Holly's husband, Zelig Meyerling, an urbane man in his midforties, reassured Matt. "Nothing is ever definite, but somehow arrangements are consummated."

"No wonder the country was in such a mess when

7

Zelig was secretary of state," Matt's uncle Jonathan muttered to his wife, Ellen.

Zelig did not hear the remark, but Patrice did. How can Uncle Jonathan, of all people, take a snobbish attitude toward Matt and Kathleen? she wondered. After all, Aunt Ellen was his secretary before he married her, and everyone knew that they had had to get married because her cousin Peter had already been conceived. Peter Stockwell's remarks to his cousin Matt were terse.

It isn't so much that Peter's mind is muddied up with outmoded class distinctions as his father's is, Patrice thought, but that he always withholds approval until he's weighed the effect of the match on his own self-interest.

Peter was single-mindedly ambitious, an attitude he had learned from his mother. Patrice didn't like him. At age twenty-seven he was almost five years younger than she and unmarried. Harvard Business School had given him a certain polish, and no one could deny his sharp intelligence, particularly in business; but his underlying personality had changed little from the childhood bully Patrice remembered him to be.

He even looks like a bully, she thought. Not even Peter's twice-a-year made-to-order suits from his Edinburgh tailors could conceal his somewhat brutish physique. Of medium height, Peter had exceptionally wide shoulders, a powerful barrel chest, and broad hands shaped naturally into fists. His features were heavy, dark, and brooding, his coal-black eyes ever-watchful. Some women, Patrice knew, found him attractive. But she wasn't one of them.

Still, she reflected wryly, he loves his mother. It was true. Peter suffered his father, Jonathan, who was recognized by those closest to him as the family fool, but he adored his mother. If there were a guiding light in Peter's life in his scramble for power and control of the Stockwell holdings, it was Ellen Smith Stockwell.

During the years Patrice had been growing up at Riverview, Aunt Ellen had been a faint shadow. It was one thing for a mere secretary to marry into the mighty Stockwell family; it was quite another to be accepted by them. Of course, the circumstances of the marriage—a son born to her and Jonathan not quite seven months after the wedding—were never mentioned. Nor were there ever any allusions to Ellen's humble background—her most common of maiden names, "Smith," summed it up very nicely for the Stockwells. What more was there to say?

Ellen had quickly learned that if the Stockwells ranked with the Rockefellers as the most prestigious family in New York State, then her husband, Jonathan, was least among them. Jonathan, the governor's youngest son, had no talent for politics, no head for business, and no gift for society. From the time he'd reached manhood, he'd been relegated to the background, and his wife was expected to join him there.

Obediently, Ellen had faded into the woodwork. She had earned a certain grudging admiration as an exceedingly devoted mother, but other than that she was politely ignored. It was only when Peter had surprised the family by succeeding spectacularly as his father's surrogate in various Stockwell enterprises that the family realized how assiduously Ellen had been grooming her son to take his rightful place in the dynastic pecking order. Peter's ability and perseverance in business placed him on a par with his uncles.

With her son's rise to power, Ellen had emerged from the shadows, and now she was no longer the colorless woman she had once seemed. Although her years showed, as her son's success had increased her confidence, she had taken more of an interest in her personal grooming. While she herself had little sense of style or of what to do with her slim-hipped, rather linear figure, of late she had put herself in the hands of those with expertise. The result had forced even the Stockwell family to take notice. Tonight muted shades of warm pink and tangerine lent color to her somewhat sallow complexion, and a clever use of eyeliner brought out the deep, lustrous black of the pupils she had passed on to her son. Her eyebrows, which she'd once plucked into a thin-lined

1920's vampish style, had been allowed to grow out and were now shaped fully to round the narrowness of her face.

Yes, indeed, Patrice thought as she watched Ellen plant a dry kiss on her Matt's cheek, Uncle Jonathan's wife may have been a frump, but grown-up Peter's mother has come a long way.

"Every day is Mother's Day for her," Carrie Tyler sang low and cynically in Patrice's ear.

Carrie's irreverence was to be expected. At age twenty she was the youngest family member present, and she delighted in shocking. While showing a lack of respect for Aunt Ellen was only a minor flouting of convention, Carrie was certainly not one to forgo it.

"How are you, Carrie?" Diplomatically, Patrice changed the subject. She had no taste for family sniping even when she agreed with the opinion expressed.

"Bored. I don't know why I let Max and Diana talk me into coming tonight."

Max and Diana Tyler, chatting together across the room, were Carrie's cousins. They were brother and sister, much older than Carrie, and the only members of the Tyler family who really kept in close touch with the Stockwells. Max was on the board of Stockwell Enterprises, and Diana had an ongoing friendship with both Patrice and Holly Meyerling, although she was some five years older.

"Riverview needed an injection of youth and beauty," Patrice answered. She didn't approve of Carrie, who tended to be frivolous, undisciplined, and wild, but she did like her. There was something about Carrie's impetuous, devil-take-the-hindmost attitude that Patrice, who always felt called upon to behave so damned responsibly herself, couldn't help admiring.

"An injection of LSD laced with aphrodisiac wouldn't hurt, either." Carrie didn't deny the compliment Patrice had paid her. She took it for granted that she deserved it. People had been admiring her beauty since she'd started developing breasts at the age of twelve. Besides,

10

she had a twin sister, Beth, who looked exactly like her, and that halved the impact of any flattery Carrie received.

Still, there was no denying their beauty. The twins were long-legged, coltish young women possessed of the grace of natural athletes. Like all the Tylers, including dapper, fortyish Max and slightly plump Diana, they had almond-shaped hazel eyes and eye-catching red-gold hair. Carrie wore her hair long and loose, while her twin, Beth, combed it neatly and tied it back, but both styles served to frame lively, youthful visages with haughty cheekbones and berry-red lips. Separately, Carrie and Beth drew admiring glances; together, they stopped traffic.

"What do you hear from your sister?" Patrice asked Carrie now.

"Crete is beautiful. Deke is wonderful. Life is marvelous. Love conquers all." Carrie shrugged cynically.

"Well, I'm glad Beth's happy."

"Oh, she's happy all right. I couldn't stand it. Love is so damn dull."

"If love is dull, then what's exciting?" Patrice asked.

"Lust, cousin. Lust is what's exciting." Carrie spun around, and the black silk skirt flared out from her hips to reveal tan-gold thighs and black silk bikini underwear.

"I think you've caught Peter's attention," Patrice murmured, privately certain that Carrie had intended to do just that.

"Peter! Ugh!"

Patrice was unconvinced by Carrie's reaction. "Well, he *is* the only unattached man in the room."

"That's true." Carrie pretended to shudder. "Well, I guess I'll just have to make do." She dazzled Peter with a smile as he moved toward them, his mother's disapproval a subtle cloud hovering behind him. "Peter, darling," Carrie greeted him. "It's been such a long time. What have you been up to? And why is it I never hear from you, you naughty boy?" She linked arms with Peter and led him to a rooster-brocaded divan just large enough for two.

"I swear that girl has been taking lessons from Buffy."

Diana Tyler regarded her young cousin with amusement and some dismay as she moved to join Patrice.

Patrice winced. Buffy, who had been the much younger second wife of Patrice's grandfather, Governor Matthew Adams Stockwell, was not someone she cared to discuss. The reason was simple. Patrice was in love with Buffy's present husband, Jack Houston.

Although Patrice had had affairs with more than one man since her marriage ended, her romance with Jack was the only one that had been truly meaningful. It had ended long ago, but she had not gotten over it. Jack was the wrong man if ever there was one—a man who was married, a man not above using her for his own purposes, but she loved him.

She had been hurt badly by Jack, not once but twice, and the second experience had made her draw back from seeking any new romance in her life. Instead she devoted even more of her time to business. "That old antifeminist sterotype," she had once confided to her cousin Holly. "That's me. The woman who works her tail off to take her mind off the man who got away."

Patrice's rise to the top in the advertising industry had been meteoric, and when her father, Governor Stockwell's eldest son, had retired to live abroad, Patrice had replaced him on the board of trustees of Stockwell Enterprises. She had plunged willingly into the complexities of the family business, serving alongside both her cousins Peter and Max Tyler, her uncle David, and a lawyer who represented the late governor's sister. Buffy Houston was also on the board, along with two other members.

In her new role Patrice proved an insightful and effective businesswoman. High finance fascinated her. She had always been more ambitious in that area than her brother Matt, who, although marked by tradition to take their father's place, had refused to do so. Patrice's grasp of the complexities of a holding company—with such far-flung interests as petroleum, semiconductors, real estate, fine arts, insurance, publishing, construction, and commodities investment—quickly earned the respect, sometimes grudging, of her fellow board members. Patrice became a workaholic.

Her cousin Holly, her best friend, despaired. She knew it wasn't just "a man" Patrice lacked. If that had been the case, there would have been no problem. With Patrice's small but voluptuously rounded figure, pretty, vivacious face, chestnut hair, and outgoing personality, Patrice would have no problem finding a man. It wasn't "a man" she wanted. It was "*the* man." It was the one and only, the man she was hooked on, the man Patrice couldn't get over. Jack Houston.

"I guess Buffy and Jack are still on St. Martin." Diana Tyler spoke now into the silence that had greeted her mention of Buffy to Patrice. Diana didn't know anything about Patrice's affair with Jack. None of the family members present did except Holly.

"I guess they are." Patrice was saved from any further discussion of Buffy and Jack by the arrival of Kathleen O'Lunney.

When they reached Riverview, Kevin O'Lunney had turned Kathleen over to Berkley, the butler, and then retired to his quarters above the garage. Now Matt Stockwell went quickly to Kathleen as Berkley escorted her into the sitting room and discreetly withdrew.

Everyone in the room knew Kathleen. As Kevin O'Lunney's daughter, she had made frequent visits to Riverview since she'd started college about three years ago. Patrice and Holly were fully aware that a romantic relationship had been evolving between Matt and Kathleen for some time, and the others, when they took the trouble to notice, were at least aware that the two had been seeing each other. But like Uncle Jonathan, they had not realized until tonight how far matters had progressed—that the subject of marriage was being discussed between a member of the family and the daughter of Riverview's chauffeur.

What a field day the papers will have with this, Patrice couldn't help but think as she crossed the room to greet Kathleen. Princess Di, move over. And watch those ratings soar for *Upstairs Downstairs.* "I love your dress," she told Kathleen aloud. "The color goes perfectly with your hair."

"Mud brown for carrot tops." Kathleen liked Patrice, and now she grinned at her as her hands nervously clutched at the chiffon skirt. "And white dot freckles to match my own."

"It's a Bill Blass, isn't it?" Holly asked.

Store-bought, thought Ellen Stockwell with malicious pleasure. Always conscious of how Riverview had for so many years regarded her as a parvenu, she was more sensitive than any born Stockwell to the intrusion of hoi polloi into the family. New to fashion herself, she was especially critical of others not born to it.

"Yes. It's a Bill Blass." Kathleen felt uncomfortable with the discussion of her gown; the talk made her feel clumsy and awkward in it. She was too strapping and healthy a lass for such frou-frou. She wasn't meant for ruffles flapping off her shoulders and hips and her bare knees hanging out. Nor for the permanent that had tamed her unruly bright red hair into such an unnatural sleekness.

The discontent, which had nagged vaguely at Kathleen all through the ride to Riverview, was focused for her now by Carrie Tyler's presence. Carrie was the only woman her own age in the room. When it came to wearing the latest styles, Carrie was everything that Kathleen was not. Slender, lithe, graceful, sexy, and—most enviable of all—with the kind of cheekbones Kathleen would probably only develop when she had one foot in the boneyard. It was true, you had to be born with such qualities, along with the silver spoon in your mouth.

Carrie, noticing Kathleen looking at her, came over. "Why would you ever want to marry into a stodgy family like ours?" she asked bluntly.

Kathleen's face quickly turned red.

"Oh, dear. Matt shouldn't have—"

"Thanks a lot, Carrie." Matt scowled at her.

"Well, it's true. *I* was born a Stockwell relative. I can't help it. But Kathleen has a choice. If you're hooked on this lummox—well, he's really not so bad, considering the rest of the family—then move in with him. Live together. But marriage? My God, Kathleen, you'll have to go to family dinners. You'll die of small talk."

"Well—" Kathleen recovered and forgave Matt with a squeeze of his hand. "When things get too bad, I'll just run over to the garage and see Pa."

"There's always more fun in the servants' quarters." Carrie winked approval. "And don't miss out on that new footman, either, the one with the nifty pectorals."

"Carrie!" Matt took a deep breath.

"Oh, I think not." Kathleen linked arms with Matt. "These are all the pectorals I want."

"Tell me that after you've been at Riverview six months." Carrie winked again at Kathleen and moved back toward Peter.

"She really has taken Buffy for her role model," Diana remarked wryly to Patrice.

"Carrie has a long way to go before she'll be in Buffy's league." It was Holly who responded. "Not that I think that's necessarily a worthwhile ambition. Besides, they really are dissimilar. Carrie's a . . ." Holly groped for the right words, then said with a smile, "Carrie is a volatile vamp, while Buffy, with all her affairs, has always been a stable siren."

A stable siren. More like a thoroughbred bitch, Patrice thought. But once again made uncomfortable by the topic, she drifted away from Holly and Diana. She was standing by the door to the sitting room when Berkley reappeared. "Dinner?" Patrice inquired, thinking he had come to announce that it was ready.

"No, Miss Patrice. Not quite yet. There's a telephone call from Mr. De Vilbiss in California. I informed him that the family was just about to sit down to dinner, but he said that it was important. He asked to speak to either you or Mister Peter."

"I'll take it, Berkley."

Wondering what Halsey de Vilbiss, the only non-

15

family member of the Stockwell board, could want that was important enough to interrupt Sunday dinner, Patrice went into the study and picked up the telephone. "Hello, Halsey. What is it?"

The voice on the other end informed Holly that there had been a death in the Stockwell family.

3

BUFFY HOUSTON WAS lying on the beach in St. Martin when the news of Sarah Stockwell Tyler's death was brought to her. Her husband, Jack, was lying beside her when the houseboy came up to them with the telegram. The couple were sunbathing in the nude, as was the custom at Rouge Beach, but the boy, a native of St. Martin, was neither embarrassed by the nudity nor inhibited about admiring it openly. His eyes on Buffy's naked body made her tingle with pleasure. It was always nice to know that at fifty-one years of age her unclothed figure was still voluptuous enough and her bare flesh still firm enough to command appreciation from youth.

"Buffy in the buff," Jack had recently remarked to a friend, "is the eighth wonder of the world—and the most sensual."

But Jack was her husband, and seventeen years younger than she. His compliments were gratefully received, and yet—Buffy's insecurities required reassurance from other male eyes than her husband's, even if those other eyes belonged to a mere houseboy.

For an instant she saw her reflection in them—a body that was voluptuous in the classical sense, a tall figure with long, shapely legs, well-defined hips, a narrow waist,

16

and a full, still firm, and arrogantly thrusting bosom with deep cleavage. Her belly was flat, her derriere compact, high and pert. As evenly tanned as it was shapely, Buffy kept her tawny-smooth flesh in peak condition by regular massage and exercise. Truly, hers was a form worthy of an Amazon queen.

The face above the Junoesque form was genuinely beautiful. Buffy's profile, strong yet quite feminine, would not have been out of place on a Greek coin. Full face, its components added up to a beacon of sensuality attracting men to irresistible, but sometimes dangerous, shoals. Many a man had run aground following the inviting light in Buffy's long-lashed violet eyes. They had gone down clutching in vain for her thickly curled, luxuriously coiffed, long blue-black tresses.

Some people thought that her former husband, Governor Matthew Adams Stockwell, had been among them, but of course that relationship had been much more complicated. The governor had truly aroused Buffy as no other man had—not even Jack Houston. Already married when she'd first met the governor, Buffy had been a restless Westchester society beauty in her early thirties. Matthew Adams Stockwell was already governor of New York State and a leading candidate for the Republican party's presidental nomination when they'd begun their affair.

Neither had anticipated how powerfully sex would seal the attraction between them. Buffy had left her first husband without a backward glance. The governor had left the wife he had loved and informed the world that he and Buffy would marry just as soon as their divorces were granted. The scandal wrecked the governor's presidential ambitions. Their subsequent marriage was launched onto stormy seas, and they became stormier and stormier, with much straying on both parts, before the governor finally died in the arms of another woman about two years ago.

By that time Buffy had become involved with Jack Houston. They were wed—her third marriage, his first— after a decent interval following the governor's funeral. Jack adored her; at least he said he did, and Buffy be-

17

lieved him, some of the time, anyway. The trouble between them flared up during the times when she didn't.

Buffy was locked into a double standard. She knew her own flirtations, even affairs, were meaningless. She loved Jack. She just needed the sort of reassurance she was finding now in the houseboy's appreciative eyes.

But Jack's interest in other women—well, that was something else. Every time Buffy discerned it, or even thought she did, she believed it was proof that Jack was finally looking at her as an older woman. His philanderings, merely mental or actually physical, had the potential to separate them permanently; hers . . . well, they were no more important than the glint in the servant's eyes.

"You may go now, Phillipe," she told the houseboy as she opened the telegram, reading it quickly. "Oh, dear."

"Bad news?" Jack inquired, careful to avert his gaze from two nubile and naked French girls farther down the beach.

"The governor's sister has died."

"Sarah Stockwell Tyler," Jack remembered. "Well, she was a very old lady, wasn't she?"

"Yes." Buffy had herself barely known Sarah Stockwell Tyler. Indeed, she had only met her after the governor had died. She was not going to pretend to be grief-stricken by her death. What the old woman's death primarily meant was the possibility of problems regarding the Stockwell financial empire. "It could be a real mess." She spoke her qualms aloud.

"Is there a will?" Jack, accustomed to his wife's train of thought, recognized the nature of her concerns.

"My God, I hope there is. Without one, Halsey De Vilbiss will be in the position of administering Sarah's fortune."

"Well, he's been doing it right along, anyway, hasn't he?" Jack pointed out.

"That's not the same thing. He's been acting as her attorney, representing her on the board. But there was never any question of his being in control. She jerked his lead many a time, and then Halsey would trip all over

18

himself going into reverse. But now, without Sarah to restrain him—"

"I don't understand," Jack interrupted. "What's different?"

"Halsey has power of attorney. If Sarah died intestate, that will continue until her estate is resolved. And with so many heirs, it could drag on for years. And during that time Halsey would have equal power on the board with all the rest of us. And he'd be accountable to no one."

"You really do dislike him." Jack grinned.

"That's because I know him so well. He was once my lawyer, remember. Believe me, that little sleazy, overdressed Southern California twerp is living proof that familiarity breeds contempt. We're going to have to go back to New York."

"*Merde!*" It was one of the French words Jack had got into the habit of using on St. Martin. He propped himself up on his elbows and looked around sourly.

The ocean was a warm blue green, the waves cresting high but breaking gently, the white froth nibbling at the golden shore. The sun was a Carribean caress, a giant ball of lemon red toasting relaxation into his naked flesh. The bluffs fringing Baie Rouge were lushly green, tangled vines embracing trees with moist, rich brown bark and giant tropical leaves. The blue sky suffered no clouds, and just as yesterday had promised this perfect day, today promised a glorious tomorrow.

"*Merde!*" Jack really didn't want to leave all this.

"You'll miss the nymphettes." Buffy read her own insecurity into his scowl.

Miffed at the assumption—there was some truth to it, but only in the way any normal man would enjoy looking at naked and shapely young French *filles*—Jack deliberately responded by directing his gaze back to the naked French girls he'd been looking at before. They were very young, their bottoms and their breasts plump and rosy; their movements as they squealed and cavorted in the surf were undeniably provocative. Laughing, they started to wrestle, and one fell to the sand facing Jack with her

19

legs flung wide apart. Without his willing it, his naked phallus stirred.

Buffy noticed; she missed nothing. Fury tightened her features, but she kept her voice carefully under control. "You don't have to come with me," she said. "I can go to New York myself. You can just stay here on St. Martin and enjoy yourself."

"Don't be silly." Jack was even more annoyed because he felt a twinge of guilt. "Of course I'll go with you. Why shouldn't I?"

"Because you'd obviously rather stay here and ogle Lolitas," Buffy told him. "That's why."

"Don't be ridiculous."

"I'm not being ridiculous. I'm just facing facts. You can't deny you look at these sweet young things with their bouncy thingamabobs whenever you get the chance. And I don't blame you. After all, you are stuck being married to Grandma Moses, as it were."

"Buffy, are we going to go all through this again? I adore you. You know that. I knocked myself out getting you to marry me. I love you. Why can't you accept that? If I didn't, why would I put up with your jealous nonsense?"

"Money." Buffy delivered the coup de grace. "That's why, darling. I have a lot of money, and that's undoubtedly what you married me for."

"Merde! Merde! Merde! That's not true, and you know it. I don't care about your money. I love you. The most frustrating thing in my life is that I can't get you to accept it."

"Well, maybe if you'd agree to wear blinders on the beach—" Her tone implied she was relenting a tad.

"I don't need blinders," Jack growled. "You're the only one I want. Only you." And to prove it he swung his naked body over hers and kissed her deeply.

This time when his phallus stirred, Buffy had no doubt that it was with desire for her. She had to stop herself from responding. True, it was a nude beach, French and

20

permissive, but there were limits. Flustered and laughing, she pulled away from Jack and regarded him.

God, he was attractive. His bronze naked body was perfectly proportioned. His shoulders were wide, his chest deep and tapering to a narrow waist and slim hips. His arms and legs were strongly muscled, evidence that he was an athlete who enjoyed using his sinew. He had intense blue eyes, very white teeth, and a square, Hollywood-cowboy kind of jaw. In no way was Jack Houston a pretty boy, but he was a very charismatic and virile-looking sort of man.

No wonder I worry, Buffy thought. Women adore him on sight. The handsome bastard!

Jack was every bit as romantic a character as he looked. At different times he had been a professional athlete playing soccer in Europe, a safari guide in Kenya, a lumberjack in the Pacific Northwest, and a soldier-of-fortune in Angola. Less adventurously, he had also earned a living as a travel writer, a mailman, and even as a bellhop at New York City's famous Algonquin Hotel.

And, Buffy remembered now with a twinge, he had even gotten himself involved with organized crime. The involvement had been short-lived and unsuccessful, but—

"Maybe you really shouldn't go back to New York with me," she said.

"Why not?"

"You know very well why not, darling."

It was true. Jack did know. He preferred not to think about it, but underneath he knew.

There were those in New York who had sworn to kill him.

4

At least, Patrice consoled herself, Jack Houston wouldn't be at the board meeting. The window-shopping Christmas crowd with their umbrellas tilted against a sheet of icy December rain held Patrice to a snail's pace as she navigated lower Broadway toward William Street and the Stockwell Building. Jack was back in New York, staying at Riverview, but she hadn't seen him yet since she maintained an apartment in Manhattan. And he wasn't a member of the board of Stockwell Enterprises so would not be present at the meeting for which she was bound.

Patrice turned up her collar against the wet wind, hiding her ubiquitous bow. Buffy, though, would be present. Patrice sighed. Business meeting or not, it was always hard for her to be in the same room with Buffy for any length of time. If Jack's return was a reminder of how Patrice's heart had been victimized, then Buffy was the living evidence of her defeat in love.

Skirt whipping around her knees, Patrice paused in front of the sleek, smoked-glass facade of the Stockwell Building and closed her umbrella. Then, with a grimace that tilted her small chin at a determined angle, she squared her shoulders and entered the lobby. The automatic glass doors slid silently shut behind her.

Taking off her Burberry and shaking the water from it, she paused before crossing to the banks of elevators behind the twin desks of the security guards. She looked up at the abstract wall mural by Stefanelli that was the focal point of the Stockwell Building's huge lobby. The

22

artist had been one of the younger members of the New York School whose work had been appreciated early on by Patrice's grandfather, the governor. Although Patrice had not liked her grandfather, she did like the Stefanelli, and whenever she looked at it, she grudgingly admitted that the governor's reputation as a knowledgeable connoisseur of avant-garde modern art was well deserved.

Besides the Stefanelli, the governor had acquired many early works by Franz Klein and Willem de Kooning, and other, younger artists who frequented Greenwich Village's Cedar Tavern from the late 1940s through the early 1960s.

While some of the governor's collection was in the form of Picassos and Braques and the like, whose worth had been recognized at the time of purchase, the bulk of his paintings consisted of works by neoabstractionists whose genius had been slow to gain recognition.

Artistic merit aside, the governor's investment in their work had been shrewd beyond most collectors of that time. After his death, his modern art acquisitions had been appraised at a value in excess of the better-known Rockefeller collection. Many pieces were now worth impressive multiples of what he had paid for them. And today it was an impressive asset of Stockwell Enterprises.

The Stefanelli was unusual because it was on public display. Most of the art holdings were sequestered at Riverview. Indeed, some of the paintings had only been unpacked for inventory and appraisal following the governor's death, and then—for lack of space to hang them—they'd been recrated for protection.

Most of the Stockwell family was uneasy with the neoabstractionists. The older members in particular preferred the nature scenes, earth colors, and easy recognizability of earlier landscape painters. Only Patrice and her cousin Holly, whose mother had been an artist and worked somewhat in the style of the Cedar Tavern painters, really liked the abstracts.

Although the controlling family did not really appreciate the Stefanelli, the mural would continue to dominate

23

the lobby. There were two reasons. First, the governor had still been alive when the new company headquarters had been erected, and he had wanted it there. None of his children, nor grandchildren, nor other relations would have dreamed of challenging his artistic judgment. Second, and inescapable, the Stefanelli truly blended superbly with the ultramodern architecture and decor of both the building and its lobby.

Below the twenty-seventh-floor executive suites, revived art-deco predominated. Like the building's facade, the interior consisted of glassine glitz, smoothness, and glitter; metallic surfaces; and the perpetual daylight of hidden fluorescents—a computerized environment for programmed paper pushers and junior executives with upwardly-mobile tunnel vision. For twenty-six floors the edges were as deceptively modernistic as the competition was killing.

On the twenty-seventh floor, however, resided the real power of Stockwell Enterprises. Wealth was grounded in visible tradition. Scenic watercolors of Riverview painted by various Hudson River Valley artists hung in the reception area, augmented by hand-loomed curtains, fading tapestries from Belgium, and a priceless Far Eastern carpet around which were placed antique overstuffed armchairs from Provence and a Louis XIV writing desk, which was the mate of one still on view in one of the Sun King's chambers at the palace of Versailles. A sort of timelessness prevailed in the twenty-seventh-floor offices, and, as always, Patrice succumbed to it as she crossed the area, nodded to the middle-aged receptionist, and let herself into the conference room.

The low-key, muted atmosphere of old money was carried into the boardroom. The oval oak table, around which Patrice and the other members of the board would seat themselves, was over two hundred years old. The chairs, none too comfortable, were straight-backed Duncan Phyfe antiques. Portraits in oil of various Stockwell forebears by Gilbert Stuart, John Singer Sargent, Benjamin West, John Singleton Copley, and later masters were spaced unobtrusively about the deep-grained mahogany walls.

"Good afternoon, Patrice." David Lewis, the only person in the conference room, rose to greet his niece as she entered.

"Hello, Uncle David." Patrice was not overly fond of her gruff, straitlaced uncle, but she made the effort to be pleasant. "Merry Christmas."

"You're a week early for Yuletide greetings." David Lewis frowned. "You'll forgive me if I don't return them. As a matter of principle, I don't like to rush the season."

"I'll forgive you." Patrice was saved from having to formulate alternative pleasantries by the arrivals in quick succession of the other members.

The makeup of the board, six in all, was the result of a probate compromise following the deaths of Governor Matthew Adams Stockwell and, shortly after, his first wife, Mary. The original compromise, however, had itself been modified by certain substitutions. Patrice served in place of her father, James Linstone Stockwell, who was presently living in Greece. For reasons of competency— never admitted, let alone discussed—Peter Stockwell had replaced his father, Jonathan, on the board. The remaining members consisted of David Lewis, married to the governor's eldest daughter; Buffy; Halsey De Vilbiss, Sarah Stockwell Tyler's representative; and Max Tyler, who represented the other Tyler heirs to the Stockwell fortune.

Before the death of the governor and his first wife, the affairs of Stockwell Enterprises had been run by James Linstone Stockwell and his brother-in-law David Lewis with the silent acquiescence of Jonathan Stockwell. In recent years Peter Stockwell had joined the three men in an active role. If David and James had only grudgingly accepted Peter, David Lewis in particular had never completely reconciled himself to the new six-person board. Nevertheless, he had no choice but to work with it.

In the beginning, the chairing of the board had been rotated among the members. But it had soon been recognized that this led to a lack of continuity in the board's agenda. Now the chair was elected for a one-year term. In deference to his greater experience—if decidedly not to his personality—the first chairperson voted in had been David Lewis.

At age fifty-six, with a sparsely fleshed physique, a military bearing, and an austere presence, David Lewis was a private man, highly efficient and not given to expressions of affection. He was first and foremost a man of business, and if he kept an emotional ledger of his loves and his sorrows, then only he was privy to its entries. On occasion he could also be a person of harsh judgments and unforgiving temperament.

Now, with all of the board members present, David Lewis called the meeting to order. "I've put the agenda on the back burner," he announced autocratically. "We will begin with a document relevant to the recent death of Sarah Stockwell Tyler."

"Document?" Halsey De Vilbiss reacted suspiciously. "What document?"

Uncle David, Patrice realized, had hit a nerve.

"A document delivered to me as chairman of the board of Stockwell Enterprises by courier," David Lewis responded, not bothering to hide his dislike of De Vilbiss. "It came from an investment bank in Nome, Alaska, acting on instructions from the deceased to be followed in the event of her death."

"I don't understand. Why you?" De Vilbiss was agitated. "I'm Sarah Stockwell Tyler's attorney."

"The document will explain that."

De Vilbiss leaned back uncomfortably in the Duncan Phyfe chair. His customarily debonair pencil-line mustache drooped, and despite his Pacific Coast tan, the downturn of his thin face and the unhappiness in his eyes gave him the unhealthy look of a warm-weather newt caught in an unexpected frost. His bony hand rifled his impeccably blow-dried hair, and the resulting displacement of its careful contour marked the lawyer's concern.

Apprehension, Patrice noted, made the Los Angeles

attorney look even more out of place in the Stockwell boardroom than usual. His customary confidence was absent. Halsey De Vilbiss had the anxious look of a shyster with a losing client—himself.

"The document," David Lewis continued, "is addressed to the Acting Chairman of the Board of Stockwell Enterprises. It is dated November eight, 1982, some three weeks before the death of Sarah Stockwell Tyler. It is signed by Sarah Stockwell Tyler and witnessed by two officers of the bank." He cleared his throat. "It reads as follows:"

To the Board of Stockwell Enterprises:

Let us dispense with formalities. Of the six members of the Stockwell board, one of you—Max—is my grandson, two of you—Patrice and Peter—are my blood relatives, two more—David Lewis and Buffy Houston—are related to me by marriage. Only one—Halsey De Vilbiss—has no family ties to me at all, and he is my attorney.

Relationships aside, it is Mr. De Vilbiss with whom I have maintained the closest contact. He has managed my business affairs, and represented me on the board, and done an excellent job in both areas. His ability is unquestioned; his ambition is another matter entirely. Which is why I do not trust him, as we say in Alaska, as far as I, at the age of eighty-seven, can throw a snowflake upwind in a blizzard.

I don't attach blame. Mr. De Vilbiss's ethical problems are due to his background. In Southern California, where the seasons never change, how can Mr. De Vilbiss be expected to pinpoint where a client's interests leave off and his own interests begin?

Nevertheless, Mr. De Vilbiss is a highly effective advocate, and I recommend that after my demise he continue to administer my estate. I advise an ongoing but informal scrutiny of his efforts by his five fellow board members. This perhaps uncomfortable situation should go on only until the heir to my estate takes over his rightful position.

He is my great-grandson, Tyron Fitzwilliam Connely of County Kildare, Ireland, a Stockwell by blood just as surely as I am myself. I have designated him in my last will and testament (copies of which are on file with the directors of the Merchant Investment and Trust Company of Nome, Alaska) as my sole legatee. It will be Mr. De Vilbiss's duty to find him.

But what of my other descendants? After all, I have children, one still living, grandchildren, great-grandchildren. Why have I cut them out of my will? Why have I favored Tyrone Fitzwilliam Connely and left them nothing?

Let me explain. I have not acted with malice. Nor do I believe the designation of Tyrone Fitzwilliam Connely as my sole heir is favoritism.

Upon the deaths two years ago of my brother and soon after his wife, Mary, my branch of the family, the Tylers, all descended from me, were provided for with extreme generosity. The former Mary Linstone was particularly magnanimous with her Tyler nephews, their children, and their grandchildren. There was a good reason for this. As well as being my descendants, they were as I have told them the descendants of Mary's brother, Ellis Linstone.

Yes, Ellis Linstone was my lover—my first lover—but not by any double-digit calculation my last.

Do not be shocked. I am an old lady, eighty-seven on my last birthday. Time is too short for delicacy, and I have lived too long for shame. Self-forgiveness is the brightest candle on any geriatric birthday cake. The icing is that yesteryear's wickedness has lost its power to embarrass. My revelations may scandalize even today, but in the long run nobody really gives a damn.

So . . . Ellis Linstone was my lover. Born a Stockwell, I lived at Riverview. He lived at Heather Crest, the Linstone estate adjacent to our property. We were the same age and knew each other all through our childhood. We were sixteen when we fell in love. We were barely eighteen when Ellis made me pregnant.

Pregnant: a tragedy leading to a greater tragedy. To say

merely that times were different then would be a great understatement. The moral tyranny under which we lived cannot truly be comprehended by today's generation. Our situation constituted an unmitigated disgrace for ourselves and for our families. Such an all-encompassing shame may not be measured by modern permissive standards.

Ellis and I reacted according to our different natures. He was strong. I was weak. Darwin is wrong. The Bible is right. It is the weak who survive, the intimidated who inherit the earth. Unable to face his own humiliation and mine, as well as the dishonor he had brought upon both our families, Ellis hanged himself. That was sixty-nine years ago. I still do not forgive him.

I was pregnant, but not yet showing. If I was to avoid running the Hudson River ice floes with a bastard babe in my arms, I had to do something and do it quickly. My first impulse was knitting needles, but I was terrified of pain.

Fortunately an alternative turned up in the person of Averill Tyler, a childless widower some thirty years older than myself. He owned one of the smaller estates in the Hudson River Valley. At table one night I heard my father remark to my mother that Mr. Tyler was in deep financial difficulty and had come to him for a loan. Such was the answer to a pregnant maiden's prayers!

My father did not think Averill Tyler a very good risk and was disinclined to make the loan. However, when I confessed my condition, Father was persuaded otherwise. As someone—I believe it was Madame Pompadour—once said: The rest is history. Father made the arrangements, and Averill Tyler and I were married a little less than a month later.

Within six months I gave birth to twin boys. Mr. Tyler of course realized that he was not their father. At first he suffered this knowledge in silence. Before long, however, he was voicing sarcasm regarding their illegitimate origins. The real reason for his attitude, though, was my refusal to perform my wifely duties.

I refused because Averill Tyler was the most inept, short-winded, clumsy, uninspiring lovemaker to whom any woman has ever had the misfortune to be married. Mostly, as a husband, he was a brain-deadening bore. In bed, however, he gained status. There he became a disgusting, inconsiderate, loveless brute.

So I left him.

I decided to take this action following a number of visits to the small room above the stables occupied by Brian Mulrooney, my husband's coachman. Brian was a handsome Irish devil with curly hair and the kind of smile that warmed you while it removed your clothes. We seduced each other—which is accurate, if not too helpful in assigning blame—and in the hay that seemed always to be drifting about Brian's room I rediscovered the passion I had known with Ellis.

Adultery is a reasonable response to marital misery, and flight is its reasonable end product. I believe that today, after a long, eventful life, just as I did at the time. I would still choose sinful flight with Brian Mulrooney over the dull death of marriage with Averill Tyler.

But what about my twin sons? After all, they were little more than a year old when I ran off. How could I just leave them like that?

If I say that the satisfactions of motherhood are overrated, you will doubtless think me heartless. Still, ask the woman who's raised her children, buried her husband, and sits alone by the unringing telephone. Ah, but I am rationalizing. The truth is that I knew my parents would take them and raise them as their own. They would be better off with my mother and father than as the ''little bastards'' of Averill Tyler and his miserable wife.

And so I left them. I missed them, after my selfish fashion, but I never regretted going. The self-sacrificing mother is not a punishment I would ever wish on any child of mine.

Brian Mulrooney and I made our way across the continent to Alaska, drawn there by hazy, romantic notions of fortunes awaiting the pioneer spirit. Disenchantment pushed me into day work as a laundress, and waiting tables, and—as I roughened—into showing my legs and the top of my bosom in dance halls. I—who had been raised with servants to cater to my every need—solicited the clink of nuggets dropped in the cleft of my bodice from drunken prospectors paying tribute to my ''sassy classiness'' in contrast with the other, somewhat more sluttish dance-hall girls.

We were in Nome when we realized that I was again pregnant. Brian wanted to marry me, but I already had one husband and would not risk jail by committing bigamy. So we compromised. Brian bought a ring, and we simply pretended to be married, and when the baby—a girl—came, he gave it his name on the birth certificate.

Maureen was born in 1917. The country was at war in far-off Europe. Even in Alaska patriotic fever was at its height, and Brian got caught up in it. He'd been born in Ireland and hated the English, but that made no difference. Nothing would do but that he enlist and go off to fight the Germans. Not being legally married to Brian, I didn't get any allotment. I had a baby and myself to feed and clothe and house. When the chance came for employment at Nome's most high-class brothel, I jumped at it. Better degradation and three squares than purity and an empty belly.

When the war ended and Brian came home, he was furious. Scrubbing clothes and displaying myself in a dance hall was one thing; whoring was something else again. We had a fierce fight. When it was over, we were through.

Brian left in the dead of night and took Maureen with him. The note he left said that he'd not have his daughter know a whore for a mother. It didn't tell me where he was taking her. I never saw either Brian or my baby daughter again.

The years went by. In the brothel I met a gold prospector who had made a small strike, a man much older than myself. He made me an attractive offer, and I went to live with him. More time passed. He died, leaving me a small income, one that was sufficient to my needs if I scrimped. One day I turned around and there I was, an old lady, still scrimping.

That was my situation when my brother the governor and his wife died. I had not had any contact with my family through all those years. Indeed, I had all but forgotten that I had started out in life as a Stockwell. To be reminded with a fabulous inheritance was most pleasant.

I was no longer poor, but I was still old and getting older. With the money, I felt a compulsion to put certain aspects of my life in order. My children by Ellis Linstone had been well provided for by the governor and by his wife, who was Ellis's sister. But what of my daughter, Maureen?

Remorse may lie dormant, but it is cumulative. I became obsessed with finding Maureen and seeing to it that she shared in the fortune bequeathed to me. I hired a top-rated private detective agency to track her down.

The first thing they found out was that Brian Mulrooney was dead, killed by strike breakers during the copper mine labor wars in Arizona. Maureen wasn't with him at the time of his death. Shortly after leaving me, Brian had sent the child to County Kildare, Ireland, where he was from originally, to be raised respectably by his family.

In 1935, at the age of eighteen, Maureen married Errol Fitzwilliam, a local boy only slightly older than herself. Errol Fitzwilliam, involved with the IRA, was shot and killed illegally crossing the Northern Ireland border by a patrol of Black and Tans. Six months later Maureen, a widow after less than a year of marriage, gave birth to a daughter.

The child was named Margaret and called ''Maggie.'' She was raised by Maureen, who never remarried and was widely known and respected in the area as ''the widow Fitzwilliam.'' Maggie grew up to marry a County Kildare potato farmer named Timothy Connely. In 1955, when she was twenty years old, Maggie Connely, my granddaughter, died in childbirth.

Maggie's son survived. He was given the name Tyrone

Fitzwilliam Connely. When he entered school, the boys took to calling him "Fitz," and the name stuck.

Fitz was eight years old when his father's potato crop failed. Timothy Connely couldn't meet his bank loan payments, and his farm was sold at public auction. He and Fitz were now homeless.

Timothy Connely migrated to America, leaving his son with his grandmother, the widow Fitzwilliam. Maureen raised Fitz, both mother and father to him, until 1975, when she died of cancer. Fitz had no other close Irish relatives. He decided to go to America and join his father, Timothy Connely. After his grandmother's funeral was paid for, there was barely enough money to pay his plane fare. Fitz arrived at Kennedy Airport two days before his twenty-first birthday.

Fitz located his father through County Kildare contacts in the Hibernian Society. Timothy Connely was working in Chicago in a meat-packing plant. After they were reunited, Timothy got Fitz a job in the plant, and the boy moved in with him. They lived together and from all descriptions hit if off well and became very close.

Tragically, the relationship ended with Timothy's death in an automobile accident. He and Fitz were both passengers in the car. They were on their way to Hammond, Indiana, about an hour from Chicago, for some sort of commemoration having to do with the fight for Irish independence when they were hit by a van whose brakes had failed. Timothy, in the front seat, was killed outright. Fitz, in the back, got off with only two broken ribs.

Fitz's trail ran out for the private detectives with the hospital records of the accident and the death certificate for Timothy Connely. At the time of this writing, they have been unable to locate my great-grandson. Fitz has simply vanished.

At my behest, the detective agency has been continuing the search for my sole heir, Tyrone Fitzwilliam "Fitz" Connely. In the event of my death, I wish it to go on until he is either found, or it is established that he is dead.

Halsey De Vilbiss shall have the responsibility of seeing that my wishes in this matter are carried out.

My will also mandates that Halsey De Vilbiss will continue to manage my considerable holdings in Stockwell Enterprises. He will continue to sit on the governing board until such time as Tyron Fitzwilliam Connely claims his inheritance. When and if that occurs, he will serve only at the pleasure of my great-grandson, just as in the past he has served only at my pleasure.

Despite my qualms regarding Mr. De Vilbiss, I am recommending in a separate letter to my great-grandson, which the bank is holding for him, that he keep Mr. De Vilbiss on as his proxy in the management of what will be his considerable share of Stockwell Enterprises. My presumption is that Tyrone Fitzwilliam Connely will not be an experienced businessman, and—I repeat what I said at the beginning of this letter—Mr. De Vilbiss is admirably competent. He will be a great help in the management of all of my great-grandson's business affairs. Still, the question of whether he stays or goes must ultimately rest with Fitz Connely.

Good-bye to all of my relatives—Stockwells and Tylers and Linstones. Good-bye to all who held me dear and to all who held me cheap. I was born and I died and in between, for the most part, to borrow a phrase of far younger vintage than I am, I had a ball.

Without regrets,
Sarah Stockwell Tyler

After David Lewis finished reading the letter, a silence descended upon the boardroom. The time-darkened oil portraits of the various Stockwells who had built the family fortune stared down with stiff neutrality as if they, like the board members present, were mulling over the ramifications of what they'd just heard.

Patrice toyed with the floppy bow at the collar of her tailored blouse. Her mind was ticking off a variety of points. The first, naturally enough, had to do with the

34

tricky position in which the letter had left Halsey De Vilbiss.

Despite Sarah Stockwell Tyler's desire to restrict Halsey to the straight and narrow, it was obvious to Patrice, as it must have been to the others, that it would be to his advantage if Fitz Connely was *not* found. With the heir unaccounted for, Sarah's estate would be in limbo and Halsey could continue to administer it and to exercise control on the Stockwell board. If Fitz was found, there was always the chance that he might exercise his prerogative despite his great-grandmother's advice and discharge Halsey immediately. Halsey would not relish the prospect of finding himself out in the cold.

On the other hand, Patrice reflected, Halsey De Vilbiss could be quite ingratiating. Locating Fitz might earn the heir's gratitude and trust. The lawyer's influence with Sarah Stockwell Tyler had come about in just that way. Halsey really did have the background and expertise to handle Fitz Connely's inheritance, so why shouldn't he go on representing him on the board just as he had represented his great-grandmother?

What about the other members of the board? Patrice wondered. Who, she tried to guess, would want Halsey gone and replaced by someone with perhaps more integrity, but certainly less experience, and who would not? Patrice's eyes fell on Max Tyler.

Max was an anomaly. Forty-one years old, gay, he had started his own insurance company to write policies for gay people and—in the face of raised eyebrows from all the hard-headed Stockwells—made a great success of it. Low-key, witty when he wanted to be, he had turned out to be as good or better a businessman as any of his straight, and wealthier, Stockwell relatives. With his apricot Tyler hair and almond-shaped hazel eyes and a slim body kept in muscular trim by regular visits to the gym, he was an attractive and personable man. His homosexuality was not unrelated to his dislike of Halsey De Vilbiss. The California lawyer was not given to confronting Max, but Max was aware that he made remarks behind

35

his back. And Halsey invariably allied himself on the board with Peter Stockwell, who did openly bait Max with insults regarding his sexual orientation.

Practically, however, there were obvious reasons why Max might not want Tyrone Fitzwilliam Connely found. Max represented all of the Tyler shareholders' interests on the board of Stockwell Enterprises.

The combined stock, which was the end result of complicated familial relationships, added up to a major and influential share of Stockwell Enterprises. However, since Tyrone Fitzwilliam Connely was as much a Tyler as Max's clan, he might be able to claim his rightful share of all that they had inherited in addition to the substantial block of stock left him directly by his great-grandmother. This constituted a threat to all of the Tylers whom Max represented, and it posed a threat to his own position on the board as well.

Indeed, if Fitz Connely could make such a claim stick, his combined shares would come perilously close to giving him control of Stockwell Enterprises. That, Patrice realized, would threaten not only Max, but all of the other board members as well. Including, she realized, herself.

Patrice smiled inwardly. Her hands were tied by heredity. She was her father's daughter. Indeed, she was on the board as her father's replacement and felt obligated to consider his views in most situations. There was no doubt what James's position would be in this matter. Integrity demanded that every effort be made to find Fitz Connely and give him his rightful place on the board since that had been his great-grandmother's wish. James always believed in doing the right thing when possible. His daughter could do no less.

David Lewis, however, behaved more pragmatically than her father. What would his attitude be? He didn't like Halsey De Vilbiss, considered him a Southern California parvenu, and might not object to his being replaced. Still, Uncle David was bound to be concerned about the nature of the replacement. Whatever else Halsey was, he had proven himself adept in the heady world of corporate finance. Would David Lewis really want to exchange Halsey's expertise for a presumably uneducated Irish immigrant, a greenhorn still wet behind the ears? Such a novice might prove a disaster on the board. Just which way, Patrice wondered, would David Lewis's bias point him?

Patrice's musings were interrupted by Buffy Houston. The glamorous and frequently outrageous Buffy left no doubt as to where she stood regarding Fitz Connely. "For God's sake, Halsey," she told him, one hand on her voluptuously curved hip, "do make a *real* effort to find this heir. Maybe he'll be able to liven up these wakes we call board meetings." Buffy's smile did not bother to hide her distrust of Halsey, nor, for that matter, her dislike of all her one-time Stockwell in-laws. "Besides," she announced, "I never met an Irishman I didn't adore. And the younger the better."

How like Buffy! Despite herself, Patrice was grudgingly admiring. All the time Buffy had been married to the governor she had been disapproved of by the haughty Stockwells, and now Buffy felt free to let them know that that dislike was a two-way street.

Peter glared at Buffy openly, the hostile look reminding Patrice that Peter's instinct would always be for the jugular. And this taste for blood was what he had in common with Halsey. The two were invariably allies in prodding the board toward cutting corners for profit. Peter would not want to see Halsey replaced by someone who might have greater scruples. Their cooperation at board meetings demonstrated just how well one hand washed the other.

Patrice noted that the hands were now soaping up. Halsey initiated a discussion about acquiring the services of Productivity Insights, Inc., for certain Stockwell Enterprises subsidiaries. Halsey was in favor of this, and Peter supported him.

As Halsey explained the services of Productivity Insights in such terms as "motivational input," and "personnel malleability," and "increased productivity," Max,

37

in opposition, called the services "mind control" and claimed that Productivity's claims of success were "fraudulent." Buffy looked bored by the discussion, while David Lewis appeared puzzled.

"I don't understand," David Lewis blurted out finally. "Why should we give a three-million-point-two annual contract to some outside company to manipulate our work force when we already spend that much to insure top management by our own personnel departments?"

"New methods," Halsey De Vilbiss explained patiently. "Times change and we have to keep up with them. Training programs slanted toward developing on-the-job motivation by focusing on narrow self-interest are proving highly successful with outfits like Firestone Tire and Rubber, Pacific Bell, and the Puget Sound Naval Shipyards."

"But how do they work?" David Lewis was still not clear. "What do they actually do?"

"Workers are taught meditation, relaxation, self-hypnosis, how to induce trancelike states of mind," Halsey replied glibly. "They attend group therapy seminars designed to resolve personal problems and to redefine values that interfere with their work performance. When such blockages are rooted out, their productivity increases remarkably."

"But how are they rooted out?" David Lewis sounded impatient.

"Firewalking." Max injected the word quickly before Halsey could answer. "Barefoot on live coals. That's how." Noticing the raised eyebrows, he leaned forward and said earnestly, "They actually used that as part of an executive training program in a major West Coast corporation."

"Well, it would wake them up," David Lewis observed thoughtfully. "God knows some of our executives could use that."

"But why Productivity Insights, Halsey?" inquired Patrice. "I've never heard of them. I've heard of Werner Erhard's Transformational Technologies. I've heard of Pacific Institute, Edge Learning Institute, but not Productivity Insights.''

''Well, they're relatively new,'' Halsey admitted. ''But,'' he added quickly, ''they have some really innovative techniques well in advance of other employee-motivation programs. They're a really up-and-coming organization.''

''In which''—Buffy spoke for the first time, her tone just a little too sweet,—''Halsey here happens to be a major stockholder. Isn't that right, Halsey?''

Halsey's answering smile was a scimitar aimed at Buffy's throat. ''Yes,'' he admitted. ''I do have some shares in the company.''

''I don't see what difference that makes.'' Peter came in quickly; he was going to need Halsey's support later in the meeting. ''Our concern should be how reliable Productivity Insights is and how well their programs can work for us.''

''They offer an initial contract which we can cancel if in our own judgment the results don't measure up to our expectations.'' Halsey spread his hands. ''In effect, they are guaranteeing the results. And,'' he added, ''I'd just like to point out that such a guarantee renders my interest in Productivity Insights irrelevant to this discussion.''

Yes, Patrice thought, considering how the board looked down on him, Halsey could be remarkably persuasive. They voted finally to allow four major Stockwell subsidiaries to sign on for the Productivity Insights program. Only Max—still growling, ''Brainwashing!''—remained opposed.

Now Peter moved to call in the marker his support of Halsey had earned. ''Real estate,'' he said, and the way he said it laid claim to his status on the board as the acknowledged expert in this area. ''I have a proposal here''—he tapped his cordovan-leather Mark Cross briefcase—''with specifications for a major one-billion-dollar New York City development project.''

''One million dollars.'' David Lewis had misheard.

"Well, I don't think we should spend too much time discussing anything that paltry."

"Billion, sir," Halsey corrected him for Peter. "A one-billion-dollar project."

"To be constructed where?" Max Tyler was instantly alert.

"East Side," Peter replied. "Midtown south on the river. Forty-eight acres. A waterfront development with federal, state, and city money available for landfill. And I am in the process of negotiating for maximum advantages under Koch's city tax abatement program."

"Great." Max was sarcastic. "And what about the people who already live in those areas?"

"Since the project will be built out into the river, mostly they won't be bothered." Halsey, who already knew of the plan, defended Peter. "Only a few SRO units will be disturbed."

"How few?" Max shot back. "How disturbed?"

"Perhaps a hundred fifty units," Peter admitted. "The buildings housing those SROs are on sites that will be needed for anchorage. They'll have to come down."

"SROs?" Buffy was not familiar with the term. "What's that?"

"Single room occupancy." Max enlightened her. "Unmarried people with low incomes. When it comes to losing their homes, they don't count." His sarcasm heated up. "And while other tenants may not be thrown out of their apartments—some of the last middle-income rental housing on Manhattan Island, by the way—this development will block off their light and air. Won't it, Peter? I mean, just how high are you planning to go?"

"Sixty stories. More if we can get a building code zoning waiver."

"High-rise monstrosities and cramped apartments." Max was disgusted.

"Land is at a premium in Manhattan," Halsey reminded him. "You have to build small units, and you have to build up. The higher the building, the greater the profit."

"Halsey's right." Peter shrugged. "Progress always has its price."

"And if the price is right," Max responded, "in the words of old John D. Rockefeller—now evidently the Stockwell Enterprises motto—'the public be damned.' "

"You're not being fair, Max." Quietly, Patrice's hand moved to cover her frivolous bow as she took issue with him. "New York City has to expand its financial base. Redevelopment is a primary way of doing that. It creates construction jobs. It creates space for new businesses, which in turn create other kinds of jobs. And it creates housing units for the work force, thereby helping to alleviate a crisis situation in the city."

Max looked at Patrice with almond-shaped eyes that were narrowed with hurt. When it came to matters of social conscience, he had come to expect her to be on his side. Now he was disappointed. He sighed. "Listen, the city has been cutting deals—low-cost land, demolition permits, zoning waivers, and particularly tax abatements—with the Trumps and the Helmsleys and the Zeckendorfs ever since our current mayor took office. 'Expanding its financial base,' as you put it, has destroyed Manhattan's lower- and middle-class housing stock, pushed small-service businesses into bankruptcy with outrageous uncontrolled rentals, and lowered the quality of life in our city in a wide variety of areas, including public transportation, education, social services for homeless and hungry children, and the very air we breathe.

"Half the construction jobs redevelopment creates," Max continued, "go to workers from outside the city and are temporary. When the project is finished, much of that imported work force can be expected to end up on New York's unemployment lines. Experience tells us that the new businesses that move into the development will be white-collar service outfits rather than manufacturing enterprises and will therefore create few jobs. Many of those will be elitest middle-management positions, and those who fill them will move here from other places, and they will doubtless occupy some of the housing units Peter will build. 'In any case, those units will be beyond the reach of the lower- and middle-class native New Yorkers who have lost their housing to so many other redevelopment projects. Believe me, Patrice, Peter's units will not be designed to alleviate New York's rental housing crisis. His buildings will be condo, and the units will go for upwards of a quarter of a million dollars.''

''Is that true?'' Patrice turned to Peter. ''Is the residential part of the package going to be high-priced condo?''

Peter spread his hands. ''That's where the profit is.''

''And there is a housing shortage,'' Halsey interjected quickly, once again supporting Peter. ''These are housing units, and they are badly needed.''

''For the rich!'' Max exploded.

''The upper-middle class must have a place to live, too.'' Halsey's phrasing was meant to be conciliatory.

''You have to earn a hundred thousand a year, or you won't pass the condo credit check.'' Max snorted. ''Upper-middle class my ass!''

''I'm never sure about these discussions with you, Max.'' Peter's voice was cold. ''Was that an offer? Is it your own sweet, gay way of trying to make friends?''

Before Max could respond and the situation escalate, David Lewis intervened. ''We are businessmen, not social workers,'' he reminded them. ''Could we get down to brass tacks? I'd like to see the financial specifications for this project, Peter. I think we should all have a look at them.''

Peter opened the Mark Cross briefcase and distributed six neat computer printouts of the plans for the redevelopment project. The stapled sheets spelled out the construction breakdown for forty-eight acres, proposing ten luxury apartment towers of sixty stories (a footnote raised the hope of adding sixteen more stories to each building), two forty-story office buildings, a sprawling twenty-story hotel, and a covered mall with shops, restaurants, and a motion picture theater complex. Most of this would be built on a sixteen-block, two-hundred-million-dollar platform to be anchored over landfill in the East River.

42

There was no denying it, Patrice realized. The scope of the project was breathtaking. It would take six years to complete, but when it was done it could be one of the proudest sights in the city. In the end, with all of the board members except Max, she voted to authorize Peter to go ahead with the project.

"Merry Christmas, Max." Patrice pecked him on the cheek as she exited the boardroom.

"Merry Christmas," Max echoed automatically. "Merry Christmas to all—or at least to those who can afford the rent!"

5

THE OLD MAN sat up in his Yonkers nursing home bed and guffawed. "You'll never guess what old Santa's bringing you for Christmas, Jackie."

"I almost forgot Christmas is coming up, Grandpa." Jack Houston was not in the spirit. "I've had other things on my mind."

"Like not ending up with your torso all hacked up to fit in the trunk of a car dumped in the wilds of Queens, boy?" The old man cackled. "That the sort of thing been troubling your mind?"

"It's not funny, Grandpa. If I hadn't listened to you—"

"I'm not Harry Truman, and the buck doesn't stop here, boy. You had wife trouble, and you thought having as much money as that almighty Stockwell widow ball-and-chain of yours would solve it. All I did was point a direction and set up a few contacts."

"Only the contacts were organized crime bosses."

"Hell, boy, you didn't have time to go out and steal it legally the way those Stockwells did in the first place. You wanted to be as rich as she was snap-crackle-pop without reading the label on the box. Well, that label read 'Risk,' boy. You're out of diapers, and when you asked for help, I figured it was up to me to give it, and up to you to be responsible for yourself."

"I guess you're right, Grandpa." Jack sighed. "I'm sorry."

"It was a damn good plan," the old man mumbled truculently.

"Only it didn't turn out," Jack said bitterly. "It fell through. And when it did, those connected contacts of yours decided it was my fault, and ever since I've had to keep looking over my shoulder for their hit man."

"Well, you cost them a lot of money, Jackie. You were the inside man, and inside is where it all fell apart." The old man's gaze started to wander, as it did when his attention strayed, which it frequently did. "Always falls apart." he mumbled. "Always. Before you can even get it on the spoon."

"Grandpa?"

"Jell-O. Every damn night, and it slides off quick as you can scoop it up. Lousy Jell-O."

"I know it wasn't your fault, Grandpa. Really I do. I just get tired of living in fear. If you knew how scared I was to come back to New York—"

"I hate Jell-O!"

"Knowing they're out to get me—"

"Merry Christmas, boy! Ho-ho-ho!" Suddenly the old man shot up in the bed again, his problems with Jell-O forgotten, and focused on Jack. "Ready for your present now?"

"Sure, Grandpa." Jack was used to making fast adjustments to the old man's mercurial thought processes.

"Then here it is, boy." The old man reached under the covers, then brought his hands out quick and high and held them up empty. "Merry Christmas, Jackie."

44

Jack stared for an instant. Then he shrugged. "Thank you, Grandpa."

"Putz!" the old man roared. "They're empty. Can't you see that?"

"I guess it's time for me to go now, Grandpa."

"Now don't you sulk, boy. Time you grew up and learned to take a joke. Anyway, I do have a Christmas present for you. One that's really gonna gladden the old heart cockles. So come on over here and sit on Santa's knee."

Jack sat down gingerly on the edge of the bed.

"Well, close enough, I guess. Now, boy, hear this. The Padrone is dead."

"Huh?"

"That's your Christmas present, boy. He's dead. New management. Your name's been crossed off the hit list."

Jack blinked. "Let me get this straight. Are you telling me that the Don has died?"

"No, putz! Not the Don. He's my friend. I wouldn't be rejoicing if he bought it. It's the Padrone ate lead."

"And who," Jack asked carefully, "is the Padrone?"

"Top man. The Don's boss. Long as he was calling the shots, the Don had no choice but to put the dogs on you. But now that he's gone, and the new Padrone doesn't care, the Don can let you off the hook."

"Is this for real, Grandpa? They called off the hit men?"

"You got it, Jackie boy. Your butt is no longer on the chopping block courtesy of the Don and Mister Helmut van Huyck."

"Helmut van Huyck?"

"He's the new Padrone."

"A Dutchman?"

"Shut your mouth, boy. Don't ever call him that. The Padrone considers himself an American born and raised, and anybody who calls him 'Dutchman' is asking for a long walk off a short pier in a cement overcoat. You could go right back on the hit list, Jackie."

"I'll never call him anything but Mr. van Huyck

45

again," Jack promised. "But are you sure, Grandpa? Really sure?"

"You're a putz, Jackie, but you're my flesh and blood. I wouldn't kid about your life. It's true. The Don called me. You're in from the cold."

"That's great news." For the first time since he'd entered the room, Jack smiled. "Really great. I'm going to leave now, Grandpa. I can't wait to tell Buffy."

"The Stockwell widow? Oh, I know"—the old man cut his protests short—"she's your wife and you love her— whatever the hell that means. Well, go on, then, boy. Run back to Mama."

"It really is a great Christmas present, Grandpa." Jack started for the door.

"Jackie." The old man stopped him. "I forgot to tell you. Fellow's been calling here looking for you. Says he's an old buddy of yours. Name of Kevin Doyle.'

"Kevin Doyle!" The name brought Jack up short. "Christ! I thought he was dead. The last time I saw him six years ago in Angola they were carrying him off on a stretcher with a hole in his chest you could put your fist in. I guess old Kevin was just too mean to die. Did he leave a number where I can reach him?"

"No. But he gave me the name of a bar. He said he hangs out there most nights and you should look him up. And if he's not there, the bartender can get a message to him. I didn't tell him anything about where you were because I figured he just might be one of those gunsels looking for you before the old Padrone bought it."

"That was probably good thinking, Grandpa. What's the name of the bar?"

"The Fair Colleen Pub. He said it's down in the Village."

"Thanks, Grandpa." Jack repeated the name. "The Fair Colleen."

6

"WHOEVER SAID COLLEENS were fair," Matt Stockwell teased Kathleen O'Lunney, "might have been referring to looks, but never to the way they play Scrabble."

"No matter the ethnic," Kathleen shot back, "let any woman best a man and he begins to spout blarney."

The sassy way she tossed her head, sending her bright red ponytail flying, reminded Matt of the Morgan filly he'd just bought for his horse-breeding farm. Like Kathleen, the Morgan was independent and high-spirited, but tender of eye and responsive to affection. Some women might not be flattered to be compared to a horse by the man they loved, but Kathleen, Matt knew, would understand.

Horses were Matt's life, and the breeding farm, five miles east of Riverview and eight miles from the Hudson River, was a dream come true. It was all his—worked for, saved for, bought and paid for—separate from Riverview and from any involvement with Stockwell money. He had acquired it by his own sweat before the bequest from his grandfather and grandmother two years earlier, and even today Matthew was careful to keep the money he'd inherited separate from his horse-breeding business. It was a source of pride that the farm showed a modest profit on its—and his—own terms.

He and Kathleen were sitting over the Scrabble board at the kitchen table in the small, rather dilapidated house that had come with the farm. The barn had been equally dilapidated when Matt bought the property, but he had virtually redone it from roof to cellar. He kept meaning to fix up the house, too, but something more important always seemed to take precedence. "Your horses live better than you do," Kathleen would tease him. "And when I marry you they'll live better than I will as well."

Matt loved the way they bantered. They were always free with each other, easy and relaxed, and their sexual passion, which had been intense from the beginning, continued to grow and deepen.

Now Matt searched the dictionary beside the Scrabble board on the kitchen table. "Aha!" he said. "Just as I thought. Not listed. O-e! You made it up, you treacherous wench!"

"No such thing!" Kathleen was indignant. "O-e is a perfectly good word. An oe is a Faroe Islands whirlwind."

"Well, it's not in the dictionary."

"A *Webster's Second*." Kathleen shrugged her round, healthy shoulders contemptuously. "The only definitive *Webster's* is the *Third* edition. You'll find it there."

"Since I don't have one, that's a pretty safe cop-out."

"It's not a cop-out." Her eyes, loving and lambent, flashed with mock anger. "I know what I'm talking about. I'm an expert, remember. I'm majoring in linguistics."

"Linguistics!" Matt snorted. "You make me play Scrabble to hold my lust at bay." He came around the table and kissed her. It was a long kiss, and his hands moved over her responsive body lovingly and hungrily.

"Not tonight." Kathleen pushed him away reluctantly. "Pa expects me back at Riverview. Strict curfew for the servant classes."

"Unfair to the lusty young master."

"You gave up your claim to being a Riverview master when you went over the hill," Kathleen reminded him. "Sorry," she said instantly. "I didn't mean that the way it came out."

"It's okay." It was a long time, Matt thought, since he'd fled Riverview, and his country as well. He had stayed in Canada more than three years and been back

48

almost seven. Even so, his defiance of the draft continued to pigeonhole him with some people. Kathleen wasn't one of them, but still . . . He grimaced.

"I really am sorry." Kathleen took his face gently between the palms of her hands. "I must have sounded like your Uncle David."

"How would I know how Uncle David sounds?" Matt was bitter. "Since he refuses to talk to me."

"I'd hoped he and your aunt Alice might be there the other night when you had me in to meet the family."

"Not likely. To Uncle David I'll always be a coward and a traitor to my country, in contrast with his dead son, who died a hero's death in Vietnam. The fact that Mark didn't want to go to Vietnam and wouldn't have gone—would be alive today, as a matter of fact—if his hawk father hadn't insisted he serve doesn't count. Mark is dead. I'm alive. Uncle David's son is a hero. His nephew is a scoundrel. Mark's been dead almost twelve years, but Uncle David won't change. He won't come to a family function if I'm there. And if he does run into me at Riverview by accident, he looks right through me and won't talk to me."

"You'd think at least your aunt Alice—"

"Aunt Alice is under Uncle David's thumb. She never got over Mark's death, but she doesn't hate me like Uncle David does. I think she just doesn't have the energy to stand up to him. They're not alone," Matt observed. "Lots of people will never be able to put Vietnam behind them. In more ways than one," he added, his mind going off on an even more personal tangent.

Kathleen was familiar with the tangent. "Is there anything new?" she asked carefully.

"Not really." Matt, too, tread cautiously. Bruce, his seven-year-old son—or, more accurately, Bruce's mother—was a touchy topic between them.

Wendy MacTavish and Matt Stockwell had lived together throughout most of the time he was in Canada. When her strict, peacenik-hating, Scotch Presbyterian father had thrown her out of the house for taking up with a draft dodger from the States, Wendy had moved in with Matt. Shortly after she became pregnant with Bruce, she had left him.

Even now it hurt Matt to think about their breakup. He had been insensitive, scared of the responsibilities of fatherhood, and had regarded the pregnancy as a problem rather than a blessing. He had pushed hard for her to have an abortion.

Wendy hadn't argued against him. She had neither agreed nor disagreed. One day she was simply gone. For a long time Matt had tried to find her in vain. Finally he had given up. The Vietnam War was over; for the most part passions among both doves and hawks had cooled; Matt went back to the States without seeing Wendy again or ever having seen the child she'd borne him.

Then, quite by accident, two years ago he had bumped into Wendy in a diner near Albany. As a result of that chance meeting, Matt had learned that he had a five-year-old son named Bruce. Naturally, he wanted to see him.

There had been difficulties with that. Because of the war, which Wendy abhorred, she had strong negative feelings regarding the Stockwells, who had enthusiastically supported it. Once she and Matt had shared that anger. Indeed, his bitterness toward his family and Wendy's sympathy with it had been an important part of their relationship. Now Wendy did not want Bruce to come under the seductive influence of Stockwell wealth and power.

Subsequently, a visit to Wendy in Canada by Matt's father had softened her attitude. She had agreed to allow Bruce to spend time with his father and even to visit his Stockwell relatives at Riverview. It was two years since that agreement had been reached, but it had yet to be implemented.

Matt still had to travel up to Canada to see Bruce, who was now seven years old. On these trips, naturally, he saw Wendy. There were things they had to discuss about their son and about the obstacle to his coming to New York. Sometimes Matt even took Wendy out to dinner so they could talk things over out of Bruce's hearing. He never lied to Kathleen about these contacts with Wendy. And he understood very well how unhappy she was with them.

"I really don't understand why the situation can't be resolved." Kathleen broke the silence, still choosing her words carefully. "If Wendy is willing, as you say she is—"

"It's not Wendy. It's her father. She went back to him with Bruce because she had no money after he was born and had no place else to go. Her father took her back, but there were conditions. The main one was that her child should have no contact with his 'cowardly draft-dodging, rich-boy' father. Wendy was forced to agree."

"But you do have contact with Bruce. You go up to Montreal to see him every other week, sometimes more. And to see his mother, too," Kathleen added pointedly.

"I can see Bruce in Montreal because Wendy can arrange that without her father knowing. She can't arrange for Bruce to come down here because she couldn't keep it from him."

"So says Wendy." Kathleen could not keep the sarcasm out of her voice.

"It's over between Wendy and me," Matt responded bluntly.

"So says Matthew."

"Kathleen!"

"You were very much in love with her once. You told me so. How do you expect me to feel when you keep traveling up to Montreal to see her?"

"I don't go to see her. I go to see my son." Matt's voice was weary.

"But you do see her. And sometimes without your son."

"To discuss Bruce. Because he's Wendy's son, too. She's concerned about his welfare, about his relationship to me, just as I am. What do you want me to do, Kathleen? Lie to you about seeing Wendy?"

"No. I don't want you to lie." Kathleen sighed. "It's

51

just that I want us to be married, Matt, and soon, if you please. But I'll not marry you until you've settled things so Wendy is out of our lives. I'll not be starting a marriage with my husband all the time traipsing off to see another woman." As emotion took over her voice, Kathleen's brogue increased.

Matt noticed. "You always get so damn Irish when you're angry with me," he said.

"Irish it is, then! And Irish it will be, Matthew Stockwell, until I am the one and only colleen in your messed-up life!" Kathleen kissed him quickly on the lips, a rather cool kiss. "I have to be going."

Matt walked her to her car, unhappy with the strained parting, and watched the taillights of her old Plymouth vanish around the bend in the country dirt road leading to Riverview.

7

At Riverview, Patrice and her cousin Holly Meyerling were almost through sorting the Christmas decorations for the servants to hang. It was still a week away from putting up the tree itself, but the holiday spirit was in the air. Berkley could have assigned the chore to one of the staff, but separating out the strands of lights and tinsel and the imported, handmade painted figurines of angels and snowmen was a task that took Patrice and Holly back to their childhoods, and they couldn't resist doing it themselves. Indeed, their mood, the pace of their chatter and their frequent laughter, was more girlish than suitable to two young women in their thirties.

"What do you hear from Zelig?" Patrice playfully slapped Holly's hand away from a blown-glass shepherd's crock she was about to reach for herself.

"Not much. He's very busy with the National Security Council. Unofficially, of course. All very hush-hush. Something to do with Nicaragua. There's a vote coming up in Congress and I think the administration expects to lose. So they're making contingency plans. From what I can gather, Zelig is trying to talk them out of them." Holly screwed the last tulip-shaped red-and-green bulbs into their sockets.

"That just about does it for now." Patrice reached behind to the small of her back and massaged so hard that the bow she was wearing came undone. "We've been sitting too long," she said as she retied it. "I'll never be able to unbend."

"Sure you will, old lady." Holly slipped effortlessly to her feet and reached out her hand to help Patrice.

"God, how I hate you tall, slender types." Patrice accepted the hand and stood up, groaning. "You have no joints."

"Ball bearings," Holly told her.

"I'm going to go soak in a hot tub and then lie down until dinner with a good book."

"What are you reading?"

"Nothing, actually. I thought I'd browse through the library and find something." Like all the Stockwells of their generation who had grown up at Riverview, Patrice took for granted the well-stocked private library housed in the mansion's north tower.

"I've been reading the Seabury diaries I found there," Holly told her.

"For your history of Riverview?" Holly had for some time been engaged in researching and compiling notes on their family and its ancestral home. While Patrice was studying for a more traditional Stockwell career—business administration—at Columbia, Holly had taken her master's in history at Bryn Mawr. She had even traveled to Amsterdam to study the records of the Dutch East India

53

Company's role in the pioneering of Riverview. "What," Patrice asked now, "are the Seabury diaries?"

"A sort of informal record kept by our great-great-great-grandmother, Edith Seabury. She married Charles Cabot Stockwell. He's the one who rebuilt Riverview after the fire of 1838. Their story is really romantic. I have the diary she kept for the period when they first met in my room if you'd like to look at it, Patrice."

"All right. It does sound interesting."

So it was that an hour later Patrice sat propped up in her bed in a dressing gown and with a towel tied like a turban over her drying hair as she opened a carefully preserved and bound diary from the year 1848.

Mrs. Amelia Jenks Bloomer of Seneca Falls, New York, and her younger, unmarried companion, Miss Edith Seabury of New York City, were not as impressed by the spanking-new steamer carrying them up the Hudson River that hot June day in 1848 as were many of the male passengers on board. Between themselves they agreed that while the screw propeller powering the ship might increase speed and be more efficient, it was much less interesting to watch than the paddle wheels that had driven riverboats since Robert Fulton had first sailed the *Clermont* up the Hudson forty years before. And—although it was well before their time—the two women also agreed that the most picturesque ships of all to sail the river had undoubtedly been the original three-masters that had relied on wind and current and had not polluted the air with the foul-smelling steam of burning coal.

By the time Bear Mountain came into view, the women had abandoned the afterdeck to the men hanging over the rail and peering at the propeller as they explained to each other its principles of operation. Seating themselves in deck chairs, Mrs. Bloomer, who had made the journey from New York City to Seneca Falls before, proceeded to tell her companion what to expect. "The trip to Albany is the pleasure part of the journey, my dear, and you should enjoy it while you can," she told Edith Seabury. "When we transfer to the barge for the Erie Canal, you can forget about comfort."

"Barge?" It was Edith's first river journey, and her deep-set blue eyes widened. "I thought we were traveling by flatboat."

"That is what they call it. And there are cabins of a sort, although one is hard put to stand erect in them. But the truth is they are really only cargo barges that have been gussied up to accommodate passengers. They're poled by crewmen and pulled by mules, and the journey is slow, and hot in summer as we change direction from north to west, and very grimy. You would be wise to cover your head well lest the soot and dust turn your lovely golden hair the color of river mud."

"Well, I don't really care," Edith declared. "Our purpose is surely worth whatever discomfort is involved."

"Surely." Mrs. Bloomer's tone was dry. She genuinely liked Edith, but she had herself been a woman activist of sorts for close to half of her thirty years and was a little leery regarding the enthusiasms of one who had but recently awakened to such concerns at the age of twenty-two.

Still, Edith Seabury was a very unusual young woman. A merchant's daughter, his only child, because her mother had died in childbirth, Edith was quite the apple of her father's eye. The family, while not wealthy, was reasonably well off, and Edith had been raised comfortably in their respectably upper-middle-class Greek revival townhouse on the Bowery. She had attended an exclusive academy for young ladies with girls from established old Dutch and English families and went riding with them on the open farmlands just to the north of what would one day be Union Square.

Now, at the age of twenty-two, Edith was an aspiring artist at a time when convention barred women painters from being taken seriously. Unlike most young ladies her age, she was not married. With her blond hair and blue eyes, grave, aquiline features, and stylishly rounded figure, she was considered something of a beauty by the young men who had come calling at the Seabury home. More than one had been interested in her, and her father, at Edith's request, had turned down three proposals of marriage for her, the first when she was barely seventeen. Before many of her suitors could reach the stage of asking her father for her hand, she had herself turned off the glint in the eyes of other eligible young men.

It was not that Edith disliked men. She was attracted to the opposite sex. But her permissive rearing had given her a rare insight: she knew that there could be more to life than wifehood and motherhood. When—and if—the right man came along, her mind would be open. Until then, as she had recently discovered, there was woman's work to be done. Her father, secretly delighted to have Edith with him for as long as she wished to remain unmarried, was remarkably supportive of both her painting and her recent feminist interests.

Edith had met Mrs. Bloomer at a small gathering of women held to hear her speak. While not as well known as Elizabeth Cady Stanton or Lucretia Mott, Mrs. Amelia Jenks Bloomer had gained some renown as an advocate of dress reform for women. She was outspoken regarding the tyranny of tight corsets, stays, and hoop skirts, arguing that they were the most visible evidence of the constricted role of women in the world.

On the occasion where the two women had met, Mrs. Bloomer had bypassed dress reform to tell her small audience about a convention of women to be held in Seneca Falls on July 19 ''to discuss the social, civil, and religious rights of women.'' Much impressed, Edith had gone up to Mrs. Bloomer when the talk was over and asked if it would be possible for her to attend the convention.

The two women were in their cabin dressing for dinner when the chug-drone of the screw propeller ceased and the ship began angling in toward the shore. ''I didn't

56

think we were scheduled to make another stop so soon after Poughkeepsie," Edith commented.

"We're not." Mrs. Bloomer was sure.

As they went back up on deck to investigate, the steamer was pulling alongside a small, private dock and a gangplank was being lowered. A tall, slender man of about thirty wearing the uniform of a United States Army captain stood waiting there. When the plank was secured, he boarded the vessel with a confident stride. Edith caught a close-up glimpse of a sandy mustache and a sportsman's ruddy cheeks as the gentleman was conducted to the steamer captain's cabin.

Getting under way again proved trickier than stopping had been. First the gangplank snagged the dock and two crewmen had to go down to free it. Then a rope ladder had to be lowered and secured so that they could get back on board. The tide seemed to be working against them this close to shore, and several sailors with poles had to push the ship back out into the center of the river before the screw propellers could be started again so that the ship could continue upstream.

Edith and Mrs. Bloomer settled into deck chairs and watched while all this was happening. "That was Captain Charles Cabot Stockwell who boarded," Mrs. Bloomer informed her young companion. "River steamers don't change their schedules for just anybody, you know."

"What makes him so important?"

"Well, for one thing, he owns the steamship line on which we are traveling. For another, he is a genuine hero of the Mexican War from which he has just returned. Not that we would have stopped for just any old hero." Mrs. Bloomer was sardonic. "The main thing is that he is a Stockwell of Riverview."

"Riverview?"

"That is Riverview." Mrs. Bloomer gestured toward an imposing mansion on a distant hilltop overlooking the river.

"It looks new."

"It is. The old place burned down ten years ago. A

57

terrible fire. His father and his brother died in it, I believe. Charles Stockwell, the only surviving son, rebuilt it."

"I can't say much for his taste." Edith gazed disapprovingly at the edifice in the distance. "Gothic revival. Ugh. It's a monstrosity."

"For your information, my dear young lady . . ." The deep, cultured voice coming from behind them took Edith by surprise. She twisted around in her deck chair to find Charles Stockwell's mustached visage gazing down on her from the porthole of the captain's cabin. "That monstrosity was designed by Alexander Jackson Davis. Do you know who Alexander Jackson Davis is?"

"I do, sir." Rattled though she was, Edith did not hesitate to answer forthrightly. "Alexander Jackson Davis is a fashionable architect most highly regarded by wealthy people. Artists—more critical, perhaps—find his designs highly derivative, if not downright imitative."

He raised an eyebrow. "You are qualified to speak for—ahh—artists."

"As it happens, I am, sir. I am an artist myself. A painter."

"I see. A female artist. Well then, the only thing left for me to say is that not having had the benefit of your advice before rebuilding my home, I shall just have to live with the inferior design of Alexander Jackson Davis as best I can." The nod of his well-sculpted head in the porthole conveyed an overly courtly bow as he withdrew.

Edith and Mrs. Bloomer went back to their cabin to finish dressing for dinner. "A very attractive man," Mrs. Bloomer commented when they were alone.

"I really didn't notice."

Mrs. Bloomer arched an eyebrow. "Well, he certainly noticed you."

"I'm not interested," Edith said curtly, but despite her disclaimer, she blushed slightly. "My focus is on bettering the lot of women, not attracting the attention of men."

"Ahh." Mrs. Bloomer nodded wisely. "Such dedication."

* * *

Mrs. Bloomer guessed that Charles Stockwell must have had a word with the steward when she and Edith were seated on either side of him at the captain's table for dinner that night. Edith, however, was unresponsive to Captain Stockwell's efforts at conversation. When Mrs. Bloomer proved more friendly, he redirected his efforts toward her.

"How far upriver are you ladies traveling?" he inquired.

"Oh, we're transferring at the canal. Seneca Falls is our destination. And you, sir?"

"I'm going to Buffalo and then on to Detroit to inspect some family holdings. Mines and foundries. Some timberlands in the area, too. Like you, I shall transfer at the canal. Observation of the Erie operation is also on my itinerary."

"Is the Erie Canal also a Stockwell family holding?" Mrs. Bloomer inquired lightly.

"As a matter of fact, the Stockwells do own major shares in the Erie." His words were a simple statement of fact—not a boast, yet unapologetic for the largesse that was his.

Mrs. Bloomer smiled. "I suspected as much."

"You see, I've been away, and so it's been a very long time since I've had a chance to survey my properties."

"You've been away in the war." Mrs. Bloomer's gaze took in his uniform.

"Yes. I lost weight." Captain Stockwell had too much natural poise to be embarrassed. "None of my clothes fit me. And so I flaunt my uniform until I can find leisure for my tailor. But then I did don it in a good cause."

"The Mexican War"—Edith interjected herself into their conversation—"can hardly be called 'a good cause.' "

"You did not approve of the war, Miss Seabury?" His warm brown eyes indicated that he was happy she had

59

joined their discussion even if it was to oppose what he said.

"I did not. It is my belief that wars of conquest should be left to Europe. I hold my country to a higher standard."

"Then you do not embrace the concept of manifest destiny, Miss Seabury?"

"A fancy phrase for stealing other people's land. All it really means is that might makes right."

"Yes, well, I can assure you that might makes right was General Santa Anna's belief. And that is why he had to be opposed."

"Sophistry, Captain Stockwell. That is purely justification after the fact. The truth is that we have coveted Texas and California for some time. The war was simply a pretext to seize them. Manifest destiny indeed! Why should the boundaries of the continent be configured to our national interests any more than to Mexico's?"

"Because there has not been in our time a Mexican government capable of keeping itself in power. Mexico has been ruled by France and Spain, and the likelihood is that one or the other of them will rule it again. We dare not have a European monarchy in possession of areas threatening the security of our country."

"Canada belongs to England," Edith reminded him. "Perhaps," she added sarcastically, "your trip to Detroit—which is, after all, on the Canadian border—presages new hostilities, Captain Stockwell."

"You have found me out." He was equally ironic. "We march on Ontario just as soon as I can resharpen my sword."

Mrs. Bloomer chuckled.

"And do you agree with your friend about the war?" Captain Stockwell asked her.

"Oh, I leave wars to men," Mrs. Bloomer replied. "They do enjoy them so, and it keeps them out of mischief."

Now it was Edith who laughed.

"And what areas would you allocate to women?"

Mrs. Bloomer looked him straight in the eye. She was no longer smiling. "Universal suffrage and abolition," she told him flatly.

"Well, there is much to be said for abolition."

"Are you an abolitionist, then?" Edith's tone implied she was sure he was not.

"I think that slavery should be allowed to die out."

"And just how long do you think this death scene should take?"

"You do me an injustice. I have just come from one war. The last thing I want to see is another one which pits one-half of our country against the other. My sister lives in the South with her husband, and I have no desire to take up arms against him. Slavery is an evil, but we here in the North have much to answer for in its establishment. It was our ships, our investments, that brought the Africans to this country as slaves. We have no right to be holier-than-thou toward our southern brethren. I want to see slavery ended, but I want to see it ended peaceably. These things take time."

"Black people under the lash have run out of time. They have not leisure for the patience of northern moderation, sir."

"And yet only moderation may prevent a national tragedy."

"Captain Stockwell is definitely not an abolitionist," Edith informed Mrs. Bloomer.

"Perhaps he is a suffragist," Mrs. Bloomer suggested wryly. "What say you, sir?"

"Alas, no. I have too high a regard for women to trouble them with the messiness of politics."

"Have you ever seen a woman give birth to a baby, Captain Stockwell?" Mrs. Bloomer asked him, not unkindly.

His cheeks flushed at the question. "No. I have not."

"It is not neat. If we women can handle that, I suspect we can handle the mess of politics."

"He would rather our hands were tied against our rights as our bodies are bound against the freedom of movement to function physically as men do.'' Edith paraphrased Mrs. Bloomer's crusade to free women from the bondage of their confining clothing.

"I beg your pardon?'' Captain Stockwell was genuinely bewildered.

"Edith is referring to the whalebone and bindings which protect women from the messy spilling-over of their flesh,'' Mrs. Bloomer explained. Her tone was firm, but she was still not hostile toward him.

He glanced from one lady to the other. His look was admiring, and his words were intended to be gallant. "Surely that fear can have no application to either one of you ladies,'' he said.

His words coincided with the serving of dessert. Shortly thereafter, Edith and Mrs. Bloomer excused themselves to take a turn around the deck before retiring. Watching them go, Captain Stockwell was left with the feeling that he had made something less than a good impression on the combative Miss Seabury.

He was right. As soon as they were alone, Edith exploded to Amelia Bloomer. "What an insufferable fellow!'' she exclaimed.

"You're too hard on him, Edith. He is only a man, a prisoner of his gender. He can't help being male, after all. As men go, you will find many far worse. To tell the truth, I thought you were rather hard on him. He's obviously attracted to you, and he seemed to me to be bending over backward to be pleasant.''

"Pleasant! Is that how you define his puerile logic regarding war, slavery, and women's rights?''

"Ah, Edith. As you grow older, you will learn not to dissipate your energies in conversational battle with individual men and to reserve them for the real campaign we women shall have to wage.''

In line with Mrs. Bloomer's advice, Edith engaged in no further argument with Captain Charles Stockwell during meals. At other times she simply avoided him. By the time they reached Albany and changed to the flatboat for their journey westward on the Erie Canal, her message had gotten across. A proud man, Captain Stockwell did not force his company on her.

Indeed, after they switched to the canal barge he avoided her just as she did him, directing his attention instead to the operation of the canal and the flood of commerce it directed. Wealthy though he was, Charles Stockwell was the sort of man who felt compelled to understand the machinery of his holdings down to the last detail. Not too long before they reached Seneca Falls, this curiosity proved very nearly fatal to him.

Man-made, the Erie Canal had not for most of its three-hundred-sixty-three-mile length been dug very deeply. Although forty feet wide, its depth varied only from four to seven feet. It had never been intended for riverboats whose keels required greater depths, and, indeed, the craft that navigated the canal were all flat-bottomed to conform to its shallowness.

Despite this, the unevenness of the terrain over which the canal had been constructed caused occasional sharp drops in the level of the canal bed. These were compensated for by the locks through which the vessels had to pass. The principle of these locks was very simple.

A flatboat passing from a deeper depth to a more shallow one would be admitted to the lock at the higher water level. The lock would be closed, shutting off the flow in both directions. The water inside the lock would be drained to the lesser depth. Then the other side of the lock would be opened, and the craft would pass through at the lower level. During this process, however, when the lock was flooded, the vessel might find itself temporarily at a greater depth than at any place in the canal itself. Because of the delicacy involved in adjusting the water level, the depth inside the lock could be ten feet or more.

It was inside the lock just east of Seneca Falls that Captain Charles Stockwell leaned too far out from a water-slicked deck to observe the machinery of the drainage pumps. He fell from the flatboat into a whirlpool of water created by the draining operation. Although he had grown up on the Hudson, Captain Stockwell had never really learned how to swim. Taken by surprise, flailing to no advantage, he felt the whirlpool sucking him down. Ten feet of water may not be a very great depth, but it is quite enough to drown in. Fighting his way to the surface, blinded by the turmoil of the water, Captain Stockwell yelled for help.

As it happened, Edith was strolling on deck alone at this time. Mrs. Bloomer was in their cabin napping. Hearing the cry, she peered over the side and saw Captain Stockwell's predicament, although he was too blinded by the churning water to see her.

Edith acted with dispatch. She spied a life preserver and threw it over the side to Captain Stockwell. Her toss was strong, her aim true, and when she saw that he had it, she went and found two stalwart sailors to haul him out of the water.

Edith was not in evidence when Captain Stockwell was pulled back on board. Later, however, she was strolling the deck when Charles Stockwell, having changed his clothes, sought out the sailors who had rescued him and pressed some money on them along with his effusive thanks.

"If you are rich enough," Edith commented to Mrs. Bloomer, "you can buy anything. Even life itself."

She had spoken more loudly than she intended. Overhearing, Charles Stockwell shot a furious look at her.

His fury had not much abated the next day when he watched from the deck as Edith and Mrs. Bloomer disembarked from the flatboat at Seneca Falls. One of the sailors he had tipped was checking a rope hawser alongside him. Noticing whom Captain Stockwell was observing, he commented.

"You won't be forgetting that lady, I'll wager, sir," he said.

"Unforgettable." Charles Stockwell's response was dry.

"I should think so, sir. It's not many men have their lives saved by so attractive a young miss."

"What do you mean?"

The seaman explained.

"I'll be damned!" Charles Stockwell stared at Edith Seabury on the dock with gratitude and with new respect. "I'd no idea. I must thank her." He started to move toward the gangplank.

"No time, sir. We're casting off."

"Damn!" Captain Stockwell took a deep breath and then shouted with a voice he had not used since rallying his men in the midst of battle at Cerro Gordo in Mexico. "Miss Seabury!" he bellowed.

"Yes?" Startled, Edith responded.

"Thank you for saving my life," he thundered.

"It was nothing." Her voice was thin and clear. "Women have been saving men from their own foolhardiness since the dawn of history."

"Nevertheless, my heartfelt thanks." The boat was moving away from the dock. "And I hope we shall meet again so that I may express my thanks less boisterously."

"What?" The noises on the dock were obscuring his words.

"We shall meet again!" Captain Stockwell bellowed, pronouncing each word strong and clear.

"On the barricades!" Her thin voice barely reached his ears. "Women's time is coming!"

If Captain Stockwell replied at all, his answer was lost to the strong river breeze. Edith turned to Mrs. Bloomer and shrugged. "Perhaps I should have let him drown," she said.

"Why do you say that, my dear?"

"If men are the enemy, then that is particularly true of men as powerful and entrenched and intransigent as Charles Cabot Stockwell."

"Are you really that attracted to him?" Mrs. Bloomer teased.

"Well, he is not altogether unattractive." It was the first time Edith had admitted that—even to herself.

65

"True. And," Mrs. Bloomer added, "a man as rich and influential and powerful as Charles Stockwell could also be a very, very powerful ally."

8

"WHICH SIDE ARE you on, boy? Which side are you on?"

The chorus of voices demanding that the newcomer declare himself as he came through the swinging doors of the Fair Colleen, was raucous, off-key, and Irish as Mulligan stew. Backing it up was the tempo of stamping feet—not a pair under size ten in the place—marking time to the war cry with a spirit that threatened to dislodge the Yuletide decorations from the rafters and the dark-stained hardwood walls of the old West Village pub.

"Up the Irish!" Jack Houston's raised fist pledged allegiance.

"Up the rebels! Out the Brits!" An arm round Jack's shoulder pulled him against the bar, and somebody bought him a drink.

Jack bought a round back, and only then did he ask the question that had brought him to the pub. "Kevin Doyle been around?" he inquired.

"Kevin is it, then?" A hand big as a wrench turned Jack's shoulder like the final twist to a wheel lug and pointed him toward the holly strung at the back of the pub. "Turned sissy and table sitting." Jack was propelled through the smoke with his nose pointed right and nothing to do but follow it.

"Houston, you old—!" Halfway to the table there was

the roar of his name followed by a stream of profanity in three different languages and two patois.

Jack Houston followed the curses, and sure enough, ugly as ever, and with a smile making it worse, there was Kevin Doyle. "I'm a believer!" Jack interrupted his diatribe. "There is a Satan! Who else would save your worthless life, Doyle?"

For the next five minutes they swapped insults and obscenities, and then Kevin Doyle pulled Jack down to the table across from him and passed him a pitcher of beer. "Here's to the worst of times." Jack chugalugged the pitcher.

"Angola." Kevin Doyle drained a growler.

"How come you're not dead?" Jack asked. "When they carted you off on that stretcher, I thought sure you bought it."

"Angolan witch doctor." Kevin grinned. "Harvard med school. Patched me up and told me to get the hell out of his country and stay out."

"Had a point."

"Oh, yeah. Anyway, I got more metal than gristle in here now." He thumped his chest. "Just in case I'm ever tempted to re-up for big bucks in Africa."

"What the hell were we doing there, anyway?" Jack wondered.

"Money," Kevin reminded him. "We went soldiering for the money."

"We were on the wrong side."

"Wrong side always pays better." Kevin shrugged. "That's how come they get the best of men like us."

"Best of men in the worst of places. Or is it the other way around?"

"Search me." Kevin made a violent gesture to the waiter that translated as a demand for more beer.

"What are you doing here?" Jack asked.

"Rediscovering my roots," Kevin bellowed over a Clancy Brothers' singalong of "The Rocky Road to Dublin."

"I mean here in New York."

"A little of this and a little of that. In a good cause, though."

"Yeah. They're all good causes." Jack was skeptical.

"Well, it's true I was never one to ask too many questions. But this time it really is a good cause, Jack. For the oldest colony against the oldest colonizer." Kevin grinned. "I've gone Irish in my old age."

"IRA," Jack realized.

"It's cleaner than fighting for the Portuguese proxies in Angola."

"The other side had proxies, too," Jack reminded him. "Cubans mostly, as I recall. Only they didn't get paid like we did."

"Probably why they won. Damned idealists always do in us practical soldier types. That's what we'll be teaching the British."

"Son of a bitch!" Jack grinned. "Old Kevin Doyle really has gone and got himself a cause. Fighting on principle. Co-opted by the true believers. Who'da thunk it?"

"Come in with me, Jack. We'll have fun, just like the old days."

"The old days weren't fun. We almost got killed. When I got out of Angola, I made myself a promise. No matter how much bucks they offer me, I will not lay my butt on the chopping block again."

"This isn't Angola. You won't have to do any fighting. You don't even have to go to Ireland, Jack. All we're talking is some gunrunning. Pickups and deliveries."

"Sure. And one jump ahead of the border patrols and the U.S. Coast Guard all the way. No thanks."

"Seriously, Jack, it really is the right side. We have to get the Brits off our backs. We have to make Ireland one."

"No 'we,' old buddy. You do what you have to do. But count me out."

"It's not Angola. Truly it's not."

"Sorry, Kevin."

"Well, all right, then." Kevin Doyle spread his hands. "If you won't go soldiering with me anymore, at least you'll drink to Christmas coming with me."

"For sure."

"Merry Christmas, then. Drink up, bucko." Kevin stood up. "Hold down this table for me," he told Jack, "while I go to the necessary."

"All right." Jack watched him go. Kevin did not turn in at the men's room. He continued past it to the back of the pub where the telephone booth stood draped in seasonal tinsel of Irish green.

"Don't keep the lady waiting on account of me," Jack kidded him when he returned.

"No lady." Kevin was frank. "You turned me down, so I had to look elsewhere. I need a good man, and I need him soon."

"Did you find one?"

"No." Kevin sighed. "I did not. I was hoping to make contact with Fitz, but he's gone too damn deep underground and the time's too short."

"Who's Fitz?" Jack asked idly.

"Young fellow came over from County Kildare on one of those temporary visas years ago. His father was in the movement in Chicago. He was killed in an accident on his way to do a bit of work for us. Fitz, the son, he did the job the father left undone. Did some other work for the movement here and there. Guns, bomb makings, money, whatever. They caught him in seventy-nine, and he went to the federal prison for a year. Visa'd run out by the time he came out, so he had to go underground to keep from being deported. Been underground ever since. Young, but a really good man. It's a real disappointment not being able to make contact with him. They don't come any cooler than young Fitz Connely."

"Fitz Connely!" Jack stared at Kevin Doyle. "Is that his name? Fitz Connely?"

"That was his name. Truth is I don't know what he'd be calling himself now."

"And you said he was from County Kildare?"

"That's right."

"Does he come in here?" Jack wanted to know.

"To the Fair Colleen? I've never seen him here."

"Well, if he surfaces, put him in contact with me, will you?" Jack scrawled his phone number on a piece of paper for Kevin. "I promise you there are only good things in it for him."

"I'll pass it along if I get the chance. But that's not to say he'll call. Fitz Connely is nervous about informers, and with good reason. The last thing he wants is to be deported to Ireland."

"I'm no informer. You know that. If you do see him, make sure he knows it, too."

"All right. If I see him."

They spoke of other things then. In the back of his mind, however, Jack was still marveling at the smallness of the world. Fitz Connely! The way Kevin described him, he might well be the elusive heir to the Sarah Stockwell Tyler fortune that Buffy had told him about.

9

"ISN'T IT A small world?"

Five words. Recalling them, Carrie Tyler reflected that she should have stood warned. Banality was never a solution to boredom. A man who can't come up with a better line than that is not likely to prove a better-than-average lover.

Average. Carrie sighed. She would have settled for average. Oh, yes. Average would have been one giant step up. Or several. If Peter Stockwell could only rise to average, this interlude might not be quite such a total loss.

They had met by chance on Fifth Avenue, in the vortex of Christmas shoppers. Peter had just finished ordering a present for his mother. Of course! Who else? Carrie had been on her way home. She was staying by herself at her parents' duplex while they were away on a vacation in Europe. ''Come have a drink.'' She had linked arms with Peter on impulse, seeking relief from what had been a dull day. Almost immediately she realized what an unlikely candidate Peter was to relieve her ennui.

Two martinis. Some neck nibbling, fingers inching with infuriating slowness over the bodice of her dress, the most tentative of tentings at his crotch. His ineptitude made Carrie realize that Peter was one of those drivingly ambitious young businessmen who had almost entirely neglected the erotic side of his development. His technique was trapped in adolescence. His hands moved over her with the furtiveness of one who expected to be stopped by the flashlight beam of a movie balcony usher. Her chin on his shoulder as his tongue tickled her neck nape, Carrie had to turn away to keep from yawning in Peter's ear.

''You really turn me on.'' Hard breathing accompanied the words, and the tenting in his trousers was more firmly established now.

''Would you excuse me a moment?'' Carrie patted Peter's cheek and stood up. ''I think I'll slip into something a little more comfortable.'' Now there's an original line, she thought to herself as she locked the bathroom door behind her.

She took a small packet out of her purse and unfolded it carefully. She laid it on the ledge of the sink and arranged the white powder it contained in two neat lines. She fished out a glass tooter and, holding her left nostril closed with one finger, sniffed one of the lines of cocaine. Inhaling slowly and deeply, she sniffed the second line.

When she felt the buzz, Carrie smiled at her reflection in the mirror. She pulled off the sweater she was wearing and admired her small, beautifully shaped naked breasts. She never wore a bra. She prided herself on not needing one. She tweaked one of her berry nipples and watched it stiffen. She arranged her long apricot hair so that the nipples peeped through the tendrils. ''Oh, you passionate girl," she murmured. She squeezed the tip of her other breast. "Shameless."

Sitting down on the toilet lid, she took off her shoes and stockings, then stood up and shucked off her skirt and her panties. She stood on tiptoe to admire her lower body in the bathroom mirror. Her hips were sleek, her legs long and athletic, her bottom pert and creamy.

"Peter is a nerd." She giggled to herself. "But he is a male nerd." Extravagantly, she splashed some Lancôme Magie noire over her body and donned a floor-length paisley silk robe. She winked at herself in the mirror with one almond-shaped hazel eye. "Brace yourself, nerd, here comes Carrie." She went back out to Peter.

"That looks more comfortable." He had been fidgeting, waiting for her.

"Oh, it is." Carrie slowly opened the robe and displayed herself to him. "Don't you think so?"

"Yeah." He gulped.

"But you don't look comfortable," she told him, leaning close. "You have too many clothes on."

"Right." Peter tore off one of the buttons of his vest in his hurry to disrobe.

Watching him strip, Carrie found herself hoping that perhaps he would not prove such a nerd when it actually came right down to making love. His body was thick but not fat, laced with muscle, very strong looking, a powerful wrestler's physique that made Peter seem more earthy and virile without his clothes on. Even his heavy, darkly fleshy features hinted at the possibility of total and thrilling possession, of fulfillment. And the girth of his erect sex organ when he revealed it made Carrie moisten with anticipation.

Five minutes later she knew that her hopes had been raised in vain. She watched Peter stand up, satisfied and smug, his emptied penis drooping. Wham-bam-thank-you-ma'am!

"I hope I wasn't too fast for you." The way he said it, manliness rated extra points for MPH with the distaff side ever the laggard.

72

"It was fun trying to keep up," Carrie murmured.

"Did you—uh—you know?"

"Oh, yes." Suppose she said no? Inwardly Carrie shuddered. She might have to go another five laps with the speed king of Lovers' Lane.

"Good." Peter rummaged through his pants pockets and came up with his wristwatch. "Oh, Lord!"

"*Tempus fugit*," Carrie observed sweetly.

"How right you are." He began to dress. "Well, I hate to—umm—and run, but . . ."

"You have an appointment."

"That's right, I do. And I can't keep Mr. van Huyck waiting."

"Mr. van Huyck?"

"Helmut van Huyck. He's the man with all the contacts to get our real estate redevelopment project off the ground."

"Helmut van Huyck." Carrie yawned, making no effort to hide it now. "Sounds like a Dutch portrait painter."

"Joke if you like, but believe me, nothing goes up in New York without his okay. He's got the politicians in one pocket and the construction industry in the other." Peter finished tying his tie and took out a comb.

"And he's more fun than staying here with me?" Actually Carrie would not have teased Peter if she thought there was the slightest chance of his staying.

"I have to go. Mr. van Huyck's going to set me up with this accountant."

"Accountant?"

"Yes. One who knows how to move money without any fuss."

"To move money?"

"It's too complicated to explain." Peter came to the bed, bent over Carrie, and kissed her good-bye. "Let's do this again real soon," he said.

"Real soon," Carrie echoed hollowly, watching him leave. Over my dead body! she promised herself as the door closed behind Peter. And that's too soon!

10

WHENEVER PATRICE SAW Jack Houston, she hungered for the sight of him and seethed with the fury of rejection in his presence. Their affair had been over since he had left the States for St. Martin, but now he was back, and Patrice knew it would never be over for her.

She clutched at the bow on her blouse like a lifeline, not aware of the telltale gesture. With her free hand, she accepted the eggnog Zelig Meyerling handed her. "Thank you," she said automatically.

She had come into the sitting room intending to have a preluncheon seasonal drink with Holly and Zelig under the now decorated Christmas tree. She had not expected to find Jack there. But by the time she saw him, it was too late to withdraw.

"You will join us for lunch, won't you, Jack?" Holly asked as he, too, accepted a tumbler of eggnog from Zelig.

"Love to."

"Will Buffy join us, too?" Zelig inquired.

"She's not home. She's in Manhattan at the beauty parlor, gilding the lily for Christmas."

Thank God! Patrice was relieved. Her composure was shaken enough by Jack's presence without Buffy being there, too.

"Have you spoken to Halsey lately, Patrice?" Jack addressed her directly, apparently oblivious to the strain she was feeling.

"No. Why should I?" Patrice made an effort to remain casual.

"Then he hasn't told you about the lead I gave him?"

"He told me," Zelig interjected. "He asked me to speak to the immigration authorities. I had the decided impression that he was hoping I'd stir them up."

"Stir them up to do what?" Patrice was bewildered. "What's this all about?"

"Jack got a lead on Fitz Connely," Holly answered Patrice. "He passed it on to Halsey. I was sure that Halsey would have informed you and the other members of the board."

"This is the first I've heard of it. What sort of lead?"

Jack told Patrice what he'd learned from Kevin Doyle on his visit to the Fair Colleen.

"The IRA federal prison." Patrice shook her head ruefully. "And now Fitz Connely is hiding from the immigration authorities. Halsey must be delighted."

"Why delighted?" Holly asked.

"Because he doesn't really want him found. Without him, he maintains control, and that's what Halsey really wants." Patrice turned to Zelig. "Were you able to learn anything from your contacts in the Immigration Department?" she asked him.

"Well, he is under sentence of deportation as an undesirable alien."

"Undesirable?"

"Yes. He was running guns for the IRA. That's why he was sent to prison. He broke the laws of the United States. That definitely makes him 'undesirable' to Immigration."

"But they haven't caught him."

"No. The deportation order has never been carried out," Zelig told her. "The truth is Immigration hasn't really pursued the matter with any great enthusiasm. Irish aliens are low on the list when it comes to allocating their efforts. They don't really work very hard at running them down. It's the Latinos and Caribbean blacks they concentrate on."

"Why?" Holly asked. "I mean, compared to the Irish,

75

the Central American and Caribbean and Mexican illegals are much more wretched.''

''But that's exactly why, my dear,'' Zelig told his wife. ''You've answered your own question. The greater the horror that illegal immigrants are fleeing, the greater the problem they present when they arrive here. Nothing makes low wages as attractive as poverty and hardship and fear. The Irish have had no bed of roses, but compared to the Latinos . . .'' Zelig's shrug was eloquent.

''That's not exactly the Christmas spirit, dear,'' Holly chastised him. ''You were an immigrant yourself. How can you have so little compassion for other immigrants?''

''From Switzerland. No great hardship there.'' Zelig loved his wife, even loved her empathy for the underdog, but he did not share it. To him, the world was a hard place populated by haves and have-nots, and realism dictated that the haves should guard their borders against the have-nots who threatened their status. The United States, his adopted country, was a nation of haves. Before, during, and since his tenure as secretary of state, Zelig had devoted himself to the maintenance of that status quo.

''I hate it when you're cynical about human misery,'' Holly told him.

''Those who cry over it are usually too blinded by their own tears to provide any real relief.''

''Aphorisms in place of policy!'' Holly scowled.

''Aphorisms are policy.''

''It's true, you know.'' Holly did a rapid about-face. ''They are. That's why Zelig has always been such a renowned policymaker. What he lacks in depth, he makes up in glibness.''

''Behind every successful man there is a woman with a sharp tongue.'' Zelig, unruffled, kissed Holly fondly and completely.

''It's a good thing I'm so much in love with you.'' She patted his stomach. ''Or I would not put up with your ruthlessness for one moment.''

76

"But I'm not ruthless." Zelig spread his rather soft, academic hands. "I am only pragmatic."

"Pragmatically"—Patrice reentered the conversation—"what can be done to have the deportation order for Fitz Connely lifted?"

"Officially, nothing," Zelig told her.

"And unofficially?"

"Unofficially, everything." Zelig smiled from under hooded eyes. "Unofficially all things are possible always."

"Can you have the order lifted?" Patrice asked the question directly.

"There are some favors owed me." He shrugged. "But first the young man must be found."

"I know." Patrice made herself turn to Jack Houston. "Did your friend have any idea at all where Fitz Connely might be hiding?"

"I've told you everything he told me, Patrice."

"Actually," Zelig said, "Immigration did have some thoughts along those lines. Not leads, exactly, but thoughts. Places where Irish illegals tend to gather. Things like that. I passed it all along to Halsey."

"Who has done nothing with it!" Patrice was angry.

"You don't know that for sure," Jack reminded her. "You only think so."

"I know Halsey." Patrice had no doubts.

"Why do you care so much?" Jack asked.

"Ethics." Patrice shrugged. "I got them from my father. I can't help myself. When a thing is wrong, it's wrong. And it's wrong that Halsey should evade his responsibility to find Fitz Connely."

"If you feel that strongly," Zelig asked Patrice, "then why don't you hire your own private detective agency, give them all the information, and track him down yourself?"

"That is a very good idea." Patrice's brown eyes softened. "Thank you, Zelig. That's just what I will do. The hell with Halsey. I'll hire my own detectives."

"Well, I'm glad that's settled." Holly perched on the

arm of her husband's chair. "Now we can get down to serious business."

"Such as?" Zelig inquired.

"The inside story on Washington."

"Ahh."

"You are an insider, darling, aren't you?"

"In the Reagan White House? You know better than that. Along with Henry, I'm considered far too liberal."

"Henry who?" Jack inquired.

"Kissinger, of course," Holly told him. "Who else?" She turned back to Zelig. "But never mind this false modesty, my darling. This is your wife speaking. I want the real lowdown. And I warn you that if you hold out on me, I shall make you sorry."

"When I displease her, she makes me sleep alone," Zelig told Jack and Patrice with a mock woeful expression.

"All right, then. Now whenever the Reagans are shown on TV getting on or off their helicopter, they have a cocker spaniel with them. But it's not the same cocker spaniel."

"That is true," Zelig granted.

"Now what I want to know," Holly demanded, "is where do they rent those dogs?"

"Never!" Zelig sprang to his feet. "Military secrets, yes, but this never. I may not be a Reaganite, but I am a good Republican, and Ronald Reagan is my president. Before I would betray him thus, I would have recourse to the cyanide in the secret compartment of my pinkie ring. My lips are sealed!"

Laughing, the four of them finished their drinks and went in to lunch.

Matt Stockwell was just sitting down to a solitary lunch at the table in his farmhouse kitchen when he was interrupted by a knock at his front door. It couldn't be Kathleen; she always let herself in the back way. He always left the back door open for her.

When he answered the knock, he found Wendy

MacTavish, wearing jeans, threadbare at the knee, a man's peacoat, and a stocking cap, standing there. A backpack bulged between her thin shoulder blades.

"Merry Christmas, Matt! Can I come in?" She brushed the long, startlingly black hair from her dark eyes. It fell back over her soft white cheeks.

"Merry Christmas. Sure." Matt had been so surprised to see Wendy that he'd blocked her way. Now he stood aside. "Coffee?" he offered. When she nodded, he left her in the living room and went into the kitchen to fetch it.

"I'm sorry." When he returned, Wendy apologized. "I guess I should have called first."

"It's okay." Matt blew on his coffee and then sipped it. "What—"

"It's my father. And Bruce. We have to talk."

"Has something happened?"

"Not really." She put her own cup down on the table, the coffee untasted. "It's just that—well, the situation can't go on this way. Pa tells Bruce that his father is dead, and Bruce knows better. I mean, he's met you. He knows who you are. On Christmas there will even be presents under the tree for him from you. It's all so confusing for him, Matt! He's only a little boy. What am I going to do?"

Wendy had never been a woman to cry. She still wasn't. But Matt could not miss the genuine anguish in her voice. "You have to take Bruce and leave, Wendy. There's no other way. Come to New York. I can help you, and I'll take him until you can get settled. After all, he's my son, too. I love him."

"Don't you think I love him? But I can't just take off that way. My father's a sick man. It's not an act. I've spoken with the doctor. His heart is a very iffy proposition. Any strain—any sudden shock—I can't be responsible for that, Matt."

"Our son's welfare has to come first." Matt was gentle, but firm. "We have to do what's best for Bruce."

"That's easy for you to say. It's not your father we're talking about."

"I know. I really do know, Wendy. But why can't he be reasonable? Why can't he just accept the situation? We lived together. We had a child. From all you say he really loves his grandson, our child. Why can't he let go of his hate?"

"It's not our having lived together or our child that fuels his fury. It's that you avoided the draft during the war. He can't help it, Matt. He's an old man. He's lived his life by certain values, certain principles. You can't expect him to turn away from them now. And you represent everything in opposition to those principles. In Pa's eyes you'll never be anything but a despicable coward."

"But I don't want my son to see me that way. Don't you see, Wendy?"

"I was in love with you." Wendy turned away from him abruptly. "I still am," she said in a very small voice.

"What?" Matt was taken aback.

"I said I still am. Oh, I know you don't feel that way. I know you've got someone else. But if I haven't your love, then where, tell me, Matt, where am I to get the strength to risk my father's life?"

"What is it that you want?" Matt asked carefully. "Why did you come?"

With an effort that was more interior than evident, Wendy pulled herself together. "I came to tell you that I don't think you should come up to Montreal anymore. It's too confusing for Bruce, and it's too hard on me. I can't give him the Christmas presents you sent. I brought them back." She nodded toward the bulging packpack.

"I can't go along with that!"

"Damn it, Matt, don't you understand? I can't stand it anymore. I won't stand it!" Her voice broke. "I won't! I won't!" And then, finally, for the first time since he'd known her, Wendy's facade cracked and she began to sob.

"Wendy, don't. Please, baby. . . ." Not knowing what else to do, Matt took her in his arms.

She burrowed against his shoulder as he patted her back, trying to calm her. Eventually her sobs subsided, but she still clung to him. "Do you know," she asked, her voice low and intense, "how much I want you?"

"Don't, Wendy."

"Am I that repugnant to you now?"

"You know better than that."

"Do I?" She raised her face to his. "Do I, Matt?"

Without intending it, he kissed her. Her mouth clung to his, sweet with memory, warm with desire. Despite himself, Matt felt the old tug, the revival of the passion that had been between them during those long-ago years. Briefly his body responded, and then he ended the kiss and pushed Wendy gently away.

But it was too late. Kathleen had let herself in the back door. Now she stood in the doorway to the living room with the sprig of mistletoe she'd brought Matt clutched in both hands and stared down at the couple embracing on the sofa.

Kathleen's normally florid skin had gone as pale as Wendy's. Her freckles stood out in bright, angry blotches. As she drew in her breath, sharply and audibly, tears formed in her eyes. Exhaling, she opened her mouth as if to speak, but no words came out. Dropping the sprig of mistletoe, she turned on her heel and rushed from the room.

"Kathleen!" Despair wrenched her name from Matt's lips. "Wait! Let me explain." But it was no use.

Kathleen was gone.

11

L OVE IS PAIN, Patrice sighed to herself. She felt very bad about the estrangement between Matt and Kathleen. We'd all be better off without it. She thought of Jack Houston and grimaced with the memory. Much better off.

Matt had told his sister about the rupturing of the relationship early that afternoon, the day before Christmas. He had stopped at Riverview to explain that he wouldn't be there for the traditional Christmas Eve dinner that night. He was driving up to Montreal, hoping to be able to arrange to be with his son for at least part of the holiday.

Just after Matt left, Patrice summoned Kevin O'Lunney to drive her into the city. It was midafternoon when Patrice entered the Yule-festooned lobby of the Stockwell Building. Behind her the streets of lower Broadway were overflowing with throngs of last-minute holiday shoppers. The doorways she passed as she proceeded to Halsey De Vilbiss's office were overflowing with office parties.

Neither Halsey's receptionist nor his secretary were in sight when Patrice arrived. She supposed they were at one of the office parties. She knocked at the door to Halsey's private office.

"Come in." He stood up when he saw her. "Mrs. O'Keefe." Halsey De Vilbiss was not the most sensitive of men, but he had understood from their first meeting that he and Patrice were unlikely to ever be on a first-name basis. "I've been expecting you."

"I'm sorry if I've kept you waiting. Traffic was impossible."

"Of course. No problem." He held a chair for Patrice. When she was seated, he walked back around his sleekly art-deco redwood desk and sat down himself. "You said on the phone that you wanted to meet with me about Fitz Connely?"

"Yes." Patrice was forthright. "He's been found."

"I think you must be misinformed. Actually, our efforts to locate him have pretty much come up against a blank wall." There were small, grinning Pacific sea monsters on Halsey's tie.

"Your efforts may have. Mine have not."

"Yours? I don't understand." Halsey scowled at the intrusion of uninhibited voices caroling "God Rest Ye Merry Gentlemen" from a nearby office.

"I hired a detective agency. I gave them the same information that was passed on to you by Jack Houston and Zelig Meyerling. They've evidently had better results with it than your people."

"I see." Halsey's voice was calm, his manner, as always, unruffled. Years of success as a courtroom lawyer had conditioned him not to respond to surprises.

"In fact, their report stated flat out that with the new information it wasn't difficult for anybody to find him who genuinely wanted to find him."

"You're not implying, are you, Mrs. O'Keefe, that my efforts to locate Fitz Connely were not sincere?" Halsey inquired mildly. Only his well-manicured fingernail scraping across the raised initial monogram on the cuff of his custom-made shirt betrayed his irritation.

"Perish the thought." A nearby chorus of "Hark the Herald Angels Sing" did not dull the sarcasm in her voice. Patrice saw no reason to handle Halsey De Vilbiss with kid gloves. "But in any case it's not important now. What is important is that he's been located."

"By your private detectives." Halsey acknowledged the sarcasm with a meticulous restating of the fact.

"Yes. Thanks to the tip that Zelig got from the Immigration Department, the detectives picked up Fitz Connely's trail at a safe house in Queens used to pass along

83

Irish illegals. From there they tracked him to a city shelter for homeless men on the Bowery. They lost the trail there for a while, but thanks to Jack Houston they picked up a fresh lead at the Fair Colleen Pub."

"He's back in the Irish pipeline, then?"

"No. He was, but he isn't anymore. Evidently, he's been going through a particularly bad time. He's been drinking, it seems. The Irish pipeline—well, they're mixed up in all this IRA business, you know—don't think he's dependable anymore."

"They don't trust him?" Although Halsey's voice was without inflection, he was assessing the character of Fitz Connely. The young Irishman was, after all, a man who would be very important to Halsey's future.

"That's putting it too strongly. It's not that they think he's untrustworthy. They only worry that he can't be depended upon because he has a drinking problem."

"Large sums of money entail large responsibilities." De Vilbiss smiled slightly and raised his hands. "To put such sums in the hands of an irresponsible alcoholic . . ."

"Fitz Connely evidently has a drinking problem. That doesn't mean he's an incurable drunk. He's been having a rough time. That's all we really know. He's a young man with his life ahead of him. His inheritance could make all the difference." Patrice knew that Fitz Connely's alcoholism—if such it was—could readily be interpreted by Halsey as reason to retain control of the Tyler fortune. "He should be informed about his legacy and helped to claim it."

"You haven't told me yet where he is." Halsey ignored Patrice's lecturing tone.

"Grand Central Station."

"I beg your pardon?"

"Grand Central Station. That's where he is. That's where Fitz Connely is living."

"I don't understand."

"He has noplace else. That's what the detectives found out. He's one of the homeless. No papers. No address. A nonperson of sublevel two, Grand Central Station."

"I see. And you're sure this—umm—derelict is the heir to Sarah Tyler's fortune?"

"Everything the detectives learned checks out. But there's a problem. When they approached him, he bolted."

"Because he was drunk," Halsey guessed.

"Possibly, but also because he's on the run. When they identified themselves, he evidently jumped to the conclusion they were from Immigration. He knocked one of them down and ran away."

"Did they inform him that he might be the heir to a considerable fortune?"

"They tried, but it only seemed to confirm his impression that they were trying to trap him in some way."

"Not just an alcoholic, but paranoid, too."

Patrice bristled. "When the authorities actually are after you and deportation is a real possibility, there's nothing paranoid about being suspicious."

"You still haven't said what it is you expect me to do," Halsey reminded Patrice.

"You're the executor of Sarah's estate. I want you to go to Fitz Connely with the proof of his legacy and convince him that he really is the heir to a great fortune."

"And then what?"

"Why, bring him back to Riverview, I suppose. I mean, he belongs there as much as any of us. He is a Stockwell even if he doesn't have the name."

Halsey clasped his well-manicured hands on the glazed redwood surface of the desk in front of him. "Now let me see if I understand this. You want me to go into the bowels of Grand Central Station, back some drunken bum into a corner, and make him believe that I am his fairy godmother. And then you want me to forcibly remove him to Riverview." Halsey regarded Patrice in a silence broken only by the distant strains of "Christmas Tree, O Christmas Tree." "Well, I may be from California, Mrs. O'Keefe, a parvenu by comparison to the Stockwells of Wall Street, but I'm not foolhardy. I'll pass."

"You won't do it?"

"I don't consider putting myself in harm's way a legitimate part of the services I provide." Halsey De Vilbiss's rather beady eyes regarded Patrice from above a suntan that was—like his desk and tie—out of sync with the New York Christmas season. "You did say he knocked one of your detectives down," Halsey reminded her.

"You really are a coward, Mr. De Vilbiss." Patrice stood up, turned on her heel, and started for the door.

"And a merry Christmas to you, Mrs. O'Keefe." Halsey's next words brought Patrice to a stop with her hand on the doorknob. "Just out of curiosity, what will you do now?" he asked.

"I'll go to Grand Central Station myself tonight, inform Fitz Connely of his inheritance, and bring him back to Riverview." Patrice closed the office door firmly behind her.

"Where did you say she's gone?" Jack Houston stared at Holly.

"To Grand Central Station."

"Well, why not?" Buffy, slightly high on Christmas Eve champagne, gestured with her glass. "It's only a stone's throw from El Morocco."

"El Morocco has been closed for years," her husband reminded her.

"And Zelig?" Jack asked.

"Called to Washington." Holly said tersely.

"On Christmas Eve? How come?" David Lewis wanted to know.

"Zelig is a very important man in the administration," his brother-in-law Jonathan Stockwell told him.

"No, he's not." Holly was bitter. "The president's inside circle despise him. They only call him at the last minute when they've gotten themselves into something they can't get out of."

"Such as?" Peter Stockwell was curious.

"Central America. The Middle East. The Persian Gulf. The balance of trade. The budget deficit. You name it."

"Zelig aside, there's no reason to be so negative about the Reagan administration." Jonathan Stockwell took umbrage. "I, for one, am glad to see my country standing tall again."

There was a moment of silence as everybody stared at him. "Of course you are, dear." Finally his wife broke the silence. "And we're all very happy for you."

"I think," said Diana Tyler, "that I would like another glass of champagne before we sit down to dinner."

"I'll join you," Max chimed in gratefully.

"You haven't told us yet just why Patrice has gone to Grand Central Station," Jack, walking over toward Holly, reminded her.

"To fetch the heir. It seems he's one of the homeless people who live in the lower levels there."

"Is that safe?" Holly's aunt Alice, David Lewis's wife, was concerned. "I've heard those people are dangerous. Drunks and junkies and criminals. They mug people. Things like that."

"Well, I don't think it's safe," Holly agreed. "I tried to tell Patrice that, but she wouldn't listen. I'm really worried about her going down there late at night."

"Why late at night?" Jack asked.

"It seems that's when the transit police sweep out the station. Patrice thinks this Fitz Connely will be easier to find then. They clean the homeless out of all the nooks and crannies of the sublevels where they hole up."

"She's going alone?" Alice Lewis was growing quite agitated.

"All alone."

"What time was she planning to go?" Jack asked.

"After midnight. Around one, I think."

Jack glanced at his watch. It was still early. "I'm going to catch the ten-thirty into Manhattan," he declared. "I'll find Patrice and stick with her."

"My hero!" Buffy put down her glass with an ominous clink. Aware of Patrice and her husband's affair, and never one to mince words, she wasn't embarrassed to expose the relationship to the family. "But you and Patrice bear in mind that it's Christmas Eve, Jack," she added. "A hotel room will be hard to find."

"Come with me." Jack as usual went straight to the heart of the matter. "That will save a lot of nonsense about what I did and why I did it and who I did it to, later."

"No thanks." Buffy poured herself another goblet of champagne and drained it at a gulp. "I wouldn't want to crimp your style."

Holly and Diana exchanged uncomfortable glances. "Peter," Holly suggested on impulse, "why don't you go with Jack?"

"I think not!" Ellen firmly answered for her son. "You were just complaining about people not being here for Christmas dinner, Holly, and now you're suggesting Peter desert us, too."

"I only thought that Patrice's safety might be more important," Holly told her aunt.

"Nobody told her to go." Peter sided with his mother. "Why should anybody inconvenience themselves for her folly?"

"I'll go with you if you like, Jack." Max Tyler tried not to sound as reluctant as he felt, but it showed in his voice. It had been a long week, and he'd been looking forward to a relaxing evening.

"There's no need, Max," Jack told him. "I'll go myself. I really don't mind."

"He really doesn't mind," Buffy echoed. "He really doesn't."

The edge in her voice made everybody uncomfortable. No one wanted to continue the discussion. David Lewis changed the subject. A while later Jack Houston left for Grand Central Station to find Patrice.

The heavily alcoholic bouquet of Christmas Eve commuters overpowered that of the homeless people who camped out in the vastnesses of Grand Central Terminal. At holiday time suburban transients smelled as evil as the waiting room's permanent bath-deprived tenants.

Well past midnight, the throng of Yule revelers catching late trains was thinning out. The homeless were more visible now. An occasional face—predominantly black or Latin—peered up with cynical eyes at the tipsy toffs who tripped over their outstretched feet. The homeless clung to the last of the warmth departing with the crowd, hugging it to their thin, rag-covered bodies in anticipation of the moment when they would be driven out of the terminal into the winter night. Males of indeterminate age predominated, but there were women and children scattered among them.

It wasn't difficult for Jack to spot Patrice. The last of the Christmas Eve commuters were hurrying quickly from the area taken up by the homeless toward the gates to the tracks from which their respective trains were leaving. Patrice stood out because she was both well dressed and stationary. He went up to her.

"Jack!" Her heart leaped; her stomach twisted. "What are you doing here?"

"The family was concerned about you. I came to make sure you were all right."

"That was good of you." Were you concerned, too, Jack? Were you? The words were a shouted demand inside Patrice's head; her lips remained fixed in a silent, restrained smile. "But I really don't think I'm in any danger."

"Not at the moment. But I hear it gets rough here later, when there are no more trains and the night people take over the station."

"They don't take it over. The transit police drive them out."

"I've heard that can get violent, too."

"They do it every night. I don't think it gets violent very often," Patrice replied evenly, willing her hands to stop shaking.

"Christmas Eve isn't exactly tranquil anywhere in the city."

"Well, as long as you're here, you can help me. This is the man we're looking for." Patrice took a picture from

89

her pocketbook and showed it to Jack. "The detectives managed to snap this before Fitz Connely got away from them."

Jack looked at the photo. It was a close-up, the body lopped off just below the neck. Fitz's face was dark and brooding, but slack-lipped with drink. Although obviously youthful, a furtive wariness clouding the deep-set eyes and black, curly hair framing an expression of suspicion and mistrust robbed the face of innocence and aged it. Fitz Connely dirty, unfocused, and angry looked like any number of the city's homeless populace.

"He'll be coming from down below." Patrice gestured to the passageway running under the Vanderbilt Avenue side of the terminal. "That's where the detectives said he stays most of the time. But when the transit cops clean out that area, they drive the derelicts toward Lexington Avenue and out that exit."

"Why there?" Jack asked. "Wouldn't Forty-second or Vanderbilt be closer?"

"Those doors are locked. They only leave one set open so they can't sneak back in. That's Lexington. If you wait here, you can maybe spot him when the transit cops clean out the sublevels. I'll wait at the Lexington Avenue doors, and that way if you miss him, I'll catch him."

"All right," Jack agreed. "When does all this start?"

"It's starting now." Patrice pointed.

Uniformed transit police in a sort of loose formation, some of them with dogs on leashes—Dobermans, German shepherds—were starting their sweep through the main level of Grand Central Station. As Patrice left Jack to take up her post at the Lexington Avenue exit, the loudspeakers, which had fallen silent with the last of the commuter train announcements, began to play Christmas music loudly. In most cases the approach of the police and their dogs was in itself enough to raise the homeless from their benches and their propped-against-the-wall positions on the floors and start them moving toward the exit. In some instances, when they were asleep or nodding, an officer might tap lightly with his billy on the thin soles of their shoes to rouse them.

A few didn't move quickly enough to suit the transit police. Some billies struck harder. A few derelicts were put on their feet violently. The dogs moved in snarling, to intimidate the sullen. A certain brutality was in the air now, if not actually being perpetrated. The materialization of a couple of dedicated advocates—a short, cheerful, chubby woman in her mid-sixties from the Coalition for the Homeless who defused possible confrontations with the sheer good-humored power of her personality and a young, earnest, clean-cut representative from the ACLU whose very presence was a reminder that even the rights of the down-and-out must be observed—who walked the high wire between volatile underdogs and righteous cops with a laid-back friendliness effectively kept things cool. Well known to both sides, they created a barrier of safety— a kind of neutral zone—between the cops with their dogs and those in front of them shambling reluctantly out into the winter night.

The initial sweep was quick and efficient. The transit cops and the two advocates moved to the lower level. A little while later the subterranean derelicts began to appear on the main level. They were in somewhat worse shape than those who had congregated in the ticket-selling areas and waiting rooms, and at their appearance one or two commuters who had missed their train backed off and fled the station to the relative safety of the all-night coffee shops.

As time wore on, the groupings being ferreted out were becoming smaller. Two or three subdwellers at a time would be propelled by their elbows toward the exit in the grip of grim-faced cops. The dogs seemed more in evidence, their blood up, bristling, snarling. Their masters were in a hurry to get it over with and go home to their own Christmas hearths.

Suddenly Jack spotted the man he was seeking. Fitz Connely, his chin stuck out, was walking slowly, refusing to respond to the nightstick prodding him above the kidneys from behind, taking his own sweet time, his body language a statement of resistance. But at the same time his gait was far from steady, and his dignity was diminished by the frequent pulls he took from the half-empty wine bottle he clutched in one hand.

Jack intercepted him. "Fitz Connely—" he started to say in a tone that was meant to be both friendly and reassuring.

It was as far as he got. The young Irishman swung the bottle hard, and it glanced off the side of Jack's head. "Immigration!" He yelled the warning and then was off and running, Jack staggering behind him.

Shaking his head to clear it, Jack took off after Fitz. His quarry's lead had been cut down by the need to zigzag past various transit policemen in the main hall before he entered the long, narrow corridor leading to the Lexington exit. Running a straight course, Jack came within tackling distance just as Fitz drew abreast of Patrice a few feet short of the glass doors.

Beyond the doors the usual chaos that accompanied the nightly expulsion of the homeless from Grand Central Station was heightened by the fact of Christmas Eve. There were more taxis than was usual that late at night on Lexington Avenue, and there were repeated sounds of screeching brakes as they swerved to avoid hitting those spilling over into the gutter. The majority of those expelled from the station chose the streets and the night and the cold in preference to the city buses and vans lined up in front of the exit to transport them to the city shelters.

Behind the glass doors, just inside the station, Jack tackled Fitz. Drunk as he was, Fitz twisted away and dropkicked one of the hands grabbing at his ankle. As Jack scrambled to his feet, they grappled. Patrice tried to intercede, to explain, but Fitz Connely shoved her roughly away.

A policeman who had seen Patrice being shoved by a derelict came through the glass doors with his gun drawn. He grabbed Fitz by the shoulder to pull him off Jack. Fitz came around swinging hard, and the cop caught a fist full force in the stomach.

Instinctively he raised his gun. Patrice screamed. The policeman stopped himself. Instead of pulling the trigger, he brought the barrel down on the top of Fitz Connely's head. Fitz went down like a felled tree.

In the emptied Grand Central Station waiting room the loudspeakers played the last notes of "Peace on Earth, Good Will to Men."

12

DAWN WAS BREAKING as the Rolls-Royce turned off the road onto the long private drive leading to Riverview. In the back of the limousine, Patrice and Jack were unobtrusively trying to keep as much distance as possible between themselves and the foul-smelling Fitz Connely. It had been an uncomfortable drive, topping off a harrowing night.

Fitz had been taken to Bellevue from Grand Central. Patrice had insisted on following the ambulance to the hospital. Jack had gone with her.

At Bellevue the doctor diagnosed a minor concussion and a large amount of alcohol in the young man's bloodstream. "The wound isn't severe enough to hospitalize him, but he is a candidate for our alcoholic ward," he told Patrice. "Of course we can release him and simply turn him over to the police."

"We'll book him on assault," the officer who had ridden the ambulance told them.

"I don't want to press any charges," Jack assured him.

"Well, Officer Spinelli, the one he took a poke at, may

feel differently. And in any case, we have to hold him on a D and D. Drunk and disorderly," he explained before Patrice could ask.

"Could you hold off until I make a call?" Patrice asked.

"I'm in no hurry. Long as the doctor here doesn't mind."

"He's sleeping it off," the doctor said. "Not doing anybody any harm. Take your time."

Patrice went to a phone booth to call her uncle David. Her aunt Alice had to get him out of bed. He wasn't happy about that, but he listened as Patrice described the situation. "It could look really bad for the family if he's booked," Patrice stressed. "Once it gets that far, there will be no way to hold down the media coverage. Is there some way we can squelch it now, Uncle David? I mean, there's been no real harm."

"I'll make some calls," he told her with a sigh.

Less than an hour later the officer who had been waiting with Patrice and Jack was summoned to the phone. When he returned, he shook his head at Patrice in awe. "You must have some clout," he told her. "That was my precinct captain. He got a call from the commissioner. There'll be no charges. You can take your wild Irish souse home."

"Thanks." Patrice asked him the name of the officer Fitz had punched and wrote it down. She also took his name. Both policemen would receive a case of Scotch at their homes.

The doctor was equally cooperative. He had given Fitz a strong tranquilizer shot, which had made him as docile as a baby.

Fitz Connely listened without saying anything during the ride to Riverview as Patrice explained to him about the legacy. It was hard to judge if he was skeptical or merely nodding out from the drug. Jack's assurances that they had nothing to do with the Immigration Department and that in fact steps would be taken to legitimate his presence in the country brought a flicker of interest to his eye, but it died quickly, and the last part of the journey was spent in silence.

When they pulled up under the porte cochere of Riverview's front entrance, Jack helped Fitz from the limousine. Kevin O'Lunney gauged the young Irishman with an experienced eye and took hold of him under the other arm without asking. Together they propelled him up the steps and waited until Berkley responded to Patrice's ringing of the chimes.

"How do you feel?" Patrice asked Fitz just before Berkeley responded.

"Fair nauseous."

"It's maybe not wise to be pushing the question, Miss Patrice," Kevin suggested deferentially.

Berkley opened the door. He started at the sight of the unkempt, unshaven derelict; however, he quickly recovered and was as impassive as always as he stood aside to admit Miss Patrice, Mr. Houston, Kevin O'Lunney, and the stranger.

Fitz Connely looked around, and his jaw dropped. "Sure and it's a palace!" he exclaimed.

"It will be your home, Patrice assured him.

"My home." He swayed on his feet. His complexion turned a greenish white. His cheeks puffed out under their high cheekbones. He tore loose from Jack and Kevin O'Lunney, dashing across the floor to a priceless, waist-high Ming vase standing to one side of the sweeping, circular staircase. He grasped the vase with both hands and leaned down into it. He threw up.

Tyrone Fitzwilliam Connely had come home to Riverview.

BOOK TWO

13

TWO WEEKS INTO the new year, belowstairs and above, adjustments were still being made in regard to the presence of Tyrone Fitzwilliam Connely. The pecking order at Riverview was defined, rarely resented, a sort of insurance that things ran smoothly, a foundation of tranquillity. Servants never overstepped their bounds, and those that were served never infringed on the well-defined domain of the household staff. Nor was the demarcation between family and menials the only line drawn. The domains of butler, cook, gardener, personal maid and downstairs maid, valet and kitchen navvy, were carefully respected. An upstairs maid did not wax hardwood floors; a footman did not fold linens.

From his first day at Riverview, Fitz Connely violated the territorial imperatives of the various domains. Indeed, he rampaged over them like the proverbial bull in a china shop. Downstairs was the same as upstairs to him, the scullery no different from the drawing room, the sculptured gardens to be tramped over as freely as the wild-wood.

He made no distinction among persons. His tone to Berkley, the butler, and Gustav Ulbricht, the gardener, was the same as to Jonathan Stockwell and David Lewis. The wink of greeting he bestowed on Holly or Patrice was the same he bestowed on Juanita, the parlor maid, or Bernice, the salad chef with the remarkable bosom. There were no Brits at Riverview and no police, so everybody was fair game for Fitz's friendship, all his equal, none his lackey or his master.

As a Stockwell in all but name, he had free access to the liquor cabinets and wine cellars of Riverview. He made no distinction between ordinary dinner wines or cocktail liqueurs and the decanters of sherry in the library from which tumblers were customarily dispensed only by Jonathan Charles Stockwell or the Napoleon brandy aging in the basement stockroom, which was by tradition the exclusive province of Berkley. Anything alcoholic was a vast improvement over the Thunderbird which Fitz had so long endured, and his attitude toward it all was that of a starving waif turned loose in a bake shop.

Fitz Connely got drunk, and frequently he passed out. In keeping with his democratic fashion, his figure, sodden and supine, a slight, sweet smile on the sullen mouth, was equally likely to be found in a drawing room or a pantry, an upstairs bed-sitting room or the garage, Buffy's east wing bathtub of Carrera marble or the servants' loo.

Overindulgence in alcohol was not unknown in the history of Riverview. Like any other family, the Stock-wells had known its share of tipplers and sots. There had been tipsy stable grooms and cooks addicted to their sherry sauces. There had been ''cures'' for family alcoholics and rehabilitation or—in the most extreme cases—discharges for habitually intoxicated menials. But all of them, drunk or sober, knew their places. Fitz Connely did not. Drunk or sober, he didn't even acknowledge that there were places.

This was a problem for everybody, but no one so much

as the butler. If Riverview ran smoothly—and prior to Fitz Connely's arrival it always had—the credit belonged to Berkley. His was the efficiency that oiled the wheels, assigned the tasks, scheduled the duties, arbitrated among conflicting personalities, integrated the particular foibles and tastes and demands of the Stockwells in residence, and made it all seem as effortless as bubbles afloat on a summer breeze. To Berkley, the Irish heir was a clinker in the customarily smooth-running machinery of Riverview. Finally, and with the utmost reluctance, Berkley went to Patrice with his problem.

"If, Miss Patrice, it might just be explained to Mr. Connely that fraternization with the staff upsets the routine of the household," Berkley suggested, picking his words as if threading his way through a mine field.

"Aren't you being just a tad snobbish, Berkley?" Patrice was sympathetic, but she couldn't help being amused. It was the sort of complaint she would have more likely expected from her uncle Jonathan than the always diplomatic Berkley.

"Such is not my intent, Miss Patrice. It's just that—umm—camaraderie is not a condition well suited to the established routines by which Riverview is run."

Patrice understood without having to ask what Berkley meant by "camaraderie." She knew that Fitz shared whiskey with the servants as easily as with any family member who came along while he was drinking. "I'll speak with him," she promised.

An opportunity presented itself a little later that afternoon when Patrice came upon Fitz sipping bourbon in the conservatory. "My angel of salvation, is it?" he greeted her elaborately. "And will you join me in a nip of the Kentucky?"

"No thanks, Fitz." Patrice sat down on a Louis XIV sofa opposite him and smiled. She was not by nature a moralist, and the role of even gentle disciplinarian came hard to her. "Maybe you should take it a little easy yourself," she suggested. "After all, it can't be much fun drinking alone.'' She had tried to strike a light note and knew at once that she had failed miserably.

"Ah, well, I've no choice. Everyone is so busy, you know, with their various important tasks. Cleaning and cooking and buttling and whatever. The gentry off to the big city to see to their financial concerns. The ladies, save yourself, not in evidence before sunset. I do miss the companionship of Mr. Houston, and the decoration of his missus as well.''

Jack and Buffy had returned to St. Martin a week ago. Patrice had herself regarded their departure with mixed feelings. She felt a certain amount of discomfort and pain when Jack was at Riverview, but in his absence, she felt empty. The "decoration" of Buffy, however, she did not miss at all.

In the short silence, Fitz was perceptive. "You miss him, too, then.'' By his use of the singular he indicated that he knew Buffy was not included in Patrice's feelings. "Ah, but you should have drunk with us, then, whilst he was here. The two of us suffered for lack of your soft feminine presence.''

Patrice burst out laughing. "My 'soft feminine presence' indeed! What malarkey! And all to divert me from the topic at hand, which is that you are drinking much too much, Tyrone Fitzwilliam Connely, and you're too young a man to swig your life away.''

"And you are too young a woman to be giving temperance lectures.''

"Older than you.''

"But not that much older. Prime age for the altar, they'd say back in County Kildare.''

"I've been married.'' Patrice was honest. "I didn't like it.''

"You'd like it well enough with the right man.''

"The right man? You mean a man like you, I suppose.''

"And why not?''

"That doesn't sound like a very firm proposal.'' Patrice was surprised to find herself enjoying the banter.

"Sure and I've too much respect for you to be making any such offer in my cups."

"Well, you wriggled out of that." Patrice laughed. "Seriously, though, Fitz, you do drink too much. Why?"

"Same reason the gent climbed the mountain; because it's there."

"No, really. I'd like to know."

"When I hit bottom, it was all that made getting through the day bearable. Sure and that's why all the sweepings of humanity drink, or shoot up, or whatever. It takes out the prickle from the seconds dragging by."

"But you're not on the bottom anymore. You can fill up the seconds—the minutes, the hours, the days—any way you want," Patrice told him.

"Yes, but you see, that's now, isn't it? And now is when all this glorious booze is at hand. Tomorrow, well, that could be something else again."

"Are you saying you don't believe your inheritance? That you're wealthy now? That you're entitled to make Riverview your home?"

"I'm saying that the same fates what lifted me up can drop me on my bum again." A look of suspicion in his deep-set eyes replaced the glimmer of a twinkle that had been there when he was teasing Patrice. He ran a hand through his unruly mop of curly black hair and poured himself another goblet of bourbon. "The good Lord and Immigration move in mysterious ways their wonders to perform. And those wonders aren't always on the upside, now, are they?"

"You don't have to worry about Immigration," Patrice reassured him. "That's all being taken care of by Zelig and my brother Michael." Patrice's younger brother Michael, the congressman, had been enlisted to help solve the family "problem."

"Ah, the good Dr. Meyerling and His Honor the congressman. Pulling strings for me, whose only collar was blue when I had a clean one at all. Is it any wonder now that I can't believe my fortune? I mean, when it's dependent on the goodwill of such very important gentlemen?''

"But they really are arranging things. You won't have any more trouble with Immigration. Why are you so cynical?''

"Well now, equality is a state of mind. I haven't reached it yet. The featherbed and the money are one thing. Feeling it, that's something else.''

"That's ridiculous. You're as equal as anyone here.''

"Am I now? As equal as Berkley, for instance?''

"As Berkley?'' Patrice laughed. "Well now, I don't know. I doubt any of the family is as equal as Berkley.''

"Exactly.'' Fitz was dead serious.

"I don't understand what you're saying.''

"Sure and it's simple enough. Berkley and Ulbricht, the gardener, and Mrs. Bainter, the cook—well now, they disapprove of me, and rightly so. I drink. I get drunk. I make messes. It falls to them to see me to my bed, to clean up my messes. And that makes them more honest in looking down on me than the family, which, after all, has our blood to consider.''

"Only a few drops.'' Immediately Patrice regretted the quip. "If the servants look down on you because of your drinking,'' she suggested, "maybe that's another good reason to stop drinking.''

"The servants look down on me because they well know I'm not of the class to be looked up to. You can't fool us, Patrice. Whether we lick your boots or hate your guts, we know who belongs among you and who does not. And we know who is one of us and who is not. Between Kevin O'Lunney and myself, for instance, there's little to choose as concerns blue blood. Kevin, being a chauffeur, is the more respectable, whilst I, a bum when you found me, have no respectability at all.''

"That's the most ridiculous thing I ever heard. This is the United States of America. Those European class distinctions are meaningless here.''

"Are they?'' Fitz stood up, set his drink down, and

102

walked swiftly to Patrice. He took her in his arms. He kissed her hard and long.

Patrice was completely taken by surprise. She responded with no chance to consider what her reaction would or should be. Fitz's mouth on hers was strong with liquor. There was a powerful man-smell of cheap tobacco and sweat. He hadn't shaved recently, and the stubble of his beard scratched her cheek.

Abruptly Fitz released her. He returned to his chair and sat down. He picked up his drink.

Taken aback, Patrice stared at him in silence until she finally asked, "Why did you do that?"

"Did you like it?"

"It was silly. Kid stuff. I'm a grown woman. I expect things to be mutual. I don't like surprises, and I don't like force."

"Is it an apology you want, then?" Fitz regarded her from dark pirate eyes, unrepentant and somewhat calculating. "An apology for the taste of liquor on my tongue and the scrape of my beard? Well then, apologize I do, milady, in this land where European class distinctions are so meaningless."

"That's nonsense and you know it, Fitz. Class distinctions have nothing to do with it. You can shave. You can take a bath. You can stop drinking. And the next time you kiss me, I'll enjoy it a lot more."

"The next time is it, then?" His grin was deliberately wicked.

"I really don't understand you." Patrice was telling the truth.

"I believe you." He stood up. "I'll be leaving you now."

"Where are you going?"

"I think I'll have a wee visit belowstairs."

"But—" Patrice was at a loss for words. The whole idea of this talk between them had been to make Fitz stop upsetting the routine of the servants. How had it gone so wrong? "Do you think that's wise?" was the best she could manage.

"In this classless country? Sure and why shouldn't it be?"

Patrice stared after him as he left.

When he got there, the kitchen seemed less than congenial to Fitz. Berkley was formal, Mrs. Bainter was silently disapproving, and Bernice was unhappily restrained. The air was thick with the message that this was not Fitz's place. His open friendliness embarrassed them, and realizing this, Fitz took himself out to the garage.

He hoped to find Kevin O'Lunney. Alone among the servants, Kevin didn't treat him as an unwanted visitor from abovestairs. Perhaps it was that they'd both been raised in Ireland. Kevin, unlike the other older Riverview servants, did not snub him. At the same time, he never wrinkled his nose behind his smile the way the older Stockwells did. Kevin alone accepted Fitz for what he was—a lad from the auld sod, a rare one among many, who had stepped into the New York gutter and found it was indeed paved with gold.

Kevin wasn't in the garage. Fitz climbed the stairs to his living quarters on the floor above and knocked at the door which was answered by Kathleen O'Lunney with a book in her hand. "It's your father I was looking for," Fitz told her.

"He's not here."

"Oh. Will he be back soon?"

"Yes. Soon," Kathleen informed him tersely.

"Is it all right then if I come in and wait?"

"I guess so." She stepped aside.

Fitz went in and sat down. Kathleen went back to the chair she'd been sitting on when he knocked and resumed reading her book.

"Kevin said you've been to Ireland." Fitz broke the silence.

"Yes. When I was little. I lived there with my mother for a while."

"Well, we've something in common, then."

104

Kathleen looked up from her book. "I don't think so."

Fitz looked up sharply at her tone. "You're not happy I'm here," he realized.

Kathleen shrugged, her bright red hair catching the late afternoon sunlight coming through the window. She didn't answer.

"Now why would that be?" Fitz pushed.

"These are servants' quarters. They're private. Even from the family."

"Oh, now, I don't think of myself as family in that way."

"Well, you are," she told him flatly.

"Are the lines that sharp, then? I'd heard differently. About you, I mean."

"Whatever you heard is not your business." Kathleen came down heavily on the "your."

"Do you dislike me that much, then? But why?" Fitz asked.

"Because you're such a phony Irishman."

"Phony, is it?" Fitz was indignant. "And wasn't I born and raised in County Kildare?"

"Not phony that way. Phony with all the macho nonsense. The drinking. The not shaving. The dressing like a bum when you've got all the money in the world. You don't even bathe as often as you should. What's the matter with you, man? Where is it written that the salt of the earth if they happen to be Irish have to be slobs? Whatever you're trying to prove, it's an affront to all the rest of us who are proud to be Irish. That's what I mean by phony."

"I see that it is." Fitz was regarding her quite seriously. He understood her in a way he had not understood Patrice before.

"The Stockwells are bad enough without you encouraging their prejudices. A sloven without money is only a sloven without money, and a sloven with money is only a sloven with money. It proves nothing to cling to misery. Give it up."

"Well now, perhaps I will."

"Perhaps my bonny foot!"

"No 'perhaps,' then. I'll give it up."

"Well, such power I have." Kathleen snorted. "To wash the unwashed, shave the unshaved, banish the stink, and pour John Barleycorn down the drain. It's the tooth fairy I am with the wand to force the pledge."

"That you are." Fitz grinned at her. "I'll not blame you for doubting your powers, but they're more real than you think. I'm a reformed man, and it's all your doing, and your responsibility as well, I'm thinking."

"And there's no more solemn pledge than that of a drunkard between drinks. Well, Fitz Connely, I'd appreciate it more if you'd not contribute to either side of the stereotype."

"Your doing and your responsibility," Fitz repeated. "As of now, I'm a reformed man."

"Giving up wine, women, and song." Kathleen was sarcastic.

"I said nothing of the last two, although I've no voice, and can't blame you if my singing offends, and so will forgo that as well. No wine. No song."

"Well." Kathleen laughed in spite of herself. "If by some remote chance you prove sincere, I can only say that two out of three isn't bad."

14

HELMUT VAN HUYCK was the sort of polished pink man, sleek and silver-haired, who blended perfectly into the ultracivilized, old-world atmosphere of Le Chantilly. He nodded for the steward to spread the wine list on the table before him. "If you gentlemen will permit?"

"Please do." Peter Stockwell's voice betrayed none of his impatience to have the ritual of ordering out of the way so that they might get down to business.

The third man merely nodded. He had been introduced as Victor Grieg. Otherwise his presence had not been explained. Peter guessed that Grieg must be the accountant he had expected to meet with van Huyck last time, the one who had been out of the country on an unanticipated business trip.

"The Châteauneuf-du-Pape, I think." Van Huyck handed the wine list back to the steward. "The seventy-four," he specified.

"An excellent choice, sir." The steward faded away into the subdued wood-paneled background with an air of being about to descend to the wine cellar in one of the idealized murals of the famous French château for which the exclusive restaurant had been named.

"Do you know"—van Huyck's exceedingly pale blue eyes twinkled—"I have never chosen a wine here that the steward has not thought 'an excellent choice.' I wonder, should I question his sincerity?"

Peter smiled. Victor Grieg did not respond at all.

"When he brings it to be tasted, I could of course wrinkle my nose and chastise him for not warning me of my error. But the truth is I have always lacked the courage to find the vintage wanting. What do you think, Victor?" The twinkling eyes, their centers cold as ice, demanded that he break his silence.

"I don't think you should jeopardize the relationship."

The sound of Victor Grieg's voice surprised Peter. Grieg was a dark-suited man in his early thirties, young but not youngish. His horn-rimmed eyeglasses and razor-sharp haircut on a face that, like his body, was long and slender and slightly hollow-cheeked, gave him a well-kept, slightly foreign air. He sat very still, without fidgeting or even shifting position, unblinking as a snake in the sun. Wealthy merchant-class Balkan had been Peter's guess. Now the sound of Grieg's voice dispelled that notion. Despite his slow and careful pronunciation, Grieg's speech betrayed origins of Brooklyn or perhaps the Lower East Side.

He and Peter Stockwell might well have exchanged voices. Peter's Harvard accents would have gone much better with Grieg's aristocratic slenderness than with his own stocky, thick-muscled torso. And Grieg's harsh fire-escape twang would have suited Peter more than the narrow-boned patrician persona Grieg presented to the world.

"Quite right." Helmut van Huyck's laugh was jovial as he responded to Victor Grieg. "I could never bear the hurt in the wine steward's eyes if I rejected his faith in my judgment. I would have to stop dining here, and that would break my heart. Their beignet of wild salmon with its beurre blanc sauce tinged with blackberry vinegar is unmatched this side of Paris." He turned abruptly to Peter. "But I must apologize, Mr. Stockwell. My palate is my pride, and while I do hope that you will enjoy the dinner, we are here for business, are we not?"

"I'm sure the food will be excellent and I'll enjoy it very much," Peter responded politely. "But business is business, and there are things we should discuss."

" 'Business is business.' Why, so it is." Van Huyck echoed the sentiment as if Peter had uttered some deep truth. "Bless my soul, so it is indeed. And by all means let the discussion begin."

Peter's eyes drifted to Victor Grieg and then back to van Huyck. There were aspects of the discussion that should be highly confidential, and Peter wondered whether Victor Grieg could be trusted.

"I should perhaps explain why I asked Victor to join us." Van Huyck answered the unspoken question smoothly. "He is essential to our arrangements. Victor is our comptroller."

"Accountant," Grieg corrected van Huyck in his gravelly New York voice. "I specialize in New York City real estate accounting."

"Don't be modest, Victor." Van Huyck sat back and beamed as a silent waiter set a plate of anise-infused tuna

108

over a julienne of leeks in a vinaigrette sauce before him. He waited until his two companions also had their appetizers before continuing. "Victor will handle certain matters with which neither you nor I will wish to be involved," Van Huyck told Peter.

Peter was a little confused. It had been his understanding that he was dealing with van Huyck in order not to be involved in certain necessary but seamy matters. Now, it seemed, van Huyck was likewise distancing himself from these matters. How many redesignations of responsibility, Peter wondered, before someone's hands actually got dirty?

"Members of government." Van Huyck tasted the tuna and rolled his pale eyes with approval. "At all levels they are necessary to your development project, Mr. Stockwell. But of course Stockwell Enterprises cannot deal with them directly. The reputation of politicians and civil servants alike is by nature fragile. Any transactions with real estate developers would most certainly be subject to misinterpretation. But how very awkward and unreasonable and indeed unfeasible such restrictions are. The fact is that without such dealings nothing would ever be built in the city of New York. Yes, without such dealings there would be no progress at all because there would be no way to arrange for the profit it can bring to those involved—to the developers and to the politicians. And profit, after all, is the lubricant of progress. Don't you agree, Mr. Stockwell?"

"I agree." Peter speared a grilled freshwater prawn and waited for van Huyck to get to the point.

"So in my modest way, I function as a midwife to urban progress. I take your billion-dollar development project and I break it down into the components of its political problems. Where you consider cost analysis and breakdown, real estate acquisitions and construction costs, I consider such matters as the personalities involved in securing cooperation under the four-two-one-A New York City real estate tax abatement program, the condemnation of structures blocking your efforts, and the securing of demolition permits to destroy them, obtaining matching funds from the federal, state, and city governments for landfill, building code zoning waivers, circumventing the various bidding procedures imposed on subcontractors, etcetera, etcetera.''

''Etcetera,'' Peter echoed from the impatient depths of his barrel chest.

''A forty-eight-acre project with a sixteen-block, two-hundred-million-dollar platform over landfill such as you intend involves the cooperation of fifty or sixty people in government. These range all the way from the politicians who vote on the various measures required by the project to the heads of specific departments concerned with all of the narrower aspects on down to the various inspectors charged with monitoring every phase of construction from nonpollutant cement to the safety of I-beam welding procedures. All this is included in the service I render you, Mr. Stockwell. Are you not impressed?''

''I'm impressed,'' Peter granted. ''But I'm not surprised. When our mutual friend at City Hall was good enough to arrange our first meeting, I understood that you had great expertise in these matters, Mr. van Huyck.''

''Thank you, sir.'' Van Huyck's slight gesture produced a waiter who took away his empty plate.

''Do you have a breakdown of the costs for this cooperation?'' Peter asked.

''Victor has it. I only make the arrangements.'' Van Huyck was diffident. ''Victor does the real work. He adds up the figures and takes care of the actual money.''

''Might I see the breakdown?'' Peter inquired.

''Certainly not, Mr. Stockwell.'' Van Huyck's tongue clucked. ''I would never compromise you that way. I consider a major part of my function to be shielding you from knowledge of any details you might ever be called upon to discuss under oath.''

''That sounds ominous.'' Peter's efforts at a light tone did not hide his genuine concern.

''Not to worry. Indeed, the reason for my caution is to relieve you of any such anxiety.''

110

"The breakdown aside," Peter said, "you do have a total figure for your expenditures?"

Helmut van Huyck looked at Victor Grieg and nodded.

"Expenditures, one point two million. Mr. van Huyck's services, eight hundred thousand. Total two million, not including cost overruns." From the flatness of Grieg's tone combined with the nasality of his voice, he might have been quoting the morning line at Belmont.

"Cost overruns?"

"The occasional whistleblower. We try to anticipate. No more than ten percent." Again van Huyck was reassuring. "And Victor's services are of course included in my fee. His travel, too."

"Two million dollars. Possibly two point two." Peter could not keep the doubt from his voice. "I suppose it's worth it."

"Why, you don't suppose," van Huyck said with a display of great good humor. "You know it's worth it. The tax abatement on your investment will give you a ninety-five percent exemption from real estate taxes in the first year. And that abatement will only be reduced by five percent annually after that. The two million will be saved before you're even close to finishing construction."

"You're sure about the abatement, then?"

"IBM, AT and T, Philip Morris, and now Stockwell Enterprises. The precedent is there. Not to worry."

"Did you handle it for those corporations?" Peter was awed.

"Of course not. They are large, respectable companies. They didn't need my services. They got the abatements on their own merits. But then you don't need my services, either, Mr. Stockwell. This meeting never took place. Stockwell Enterprises, too, will get their tax abatement on the merits." Helmut van Huyck sampled his side dish of warm chicory salad.

"You mentioned travel for Mr. Grieg," Peter remembered. "What's that about?"

"Board of Estimate. City council. State legislature. Borough party bosses. Department heads. Regulatory agency heads. Bureau heads. Etcetera." Van Huyck ticked them off. "A great deal of etcetera. None of these can be direct recipients of Stockwell Enterprises' generosity. Whether personal gifts, or campaign contributions, or funds deposited in blind trusts, the money involved has to be laundered. This requires Victor to make frequent trips."

"Trips to where?"

"Victor." Van Huyck indicated that the accountant should answer Peter while he devoted himself to his roast Muscovy duck in its savory sauce of lime and bitter oranges.

"St. Martin." Victor pushed his grilled lobster to one side and explained, "You'll give me various sums of money for certain parties, Mr. Stockwell, and I'll fly with it to St. Martin. Judging by the size of the project, I'll be making a lot of trips."

"Why St. Martin?" Peter asked.

"Because it's one Caribbean island of two separate colonies run by two different countries with no guards at the borders separating the territories. The Dutch run one side. The French run the other," he continued. "It's been that way for three hundred fifty years. And that makes St. Martin ideal for our purposes."

"Could you explain that so I can understand it?"

Victor Grieg looked at Helmut van Huyck, who nodded. "I take the money you give me and deposit it in different accounts in various banks in Philipsburg, which is the capital of Dutch Sint Maarten. Later I withdraw the money in Dutch guilders. I drive across the unguarded border to Marigot or Grand Case in French St. Martin. I deposit the guilders in French banks. Now the money is francs, and I transfer it to a certain French St. Martin brokerage house. Periodically this house issues dividends in the form of dollars to its investors. Among these investors will be those government people who have cooperated with Stockwell Enterprises in facilitating the project. Some of the money will be redistributed through various New York agencies in the form of contributions to political parties and to specific political campaigns. The rest may be

112

used to purchase cars, houses, vacations, stocks or bonds, whatever.''

"These rather melodramatic machinations," van Huyck pointed out, "are further insurance against embarrassment for all those involved. Even if one of our collaborators were exposed, Mr. Stockwell, Victor will have so muddied the trail that the money could not possibly be traced back to Stockwell Enterprises."

"I don't know." Peter still had reservations. "I've never done anything like this before."

"It is the price of doing business in New York City real estate," Helmut van Huyck told him. "Believe me, there is no other way." He sat back, smiling warmly under the cold pupils of his pale blue eyes. "Now, as to dessert. The charlotte with passion fruit mousse is excellent. I can also recommend the chocolate with crème anglaise."

"No dessert for me, thank you."

"I'll pass, too," Victor Grieg decided.

"When and how shall I deliver the money to you?" Peter asked van Huyck.

"You shan't. Why bless me, that would be foolish on both our parts. Much as I shall regret forgoing your company, Mr. Stockwell, you and I shall not meet again at all. You will give the money to Victor. That is why I asked him to join us at dinner. You two will be meeting on a regular basis, I should imagine. I will keep things running smoothly for you, Mr. Stockwell, never fear. But the money will be Victor's domain. He will work out the details with you."

"I see." Peter looked at Victor Grieg questioningly.

"I'll be in touch." Grieg's voice was strictly business, his eyes as narrow as if he were lining up a three-cushion shot in a pool hall.

"No dessert, then, gentlemen." Helmut van Huyck patted the front of his vest. "Well then, you have saved me from myself. But shall we have a brandy? They have a fourteen-year-old Courvoisier that strokes the throat like velvet on the breasts of virgins."

15

"YOU'VE GIVEN UP drinking!" Carrie Tyler stared at Fitz Connely in disbelief.

"That I have." Fitz regarded her from the depths of his dark eyes. "And from your tone, you're no admirer of temperance."

They had met in the upstairs hallway. Carrie had been looking for Holly. It was a warm day for January, and she had driven her 480 SL Porsche up to Riverview on impulse, hoping Holly would go horseback riding with her. The stables had always been Riverview's prime attraction as far as Carrie was concerned.

She had run into Fitz coming out of his room. Since his arrival at Riverview, she had met him only once. On that occasion he had been dead drunk, and Carrie had been told that that was his usual condition. Now, to have him reply to her suggestion that they have a drink together with the news that he'd given it up was a surprise.

"Temperance is a form of moderation," Carrie responded. "I'm no admirer of moderation. In my experience it's just another word for dull."

"And you wouldn't be a lass to say a good word for anything dull." His gaze took in Carrie's overt sensuality. She was a knockout beauty, but there were plenty of attractive women at Riverview. Buffy was a siren, Holly a regal, ice-blond beauty, and Patrice—well, Patrice despite her composed demeanor, was warm and lovely, her thick chestnut hair, doe eyes, and petite figure an appealing contrast to her shrewd intelligence.

"Is that your room?"

"Oh, it is." His eyes wandered boldly over Carrie's provocative figure.

"Could I go in there a minute?"

"And why would you want to do that?" His voice was teasing, interested.

"Because there's something I can't do out here in the hall."

"Is there, now?" Fitz held the door open for Carrie, followed her in, and closed it behind them.

Carrie looked at him. Her initial impression was of a man wild and dark and brimming with energy. Such a man would be overwhelming. She shivered deliciously at the prospect. "So you've given up drink," she said. "Does that mean you've given up all the vices?"

"Not all."

"Would you like some of this, then?" Carrie produced some cocaine.

"Sure and I've never acquired the taste."

"It will make it better," Carrie told him softly, tacitly acknowledging what was becoming clear to both of them—that they were going to make love.

"Oh, it will be fine for me without."

"Do you mind if I indulge?"

"Each his own master; each her own mistress."

Carrie laid out the lines and sniffed them quickly. She brushed the powder from the tip of her nose and turned to Fitz. "Why don't you kiss me?" she suggested.

"Why not indeed?"

He took her in his arms, his grip a vise. It squeezed the breath from her body as he kissed her. His tongue filled her mouth, hot and demanding. His penis crawled up against her belly and hardened.

Carrie clung to him. She was dizzy. The cocaine? The way he was squeezing her? As she'd anticipated, she felt overwhelmed, and at the same time she was very excited.

His hands moved under her sweater. A callused fingertip traced the cleavage between her breasts. His thumbs stroked her naked, stiffening nipples. He pushed the sweater up. His lips left hers and moved to her breasts.

Carrie's knees buckled slightly as he sucked at one and then the other. They were still standing in front of the bed. Fitz reached under her skirt from behind, and his hand moved over her plump, writhing bottom. He found the elastic of her bikini panties and tugged them down.

"Oh, God!" Carrie moaned, very turned on now.

Abruptly Fitz stepped back and unzipped his pants. He took out his penis and placed it in Carrie's hand.

Widening her stance as he raised her woolen skirt, she told Fitz hoarsely, "I like to hold your prick. I love it. I love you. Do you love me?"

"Not a bit of it."

"You don't love me?"

"I do not. Nor do you love me, my girl. You're just horny for a bit of the old push-pull is all."

"That's right." His refusal to play the game excited Carrie even more. "I don't love you. But I want to fuck you." She rose up on the tips of her toes and tried to insert his organ. "I want your prick in my pussy!" she panted.

In response Fitz put both hands under her squirming bottom and raised her.

Carrie, locking her long legs above his hips, pushed down until he was buried inside her to the sac of his scrotum. Her arms around his neck, she began bouncing, easily at first and then harder.

Fitz felt her bury her face in his shoulder, and then he felt her teeth digging into his shoulder. When she began to squeal and bounce hard against his groin, half laughing and half crying, Fitz backed her against the wall and held her there while she held him inside her full length and prolonged her hot, intense orgasm.

When it was over, he pushed her back on the bed without withdrawing. Sensitive in the aftermath of her climax, he could tell that his movements inside her now were pleasuring her in ways that temporarily sacrificed her rationality. He bent her double and stroked her deep, riding her clitoris, until he felt Carrie on the brink of a second orgasm.

116

"Wow!" Carrie enthused a long time later when they had subsided. "Is that the effect giving up liquor has on you?"

"No," Fitz told her. "That's the effect going without sex for too long has."

"Christ, I miss you!" Matt had managed to corner Kathleen alone in the Riverview library.

"Me or the sex?" Kathleen asked, her freckled face a mask of suspicion under her bright red curls.

"That, too." Matt was honest.

"Then why not go to Montreal?" Kathleen asked bitterly. "You won't have any trouble finding satisfaction there, I'm sure."

"I don't want Wendy. I want you, Kathleen. And yes, in bed, too. Is that so wrong?"

"How can you ask that after I walked in on you making love to her?"

"I wasn't making love to her. She was upset. I was trying to comfort her."

"Oh? Daniel in the lioness's den?" Kathleen was sarcastic. "Were you removing a thorn from her mouth with your tongue, then?"

"Listen, let me explain. Just give me a chance."

"Explain, then." Kathleen folded her arms and waited. The expression on her face did not soothe Matt's fears that no explanation would satisfy her. Nevertheless, he had to try.

"Wendy was very upset about Bruce. About her father and Bruce. About the whole lousy situation and my part in it. She's being torn in different directions, Kathleen. I'm insisting on my rights as Bruce's father. Her father would be furious if he knew she was letting Bruce see me. He's a very sick man, and she doesn't dare risk the emotional strain of a row with him. At the same time, Wendy wants to do what's best for our son. The pressure was simply too much for her and she went to pieces. I took her in my arms because I felt so bad for her."

117

"You were kissing her," Kathleen reminded him.

"It just got away from us. The closeness. The shared memories. But it didn't mean anything."

"The shared memories," Kathleen repeated flatly.

"Kathleen, I love you!" Matt took her by the shoulders and looked deep into her jade-green eyes. "Not Wendy. You."

"Damn it, I love you, too," Kathleen replied in a small voice.

"Well then—" He took her in his arms and kissed her.

His touch, the crisp aroma of his after-shave, his voice murmuring in her ear, were familiar and reassuring. Kathleen felt herself melting, and the motes in the pale January light streaming through the two-story-high vaulted library windows swam before her eyes. A surge of desire to make love with Matt overcame her.

"Did you mean what you said before, Matt?" Her voice was husky and thick with desire. "About wanting me in bed?"

"How can you ask?" He chuckled. "The proof is an embarrassment."

"Tonight, then? Shall I come to your house for supper and stay the night?" She pressed against him, her generous breasts soft and warm and healthy with passion.

There was a silence. It lengthened. Kathleen looked up at Matt inquiringly. "I can't tonight," he said miserably.

"And why not?" Kathleen took a step backward, out of his arms, and looked at him from eyes that were darkening with suspicion.

"I have to go to Montreal," Matt told her. "I set up this visit the last time Wendy was here. I can't cancel now. Not at the last minute."

"I see."

"Wendy is bringing Bruce to my hotel to see me. Please, Kathleen, try to understand. He's my son."

"To your hotel."

"Don't read anything into it, Kathleen. Please—"

"And will you be dining with the mother of your son?" she inquired coldly.

118

"Yes," Matt answered frankly. "But it's not like you're making it seem. We have a lot to talk about." Immediately he regretted his choice of words.

"I'll just bet you do."

"I mean Bruce. We have to discuss Bruce."

"Bruce." Kathleen's normally wide and generous mouth was not attractive when she snarled. "The woman says 'Bruce' and snaps her fingers and you come running. Damn it, Matt, do what you want, but don't pretend. It's you that Wendy wants to see. And from the way you jump when she snaps her fingers, you must really want to be with her as well."

"Please, Kathleen. Try to understand."

"I understand all too well. You want to be with Wendy, not me. You'd rather go to Montreal than make love to me. It's not hard to understand. It's a little harder to accept, but I can do that, too.'

"Kathleen—"

"No, Matt!" She held up her hands to keep him away from her. "The message is clear. It's over with you and me."

"Come on, Kathleen."

"I mean it. It's over." She turned on her heel, tall and resolute, and walked toward the massive, carved oak door.

"Where are you going? What are you going to do?"

"I'm going to find someone else. I'm not the type to pine away from a broken heart. Oh, no. Not my style, bucko." In her hurt and anger, a bit of brogue crept into Kathleen's speech. "Sure and there are other men in the world." She exited without turning around. "Why, there are even other men right here at Riverview."

Even as she said it, Kathleen wondered why, at that particular moment, she should have thought of Fitz Connely.

16

Fitz Connely was looking up at the Stefanelli mural in the lobby of the Stockwell Building when Patrice O'Keefe spied him. She was returning from a business luncheon with the head of the advertising agency the board was considering to design the prospectus for its new real estate project. After dropping off some papers at the Stockwell executive offices, she planned to catch a cab to Grand Central and take the train up to Riverview.

"Do you like it?" Patrice came up behind Fitz as he was studying the painting.

"I recognize it." His answer surprised Patrice. He turned to her, his freshly shaved cheeks still ruddy from the seaport wind whipping through the canyons of lower Manhattan. "And hello to you."

"Hello to you, too." Without his usual stubbly beard and that phony forelock-tugging attitude, Patrice reflected, he really is quite presentable. "Recognize it? What do you mean?"

Fitz squinted at the large abstract splash of colors and smiled. "Sure and I lived with it during my wino days," he told Patrice.

"You mean it's like some kind of psychedelic fantasy you had?"

"I wouldn't know about that. But the feller who painted that knew what it was about right enough. Breakin' it down and rearranging it. The brain looking out, and then in, gathering it in, that is, chopping it up, dicing it, and rearranging it closer to the heart's desire. Stefanelli. Funny, the name doesn't sound Irish."

"It's not."

"Well now, this is America. The melting pot. You never know."

"What brings you here, Fitz?"

"A matter of business." His grin was self-deprecating. "An occasion, too, though. Isn't it my first trip into the city since you and Jack abducted me from Grand Central Station?"

"Business?"

"I have an appointment with Mr. De Vilbiss, and at his request."

Patrice was immediately suspicious. It was just like De Vilbiss to contrive to see Fitz alone without anybody else knowing. With no one to look out for Fitz, the California lawyer would make mincemeat of him. After all, Fitz was an innocent plunged into the shark pool of the business world, while De Vilbiss had always been the slickest of manipulators. Patrice could no more let Fitz take on De Vilbiss alone than she could give a toddler a loaded revolver to play with in its crib. She would have to intercede.

"Can I tag along?" she asked Fitz. "Then when your business with Mr. De Vilbiss is over, we can go back to Riverview together."

"I'm not a man to object to the sunrise, or the bloom of the rose, or the presence of a beautiful woman."

Patrice's answering smile lit up her heart-shaped face and deep brown eyes. "What blarney!" She blushed and laughed and linked arms with him.

They followed the ding-ding of elevators to the small crowds being measured by the starter into the cars. Whisked aloft, they disembarked and walked down the hallway to the door with "Halsey De Vilbiss, Attorney-At-Law" inscribed on the frosted glass. They entered the premises.

Fitz was expected. The receptionist turned them over to the secretary, who immediately ushered them into Halsey De Vilbiss's inner office. De Vilbiss did not hide his surprise at Patrice's presence.

Greeting him sweetly, Patrice slipped onto a chair. De Vilbiss made a quick recovery and returned the greeting smoothly. Fitz, aware of the tension behind the exchange of greetings, looked from him to Patrice.

"Can I offer you a drink?" De Vilbiss asked.

"Sure and I've taken the pledge," Fitz told him.

Patrice shook her head in stunned disbelief.

"Well, down to business, then." De Vilbiss took his seat behind the glazed redwood desk. He focused his attention on Fitz. "As you know," he said, "I handled most of your great-grandmother Sarah Stockwell Tyler's business affairs. I was empowered to act for her on the board of trustees of Stockwell Enterprises. It was her wish that I continue on in that capacity after her death, in effect representing her heir, you."

"It was her *recommendation*," Patrice corrected him.

"This is an informal discussion, Mrs. O'Keefe. Exploratory, as it were." Halsey's manicured fingers had a stranglehold on the pencil between them. "Its purpose is to enable Mr. Connely and myself to become better acquainted." His injured tone implied that Patrice was an interloper.

"I just want Fitz to be aware that Sarah didn't tie his hands. She left him choices."

"I understand that," Fitz said mildly. "And I've a tongue in my head to speak for myself."

Patrice flushed. If he rejected her help, how could she look out for his interests? If she didn't look out for his interests, De Vilbiss would overwhelm him.

"Exactly." De Vilbiss's smug smile was as sharp as a fresh-honed razor blade. "Now, Mr. Connely, your great-grandmother left a letter with her bank regarding this matter."

"I've seen it."

"You have?" De Vilbiss was surprised.

Now it was Patrice's turn to smile. She was the one who had notified the bank that Sarah Stockwell Tyler's heir had been found and was living at Riverview—just in

122

case Halsey De Vilbiss might have overlooked it. Of course Fitz didn't know she'd done that for him.

"And I've read it," Fitz added. "As well as the communication to the board."

"Where did you—?" De Vilbiss looked at Patrice. "I see." He took a deep breath. "Then you will appreciate that there is some validity to Sarah Stockwell Tyler's apprehension that you might lack experience as regards the world of finance."

"The world of finance is it? Tell me then, Mr. De Vilbiss, is there a different method of addition and subtraction used in the world of finance, then?"

Patrice laughed.

"There's a lot more to it than simple arithmetic." This meeting was not going at all the way De Vilbiss had envisioned.

"To be sure." Fitz scratched his head and smiled a childlike smile. "I meant no claim to an expertise in a league with your own, Mr. De Vilbiss. My investment strategy is limited to the poker table, and in all honesty, I can boast of no great returns on it."

"That's precisely my point." Halsey De Vilbiss's voice turned silky, ingratiating. "It's not a matter of intelligence at all," he said earnestly. "But it takes time to become proficient in business matters as complex as those involving Stockwell Enterprises. Mistakes can be very costly. Believe me, I have your best interests at heart."

"Believe him," Patrice murmured sarcastically.

"And it is in your best interests," Halsey continued, "that I continue to act as your proxy on the Stockwell board just as I did for your great-grandmother."

"I see." Fitz stuck his tongue in his cheek and then stroked the cheek with one finger thoughtfully. "But tell me, Mr. De Vilbiss, if you keep doing for me, how will I learn to do for myself?"

"Well, in time . . ." De Vilbiss let the evasion drift off into thin air.

"And there's something else I'm not clear on," Fitz

123

added. "What is it you receive in payment for this dedicated service, Mr. De Vilbiss?"

Patrice played happily with her bow. Fitz might be rough around the edges, but he certainly was nobody's fool. It was absolutely delicious to watch him employing an air of innocence as he hectored Halsey De Vilbiss with bottom-line questions.

"I am, of course, well paid." Halsey De Vilbiss said it lightly with an "among us boys" laugh, but it didn't quite come off.

"And just how well would that be?" The deep-set Irish eyes held De Vilbiss in their sights.

"Very well."

"I wonder now, could you be a little more specific, Mr. De Vilbiss?" Despite the hardening of his eyes, Fitz's tone was still diffident.

"Seven hundred fifty thousand dollars a year," De Vilbiss told him unwillingly. "And a percentage of dividends."

"Seven hundred fifty thousand dollars," Fitz repeated softly. "*And* a percentage of dividends. And would that be dividends of Stockwell stock, Mr. De Vilbiss?"

"That's the major part, yes. But the rest of the portfolio as well."

"And just what percentage of such dividends is that now?"

"Three percent."

"Oh. Well now, that doesn't seem so very much. Just how much would you say that comes to, Mr. De Vilbiss?"

"Under a million annually," De Vilbiss admitted reluctantly.

"Under a million is it? But not very much under, I'll wager."

"No. Not very much under."

"So the total of what you earn managing this estate I've inherited is close to one and three-quarter million a year, would you say now, Mr. De Vilbiss?"

"Yes. But you have to understand that's not unusual considering the value of the estate."

124

"Oh, to be sure. And believe me, sir, I take it as a compliment to you that my great-grandmother valued your services so highly. A very great compliment indeed."

"Thank you." Patrice saw that Halsey De Vilbiss was thrown off balance; he wasn't sure if Fitz was being sarcastic or if he really meant what he said. Actually, she wasn't quite sure herself.

"Money—the handling of it—is a lesson to be learned, to be sure," Fitz said as if speaking to himself.

"Which is why experts are worth what they're paid," De Vilbiss told him. "And I am an expert, a professional."

"So you said." Fitz held up his hand as if to quiet a baby about to squall. "And so my great-grandmother said. And wouldn't I be the fool then to turn away from such expertise?"

"May I take it, then," Halsey De Vilbiss asked carefully, "that you wish me to continue to represent the estate?"

"There's no hurry in deciding—" Patrice started to say, her protective instincts toward Fitz once again propelling her into the conversation.

"Shah now. Shah," Fitz hushed her, another infant to be calmed. "Mr. De Vilbiss and I are doing just fine."

He had not added "without your help," but the message was clear to Patrice. She pressed her full lips together in a thin line and stopped talking. Obviously Fitz thought himself capable of handling De Vilbiss without help. She wasn't so sure.

"It would be a favor to me for you to continue doing what you've been doing so well," Fitz told De Vilbiss. "And I'm hoping you'll be good enough to show me a trick or two as relates to this world of finance you grasp so cleverly."

"Well, of course, I'll be happy to answer any questions you might have," De Vilbiss assured him.

"Well now, I'll try not to have so many as to be a bother to you." Fitz rumpled his hair as if digging for the roots of wisdom. "For now, though," he said, "there's only the one thing I'd be obliged to know."

"Of course. If I can tell you."

"Oh, I've no doubt at all that you can. It's just this: When exactly is the next meeting of the board of Stockwell Enterprises?"

Well, well, Patrice thought.

"The next board meeting?" De Vilbiss looked at him blankly.

"Yes, please. I'm thinking it would be a good thing for me to be there, you see, Mr. De Vilbiss."

"Well now, I don't know. Without any previous background in the matters under discussion . . ."

"Oh, I'll have difficulties understanding the complexities, to be sure. Even so, being there among all you folk with your great experience and know-how can't hurt, now, can it? I mean, some of it is bound to rub off on me, wouldn't you say? So just when is it, the board meeting, please, Mr. De Vilbiss?"

With a scarcely concealed sigh, the lawyer told him.

Saying their farewells, Fitz repeated his faith in De Vilbiss's experience and skills and his gratitude at having them at his disposal. De Vilbiss in turn assured Fitz that he would represent his interests to the best of his abilities. Patrice restricted herself to a simple "Good-bye" and was otherwise silent until they were in the hallway outside De Vilbiss's offices.

There her restraint ceased. "You let him keep his power over the estate!" she exploded. "Why? Don't you see the kind of man he is? How can you trust him?"

"I never said I trusted him," Fitz replied softly.

"Then why let him continue to control your fortune?"

"Manage, not control. If I understand the will correctly, control rests with me and no one else. But to answer your question, then: The impression I've got of my great-grandmother is she was a wise woman who knew exactly what she was about. She saw Mr. De Vilbiss for the scoundrel he is, but she used him. I'm only carrying on the tradition."

"But if he's such a scoundrel . . . ?" Patrice was upset.

"A competent scoundrel. There's no argument on that from anyone, to my knowledge. And not downright dishonest."

"He's too clever—"

"So it's the cutting of corners that concerns you, then?" Fitz interrupted. "And maybe a pushing through here and there of something more to his own advantage than to the general good. But take the larger picture, Stockwell Enterprises, now, doesn't it act for its own advantage more than to the general good?"

"That's not the same—"

"Oh, to be sure. The corporate as differentiated—ah, there's a fine hundred-dollar word for you—from the individual. Well, of course that's still a wee bit complicated for my uneducated business brain. Still, for the time being I'll be needing Mr. De Vilbiss. He's my wee pencil flashlight illuminating the dark corners of this almighty financial world into which fate has dropped me, or so you might say."

"Well," Patrice said slowly, "as long as you're sure you're using him rather than the other way around."

"It's how I mean it to be." Fitz folded her arm in his as they entered the elevator. "And it's very grateful I am for your concern."

Confused, Patrice looked up into his dark eyes and wondered just how well she really knew this enigmatic Stockwell heir.

17

OTHER MEN HAD aroused Carrie Tyler before, but with this new man she felt it would be different—more than a brief relationship, a one-night stand. It would be a far cry from her interlude with Fitz Connely—explosive sex, quick parting, no regrets. This new romance, she was sure, would have a course to run.

She had been having dinner by herself at Romna, an obscure Indian restaurant with a deliciously saffron cuisine in the East Village. Eating pink was an addiction with Carrie more secret than cocaine. There was nothing trendy about Romna, nothing to draw the Upper East Side crowd with whom she usually ran. Its sole recommendation was the best Indian food in New York, and that was enough to justify Carrie's dining alone there once a month or so.

Never before had she run into anyone she knew at Romna. She certainly had never expected to encounter a Stockwell there—not with the price of entrées ranging between three sixty and five forty. And the last person she would have expected to see was her cousin Peter.

When he entered the dimly lit restaurant, Carrie raised her menu in front of her face like a shield. She had no wish to spoil her meal by being put in the position of having to ask her premature ejaculator of a cousin to join her. She only removed the concealment of the menu when Peter and his male dinner companion had seated themselves and she was sure that Peter's back was to her.

As she ate her samosa and then her chicken tandoori, Carrie's gaze strayed back to their table. Peter seemed to be doing most of the talking. He was hunched across the table toward the other man, whose answers seemed terse, monosyllabic, perhaps.

Facing Carrie, Peter's companion chewed effortlessly, swallowed smoothly, and his expression remained impassive. Once his gaze met Carrie's hazel eyes. The unblinking, snakelike coldness behind the horn-rimmed glasses was replaced by a momentary interest. Carrie felt as if she'd brushed against something menacing but sensual in the dark. It was an intriguing feeling—the first flash of the magnetism between them.

Carrie smiled slightly—enough to let him know it was not inadvertent—and looked back down at her plate. Save for the saffron rice, it had been cleaned. Much as she adored the saffron rice, she would not sacrifice her slenderness to it. She pushed the plate away and lit a cigarette. She looked toward Peter's table again. The man with her cousin returned her smile, and she tossed her long, loose, silky mane of apricot-colored hair by way of acknowledgment.

The exchange of smiles decided Carrie. She tamped out her cigarette and called for the check. When she had paid it, she walked by Peter's table.

"Carrie." He stood up halfway with automatic politeness.

"Why, hello, Peter." She behaved as if she had not noticed him earlier. "What are you doing here?"

"Mixing dinner and business." Peter did not explain that discretion had dictated the meeting take place in some obscure place where he and Victor Grieg would not likely be seen together.

Carrie stood there smiling and waiting while Peter got a crick in his back from his half-standing, half-seated position. "Join us," he finally had to suggest, hiding his reluctance. He signaled a waiter to bring a chair. "Will you have some wine?"

"I'd love some." Carrie's smile—a dazzle as deliberate as pushing the button of a searchlight aimed into the other person's eyes—included Peter's companion. "Aren't you going to introduce me?" she said.

"This is my cousin, Carrie Tyler," Peter complied obediently. "Carrie, this is Victor Grieg."

"It's a pleasure to meet you."

Victor's sandpapery New York tones surprised her. His appearance—well tailored, dark, suave looking—had prepared her for more cultured accents. She was further intrigued. "Are you from New York?" she asked, straight-faced.

His long, narrow body shifted in his chair, and the cunning eyes behind his horn-rimmed glasses mocked the absurdity of her question. "It's been my home since Oxford," he told Carrie, his tone equally serious.

"You're British, then?"

"My speech gave me away." Grieg's voice grew more gravelly than ever.

"I can always spot an upper-class Englishman."

"What are you two talking about?" Peter asked, bewildered.

"I knew you were a perceptive lady."

"And when did you know that?" They both ignored Peter.

"When I saw you looking at me before," Grieg told her bluntly.

"Ah, well, your face interested me," Carrie confessed.

"All of you interests me." Victor Grieg was bold.

"Why do I suddenly feel like a third wheel?" Peter asked aloud, a slight sulkiness in his voice.

"I have to visit the euphemism." Carrie stood up and started for the ladies' room. The look she shot Victor Grieg over her shoulder was a tantalizing question.

His quick nod answered it affirmatively. "She's very attractive, your cousin," he remarked to Peter. "Unusual eyes. Beautiful hair."

"Carrie? She's not really a cousin. It's sort of a complicated and distant relationship. She's a real roundheels, though, if you're interested."

"I am interested." Victor Grieg admitted.

"If you'd like me to fade away and leave you a clear field . . ." Peter was eager for Victor Grieg's goodwill. As

130

things had been worked out by Helmut van Huyck, he would have to be dependent on Grieg to a great extent.

"I would like."

"Well, I guess we have finished with our business for now."

"We have."

"Should my ears be burning?" Carrie was back.

"There are other things to talk about." Peter's laugh wasn't convincing.

Carrie sat down. Her knee brushed Victor Grieg's knee. He smiled thinly at Peter.

"Listen, you two," Peter said, "I have to run. Another appointment. That's no reason for you to hurry, though. Why don't you stay and finish the wine and . . . well, whatever."

"Good night, Peter," Carrie said without hesitation.

"Good night, Mr. Stockwell," Victor Grieg echoed.

"I'll be in touch," Peter told him. He picked up the check and carried it to the owner of Romna with his credit card. A few moments later he was gone.

There was not really very much wine to finish, and Victor Grieg and Carrie did not stay very long after Peter's departure. "Would you like me to drop you someplace?" he asked her when they were out on the sidewalk in front of the restaurant.

"Where are you going?"

"Home," he told her. "Just home."

"Then drop me there," Carrie said. "Drop me home . . . with you."

Wendy and Matt Stockwell were seated in a small French restaurant in Montreal. The decor was roughhewn, not fancy, and the service was pure Quebec, arrogant, a bit hostile to English speakers. The food was plentiful and excellent.

Matt had spent the afternoon with his son. Wendy had picked him up, and Matt had waited around the corner while she returned the little boy to the home they shared with her father. They they had gone out to dinner to discuss the seemingly unsolvable dilemma of their situation. Now, with the opening of the second bottle of wine, Wendy was becoming nostalgic.

"Sometimes I miss what we had so much, Matt," she told him frankly.

Matt did not know how to respond. That had been another chapter in his life, a chapter that was closed now. But if he told Wendy that, her feelings would be hurt. He didn't want to hurt Wendy. He owed her that much, not hurting her any more than he had in the past.

Wendy, recognizing his discomfort, changed the subject. After dinner, though, when they left the restaurant, she linked arms with him. "I'll walk you back to your hotel," she suggested. "I can use the exercise after that humongous meal."

"Swell."

"I'm sorry about you and Kathleen," she said after they'd walked in silence for a while.

"Yeah. So am I." Matt knew Wendy well enough to know that she wasn't sorry at all.

"Do you think you'll be able to patch it up?"

"I don't really know," he answered honestly.

"Do you want to? I mean, do you really love her so much?"

"Yeah. I do."

They fell silent again. As they approached the hotel Wendy brought them to a halt with a pressure on Matt's arm. "I don't care," she said. "I know I shouldn't do this with you still hooked on her, but I don't care." She took a deep breath. "I'll come up with you if you want. I'll spend the night with you if you'd like."

Matt stared at her. If he wanted. If he liked. And Kathleen had not only left him, but as much as told him she was going to look for someone else. Well, why not? Why shouldn't he take Wendy up on her offer?

"What do you say, Matt?" Wendy said finally. "Do you want to make love to me tonight?"

Did he? Matt couldn't decide. The physical urge was

there. He couldn't deny that. Why not, then? Why was he hesitating? Why shouldn't he make love to Wendy tonight?

18

" THERE'S A NEW company just went up on the big board," David Lewis was telling his fellow board members. "I'd like to buy in heavily with an eye toward a takeover. I see real potential in a virgin field. Their patents alone justify the purchase price."

"How much?" Peter Stockwell inquired.

"Two million—give or take a half million."

"Small potatoes." Peter shrugged. "Why waste board time discussing it? Just do it, Uncle David."

Fitz, who was attending his first meeting, leaned forward and whispered hurriedly in De Vilbiss's ear. The attorney shrugged and sighed. "Might we know the name of the company and its business?" he requested in a bored tone.

"Shakeout, Inc." David Lewis told him with a small frown. "Its business is vibrations."

"Begging your pardon?" Fitz put the question directly.

"All right, then." David Lewis sighed and explained. "I have an old friend who recently bought a condominium penthouse in the Sixties off Fifth Avenue for three point five million. A new building. After he moved in, he discovered that there was a rooftop air conditioner adjacent to his penthouse apartment which operated twenty-four hours a day. Now, his walls are soundproof, so he didn't hear it. However, the vibrations from the unit—it was a large one and serviced the whole building—shook

133

the Waterford crystal from his china closet and broke several pieces. A large, original Picasso, valued at half as much as the apartment itself, could not be hung because the vibrations constantly shook it off center. He was at his wit's end. And then he heard of Shakeout, Inc. He called them, and within two weeks they had solved his problem. He considered the forty thousand dollars they charged him well spent."

Patrice could not help noticing how intently Fitz Connely was staring at David Lewis. The culture shock of emigration from Ireland to the United States, she reflected, was nothing compared to the distance between New York homelessness and megabucks condo dwelling. What must Fitz be thinking?

Forty thousand dollars to get rid of the shakes, and society begrudging the wino his one fifty jug. That's what Fitz was thinking.

"But how much demand can there be for services like that?" Max Tyler asked.

"More than they can keep up with." It was Peter who answered him. "Uncle David has hit on something. There are only a few companies doing this sort of thing, and they're pulling in profits hand over fist. Jacuzzis, for instance, are a big vibration problem to the neighbors of the people who install them. The subway system shakes lower-floor apartments in buildings with iffy foundations. The aerobics craze is shaking walls all over Manhattan. Everything from paper shredders to stereo systems results in incrementally nerve-shattering vibrations creating a need for the services of high-priced outfits like Vibranetics, or the Vibration Eliminator Company, or this Shakeout firm that Uncle David wants to earmark for takeover. Acoustic sealing is big business."

"Sure and it's amazing the knowledge you all have," Fitz complimented Peter.

"Not really." Peter did not pass up the opportunity to ingratiate himself with the new boy on the block. "Real estate development is my field of expertise, and naturally that includes building specifications. You see, construc-

134

tion is cheaper and lighter in luxury high rises today than it used to be. Once upon a time the New York City building codes required twelve-inch concrete floors in structures over a certain height. Now that's been waived and the floors only have to be four or five inches thick. Soundproofing makes up for some of that, but coping with the vibration potential would eat too deeply into the profits.''

"Now who do you suppose waived those building codes?'' Fitz wondered aloud.

Nobody answered him.

"Potential vibration is a problem in all new high-rise construction, including our own projected development,'' Peter concluded. "The two million, or whatever, is a good investment. I say we approve Uncle David spending the money and move along.''

"We'll make a profit putting up shoddy buildings. And then we'll make another profit when the people who live in them have to hire this Shakeout company to come in and fix up our shoddy workmanship.'' Max Tyler was cynical. "By all means, let's buy into the company. And by all means let's invest in prison construction because it's bound to be a booming business when they catch up with all the contractors and subcontractors.''

Max's qualms were ignored. David Lewis made a notation regarding Shakeout, Inc., and then moved along. "Mr. De Vilbiss,'' he said, "I believe you wanted to give us a preliminary progress report on the Productivity Insights programs.''

Fitz stayed quiet, looking almost bored as half a dozen other matters were discussed. His interest revived, however, when Peter brought up the East Side development project. "I will need board authorization for the expenditure over a period of time—perhaps as much as a year—of between two and two point two million dollars,'' Peter told them.

"I was under the impression that seed money had already been authorized,'' David Lewis responded.

"This is a step further along,'' Peter told him. "It involved R and D vis-à-vis the various departments in all levels of government concerned." Peter did not need to explain that R&D into the government role was a euphemism for lubricating the bureaucracy. There was no reason to point out that the wheels of government did not spin smoothly without the application of a certain amount of grease. All the board members were fully aware of the workings of real estate and city government.

Max, however, took a perverse pleasure in giving Peter a hard time. "Could you be more specific, please?" he requested.

"That's hard to do. After all, I'm overseeing the big picture. I don't carry around all the small details in my head."

The discussion, noted Patrice, had Fitz's full attention.

"I'm not asking for all. Just an example or two." Max was blithe.

"City real estate tax abatement. Federal matching funds for landfills. Elevation waivers. Etcetera."

"I do hope none of the 'etcetera' involves anything which could embarrass Stockwell Enterprises," Max observed.

"Why not let Peter worry about that?" De Vilbiss said. "It's his area of expertise."

"Is it the bribing of government mucky-mucks we're talking about, then?" Fitz inquired suddenly.

There was a stunned silence at his blatancy.

"Oh, now, I'm not criticizing a bit of vigorish. Housing, isn't it? And from what I've seen in this city, the best of causes, to be sure."

Patrice regarded him with dismay. Fitz was intelligent, and sharp, too, but if he was jumping to the conclusion that the housing shortage had played the slightest part in the Stockwell board's decision to build this project, he still had a lot to learn.

"We are businessmen." Turning his baleful glare on Fitz, David Lewis responded icily. "We do not bribe public officials, Mr. Connely."

"Businessmen is it? It's clear then that in my ignorance

I must have misunderstood. It's asking forgiveness I am of all present."

In the aftermath of Fitz's apparent gaffe, Patrice's uncle David brought the board meeting to a speedy conclusion. The members left the boardroom without questioning Peter any further on the expenditure of the two point two million dollars.

19

THE BATHTUB IN Victor Grieg's black marble bathroom was oversized. It hadn't come with the apartment. "I bought it myself and had it installed," he was telling Carrie Tyler. "It reminded me of when I was a kid on Cherry Street. Oversized bathtubs were the only good thing about growing up on the Lower East Side."

There were wide ledges at all four corners of the tub. A tooter rested on one of them, along with the dregs of the four lines of grade-A Colombian cocaine Carrie and Victor had snorted. It was the purest snow Carrie had ever snuffed. Victor said it was a gift from a grower with whom he did business.

Under the circumstances—the two of them naked together in the steaming water filling the tub—the glow was particularly satisfying. They'd already made love once that night. This was the in-between time. There was no doubt in Carrie's mind that they were building up to making love again.

Would they do it in the tub? she wondered. At twenty years old Carrie was experienced; she had known sex with a wide variety of lovers in a wide variety of circumstances, but she had never made love in a filled bathtub. Would she and Victor do it facing each other as they were now? she mused. Or would they have to change position, splashing water all over the floor?

Just so I don't drown. Carrie giggled to herself, high on the coke. The possibilities were exciting.

Probably there wouldn't be much splashing. Victor was very smooth. No matter what they did sexually, his long, supple body was always graceful. "I'll bet," Carrie said aloud, "that you can do it without spilling a drop."

"Do what?" he teased, placing his hand on the inside of one of her thighs under the water. His dark eyes regarded her with a surprisingly possessive lust. "Did the coke turn you on again?" he inquired in his rasping voice. His hand moved higher up her thigh, fingertips grazing the wet pubic curls.

"You turn me on." Carrie leaned toward him, her small breasts with their erect nipples floating up against his chest. "My anaconda." Her lips parted hungrily to his kiss. "It is awfully good stuff, though," she acknowledged, sliding her hand down his long, bony chest, down the series of long muscles that were his stomach. "Tell me the truth," she murmured, finding the idea exciting. "Is that your real business? Are you a kingpin of the drug world?"

"Kingpin? Drug world?" A rare laugh escaped him. "You watch too much TV, cookie. I'm an accountant. Money's my business. Not drugs." He lifted one of her breasts from the water and kissed the erect ruby tip.

"But you do business with the Colombian growers."

"I never handle drugs, except recreationally like now. The business I do has to do with money. There's this island—St. Martin—where a lot of South American drugs change hands. A lot of money changes hands, too. Sometimes I handle the money, but never the drugs. I invest the money for people."

"For the drug people?" Carrie investigated and found his tumescent penis.

"No. For the people they do business with. Distributors. Entry-point officials. Politicians who look the other

138

way. The people without whom there wouldn't be any drug trade.'' His hands were on Carrie's hips now, pulling her in to him. ''The people who make it possible for us to snort in the bathtub.''

''But they're all into drugs, and so that means you are, too.'' Carrie was breathless. She had caught his growing erection between the softness of her thighs and was rolling it there.

''I don't just juggle currencies for the drug trade,'' he told her. ''My services come in handy for a lot of people.'' His hands were under her bottom now, tilting it up.

''Like Peter?'' Carrie asked, squirming. ''I can't get over meeting somebody like you through someone like him.''

''Maybe.'' Victor was noncommittal. Arcing up from the bottom of the tub, he guided her onto his erect penis.

''Is he the one you're going to St. Martin for next week?'' Carrie panted.

''Maybe.'' Victor positioned Carrie, who rested tantalizingly over him, and then pulled her down fiercely until he was buried inside her to the hilt.

''Take me with you.'' Licking her lips, Carrie began to move slowly, grindingly, feverishly.

''All right.'' He moved in and out of her, pushing her up and down, slowly, and then faster, harder, their soapy, slick bodies rubbing against each other. ''You can come along to St. Martin if you like.''

Under the circumstances, Victor Grieg was highly motivated to agree.

20

KATHLEEN O'LUNNEY COULD think of no good reason not to flirt with Fitz Connely. Off the sauce, as her father Kevin put it, shaved and bathed, with his curly black hair and the devil in his eye, Fitz was a lad to catch the attention of any young woman with Irish in her blood. Indeed, it was a long time since Kathleen had felt quite as Irish as being around Fitz made her feel.

Matt was still in Montreal, probably making it up with the mother of his child. The thought was a sharp knife to Kathleen's heart. Nevertheless, it left her free.

It had been warm for a winter day, and Kathleen, for all her freedom, was feeling miserable. She missed Matt, the closeness she felt as she accompanied him on the daily chores required by his breeding farm. She missed the strong, healthy smell of the Morgan horses and their nuzzling of her in quest of the sugar cubes she brought them.

In this mood, she'd sought the substitution of the Riverview stables. She'd wandered unhappily out there to watch the stableboys exercising the thoroughbreds in the corral. There she'd encountered Fitz. Like herself, he was wearing jeans. He'd come to investigate the possibilities of taking a horse out on one of the estate trails.

"No problem," Kathleen told him when she learned what he wanted. "You're a Stockwell now. Just tell the groom which horse takes your fancy and ask him to saddle the beast up."

"And if I persuade him to saddle a brace, would you care to come riding yourself?"

"But I'm not a Stockwell."

"How about as a guest of a member of the family?"

"I would enjoy a ride," Kathleen admitted with a toss of the mane of her bright red hair. The action was a flirtatious defiance of any claim she might still feel Matt Stockwell had on her.

"It's settled, then."

A half hour later they were riding along the cliff trail on the banks of the Hudson. The air was crisp but not icy, and the wind off the river was mild. Fitz matched his chestnut's pace to that of Kathleen's bay, and the horses trotted with the briskness of winter at their heels and the promise of springtime widening their nostrils.

The promise of spring affected Kathleen as well. She was young and strong and healthy. Coordinating the movements of the solid flesh of her compact body with the motion of her mount, she resolved that she would put her life in order. Matt had rejected her, and now she would put Matt behind her. Like the springtime pushing winter out, she, too, must make a new beginning.

She glanced sideways at Fitz. A new beginning . . . Well, why not? A smile cost nothing. She was only testing the water, that was all.

The sunburst smile Fitz gave her in return said Come on in, the water's fine. And the exchange of smiles prompted him to speech. "It's glad I am of this chance to be alone with you. I've been waiting to thank you properly."

"Thank me for what?"

"For pointing the way to the pride I'd lost." Fitz was serious. "I was too comfortable with the booze, you see, until your tongue-lashing made me see how low I'd sunk. Because of you I took a good look in the mirror and saw looking back at me the filthy, unshaven creature I'd become. Maybe I saw myself through your eyes. Anyway, whether it was the lilt of Irish in your voice or whatever, it got through to me where nothing else did. I really have stopped drinking, you know."

"And have you stopped singing, too?" Kathleen

141

smiled, remembering the "two out of three" of their last discussion.

Fitz laughed. "By popular request."

"But you've stuck to your guns and haven't given up women, I hope." Kathleen was flirting with him more openly now. Well, she asked herself again, why not?

"Sure and how could I in such charming company?" Fitz responded to the sparkle in her emerald eyes.

"Uh-oh." Kathleen laughed. "Virtue beware when the glib tongue of County Kildare unrolls itself."

"Don't you be questioning my sincerity now."

"I wouldn't dream of it." Kathleen reined in her horse. "Could we walk a while?" she asked. "My bottom's getting sore."

"And why not?"

Her heart was beating very fast as she dismounted. Matt and Wendy! She'd show him! And it wasn't as if she didn't find Fitz attractive. "The other extreme, then?" Obscure as the question sounded, Kathleen had chosen her words very carefully.

"Begging your pardon?"

"You've given up wine and song, but not women. I was just wondering if you're overcompensating in that area." Kathleen tethered her horse to a winter-bared Canadian maple sapling.

"Is my reputation so infamous, then?" He secured his reins beside hers.

"Not infamous. More intriguing, the way I hear it." She sat down with her back against the broad base of an old oak tree. "Bernice, the salad chef. Carrie. Juanita. Patrice. The rumors abound; the cast grows."

"Don't be libeling my friend Patrice, if you please."

"You've cut quite a romantic swath in the short time you've been at Riverview." Kathleen ignored his disclaimer. "I feel positively neglected." Nothing subtle about you, my girl. She winced at the echo of her words in her ears.

"You needn't. Sure and wasn't I given to understand you were spoken for?"

"Well, now I'm unspoken for." Kathleen patted the ground beside her. "Sit," she said. "There's plenty of room."

"Didn't you tell me that once before? But it didn't seem to stick."

"Now it's stuck." Kathleen half turned so that her face was looking up at him from only inches away. "I'm available, Fitz," she told him frankly. "If you're interested."

He was interested. His arms went around her full upper body. He kissed her, a long and thorough kiss.

Kathleen's mind was racing. It was as if it were running simultaneously on two parallel but separate tracks. She was concentrating hard on responding, feeling, on surrendering to the kiss. And at the same time there was the silent sob of hurt and getting even, of showing Matt that if he could make love to someone else, so could she.

After the kiss there was a question in Fitz's dark eyes. Kathleen tried to answer it. She took his hand, slipped it inside her down jacket, and pressed it to her full breast so that he might feel her nipple through the wool shirt she was wearing. "Don't you like me?" She only half succeeded in making her voice sultry. "Don't you want me?"

"I like you." His fingers slipped between the buttons of the shirt, caressing the soft, generous flesh. "I want you." He kissed her again.

When the second kiss was over, however, Fitz pulled back from Kathleen. "But it's my strong feeling that you don't want me."

"I want—" Kathleen started to protest.

"Hush now. You surely do. You do want." Fitz reached inside the down jacket with both hands and buttoned her shirt. "But not me. Able as I may be, there's no way I'm the one to put out your torch." He drew her to her feet. "Let's ride a bit more, shall we?"

"Why don't you just come out and say you're not attracted to me?" Kathleen was hurt and embarrassed by his rejection.

"But I am."

"Then why—?"

"Let's call it chivalry." He gave her a leg up.

"You're the kind of man who gives chivalry a bad name!"

"Doubtless you're right. Still, I think that you need some time to decide if us making love is truly what you want to do."

"And suppose I decide it is?" Kathleen demanded. "Do you think I'd leave myself open to this kind of demeaning rejection again?"

"If you truly decided that," Fitz assured her, "I'd not reject you. I'm not a man to twice turn away from the knock of such a lovely opportunity."

Kathleen believed him. If she thought it over and decided that making love with him was something she really wanted, he would be more than willing. A second offer from her would be welcomed, not refused. Strangely, that relieved the pressure for Kathleen. If she did go to Fitz again, it would not be with desperation, as she had today. It would not be just because she was still so painfully involved with Matt.

It would be because she truly wanted Fitz.

"How can you still be so emotionally involved with him?" Holly demanded of Patrice. "It's been over a year since you and Jack ended your affair."

Patrice looked helplessly at her sleek, always-so-sure-of-herself, golden-haired cousin. "I'm lonely," she replied. "You have Zelig. I don't expect you to understand." Brandy, Patrice knew, was meant to be sipped. She took a healthy gulp of hers from the snifter.

The two young women were in the east wing parlor. They had dined together alone and then come in here where it was cozier to have their brandy and coffee. Zelig was in Washington. The other members of the family had not, for one reason or another, dined at home that evening.

"I didn't always have Zelig." Holly's clear blue eyes

were genuinely concerned. Patrice wore her unhappiness like a too comfortably fitting old glove. "I know what it is to be alone. But that's not the same as mooning for someone who's beyond your grasp."

"I can't help it. I miss him." Patrice was not sullen by nature, and she didn't mean to sound that way, but she did.

"If Jack was here, he'd be with Buffy. Face it, Patrice. You still wouldn't have him."

"Well, anyway, he isn't here." Patrice sighed. Unhappiness made her seem particularly small and woebegone.

"That's right," Holly stated forcefully, believing that sympathy would not help her cousin.

"He's on St. Martin, probably making love to his rich, beautiful, sophisticated wife under a tropic moon at this very moment."

"No tropic moon," Holly told her dryly. "It's too early for the night to have fallen yet on St. Martin."

"Making love to his rich, beautiful, sophisticated wife in the dying rays of a lush tropic sunset," Patrice amended.

"You're wallowing in it." Holly took a hard line.

"I know." Patrice sighed. "I'm being impossible. But it's your fault."

"*My* fault?"

"I'd never let my hair down like this with anybody else but you."

"Oh, Patrice." The frankness took the wind out of Holly's sails. "Forget Jack Houston. Find someone else. The world is full of men."

"All the ones I meet are either married or gay."

"Not very original, Patrice. And not true, either. There are lots of desirable men out there. You're just blind to them."

"Sure there are. If you don't mind the ones who never let you get a word in edgewise, or fawn all over their mothers, or drool in their soup." Patrice poured herself another brandy. "I'm sorry, Holly. I know what a drag I must be. I'm irritable because when it comes right down

145

to it, I'm bored out of my head. Outside of business, I don't know what to do with myself. I just rattle around and get more and more impossible. And I really don't meet any men who interest me."

"Then you're not looking."

"I *am* looking," Patrice protested. "Every time I walk up Broadway I bump into telephone poles looking."

"Maybe you should look closer to home," Holly suggested.

"What do you mean?"

"Fitz Connely. That's what—who—I mean," Holly told her.

"He's too young for me."

"A couple years. The age difference is inconsequential. Besides, you don't have to marry him."

"Why, Mrs. Meyerling, what are you suggesting?" Patrice laughed nervously. "That I have an affair with Fitz?"

"Well, it would get your mind off Jack."

"What makes you think Fitz would be interested?"

"From my observations, Fitz Connely is interested in women, period."

"Thanks a lot." Patrice stuck her tongue out at Holly. "You really know how to flatter a girl."

"Oh, Patrice, you know you're attractive. I'm only trying to tell you that he's the sort of man who couldn't help noticing that."

"That's better." Patrice smiled. "Fitz did kiss me once."

"There," Holly crowed in triumph. "You see?"

"It didn't really mean anything, though. And since then I've been more like an older sister to him, guiding him through the corporate swamp, keeping him out of Halsey De Vilbiss's clutches, that sort of thing."

"An ideal prelude to seduction," Holly assured her, the wicked glint in her eye contrasting with her haughty demeanor.

"You are a cold-blooded woman." Patrice was bemused. "I could never seduce a man unless I was strongly attracted to him."

"And you're not attracted to Fitz?"

146

"Well . . ."

"You are." Holly pounced. "Admit it, Patrice."

"A bit, maybe."

"More than a bit," Holly persisted.

"All right, then. More than a bit. Actually," Patrice admitted, "he's the only man I've been attracted to since my thing with Jack ended."

"Then do yourself a favor, Patrice. Cure yourself of Jack Houston once and for all. Zero in on Fitz Connely!"

21

MAYBE HOLLY WAS right, Patrice reflected later that night in her room as she slipped under the covers. Maybe she should come on to Fitz Connely. Pondering the situation, she stared out over the book in her hand for a long time. Finally, with a sigh, she opened the autumn 1849 volume of the Edith Seabury diary she'd brought to bed with her and began to read. . . .

It was October of the year after the Seneca Falls convention, but although fifteen months had elapsed, the watershed event of the American women's rights movement was still as fresh in Edith Seabury's mind as it had been when it ended. Over three hundred people had attended the convention. Forty of them, including James Mott, husband of Lucretia Mott, who had presided, had been men. The rest had been women.

They had come by railroad and riverboat, carriage and farm wagon. Some women rode to the convention on horseback, and a few came on mules. Most of the women were married, and quite a few of them attended in defiance of their husbands' wishes. Some, like Edith Seabury, were single and characterized by the men who jeered their arrival as either "old-maid spinsters" or "hussies." The latter label was usually accompanied by a masculine elbow to the ribs and a knowing wink.

None of this impressed Edith nor stayed with her throughout the intervening fifteen months so strongly as the Declaration of Sentiments preamble to the Declaration of Women's Rights, which was patterned after the national Declaration of Independence. As read to the vigorous nods of agreement of the assemblage, the Sentiments constituted a catalog of women's grievances. These included barring women from their "inalienable right to the elective franchise," taxation without representation of single women, the denial of property rights to married women, the ownership under law by husbands of their wives' wages, discrimination against women in employment and in the professions, the superior legal status of men and husbands as opposed to women and wives under law, the exclusion of women from colleges, the barring of women from the ministries of all religions, and the double standard that male-enforced morality applied to women.

Two weeks after the Seneca Falls Women's Rights Convention, a second assemblage met in Rochester, New York. Along with Amelia Bloomer, Edith attended that conclave as well. When it was over, she returned to Manhattan with the twin convictions that the women's rights movement would spread and that its goals would be attained. She also took with her a firm personal commitment to be a part of the struggle.

As a visible badge of this commitment, Edith wore the new feminist attire, which earned her the derogatory appellation of "Bloomer girl." Designed by Mrs. Amelia Bloomer, the costume was startlingly different from traditional woman's wear: it was basically a loose, high-necked tunic with three-quarter-length puffed sleeves. Gathered at the waist, it flared to blowsy pantaloons reaching to the ankles and secured there. Usually black stockings and shoes were worn to shield any flesh below the ankle from the easily aroused masculine lust the era presupposed.

Edith and her companion, a young woman poet named Susan Archer Talley, who was a protégée of Edgar Allan Poe, were both wearing the outfits at an outdoor rally on the banks of the East River. As frequently occurred, the two Bloomer girls were subjected to whistles, catcalls, and lascivious comments on their walk to the meeting.

Edith and Susan had become acquainted a month earlier when they attended a conference on the roles and problems of women in the arts. Susan Talley had learned that the most vexing prejudice to painters like Edith was being barred from the life classes male artists attended. How could women perfect their basic sketching techniques, let alone gain recognition for their oils, when they were denied observation of that which was most basic, the human form? Edith had learned that the literary arts were similarly riddled with prejudices against women, particularly poets like Susan Archer Talley, and that it was only through the rare luck of attracting a well-known patron—as Susan had done with Edgar Allan Poe—that a woman could penetrate the male-dominated world of publishing and find her way into print. Victimization had made them friends.

They weren't able to get very close to the makeshift platform from which the crowd was being addressed, so the insults directed at them continued from the small groups of mostly Irish and German unemployed laborers who had gathered on the outskirts of the "petticoat circus." The speaker, Ernestine Rose, already known even outside the movement as "the Queen of the Platform" because of her wit and eloquence, was the daughter of a Polish rabbi. She had emigrated to the United States thirteen years previously and plunged into the movements for free thought, women's rights, and the abolition of slavery.

Ernestine Rose's speech on abolition did not sit well with the jobless German and Irish immigrant workingmen in New York, who perceived the threat of more competition for scarce jobs. Convinced that a black labor force

149

turned loose on the market would push low wages even lower and make employment even harder to find, the crowd was rapidly turning ugly in response to the feminist orator's demands that Negro slaves be freed and granted equality to whites.

Edith was frightened, but, linking arms with Susan, she stood fast. The shifting of the crowd had isolated them somewhat from the main body of women. There were angry shouts from the men around them in response to the speaker. Closer at hand, Edith and Susan became the target of mutters and curses much less good-natured than the earlier jeers at their Bloomer girl outfits.

It was obvious that the two young women were from a higher class than the men surrounding them. Working-class women could not afford the Bloomer costume. Edith's aristocratic blondness and Susan's soft southern beauty were symbolic of the hypocrisy of rich bleeding-heart abolitionists crying over black slaves when what they really wanted was a cheap labor force to do their dirty work. The fact that these were idle women calling for the freeing of the slaves struck the men—the most downtrodden of their northern preindustrial society, after all—as particularly outrageous.

Someone flung a clod of mud at the speaker on the platform. It fell far short. The action, however, inspired others among the men to scramble toward the wagon road at the rear of the throng and gather pieces of horse dung with which to pelt the antislavery feminists.

A horseman riding by, made curious by the activity of the dung gatherers, reined in his steed. Stroking his flowing mustache, he dismounted and followed the men back to the fringes of the crowd. There he saw some men jostling the two Bloomer girls.

"Here, there! Leave them alone!" Leading his horse and clearing a path in front of him with the arc of his riding crop, the well-dressed horseman made his way to the young women.

With sullen mutters, the crowd gave way before him. By his dress, his confidence, his arrogance, even, they knew he was a gentleman, one of those who controlled the few jobs that came along. It wasn't his brawn they feared, but another kind of power altogether. The most disgruntled among them didn't want to incur the wrath of one of the small, rich group of nabobs who paid wages.

"Thank you, sir." Edith could not help but be relieved at the slackening of the pressure that had been so ominously pressing in on her and her friend. "We are in your debt—" She stopped short, recognizing their savior. It was Charles Cabot Stockwell, whom she had last seen standing on the deck of a flatboat on the Erie Canal some fifteen months before.

"Miss Seabury." Charles Stockwell made no effort to hide his delight. "How nice to see you again."

"Captain Stockwell." Recalling what she considered to be his chauvinism, Edith was more reserved.

"Just plain Charles Stockwell now," he corrected her. "I've resigned my commission."

"Mr. Charles Stockwell. Miss Susan Talley of Virginia," Edith said, introducing them.

"Mr. Stockwell." Susan curtsied prettily.

Observing, two of the idle men around them grimaced and muttered. Charles Stockwell scowled at them ferociously. Hands rising in automatic acknowledgment of authority—a salute, perhaps, or perhaps even an uncompleted tugging of a forelock—they backed away.

His face relaxing into a pleasant smile, Charles turned back to the two young women. "How is your friend Mrs. Bloomer?" he asked Edith.

"She is well, thank you."

"I am reminded of her often." His cinnamon eyes slid over their garb and then away.

"And of what she has come to stand for, I hope." Edith's voice was sharper than she intended.

Around them the crowd was growing louder. Many of the ladies in the vicinity of the speaker's platform had opened their parasols and raised them against the increasing barrage of mud and dung and rotting garbage the hostile men were throwing.

151

Charles Stockwell took note. "This situation grows increasingly unsafe," he observed. "Would you permit me to escort you two ladies to some less volatile environment?"

"Thank you, no." Edith's response was quick and firm. "We have come to hear Mrs. Rose speak, and we will hear her out to her conclusion."

"I fear for your safety."

"We, however, do not. We are quite able to take care of ourselves, thank you. Isn't that so, Susan?"

"Of course." There was, however, a certain doubt present in Susan's nod of agreement.

"Well, if I cannot persuade you to leave, then I shall stay with you. I cannot in conscience leave you unprotected in these circumstances."

"This is really very considerate of you, Mr. Stockwell." Susan Talley, relieved to have him stay, responded quickly before Edith might object. "Are you a believer in the cause?" she asked innocently.

"To which of the multitude of causes do you refer, Miss Talley?"

"Well, abolitionism, I suppose. That is the subject on which Mrs. Rose is speaking today."

"I see the justice in it. I also see the danger. We must move slowly, I think, in the interests of maintaining national unity."

"National unity while black children continue being born into slavery, are raised to the rhythm of the lash flaying the skin from their bodies, are worked like animals in the cotton fields and bred like animals as well!" Edith answered him scathingly.

"I justify none of that. I want to see the slave system abolished just as you do," Charles Stockwell assured her. "I simply do not wish to see the country torn apart in the process. I don't want to throw out the baby with the bath water. Gradualism—"

"Gradualism is the refuge of moral cowards!" There was fire in Edith's blue eyes, and her chin was tilted up at Charles with the fury of a sword poised to strike.

"I am not a moral coward, Miss Seabury," Charles assured her quietly, his anger under tight control. "I will also tell you that freeing the slaves and the possibility of recruiting from their ranks a labor force at reasonable wages for my Michigan forestry preserves and foundries is a very attractive prospect to me. Were self-interest my only concern, I would be more ardent an abolitionist than you are. I, too, claim moral underpinnings for my views, and I do not take kindly to having my character called into question. Indeed, were I not concerned for your safety, I should feel bound to withdraw from your company after your last remark."

"Kindly do withdraw, Mr. Stockwell. Your efforts at protection may be well meant, but they are onerous. They smack of condescension. They serve only to reinforce the calumny that women are weak and require the supervision of men who are strong. I assure you once again, as I did before, that we are quite able to see to our own welfare. We would appreciate it, therefore, if you would leave us to our own devices."

"Very well, then." Charles raised his fawn-colored silk stovepipe hat to each of them in turn. Quietly furious, he turned and led his brindle riding horse out of the crowd.

In his wake, the mood turned still uglier. Sensing that the situation was growing dangerous, Ernestine Rose brought her address to a speedy conclusion. As the meeting broke up, Edith and Susan, arm in arm, picked their way through the surly men toward the road.

"And how would you fine ladies like it if your younger brother brought home a wench to wed with skin the color of peat coal?" The Irishman barring their path was large and burly, not young, and very drunk.

"Ja, but maybe rather a *schwarz* buck to their own bed." His companion was German, smaller, weasly, and also under the influence.

"Get out of our way, you insolent sots!" Edith brandished her parasol in much the same manner that Charles Stockwell had earlier cleared a path with his riding crop.

Standing up to them had its effect. Their bows were mocking, but nevertheless the two men separated to let the women pass. The Irishman made a lewd comment as Edith inadvertently brushed against him in her hurry. The German went further. Perceiving in her movement no barricade of whalebone corset or bustle beneath her billowing Bloomer costume, he reached out and pinched Edith hard on one buttock. She cried aloud and then whirled around furiously, swinging her parasol wildly.

Half a dozen men scrambled to avoid being struck by it. Otherwise, however, the maneuver proved unfortunate. Edith had attracted wider attention, and now a small group of men trailed after the two women as they made their way to the Bowery carriage road.

"I wish you had not told Mr. Stockwell to leave us," Susan said in a low voice to Edith.

"Do not be intimidated. They are only men."

"Nevertheless, I do find them intimidating," Susan replied, with a nervous glance over her shoulder at the youth leading the small group of men with a mincing gait meant to mimic the suggestive movements of their bodies under the loose Bloomer outfits.

"My home is on Sixth Street, only a few doors off this avenue. We will be there soon, and we will be safe. Meanwhile carry your chin high and walk with dignity. We are women, and we will not give them the satisfaction of showing fear." Edith's proud gait was meant to set an example for her friend.

A newsboy was coming toward them waving a paper with a black banner over his head to attract attention. "Poet dies in Baltimore!" he shouted. "Drink blamed for Poe's death!"

"What?" Susan stopped in her tracks, turning quite pale. "What is he saying?"

"What is it, Susan?" Edith took her arm, steadying her. "We can't stop here." She was acutely aware that the men who had been following them had now caught up and were scratching their heads as if wondering what mischief to instigate next.

"Poe. That boy said that Edgar—"

"We'll get a paper." Ignoring their tormentors, one of

154

whom was now fainting in another's arms while the rest watched and chortled, Edith summoned the newsboy. She handed him a coin and accepted a paper.

Scanning the headline quickly, she realized that Susan's dread was justified. Edgar Allan Poe, Susan's mentor—and perhaps something more? Edith wasn't sure; it was a matter of principle with her not to traffic in gossip—had died suddenly in Baltimore. He had attended a lady's birthday party, toasted his hostess repeatedly in honor of the occasion, and simply keeled over. There seemed no doubt that the overstimulation of the alcohol had proven too much for a heart already weakened by a lifetime of dissipation.

"I'm sorry, Susan." Still supporting her friend under the arm, Edith spoke with tender sympathy. "It's true."

"He is gone, then? Edgar is dead?"

"Edgar is dead. Oh, my. Oh, my." The youngest of their tormentors imitated Susan in a high, shrill voice. The others pressed in on them, once more jeering and laughing. "Poe, the poet Romeo!" they hooted, alluding to his widespread reputation as a roué. "Poe, the drunken bard of bawdiness."

The onslaught of catcalls proved too much for Susan. Her eyes unfocused and staring, she sagged against Edith, a cold sweat breaking out on her forehead. It was all Edith could do to hold her erect.

Edith looked around her, seeking some support. She recognized that Susan was on the verge of fainting. If only she could get through the crowd to that courtyard wall across from them, she might be able to prop up her friend there until she was feeling better. But the inebriated group of men would not part to give her passage. Her pleas to do so fell on deaf ears.

"Make way, you drunken rabble!" The voice of Charles Stockwell sounded loud and clear over the hubbub. After his dismissal by Edith, he had stopped off to quench his anger in a Bowery tavern. Moderate in drink as in most other things, he had limited himself to one tankard of ale and left. As he'd emerged and mounted his horse, he had noticed the small crowd farther down the Bowery. Ap-

155

proaching it at a slow trot, he'd spied Edith and her friend and, realizing their predicament, had not hesitated to act. "Disperse, I say!" His crop left welts on two loutish faces, and then all the men were scrambling from the vicinity. He rode up to the women and dismounted. "Miss Seabury," he said, "you seem to be in some difficulty."

"My friend is feeling faint." This was no time to resume her argument with Mr. Stockwell, and Edith did not attempt to do so. They needed aid. "Will you help me get her home?"

"Of course." It never occurred to Charles to upbraid her for her previous rejection of his offers of assistance. Lifting Susan Talley in his arms, he set her down sidesaddle atop his horse.

As he supported her there, making sure she had her balance, the small group of unruly drunks rediscovered its courage. "Abolitionist rich bitches!" The shout was loud and clear. A clod of mud followed it, narrowly missing Susan atop the horse. A second clod stained the sleeve of Charles's high-collared, full-skirted topcoat.

He ignored it. Holding Susan in place atop the horse with one hand, he circled Edith's waist with his free arm and lifted her to the saddle behind her friend. When both women were secure on the steed, he took the reins in one hand in order to lead it. Holding them tightly, he reached inside his coat with the other hand and produced a long-barreled dueling pistol.

As always, there was one load of shot in it. He cocked the hammer, pointed the gun at the sky, and fired. "Make way, or the next shot finds a mark!" In the shocked silence following the reverberation, his voice was loud and clear. He led the horse with the two women on it down an avenue that was suddenly sparsely populated.

Edith gave Charles directions to her home. When they reached it, he carried Susan inside. Edith requested him to wait in the parlor while she attended to her friend.

"I wanted to thank you properly," she told Charles when she returned.

"Not at all necessary. It was my pleasure to be of service." Mindful of her previous words, Charles was polite but cold.

"An apology is owed you, sir. I was very rude to you before. I impugned your character, and you have since shown it to be beyond reproach. I should like to ask your pardon."

"Gladly granted." Charles warmed noticeably to the friendly tone Edith was now taking.

"Thank you." Edith curtsied formally. "Beyond that, I want you to know that I am in your debt, sir."

Charles was amused but hid it. From time to time men had been in his debt, but never before a woman. He decided to take advantage of the situation. "In that case, I wonder if I might ask you a favor," he said. "I should like to ask your father's permission to call on you, if that would be agreeable."

"Why bring my father into it?" Edith asked. "Why don't you simply ask my permission to call?"

"Very well. May I call on you, Miss Seabury?"

Edith considered it. "You have done me a service," she said finally. "If you wish to call on me, then of course you may call on me. But I should like to ask you a question, Mr. Stockwell. Why do you want to?"

Charles was nonplussed. This young woman was very difficult. But of course that was why he was attracted to her. Evidently there was a whole new women's language to be learned. It was a language without the embroideries and roundabout flourishes customary to courtship.

Charles took a deep breath and demonstrated that he was catching on to it. "I want to call on you," he told Edith, "because I am attracted to you, Miss Seabury. Very attracted."

"That is normal. I am a woman." Edith shrugged. "You are a man. But these are changing times, Mr. Stockwell. Men are the enemy."

"Why then"—Charles bowed and reached for his stovepipe hat—"I look forward to the conflict."

22

To Carrie Tyler the island of St. Martin was everything Victor had led her to expect and more. Beaches of virgin sand, lapped by the cobalt Caribbean on St. Martin's western shores and pummeled by the Atlantic from the east, were interspersed with breathtaking cliffs of hollowed-out caves, coral lagoons, and white crystal moonscape salt marshes. Inland were the remnants of sugar cane plantations amid lush, golden-green pasturelands. Rolling pastel hills climbed to tall, sweeping, dark jade mountains.

The scenery throughout was shaded by the aptly named "flamboyant tree" with its wide-flung branches and brazen red, orange, and yellow flowers. Mahogany and cedar provided a subdued background for the deep rose shades of bougainvillea and the rainbow colors of frangipani, hibiscus, and poinsettia that danced from sunrise to sunset in the ever-changing light. When the skies darkened from blue to pearl gray to lavender to night, the ultimate brightness of the star-splashed cosmos was breathtaking.

Carrie Tyler was dazzled. She was also stirred emotionally by St. Martin. With people Carrie almost always related physically, but the island somehow aroused sensations that transcended her libido and revived long-gone feelings of her childhood.

None of this did she mention to her companion. Victor Grieg, she knew, was not a man to deal in abstracts. His logic was that of numbers, absolute, never ephemeral. He was drawn to Carrie because her sexuality was as clear to him as a ledger book. The delights of their lovemaking were as foreordained as four resulting from two plus two.

This worked for Carrie, as it did for him. In sex, above all, her philosophy was, if it's not broken, don't fix it. Carrie was not in love with Victor, nor he with her, but they did enjoy each other's flesh immensely. She would not distract from this by imposing on him the flashes of emotional insight St. Martin aroused in her. They were a thing apart from her usual superficial behavior.

Carrie was comfortable on the surface, always had been. And it was a profitable attitude for any tourist. The French and West Indian cuisine of St. Martin, the thrill of the overly brilliant casinos, the snorkeling and the sailing, all gave her pleasure. At night she and Victor made love with bodies tuned by the sun and the sea. During the day they mingled with the crème de la crème of St. Martin's visitors. Only those occasions when Victor had to attend to business—sometimes taking Carrie with him, sometimes leaving her behind—interfered with their lovers' idyll on St. Martin.

Despite Victor Grieg's slum-kid background, on St. Martin he moved easily among the rich and famous. Carrie herself had always been at home with such people. Nevertheless, even she had her moments of being impressed.

"There's Mick Jagger!" She and Victor were lying on chaise longues beside the swimming pool when she spied the rock star. "The girls at Miss Lillian's would be green with envy."

"Miss Lillian's?"

"The finishing school I went to."

Victor Grieg reached over and pinched Carrie hard on the buttock through the skimpy triangle of her silk bikini.

"Ouch! What did you do that for?"

"I did it for the boys in the poolroom on Fourteenth Street. I always promised them that if I ever made it big, I'd pinch a graduate of Miss Lillian's Finishing School on the ass."

"Liar! You never even heard of Miss Lillian's until just

this minute." Carrie rubbed the injured spot. "Besides"—she giggled—"I never did graduate. They threw me out."

"What did you do to deserve that?"

"What we did last night. And what, I hope, we're going to do again tonight."

"Not if you're going to be thinking of Mick Jagger while we're doing it."

"If you didn't want me to ogle the celebrities, you shouldn't have brought me here."

"Here" was La Samanna, the most exclusive resort hotel on St. Martin. Its clientele was made up of the sort of people to whom privacy was a high priority. Superstars and royalty, tycoons and statesmen, famous beauties and infamous dictators, the talented and the tyrannical—all came to La Samanna with their need for the relief of occasional obscurity, their loves of the moment, their desire to be pampered, and the means to pay for it.

Shielded from the road, guarded by a private security force, staffed by experts schooled in silence and discretion, La Samanna offered all the amenities that might be desired by those who could afford them. At its private lagoon and on nearby Baie Longue, notables were free to sun themselves nude without fear of autograph seekers or photographers. In private beach cottages they might quietly indulge in whatever amusements suited them without fear of intrusion by the media. The resort was, indeed, one of the few places in the civilized world where a celebrity might let down his or her hair, put up his or her feet, and belch freely without fear of shattering his or her image. The commodity most valued by the celebrities who indulged themselves at La Samanna, however, was not the release of inhibitions—indeed, wild parties and loud gatherings were rare—but tranquillity.

The resort had its own restaurant, of course, and the cuisine was superb. Nevertheless, there were so many gourmet restaurants in French St. Martin that after their first night at La Samanna Carrie and Victor made a practice of dining out. This evening, after watching the sunset, they changed for dinner and then drove in the Mercedes sports coupe Victor had rented to Le Santal, known among gourmets as one of the six truly great French restaurants in the world.

Even Carrie, usually blasé, was impressed. The main dining room of Le Santal was a striking white and blue with formally set tables, Copenhagen crystal, and Moroccan silver. Overhead, imported Parisian chandeliers were inset with tiny twinkling, multicolored seashells from the shores of St. Martin. The setting for the exquisite decor was a colonial mansion on Nettle Bay Beach.

Carrie and Victor began with the establishment's famous crab soup and crêpe Santal. Victor followed with the lacquered duck while Carrie ordered the fresh snapper flambéed with Pernod and prepared at their table. Victor was halfway through his tarte tatin dessert and Carrie was savoring a coupé of caramelized apples with ice cream when she heard her name pronounced.

"Carrie! Carrie Tyler! Whatever are you doing here?"

She looked up to find Buffy Houston standing next to their table, hand on her hip, blue-black hair coiffed to perfection. Behind her Jack Houston smiled, very white teeth in a sun-bronzed face, his white dinner jacket molded to perfection over his athletic shoulders and chest. Despite the differences in their ages, they appeared the handsomest of couples.

It was evident that Buffy's question included Victor Grieg. Carrie introduced him to the Houstons. Victor, who had been standing since Buffy appeared, asked that they join them for an after-dinner brandy and signaled the waiter to bring two chairs.

Over the liqueurs, Carrie explained that Victor was in St. Martin on business and she had come along for pleasure. When Jack inquired politely as to the nature of Victor's business in St. Martin, the eyes behind the horn-rimmed glasses stayed cool and the answer was fudged over. Buffy, intrigued but never gauche, turned the conversation with a question.

"Where are you staying?" she asked Carrie.

"La Samanna. And you?"

"We have a villa on the cliff point overlooking Baie Rouge."

"That sounds lovely."

"It is." Buffy sipped her brandy. "Are you happy with La Samanna?"

"It's utter luxury. What's not to be happy about?"

"Well, I know it's idyllic," Buffy observed. "But it's not exactly where the action is."

"It is very laid back," Carrie admitted. "There's not much in the way of partying unless you're part of a group."

"Partying?" Buffy smiled. "Would you like to go to a party? Tonight, I mean? A good friend of mine is giving one. The countess de Guillemaine."

"Oh, I don't think we could crash—"

"You won't be." Jack broke in. "Fifi is always delighted to entertain attractive people regardless of gender."

"Fifi isn't her real name," Buffy told them. "It's an affectation. One of many. Still, the countess isn't a bad sort. She really is most hospitable. And her place in the mountains overlooking Philipsburg Harbor is really a castle not to be missed."

"It's on the Dutch side?" Victor Grieg broke his silence, smiling. "I'm afraid we can't make it, then. I've got business in Marigot tonight."

Carrie pouted. Victor had told her about his meeting before, but she had put it out of her mind. In the short time they'd been on St. Martin Victor had kept four such business appointments, all with a man named Junot. Carrie had never heard his first name mentioned. Victor said he was a French Algerian who had fled to St. Martin after the revolution. The two occasions on which Carrie had met him, she had not liked him.

Junot made her uneasy. He was a tall man, heavyset but not fat, completely bald with small, reddish pig eyes. He was menacing not just in his appearance, but in his manner as well. His most casual movements betrayed an

162

unwilling restraint of violence. His flat features were always a trifle distorted, as if that restraint were to him an unnatural denial of pleasure. Junot's pleasure, Carrie sensed, would always involve someone else's pain.

After the second meeting she had mentioned her feelings about Junot to Victor. "You pegged him right." He shrugged. "He's the dark alley man. Not nice, but necessary. Very necessary."

"He makes me feel afraid," Carrie told him.

"Me too."

Carrie was startled. Victor's agreement was neither automatic nor casual. He meant it. He, too, was afraid of Junot.

Now he was meeting with Junot again. "But that's not all," he had said. "The man is flying in."

"The man?"

"Helmut van Huyck."

Victor never really showed his feelings, but Carrie could tell he was worried at the prospect of the meeting. He had taken the papers out of his attaché case and carefully arranged them into two piles. One pile he had put back. The other he had taken down to the La Samanna desk and put into a strongbox, which had then been locked in the hotel safe. He had put the receipt and the strongbox key away in his suitcase. "Just in case," he had told Carrie.

"In case what?" The edge in his voice had been very slight, but it had been enough to alarm her. "Is something the matter, Victor?"

"Van Huyck shouldn't be here." There was that name again. "Junot is a strong-arm, but maybe not as stupid as I always took for granted." He'd cut himself off abruptly. "You don't need to know any of this," he'd said.

"Are you in trouble?"

"I don't think so. Maybe. I can handle it." Victor hadn't said anything else.

Carrie's worry had waned with the lazy, sun-drenched day, the twilight lovemaking, the superb meal at Le Santal. Not used to thinking about other people's concerns,

163

she allowed Victor's problems to recede to the back of her mind. Now, she completely forgot his anxiety over the upcoming meeting in her own annoyance at its interfering with their going to the party to which Buffy and Jack Houston were inviting them.

"It really is too bad," Carrie sighed. "It's the first party anyone's asked us to since we got here."

"Six days ago," Victor observed dryly. "Still, you can go by yourself if you'd like." The original plan had been for him to drop Carrie at La Samanna while he went to the meeting with Junot and van Huyck by himself.

"How? You're taking the car."

"I'll call you a cab."

"Nonsense," Buffy interrupted. "Carrie can come with us."

"But shouldn't I go back to the hotel and change first?"

"I really don't think that's necessary, dear," Buffy commented dryly as she regarded the Bill Blass black strapless "bob" with the sheer point d'esprit miniskirt Carrie was wearing. The dress screamed youth.

It was settled. The Houstons would bring Carrie to the countess de Guillemaine's party with them, and Victor Grieg would meet them there later after attending to his business.

Carrie and Victor parted with a kiss in the Le Santal parking lot. She and Buffy and Jack rode together to the party in the back of Buffy's chauffeured limousine. It took forty minutes to wend their way through French St. Martin to Dutch Sint Maarten, past Philipsburg on the road fringing Great Salt Pond, then up into the hills to the residence of the countess de Guillemaine.

Even though she was used to the splendors of Riverview, Carrie was impressed by the countess's palatial villa. Built in the Moorish style, a pastel gingerbread castle with parapets and turrets, domes and terraces, and sculptured tropical gardens, it had wide cool hallways filled with illicit artifacts from Greece and Sicily, and the loot of conquistadores from Peru and Mexico.

The countess herself was a too thin, fortyish, effusive

woman, affected as Buffy had said, but nevertheless hospitable.

Finding herself pretty much among strangers at a party where there were already a hundred guests with more arriving all the time, however, did make Carrie a little tense. While the countess was making her feel at home, Jack and Buffy had been swallowed up by the crowd, and for the moment she found herself quite alone. Damn it! Why did Victor's meeting with that Helmut van Huyck have to be tonight? On edge, she asked a servant to direct her to the ladies' room.

There were a dozen or more lavatories in the mansion, and Carrie deliberately chose one on the second floor where she was less likely to be interrupted. She locked the door behind her and checked it before she took the vial of cocaine from her small satin clutch bag. She snorted two healthy lines and waited until the glow had spread thoroughly before she rejoined the party.

Now, when she entered the main ballroom downstairs, she felt not only good, but confident. And sexy; coke always made her feel that way. Her eyes roved over the attractive men in attendance until she spied Jack standing alone with a drink in his hand.

She studied him for a moment before she approached him. Buffy's stud, she thought. Damn good, too, I'll bet. Buffy might be a great beauty, there was no denying it, but she was—what was the phrase?—past her prime. Yes, Buffy was definitely past her prime.

Jack was younger—much younger. He was all smooth tan and rippling muscles. Just standing still there with a drink in his hand, he made all the right moves. What must it be like when he really moved? In bed, say. At the thought, Carrie's nipples hardened against the black silk satin of her tight, low bodice.

She walked over to Jack. ''Come dance with me.'' Her tone was as direct as the words.

Jack looked at Carrie curiously. Like everybody else in the family, he knew her reputation. Young and wild and uninhibited. With her apricot hair, feline face, and high-

165

breasted, long-legged body, she exuded sensuality. Taking her in his arms to dance, Jack couldn't help responding to that. Still, it was only a dance, and he did love Buffy.

Carrie felt his response. It excited her. Victor was forgotten as she pressed against Jack. His chest was hard against her breasts. His hard thighs and belly were responsive to her rubbing.

"It's warm in here." She clung to him and was disappointed when he backed away. "I'm feeling a little dizzy. Do you think we could get some air?"

"Sure." He was concerned. Supporting her with his arm around her slender waist, he led her to the French doors leading out onto one of the terraces.

The air was heavy with the perfume of blossoming hibiscus. There was nobody else on the terrace. Carrie clung to Jack as if she were wobbly on her feet. One of her hands was inside his white dinner jacket, clutching at the ridge of muscle just behind his rib cage.

"Are you feeling better?" Jack was still supporting her, uncomfortably aware of the soft, pliant body arching into his.

"A little." Carrie's hands slid up and locked around his neck then. She widened her stance and leaned into him, belly to belly. She raised her face; her lips parted. When he did nothing, she pulled hard on the back of Jack's neck with both her hands until his lips met hers. And during the kiss, atingle with cocaine, she slid one hand down and groped to find the hardening at his groin.

Jack tried to break it off, but Carrie had a tight grip on him, and all of her movements—the tongue in his mouth, the hand at his groin—were demanding. She would not be rejected gently. He raised his hands then, flattened them against her breasts, and pushed to force them apart.

"You Lolita-hungry son of a bitch!"

The champagne glass nicked Jack's ear as it went flying past. The bubbly liquid spattered his face and his white dinner jacket.

It took him a moment to register what was happening.

166

It took another instant to focus. When he did, he was just in time to see his wife plunging back through the French doors into the ballroom.

Buffy was as furious as he had ever seen her.

By the time he made his way through the ballroom and out the front door to the parking area, she was gone. So, too, were the car and chauffeur that had brought them there. Jack found himself in the humiliating position of having to go back inside to ask the countess if he might borrow one of her cars in order to follow his wife.

A sophisticated woman of the world, the countess asked no questions. She simply asked the majordomo to fetch the keys to the Jaguar for Jack and to have a servant show him where it was parked. Jack was glad of the servant's guidance since the parking lot was large and sprawling and dark, and there must have been a couple of dozen Jaguars interspersed among the hundred and fifty or so cars parked there.

Upset, a little drunk, feeling wrongfully accused and too quickly judged, Jack navigated with cowboy reckless-ness the series of roads from the mountains of Dutch Sint Maarten to Buffy's French St. Martin clifftop villa. He could see the light on in their bedroom window from the paved Marigot road before he turned onto the treacher-ous, winding, rutted dirt road veering off from Rouge Beach and up the side of the cliff. Then it was lost to view until he roared into their driveway in a cloud of starlit dust and gravel and braked to a screeching halt.

Taking the steps to the upstairs bedroom two at a time, he arrived out of breath to find Buffy folding garments into a large suitcase. Even in her rage, she selected and packed the clothes carefully. Her maid was not there to help her. Since they'd expected to be out for the evening, all of the servants except the chauffeur had been given the night off. Now the chauffeur was in his room over the garage, and they were alone in the house.

Buffy made a show of taking no notice of Jack when he entered. He watched her pack in silence for a while, try-ing to think what to say. Finally he crossed over the small

167

bar adjacent to the wardrobe closet in their bedroom and poured himself a large Scotch. He belted it at a gulp. "This is ridiculous," he said. Immediately he knew those were not the right words.

"I'm sorry you think me ridiculous." Buffy was calm—too calm—icy calm.

"I didn't mean you, and you know it. I mean the situation."

"Older wife finds younger husband making love to jail bait," Buffy capsulized. "Yes. Such situations usually are ridiculous."

"I was not making love to her. And she's not quite that young. She's out of her teens, after all." Wrong choice of words again. Jack poured another Scotch and downed it. The raw whiskey punished his clumsy tongue.

"Out of her teens." Buffy repeated the phrase without inflection. "But only by a hair."

Jack tried a different tack. "Why are you packing?"

"I want to get out of this house. Away from you."

"And if I hadn't gotten here as quickly as I did, I'd just have found you gone," Jack concluded.

"As if you'd care."

"Of course I care. Damn it, Buffy, I love you."

"You love my money, you mean. And you lust after every young tramp that comes your way."

"I do not lust—"

"I know what I saw, Jack. Don't bother to lie."

"Listen"—Jack found courage in another drink—"she threw herself at me. I didn't even respond. It all happened so quickly I didn't know what was coming off until she kissed me."

"Which is why both your hands were fastened securely on her cute, panting, hot little breasts." Buffy stressed the word "little."

"I was just trying to push her away." Jack's head was spinning. It really had happened so damn fast. How the hell had Carrie gotten him into this mess, anyway?

"Of course you were."

"It's true."

168

"And I am the virgin Marie, queen of Rumania." Buffy's tone was more scathing than ironic.

"All right, then! All right!" Jack shook his head against the fog of whiskey. "I'll prove it to you!" Grabbing the bottle, he started out of the room.

"Where are you going?" The question was Buffy's first real lapse from her pose of detached coolness.

"Back to the party. For Carrie." Jack meant he was going back to fetch her and bring her to Buffy's villa to explain that what had happened had been neither his idea nor his fault. In his alcoholically muddled condition, it seemed to make perfect sense.

Buffy, however, heard only that he was leaving her to return to Carrie. Now, as she heard him starting up the Jaguar in the driveway, her facade collapsed. Her sense of loss was a vise gripping her heart.

Yes, Jack really did want a younger woman. She'd always known it, never wanted to face it. But here it was. And instead of clutching him to her, she had pushed him away. She had pushed him back into the arms of that nymphette. And, all too obviously, that was where he wanted to be.

I won't cry. I won't. Buffy bit her lip. It's a blow to your ego, she told herself. That's all. Just a blow to your ego. It's not as if you really love him any more than he loves you.

But I do.

Oh, damn it. Now she did start to cry. I do love him, the bastard! I love him!

Stop, she told herself. Stop crying. Stop loving him. Loving Jack makes you vulnerable, and you get hurt every time. Patrice O'Keefe. And now damn Carrie with her almond-shaped naughty child's eyes. So stop crying. Stop loving him. Stop!

Buffy stopped crying. She blew her nose. She went into the bathroom and washed her face with cold water. She called the Queen Juliana Airport. There was a flight leaving within the hour for Puerto Rico. They would call ahead to put her on standby for the first available plane to New York.

Jack floored the Jaguar gas pedal for the drive back to the countess's estate overlooking Philipsburg. Much drunker now than he had been earlier, he loop-the-looped the roads. He was on automatic pilot, his mind wrestling with the half-formulated conviction that if he could just get Carrie and bring her back to Buffy's villa, she would tell Buffy the truth about what had happened and absolve him of blame. Concentrating on this plan, he pulled the Jaguar screechingly into the huge lot stretching out from the mountainside mansion, got out, and hurried toward the ballroom.

The party had spilled over from the ballroom to the various terraces. The dance floor was crowded, and the lights had been lowered. Jack squinted through the murk, trying to find Carrie. When a footman passed him with a tray of cocktails, he automatically took one and drank it. As upset as he was, he didn't realize how much liquor he was putting away, how very drunk he was getting.

There she was! He spied Carrie just coming off the dance floor with a young man. He made his way to her.

"Jack." She greeted him with interest. "You came back." Carrie had made another trip to the bathroom to snort cocaine in his absence, and she was flying. "I'm glad." She turned to the young man with whom she'd been dancing. "Jack and I are going to dance." She dismissed him. "Or make love." She giggled. "Which is it, Jack?"

"Listen. I have to talk to you. It's very—"

"Dance or make love." Carrie giggled, falling against him. "Only choices you get, Jack. No talk. Now make up your mind."

"Dance, then." He led her onto the floor. When they were hemmed in by the crowd, he once again began speaking urgently. "You have to come back to Baie Rouge with me," he started to say. "You—"

"Back to your place? I'd love to. But we'd better get going quick because Victor's liable to turn up any minute, and that could be awkward. I suspect he could be jealous. Possessive, really. He grew up poor, and he doesn't share willingly. Now I'm not like that at all." Carrie began to sing. "When I'm not with the man I luh-huve, I luh-huve . . ."

"Damn it, Carrie, you don't understand. Just listen to me a minute." Jack explained to her that she had caused a really serious problem with Buffy, and now he wanted her to come with him and explain that he'd been innocent. "Even if she won't believe me, she might believe you."

Carrie stopped dancing. She stared up at Jack. "Let me get this straight," she said. "You want me to go back to your place with you so I can tell your wife our hanky-panky before wasn't really hanky-panky on your part but only on mine. You want me to tell her that *I* forced my intentions on you and that you were really only an innocent victim in the love scene she saw. Is that what you want me to tell her?"

"Well, it's true, isn't it?"

"You must be out of your mind." Carrie laughed harshly. "Do you really think I have to force myself on any man?"

"But you did force yourself."

"The hell I did!" Carrie turned away from him angrily and started to push her way through the crowd on the dance floor.

Jack reached out quickly and grabbed her arm so she couldn't leave.

"Let me go."

He held the arm tighter.

"You're hurting me. Let go."

"No. You're going to come with me and—"

"I think you better let her go." Victor Grieg materialized in front of Jack. He had seen Carrie dancing with him and elbowed his way to them to let her know he'd arrived. Now he attempted to intercede.

"You don't know anything about this." Jack kept his tight grip on Carrie's arm. "It's between Carrie and me."

"Make him let me go, Victor." Carrie's voice was pained and shrill.

People around them were beginning to take notice of the scene developing.

Victor put his hand on Jack's arm. "Let her go."

Jack gripped her more tightly.

"Ouch! That really hurts," Carrie cried.

Victor delivered a short, powerful karate chop to Jack's forearm, forcing him to release Carrie. At the same time Jack's other hand reacted instinctively with a counter-blow, and his return chop caught the more slender Victor in the ribs. With an oath, Victor jabbed with a left and swung with a right. Neither connected. His knee, however, caught Jack square in the crotch. Jack clinched with Victor, delivering short jabs to the rib cage as he waited for the waves of pain to subside. Finally some men interceded to pull them apart.

"This fellow started it. He had hold of her arm." The majority opinion faulted Jack.

He opened his mouth to explain but closed it quickly. Suddenly he was overwhelmingly nauseated, and he realized at that moment how very drunk he must be. "Sorry," he said through clenched lips. " 'Scuse me." Elbowing his way through the crowd, he exited the villa.

Once outside, he threw up in the bushes. It didn't help. He still felt very drunk. Slowly, he weaved his way back to the parking lot to get the Jaguar and drive back to Buffy. Somehow he had to make her see he was innocent.

Squinting into the dark parking area, Jack couldn't for the life of him remember where he had parked the Jaguar. He wandered over the lot feeling drunk and sick and disoriented. It was a full half hour before he found the car.

When he did, he discovered it had a flat tire. It must have been a slow leak aggravated by the way he'd barreled over the ruts on the dirt roads. Now the tire was a pancake. Cursing to himself, Jack opened the trunk, found the tire jack, lug wrench, and spare, and set about changing the tire.

Just as he was finishing, he spotted Carrie and Victor

Grieg coming across the parking lot. Grieg must have pulled in not long after him, and his car was parked near the Jaguar. Jack watched them walking toward him.

The exertion of changing the tire had not made Jack any more clear-headed. On the contrary, the strenuous exercise had made him feel as drunk as before the fight. In this condition he decided to make one last effort to get Carrie to come with him and explain the truth of what had happened to Buffy. He popped up in front of them and began to talk rapidly.

"Listen, Carrie, you have to—"

"She doesn't have to do anything." Victor's blood was still up from their earlier confrontation.

"Listen, just butt out, will you? I only want her to—" Carrie was backing away, and Jack made the mistake of reaching out to stop her.

Victor Grieg had grown up fighting on the streets of New York. Early on he had learned the strategy for winning. Always throw the first punch, and throw it hard. Then follow up strong while the other guy is still psyching himself up to fight. Now he threw the first punch, and the signet ring he was wearing opened up a half-inch cut on Jack's cheek.

Jack was himself an experienced brawler. Like Victor, fair play didn't enter into his calculations. He deliberately went down with the punch and as he was falling whacked Victor on one shin with the lug wrench. Victor tore the wrench from his grip and delivered a short, powerful blow to the kidneys.

Screaming for help, Carrie ran back into the mansion. Behind her the two men struggled, rolled on the ground, parted, punched, came together again. The sounds of their blows and their grunts and their curses filled the night air.

Inside, Carrie ran up to the countess and blurted out what was happening. The countess summoned half a dozen servants, and Carrie led the way back outside. Concerned and excited, Carrie was several feet in front as she led the others through the parking lot to where she had left the two struggling men. Suddenly she stopped short, shocked into complete sobriety by what she saw. Then she screamed.

In the wake of Carrie's scream, the countess and her servants rushed past her and toward the Jaguar. They stopped short of it. The countess turned around, looking for Carrie, wanting to comfort her. But she wasn't there. She had fled.

Carrie had vanished into the night.

The countess turned back to the scene beside the trunk of the Jaguar. Victor Grieg was lying on the ground with his skull split like a chestnut opened by a nutcracker. There was a pool of blood spreading on the ground where his scalp had been. Jack was standing above him with a look on his face that was a combination of horror and drunken confusion.

At Jack's feet lay a bloody tire iron.

23

FITZ CONNELY WAS seated at a table under the trompe l'oeil ceiling of the Riverview library with several of the record books from the Stockwell archives spread out before him. The pool of light from a brass reading lamp was the only illumination in the room when Patrice entered. Hearing her footsteps, he squinted into the shadows, unable to make out who was there.

"It's me." Patrice stepped forward so he could identify her.

"And so it is." His smile of greeting lit up his face.

"What are you doing here?"

"Reading up on my benefactor." He held up the volume for Patrice to see. It was labeled to cover the period of the early 1900s. "And you?" he asked.

"I've been reading about the Stockwell who rebuilt Riverview after it burned to the ground. And about the most remarkable woman he married—a suffragist and abolitionist and artist—and about their courtship. She kept a diary. I've come for the next volume."

"Very romantic is it, then?"

"Very." Patrice laughed. "But then I'm a sucker for romance."

"Ah." Fitz smiled back, dark eyes signalling his interest. "Now that's what you might call encouraging."

"You might." Patrice's tone was more flirtatious than the words themselves. Holly had indeed guessed the truth. Patrice was interested in Fitz. In his presence, she sensed even more strongly that he was a man who might make her forget Jack—for a night, anyway. But the look Fitz gave her now, in response to her tone, made her suddenly feel very vulnerable. Flushing slightly, she changed the subject. "You'll ruin your eyes reading in this light," she told him, toying nervously with the black string bow at her throat. "Why don't you take the book back to your room to read?"

"I don't want to be lugging it back and forth."

"You could have gone upstairs and read in comfort." Patrice nodded toward the hand-carved spiral staircase that had once graced a lighthouse off the coast of Scotland. "There are a couple of armchairs and comfortable reading lamps up there."

"Sure and I didn't know there was an upstairs, tall as this chamber is." Fitz glanced up at the optical illusion of the dome two full stories above them.

"There's a studio on the third floor. Holly uses it."

"Well, I wouldn't have gone anyway, then, would I? Not wanting to intrude on Mrs. Meyerling, I mean."

"You wouldn't have been. Holly's in Washington with Zelig. And she wouldn't mind your reading in the studio." Looking at Fitz, the high, angular planes of his face and the brooding eyes, Patrice had a sudden impulse.

175

"Come on," she suggested. "I'll show you the studio if you'd like."

"I'd like very much." Fitz followed her across the vast chamber to the spiral staircase and then up the winding treads. When they emerged at the top and Patrice turned on the light, he stopped, surprised and pleased. "Right cozy it is," he exclaimed.

"That's Holly's doing. And her mother's. Her mother, the governor's daughter, was a painter before she died. She fixed it up as an artist's studio for herself, and then Holly redid it so she could write here. She's working on a sort of family history. If it was me"—Patrice laughed—"I'd spend my time up here staring out this nifty dormer window." She flopped down among the overstuffed pillows on the window seat. "There's a magnificent view of the grounds from here in the daylight," she told Fitz.

"Well, it's not the fanciest, but I'm thinking it's the nicest room at Riverview." Fitz squeezed in beside Patrice and grinned. When her fingers began automatically twisting the string bow, he reached out and stayed them. "Sure and you'll tie yourself in knots," he told her.

Disconcerted, Patrice stood up. "Would you like a drink?" she asked him. "Holly keeps a small bar up here." Her face turned crimson; she had forgotten that Fitz had given up alcohol.

"All the amenities is it, then? But I've sworn off," he reminded her. "So don't be tempting me now." His voice was soft and filled with innuendo.

Or was she imagining it? Patrice couldn't be sure. "Well, I didn't swear off," she told him, trying to recover her composure. "So if you don't mind, I will have a drink."

"I don't mind. A nip for a lass never did hurt the situation."

"What situation?" Patrice knew when he stood up and started toward her that Fitz was going to kiss her. She made no attempt to stop him. It was a long, warm kiss, and she responded to it. "Why did you do that?" she murmured, still in his arms when it was over.

176

"I thought you might like the opportunity to make a comparison between kissing a scarce washed drunkard with a scratchy beard and a spanky-clean-shaved, fresh-bathed, upright citizen. As I recall, those were the conditions you set for the enjoyment of our second kiss."

"Did I really?" Patrice made no attempt to move out of his embrace. She turned her face up to him, and they kissed again.

"Well, what do you think?" he asked, one hand holding her in place, the other stroking her long auburn hair.

"About what?" Patrice was aware that her heart was beating more quickly than usual.

"Better now, is it? The osculation, I mean."

"Much better." A casual affair. That, Patrice remembered, was what Holly had prescribed. Well, why not?

Patrice did not protest as Fitz's caresses became more intimate. His fingers were steady as he unbuttoned her blouse. A thrill of anticipation swept through her when he touched the bare flesh of her swelling bosom.

Yes, a casual affair. No love nonsense this time. Just physical release, physical satisfaction. That was the ticket. Fitz was a nice young man, and he was sexy, too. It would be fun to make love with him . . . just as long as she didn't get too involved.

"Am I going too fast for you, then?" His breath was warm in her ear.

"Not at all. I enjoy sex." Patrice had not meant to sound quite so defiant, nor quite so lacking in warmth.

Fitz paused. "I'd say a kind word for tenderness, too," he said slowly. His hand was no longer on her breast.

"I have nothing against tenderness." Why had he stopped? Patrice was irritated. His hands on her flesh had been exciting. Now the excitement was waning away with their exchange of words. "And I'm too old to pretend I don't enjoy making love."

"Is it making love, then, or just the rutting?"

"Don't be crude."

"I'd meant only to be accurate," Fitz apologized.

177

"Do we have to talk about it?" Patrice said sharply. "Can't we just do it?"

"Oh, sure and we can. But wouldn't it be friendlier with a bit of that tenderness I mentioned?"

"What is it you want, Fitz? Sex or affection?"

"Is it not possible to have a bit of both?"

"I'm willing to go to bed with you. But I'm not going to pretend that I'm in love with you."

"There's a rainbow of affection. Love's the pot of gold at the end. I'm not asking for the gold. But without a bit of the rainbow, I'd just as soon pass up this lovely opportunity."

"You don't want to make love to me?" Patrice was hurt and insulted. "Then why did you start—"

"Not in cold blood, I don't. And as to why I started, well, I have some feeling for you. But I thought it was returned."

"Well, it is. I'm aroused." Patrice's face turned bright red with the declaration. "You aroused me."

"On a par with milady's massage vibrator is it, then?"

"Just what do you want me to say? Why can't you accept this for what it is? I'm a woman, and you're a man, aren't you? Surely you're not going to tell me you were madly in love with every woman you've gone to bed with."

"True enough. But I never made one my plaything, either, nor willingly was hers."

"I didn't mean to—"

"There's a wall of ice, and I'll not blunt myself on it," Fitz told her firmly.

Patrice stared at him. Damn him! She wanted to feel with her body and with no other part of her. Men did that all the time, didn't they? "Couldn't we just have fun?" she asked in a small, woebegone voice.

"If we could, I'd not be against it. I'm not asking for Romeo and Juliet any more than you are. Fun would be fine. But that ice wall excludes fun as surely as the affection you've shut out."

"I haven't—" Patrice's voice broke suddenly. Damn

him! Of course she had. But why did he have to rub her nose in it? She just didn't want to get emotionally involved. She didn't want to get hurt again, to open herself to the pain of another Jack Houston. Tears slid down her cheeks. "You're right," she sobbed. "I'm a cold-blooded bitch. I'm just using you. I've got nothing to give in return."

"Ah, but now you have." He surprised her. His voice was tender again. Tender and affectionate. He took her in his arms and held her against his chest.

Patrice felt herself relaxing. As her tears subsided, the warmth she felt became genuine. Her flesh was pliant to his touch. Her tears had released her, opened her to feeling. She felt an emotional bond between them that had been absent before. This time as Fitz's caresses aroused her, she felt an emotional joy to match the physical anticipation.

"That's a fine, soft rug, and roomy, too." He led her from the window seat and gently pulled her down with him. They undressed each other slowly. Their kisses lingered on each other's naked bodies as they lay pressing together on the rug. The thrill of anticipation was caused by more than just their flesh touching.

It was their best moment, a moment filled with promise; it was shattered by the ringing of the telephone.

"Damn!" The expletive exploded from both their mouths in unison, and then both laughed ruefully.

Patrice got up to answer. She stood naked with her hand on her hip and Fitz's eyes hot and admiring on her flushed body. "Yes?" she said into the mouthpiece. "What is it?"

It was Berkley. He had thought Holly might be in her studio. He had a call for her from St. Martin.

"From St. Martin?" Patrice repeated uncomprehendingly.

"It's someone making the call for Mr. Houston, Miss Patrice."

"I don't understand. Why isn't he calling for himself?"

"I couldn't say, Miss Patrice. Perhaps if you'd talk to the gentleman yourself . . ."

"All right. Put him through."

There was a clicking sound in Patrice's ear, and then an unfamiliar voice came on the line. The man introduced himself as the captain of police in Philipsburg. "I've been asked to call you for Mr. Jack Houston," he began.

"I don't understand. Why can't he call himself?" Her heart was pounding with anxiety. "Has there been an accident or something? Is Jack all right?"

"No accident, *mefrou*." The voice had a faint Dutch accent. "Mr. Houston cannot call himself because he is under arrest. He is in jail."

"In jail? I don't understand." At least Jack was alive. At least he was unharmed. "What's the charge?"

"Murder, *mefrou*." The voice in Patrice's ear communicated how serious the situation was. "The charge against Mr. Houston is murder."

BOOK THREE

24

T HE SUDDEN AND unanticipated arrival of Buffy Houston at Riverview took the household staff by surprise. Buffy had been fortunate in catching an immediate connecting flight out of Puerto Rico, so there had been no time to call ahead. It was only after she landed at Kennedy that she was able to telephone to say she would be arriving at the estate in approximately two hours.

Although it was four A.M. when Berkley took the call, he did not hesitate to wake those servants necessary to prepare the Houstons' suite of rooms for the arrival. Under Berkley's supervision, two upstairs maids were roused to change all the linens and to lay out fresh towels for the Houstons' private bathroom as well. A small bar was set up in their sitting room, and a table was laid for the serving of either breakfast or a tray of sandwiches, whichever repast might be requested to offset the rigors of the journey just completed.

There had been a light drizzle the night before, so a footman was assigned to wash the windows of the large master bedroom, the sitting room, the dressing room, and even the bathroom. Another footman gave the floors and woodwork a fast going-over with a quick-drying wax. He was followed by the maids with dust rags and carpet sweepers. Vacuum cleaners were not used lest they disturb the other members of the family still sleeping in their beds. By the time Buffy arrived, all of this had been completed to the satisfaction of Berkley's critical eye, and the servants who accomplished it had receded to their customary out-of-sight-out-of-mind status.

Buffy's mind did not register any of the results of the hectic preparations. She was physically exhausted from her own frantic trip and emotionally strung out from the scenes that had led up to it. She peremptorily waved away Berkley's suggestions of breakfast or a light snack and went straight to bed. Exhausted, she slept through the next day until late afternoon.

When she woke she had a long, hot bath to compose herself. She dressed slowly and put on her makeup carefully before going downstairs to face the family. Only when she was satisfied that her facade—armor, really— was securely in place did she descend. In Buffy's mind every meeting with her former in-laws—the family of Governor Matthew Adams Stockwell—was a potential confrontation.

Coming down the wide, sweeping circular staircase, she encountered Berkley. The butler stood aside in the niche where the Medici bust by a pupil of Raphael rested on its pedestal. His bow discriminated between respect and obsequiousness. ''Miss Patrice has asked if you would be good enough to join her in the parlor of the east wing, Mrs. Houston.'' He relayed the message with cool precision.

Buffy did not fail to register Berkley's tone. It was one she had come to know well during the years she had been married to the governor. It was never anything but polite, and it was never anything but cool. It was summed up by the fact that Patrice, who had kept her married name after her divorce, was never ''Mrs. O'Keefe'' but always ''Miss

Patrice," while Buffy had always been either "Mrs. Stockwell" or "Mrs. Houston." Even the Governor's eldest daughter, who was actually older than Buffy, was called "Miss Alice." It reflected quite clearly the attitude of all the Stockwells toward her. She would never be anything but an outsider to the family, or to the staff of Riverview.

"Thank you, Berkley." Her answer was as calculatedly cool as his attitude. Still, Buffy thought as she continued down the stairs, she would never be able to get as much snootiness and snottiness in her voice as Berkley did. You had to be born a third-generation butler for that.

As she made her way to the east wing parlor, Buffy's pace was measured. Why would Patrice want to see her? It couldn't be to welcome her home. She and Patrice were hardly friends. Buffy believed in being as sophisticated about her husband's former lovers as about her own, but she stopped short of cultivating comradeship.

Besides, long before she had taken Jack away from Patrice—twice, actually, once before and once after their marriage—it had been obvious to Buffy that the petite granddaughter of Governor Stockwell deplored Buffy because she had broken up the governor's marriage. So why the request from Patrice now to join her? Probably, Buffy decided, Patrice had deduced that her coming back to Riverview alone signified trouble between her and Jack, and she couldn't pass up the opportunity to gloat.

"There you are, darling." Buffy swept into the east wing parlor with her usual panache. "Berkley said that you wanted to see me. I've been trying to imagine what about, but I can't. So now you must tell me before I simply die of curiosity."

"Will you have a cocktail?" Patrice resisted being caught up in Buffy's effusiveness.

"Of course. Martini, please. Very dry."

Patrice mixed a shaker of martinis and poured them each one. She waited until Buffy, comfortably settled on the Louis XIV sofa, had sipped hers and nodded satisfaction before revealing the reason she'd asked Buffy to join her. "It's about Jack," she began. Patrice ignored the eyebrow Buffy raised and told her tersely about the call from the Dutch police on St. Martin. "So Jack is under arrest, charged with murder," Patrice concluded.

"I see." The expression on Buffy's face had not altered, and as she finished her martini, she held out her goblet for a refill.

Thinking Buffy might be shaken by what she had just heard, Patrice fetched the shaker from the sideboard, re-stirred it, and poured a second cocktail. She waited until Buffy had sipped some of it before speaking again. "What will you do?" she finally asked. "What can I—we—do to help?"

"I don't know," Buffy said very slowly and deliberately, "that I shall *do* anything. And whatever you may choose to do, my dear Patrice, is your own affair."

Patrice stared at her. She hadn't expected such a response, not even from Buffy. The older woman's personality had always been distasteful to her, but she had never had any reason to think Buffy cold-hearted. As stormy as her marriage to Jack had been, Patrice had always assumed that Buffy loved him. Why else would she stay married to him, after all? Yet Buffy's tone now was as detached and dispassionate as if she'd just heard news about some stranger, rather than a husband in serious trouble.

Perhaps she was in a state of shock. Little as she liked Buffy, Patrice nevertheless felt compelled under the circumstances to grant her the benefit of the doubt. "Bail will have to be arranged," she said tentatively.

"If you'll tell me how much, I'll write a check."

"A check." Patrice stared at her. "I see." She took a deep breath and brought her voice back under control. "Jack will need a good criminal lawyer."

"I'll pay for that, too." Buffy's classically sculpted visage regarded Patrice haughtily. "I'm sure, dear Patrice, that you will see that he is represented by the best."

"I don't understand!" Patrice blurted out. "Aren't you concerned?"

184

"I am concerned," Buffy told her. "And that is all that I am. I do not feel compelled to become involved."

"But Jack's your husband!"

"Well now, Patrice, you haven't always been so quick to remember that, have you?"

Patrice ignored the gibe. "He's in trouble."

"Of his own making."

"Perhaps that's true. But you don't really know."

"But I do." The ice sheet of Buffy's calm was undisturbed.

"What do you mean?"

"The man they told you Jack is accused of killing was named Victor Grieg. Isn't that right?"

"Yes." Patrice couldn't see why the victim's name was important.

"Jack and I met him together on St. Martin. He was with Carrie Tyler. They were obviously lovers."

"I don't see—"

"The reason I left St. Martin so abruptly was that I walked in on Jack and Carrie in each other's arms."

"Oh." Patrice sat down slowly in a Regency chair with delicately curved legs. It was all beginning to fall into place. "Then you think—"

"That Victor Grieg discovered Carrie was being untrue to him with Jack, and that started the fight that resulted in Jack killing him." With her conclusion, Buffy was no longer bothering to hide the bitterness in her voice.

There was a pause before Patrice spoke again. "Even so," she said, "Jack is your husband. He really is in deep trouble. He needs you to stand by him."

"There is a certain irony in your telling me that, don't you think?" Buffy's voice was too sweet. "But I'll tell you what. If you don't mind sharing him with Carrie—and why should you, after all? You never minded sharing him with me—then *you* stand by him."

"I'm not his wife." Patrice restrained herself with difficulty.

"And I am not his patsy." Buffy finished her cocktail and got to her feet. "So nice chatting with you, Patrice."

Head high, she glided gracefully toward the blue-and-gilt-paneled door of the east wing parlor.

Her exit was truly imperial, a great actress vanishing stage left as Catherine the Great.

Buffy's performances, however, always required an audience, if only an audience of one, even if that one was someone she resented as much as she did Patrice. Once in the privacy of her rooms, her facade crumpled. Alone, she cried and pounded her fist into the petit-lace spread over the pillow and gave free rein to her emotions.

Damn you, Jack! You couldn't stay away from her, could you? You couldn't resist her goddamn youth! Firm thighs! Breasts that don't sag! Damn her! Damn you!

Buffy rose to her knees on the bed and looked in the mirror. Her cheeks were stained with tears. Her eyes were red. Her mascara had run. Rivulets had washed away her makeup, revealing lines of strain and age. The face looking back at her was beautiful, but it was also unmistakably mature.

You're a wreck, she told herself. An old wreck. Old. How can you blame him for wanting younger women? You always knew he would leave you for one, and now he has. But it hurts. It hurts. It hurt so badly that Buffy could not focus on the price that Jack might have to pay for his presumed infidelity. It hurt so much that the two martinis she had drunk with Patrice no longer deadened the pain. She went to the small bar in her sitting room and poured herself a large glass of vodka. She drank slowly but steadily until the glass was empty.

She decided then that she would not join the family at dinner. She did not have the resources tonight to cope with their carefully veiled, polite, but unmistakable hostility.

Taking off the dress she had only just donned, she put on silk pajamas and a housecoat. She poured herself another tall glass of vodka. She thought about Jack—Jack and Patrice, Jack and Carrie, Jack and whoever, just as long as they weren't over the hill the way she was. She drank the second glass of vodka and poured a third.

186

Much later when Buffy went to pour from the vodka bottle, she found it was empty. She put it down and picked up a bottle of bourbon at random. She started to decant the amber liquor into the glass she'd been using. Then she caught herself. Mustn't mix drinks, she recalled hazily. Never mix, never worry. The governor used to say that. Mix bourbon with vodka, that's a ticket to the upchuck. So no to the bourbon and find another bottle of the Russian.

Buffy rummaged through the liquor cabinet under the small bar. There was no more vodka. Remembering that there was always a bottle in the cellarette in the small family dining room downstairs, she decided to fetch it.

The hallway outside her room was quiet. Buffy had lost track of time, but she didn't think it could be so very late. Past some bedtimes, she would have guessed, but not all. The servants probably would have retired already; they had to rise early to deal with their various masters' various morning demands. That alone would account for the house seeming so quiet.

Half tiptoeing and half lurching, Buffy made her way down the sweeping staircase. Crossing the foyer to the small dining room, she saw light coming from behind a partly opened door. She caught a glimpse of Patrice sitting on an armchair and going over some papers she had taken from her briefcase. Her glasses were on, and her head was bent intently. Buffy continued on without being seen by her.

Foggy as her brain was with all she'd had to drink, she nevertheless found the bottle of vodka without any trouble. Clutching it to her breast, she made her way back upstairs.

Eager to return to her room and continue blotting out the perfidy of her husband, Buffy picked up speed as she reached the upper landing of the staircase. In her hurry, she didn't see Fitz coming down the upstairs hall before she ran into him.

"Oops." With the impact he grabbed Buffy by both elbows to steady her. "Sure and you should blow your whistle comin' round the bend."

"Just keeping you on your wild Irish toes." Buffy giggled. "Not bad," she decided, "for the spur of the moment." She focused on him, and her eyes approved. "Let's drink to it," she suggested. "My quick wit, I mean."

"Thanks, no. It's the water wagon I'm on these days."

"What do you mean? You're Irish, aren't you? Have you no respect for stereotypes?" Buffy waved the bottle at him and lurched.

"Stereotypes? Well, you're not Irish, now, are you? But you're surely three sheets to the wind. And the hallway's no place to be sailing with such ballast." Fitz took her arm and guided her to the door of her rooms.

"Absolutely right. More comfortable drinking inside." Buffy stumbled as Fitz let go of one of her arms to turn the doorknob.

He caught her as the door opened and supported her into the room. Giggling, Buffy reached behind her with her free hand and pushed the door closed. "Trapped now," she told him. "And you have to have a drink with me. If you don't, I'll scream rape."

"Ah, now, you'll do no such thing. You're too much a lady to force a man to drink when he doesn't want to." Fitz turned and started to leave.

"Wait. I'll make a deal with you. If you stay while I have a drink, I won't make you have one, and I won't scream rape, either."

"Well, all right, then."

Buffy struggled to open the bottle of vodka. When she'd succeeded, she poured some into her glass and drank it. Fitz stood and watched her. "Why don't you sit down," Buffy suggested, patting the cushion of the settee beside her.

"Ah, well, it's late now, and I should really be on my way."

"Don't you like me?"

188

"You're a fine lady."

"But you don't think I'm attractive?"

"Oh, but I do. A great beauty, and no exaggeration." Fitz was truthful.

"A great beauty, but over the hill. Too old for a young man like you."

"Not at all."

"Then why don't you come sit down next to me?"

"Well now—"

"It is because I'm too old, isn't it?"

"No." Fitz was honest. "It's because you're too drunk."

"You're just like my husband. You're all alike. All you want is nubile young girls. A mature woman doesn't make it. You might have to deal with wrinkles. You only want smooth flesh."

"Ah, now, you're upset. And it's not me you want, it's Jack. Sure and whatever it is, the trouble between you two, it will work itself out." Fitz was trying hard to be kind.

"My flesh is smooth! My behind is not corrugated! In no way does it resemble a washboard!"

"I never suggested—"

"Make love to me, Fitz!" It was more a demand than a plea. "You won't be sorry."

"You need some sleep, Mrs. Houston. No more booze and a good night's sleep. You don't want me. And in the morning, with a clear head, you'll see your way back to the man you do want."

"He doesn't want me. You don't want me. Nobody wants me." Buffy collapsed on the settee, sobbing. She gave way to a crying jag.

Fitz moved quickly. He picked her up, carried her into her bedroom, and laid her on the bed, covering her with the blanket. Buffy's sobs were already subsiding as he turned out the light. He also turned out the light in the sitting room and started to leave but stopped abruptly. Turning around, he crossed quickly over to the wet bar and took the bottle of vodka. Best, he thought, if it wasn't

189

there to tempt her if she got up. He slipped out the door to the hallway and closed it behind him. He never noticed Patrice coming up the stairs as he made his way back to his own room.

Patrice, however, did see Fitz and the bottle in his hand quite clearly. She had heard the door opening, presumed it was Buffy, and, not wanting to be confronted by her, had shrunk back into an alcove. She stood there, unseen, as Fitz passed by.

After his bedroom door closed behind him, she continued to stand there, silently furious. Jack was facing a murder charge, and his wife couldn't wait to commit adultery with another man. And with Fitz! Well, it hadn't taken Buffy long to get him off the wagon and into her bed.

Patrice really had thought Fitz was different. She'd believed him when he'd said he wanted to feel something and know that the other person felt something, too, before jumping into bed. But obviously Patrice had once again allowed herself to be fooled. Fitz didn't care about her. He just wanted sex.

All men were alike. Fitz Connely. Jack Houston. All men, Patrice snarled to herself as she crept back to her room.

But, damn it, why did Buffy always attract the men to whom she, Patrice, was most attracted?

Patrice's bitterness toward Buffy had not abated when the family gathered in the spacious west parlor two nights later to discuss the handling of what the newspapers were already referring to as ''the St. Martin high-society murder case.''

The media was treating the story as a love triangle in which jealous passion had resulted in the killing of the lover of ''young and beautiful Stockwell debutante heiress Carrie Tyler'' by ''the new and much younger hubby of Governor Matthew Adams Stockwell's widow.'' Buffy, furious at this treatment, was brazening the situation out

190

before the family. To Patrice she appeared every bit as callous and unloving as her initial response had indicated.

All of the Stockwells and Tylers who were in New York were present. Fitz Connely, not accepted yet as a member of the family, was not. Neither was his lawyer, Halsey De Vilbiss. This was strictly a family matter.

Jack's welfare was paramount to Patrice. The others—Buffy aside—were mainly concerned about the family's position. Scandal was no stranger to the Stockwells of Riverview, but their status—both in society and on Wall Street—could only suffer from being linked to so tawdry an affair.

Now Patrice's attention turned to her uncle Jonathan. Jonathan's recommendation was that they all stick their heads in the sand until events blew over. "It's not as if Jack is actually a member of the family," he said. "Marriage to the governor's widow hardly qualifies him for that status."

Buffy's only reply was a razor-edged smile; Jonathan was a fool and not worth the effort to correct.

"Still, Carrie's a member of the family," Diana Tyler responded. "She's involved and will come in for more and more attention as Jack's trial draws closer."

"Have you heard from Carrie?" Alice Lewis asked.

Diana frowned. "No. Not a word."

"Max?" Alice turned to Max Tyler.

"No." Max, too, shook his head. "She disappeared right after the murder and hasn't been seen since."

"The authorities on St. Martin—both the Dutch and the French—have been trying to find her without success," Patrice told them. "At least that was the story as of this afternoon when I last spoke with them."

"You are au courant, my dear." Buffy was sarcastic.

"I care enough to take the trouble to find out what's happening." Patrice twisted her waist-anchored ribbon bow savagely. "Unlike you," she added bluntly.

"If we desert Jack," David Lewis observed thoughtfully, "that will make the family look even worse in the media."

191

"I agree with that," said Matt.

David Lewis scowled faintly. It was the only sign he gave of having heard Matt Stockwell. Whenever he found himself in a room with "that cowardly draft dodger," he responded by ignoring Matt's presence.

Matt flushed at the reaction or, rather, the lack of one. "Maybe you should rethink your position, Uncle David," he suggested sarcastically. "I mean, if my agreement is so distasteful to you . . ."

David Lewis turned his back on Matt and went to the sideboard to pour himself a brandy. Patrice felt sorry for his wife. She looked embarrassed and unhappy.

"I agree with Uncle David, too." Holly calmly smoothed over the awkwardness. "The family should stand united in support of Jack. Uncle Jonathan, I think you're wrong. Jack is one of us. A united front will cool off the media coverage to some extent. Also, there are certain practical things to be done. I spoke with Zelig in Washington last night, and I took the liberty of discussing some of them with him. I hope that was all right?" Holly directed the question directly to Buffy.

Buffy nodded, shrugged, lit a cigarette.

"Jack will need a lawyer, of course," Holly continued, "and Zelig has offered to make inquiries through his diplomatic contacts in the Caribbean as to who the best person for the job might be." Again she looked questioningly at Buffy.

"Very sensible."

"Stockwell family influence will be important to your husband." It was David Lewis who pointed this out to Buffy. "As an American who has committed a capital crime, he will no longer be regarded as a tourist, but rather as an alien. Not even an alien-in-residence, mind you, because your villa is on the French side, and he's been arrested by the Dutch. Given the severity of the charge, it would not be unusual for a Dutch court to deny him bail. He could languish in jail for as long as it takes to bring the case to trial."

"The police captain I've been in contact with," Patrice

192

added, "told me that their judiciary is small in number and has a backlog of cases. It could be months before trial, maybe even a year."

Inwardly, Buffy winced. The picture of Jack as a caged bird was so out of keeping with his free-spirited personality that it truly hurt her to contemplate it. She was furious with him, but still . . .

"What can be done to get him out of jail?" she asked aloud. Her tone betrayed nothing of her feelings. She might have been inquiring about the availability of a hairdresser.

"Zelig has been talking to Michael," Holly informed Buffy. "Between them they think they can pull the strings necessary to have bail set quickly."

Michael, Matt and Patrice's younger brother, was a congressman well on his way to higher office. He would not, Patrice knew, want the case to reflect on him politically. It came in handy, she thought, having a brother with congressional pull and a cousin by marriage with the prestige to ask and receive favors from the administration.

"Usually," Holly was explaining now, "the U.S. legation on St. Martin wouldn't interfere. They might go through the motions of representing him as an American citizen, but their primary concern would be maintaining friendly relations with the Dutch government. Zelig, however, has seen to it that they will more actively support Jack. He has—in his words—'called in some favors.' "

"At the very least, his wife should be by Jack's side." Speaking for the first time, Ellen, Jonathan's wife, surprised everyone present. Ellen was becoming more and more assertive, and the older generation, at least, had trouble adjusting to her new role.

"I have no intention of playing that part." Buffy was defiant.

Her tone made them all stare at her momentarily. Patrice broke the silence. "So much for filial obligations." She did not bother to hide her bitterness. Privately she thought to herself that Buffy would simply rather stay at

Riverview hopping in and out of bed with Fitz than attend to a husband in jail. Confused by her feelings, she wasn't sure just how much of her fury toward Buffy was because of her desertion of her husband and how much was because she'd seduced Fitz.

"I told you, Patrice"—Buffy's composure was infuriating—"feel free to go to St. Martin yourself and stand by Jack to your heart's content. I don't mind. But I won't go."

"Well, somebody from the family should be there with him," Ellen insisted disapprovingly.

"I'll go," Peter announced.

Ellen's jaw dropped open. The last person she had expected to volunteer was her son. "But why?" she blurted out.

"Because, Mother, as you've just been saying, the family should be represented there. I think I'm qualified to do that as well as anyone." He regarded his mother sternly, trying to convey through his eyes a message not to question him. The reasons, known only to Peter, had not so much to do with Jack's situation as with Victor Grieg. Only Peter knew that Grieg's "business" in St. Martin had been the laundering of money received from Stockwell Enterprises. And he was concerned that an investigation of the murder might uncover Grieg's connection to organized crime and those unsavory transactions that might compromise Stockwell Enterprises. Accepting bribes was a crime; so, too, was paying bribes; Peter was anxious as to his own culpability. He had to go to St. Martin to do whatever had to be done to cover the money trail.

"But Peter," David Lewis pointed out, "I thought you had your hands full with the East Side development project."

"There's a lull right now." Peter was nothing if not glib. "I've got time. And I'm concerned that the family's interests be protected and the scandal contained. I may know some people down there," he added ambiguously, "who can be helpful."

Patrice's mind was racing as the rest of the family agreed that Peter would be just the one to go to St. Martin. What was he up to? She was very suspicious. Peter was never to be trusted. He always had some angle that was strictly his own, and he didn't give one damn about Jack. She was sure of that. Why the devil was he doing this?

"I'll go with you, Peter," she decided.

Buffy's laughter tinkled over the reactions of the others. Why should two people go? they queried logically. Holly, who thought she knew why and disapproved, in particular tried to dissuade Patrice.

But she would not be moved. Jack would need a friend—not Peter, a real friend. The hell with what anybody thought. In particular, the hell with Buffy. "I'm going," Patrice repeated.

And that was that.

Patrice was in her room later that night when there was a soft knock at the door. She knew who it was before she answered. She put on a robe and confronted Fitz.

"What do you want?" She blocked his way, her tone hostile.

His eyes were quizzical. "A word, if you've no objection."

"Yes?"

"Standing in the hall is it?" Fitz laughed. "Sure and that's no place for a private conversation."

"All right." Patrice stood aside reluctantly. "You can come in. But only for a minute," she added.

"I am less than overwhelmed by the warmth of your welcome," Fitz told her when he was inside the room with the door closed behind him.

"I'm sorry." Her tone implied she was no such thing.

Fitz was patient. "And might I know the reason for it?"

"It's just the way I feel." Patrice's shrug was meant to stonewall him.

"That was not the way you felt the other night when we were interrupted by the bad news regarding Jack Houston."

"That was then. This is now."

"True enough. Still, as of then, as I recall, we had established a certain affection between us," Fitz reminded her. "It's obvious something has occurred to make you feel differently. I'm only asking what that something might be."

"I saw you coming out of Buffy's room the other night," Patrice told him bluntly.

"Did you now?" Fitz thought that over a moment. "If it's jealousy, then," he told her slowly, "I am flattered."

"It isn't. Don't be."

His mouth set in a grim line and his eyes flashing his anger, he asked, "Was I obligated to some faithfulness you've jumped to the conclusion I've broken?"

"Not at all," Patrice told him coldly. "You don't owe me a thing."

"I didn't think I did. Leastwise, I recall making no promises regarding any fidelity."

"You didn't." Her tone remained unrelenting.

"Why are you so angry with me, then?"

"I'm not. I'm merely . . . indifferent."

Fitz tried a different tack. " 'Indifferent' is it? Ah, well, then it's worse than I thought. Listen now, might it make some difference if I told you that nothing happened with the lady?"

"Ha!"

"She'd had a wee bit too much to drink. I helped her to her room was all. And then I left. That's all there was to it."

"And now I'll tell you about the maiden who took a frog to bed with her and woke up in the morning to find a handsome young prince." Patrice's sarcasm was scathing. "To this day her mother doesn't believe that story."

"And you don't believe me." Fitz nodded. "But what I'm telling you is the truth." He studied Patrice for a long moment. Her cocoa-brown eyes were tired. Her chestnut

196

hair was tied back rather than combed, adding to the picture of strain. Her small hand was clutching her robe closed high at the neck. She looked defiant, but small and vulnerable, too. "All right, then," he said finally. "I'll not try to convince you. But answer me one thing if you will."

"What's that?"

"If you're not jealous, then why should it matter to you whatever happened between myself and Mrs. Houston?"

"You just answered your own question," Patrice told him. "She is 'Mrs. Houston.' And her husband was a good friend to you when you needed one. Letting Buffy seduce you is no way to repay that friendship."

"The lady seduced *me*, then? I didn't overwhelm her with my wicked Irish charms?" Fitz, too, could be sarcastic.

"Either way it's a betrayal of Jack."

Once again Fitz studied her for a long moment. "I'm told you'll be leaving for St. Martin directly after the board meeting tomorrow." He was not really changing the subject.

"That's right."

"I'll miss you. I am sorry that we are parting this way."

Patrice made no reply.

"You'll be a great comfort to Jack, I'm sure."

Despite herself, she blushed.

"Wish him the best of luck for me." Fitz started for the door.

"I will."

"He's a fortunate man to have such a loving"—Fitz paused, before finishing the sentence—"friend."

As the door close behind him, Patrice's emotions were in turmoil. Was it really possible that she might be wrong about him and Buffy? Was it so obvious that her feelings for Jack were much more than mere friendship? And what about the feelings that she and Fitz had shared?

Fitz would, Patrice realized sadly, have no trouble finding some other woman with whom to share his affection.

197

25

ON THE PLANE to St. Martin, Patrice was still mulling over the question of her anger. Was she more angry at Fitz for sleeping with Buffy than any other issue? Was it only jealousy?

Buffy was the sort of woman—the sort of beauty, to be accurate—most men desired. She exuded sexuality the way the maple trees exuded sap in autumn. It was, perhaps, inevitable that Fitz would be attracted to her. But Patrice felt the anger welling up inside her all over again. How could Buffy cheat with Fitz while her husband was languishing in jail? Regardless of what Jack might or might not have done with Carrie, how could Buffy abandon him when he was in such deep trouble? If he was my husband, Patrice told herself, I could never behave that way.

If he was my husband . . .

Patrice sighed. She was still in love with Jack. No matter her casual interest in Fitz, it was clear to her that it was Jack she really wanted. Probably, she reasoned, she had been so angry with Fitz because like all men he'd been such a marshmallow in Buffy's hands. He'd let Buffy make him a party to her betrayal of Jack. That's how hooked I am on Jack, Patrice thought. I'm furious with the man who cooperated with his wife's betraying him, instead of feeling betrayed myself. But that's crazy. Patrice smiled wanly to herself. Love is crazy. Nevertheless, she loved him. She would do everything possible to help him get out of this mess he was in. And this time she would pursue him aggressively. His marriage was obviously a farce so why not? She would use all her wiles, and she would succeed. She would take Jack away from Buffy.

Patrice nodded once, firmly, to herself. That was decided. Jack would be hers. She turned back to the Seabury diary and began to read. . . .

Edith Seabury was seated before her easel in the small room on the fourth floor of the home she shared with her father. When the house had been built in 1835, fifteen years earlier, the entire fourth floor, or attic, had been intended as servants' quarters. But because it was in the center of six row houses, the elegant interior, although spacious, was dimly lit. Only the topmost floor caught the light through the slanted dormer windows, so Edith had appropriated it for a studio, relegating the two delighted parlor maids who had shared the room to a much larger chamber on the floor below.

The house, with its fine mahogany furniture, crimson silk draperies, and imported Eastern carpeting, reflected the status of Edith's father. Linus Seabury was a successful dry-goods merchant who had expanded his activities into the flourishing New York import-export trade. He was not a wealthy man in the manner of the Stockwells and other gentry who dwelt in the great Hudson River Valley mansions. But he was well off, and the Seabury house was by the New York standards of the day comfortably luxurious, if not ostentatious.

A gentle man, a widower with an ongoing air of tragedy, Linus Seabury doted on his only child. He pampered Edith in a manner that made his friends and neighbors roll their eyes and give thanks to the Lord that the child was female. If Linus had had a son, they said, the boy would surely have turned out a wastrel and probably a fop and a rake. As it was, there was general agreement that his spoiling of Edith had undermined the docility necessary to a proper wife and mother. They blamed his coddling of her for the outlandish way she had turned out: a suffragist, an abolitionist, even, it was whispered, an artist—in short, a rebellious female spirit who meddled in things traditionally the sole province of men.

This criticism from his friends and peers concerned Linus, but it did not make him any harsher in the handling of his daughter. No matter how he worried privately about Edith's future, now that she was grown he treated her as an adult and with consideration. He did so now as he tapped at the door to her studio. "It's Father, Edith," he announced. "Am I disturbing you?"

"Come in, Father." Edith stood up from her easel and greeted him with a kiss on the cheek. "You're not disturbing me at all. I can't find the bones in my oils, and the best of the afternoon light is fading anyway."

"Bones?" Linus Seabury was frequently perplexed by his daughter's references to her painting.

"This is a harbor scene," she explained, showing him the canvass. "I spent three days sketching it last week. Now I'm doing a painting from the sketches. The ships and the water are coming all right, but the figures of the two seamen I show in the rigging here, and here"—she pointed—"lose definition in the transposition from charcoal to oil. I simply don't know enough, you see."

"I see." Linus Seabury's tone was placating. Actually he wasn't at all sure that he did see.

"I should have gone to medical school and studied anatomy."

"Medical school? Anatomy?" Linus Seabury's brow did not unfurrow.

"As an alternative to a good painting life class, which I am barred from because I am a woman!"

"Whenever your work goes badly, your frustration puts outrageous ideas in your head," her father chided her gently.

Edith sighed. "If I can't learn through artistic instruction how bodies are constructed, then why not through medical instruction?"

"Because, as you should know, the bars against women attending medical schools are equally strong."

"Elizabeth Blackwell did it." Elizabeth Blackwell, despite having been ostracized and persecuted by fellow students and many of her teachers had graduated at the head of her class. "She showed them," Edith added.

"One woman, and a remarkable one at that. But despite her accomplishments, the medical schools are not exactly opening their doors to women students. No, Edith, I don't think the solution to your problem lies in that direction."

"You're probably right." Edith sighed. "I should throw it all up and marry the first man who will have me and devote myself to producing children rather than paintings."

"It might be possible to produce both with the right man," her father suggested. "Say Charles Cabot Stockwell."

"The subject of marriage has not come up with Charles, Father. I hope it never does. We are friends. I wouldn't want to spoil that."

Edith had been accompanying Charles to concerts and the theater and dinners for almost a year now.

Charles always behaved like a gentleman on their outings, humorous sometimes, even teasing, but never less than respectful. He never touched her except to take her arm in his when they strolled. He made no attempt to kiss her or do anything else that might have been construed as furthering his courtship. Yet she could not help but know that his interest in her was romantic. The message nestled with the laughter in his cinnamon eyes.

"Why would a proposal of marriage from Charles spoil your friendship with him?" Linus Seabury asked.

"In my observation, marriage and friendship are almost always incompatible. Marriage stamps women as chattel. How can a man feel friendship for that which he owns?"

"Surely you put it too strongly." Her father's eyes were troubled. "I was your mother's friend and she mine. Marriage did not alter that."

"You were not married very long." Edith bit her lip. That had been a stupid and unkind thing to say. She loved her father and knew the day did not pass but that he reexperienced the pain of his wife's long-ago death. "If all men were like you, Father," she told him lovingly, "then no woman would ever balk at marriage. But most, alas, are not."

"Charles Stockwell seems a very decent man indeed."

"Perhaps. But then he is still a bachelor. And in any case, the subject has not come up. I am content to leave it so."

"He is, I am told"—now her father's eyes twinkled mischievously—"a catch. Indeed, it seems that has now been officially confirmed."

"Officially confirmed? What do you mean, Father?"

"It seems that a volume has just been published listing the most important people in society, and the name of Charles Cabot Stockwell is prominent among them. It is called *Who's Who*. The idea, I understand, is to update it every year."

"Toward what end?"

"To insure the ongoing quality of high society, I imagine. The leaders of the elite do change from year to year, you know. Some will fall from grace for one reason or another. Others will be elevated to the heady heights."

"And we call ourselves a democracy!" Edith jeered. "Next thing we will be dubbing our gentry with the sword tip and bestowing titles upon them. The royalists are ever with us."

"Well, if that's true, it's better to be one of them than to be the daughter of a plebeian merchant."

"Are you so eager to marry me off, Father? Am I taking up too much room in your house?"

"Never, Edith." He knew that the remark was not meant seriously and did not take it so. "I just thought how nice it would be to see the name of a daughter of mine listed in this *Who's Who*."

"In recognition of my own accomplishments as an artist, it would be very nice. But to be there merely as the appendage of a rich man? Where is the honor in that?"

Nevertheless, the subject of the new *Who's Who* remained on Edith's mind that evening when Charles arrived to escort her to dinner at the Manhattan town house of some Hudson River Valley friends of his. She mentioned the tome during the carriage ride. "There are no women mentioned except as the mates of accomplished men," she complained. "Neither Lucretia Mott, nor Elizabeth Cady Stanton, nor even Dr. Elizabeth Blackwell are listed. There are no women artists mentioned at all."

"That's not surprising," Charles pointed out. "None have gained recognition."

"Because recognition is by males, of males, for males. The art world is a world for men only."

"That's absolutely true."

"It's not fair."

"It surely is not," Charles agreed.

"The opposition is too great for a woman artist. I should give it up."

"You most certainly should not. You are much too talented to speak of that." Charles was very earnest.

Too earnest? Edith wondered. Sometimes she thought that his encouragement of her painting—and he was most encouraging and most constantly so—was because he preferred her to keep busy at her easel rather than to be out on the streets demonstrating with her sisters in the causes of abolitionism and suffrage. While her painting might be looked upon by his circle as a hobby, a social conscience for a woman was definitely frowned upon in the upper-class society in which Charles moved. Could she really expect him to be free of the prejudice?

She was silent so long that Charles concluded she was brooding on the lack of recognition for her art. He had been supportive; now he thought it best to change the subject. "Have you heard from your friend Mrs. Bloomer?" he inquired.

"A letter two days ago. She is helping to recruit women to the suffragist cause in upstate New York."

"She has given up designing clothing?"

"Yes." Edith's answer was so clipped as to suggest hostility.

"I see." The reaction puzzled Charles. "I had noticed you no longer wear the Bloomer costume," he offered tentatively.

"It is called a 'Camilia,' " Edith corrected him. "And you are right. I no longer wear it."

"Nor do I see it as much in evidence with other women as it once was."

"True."

"Why is that?" Charles asked.

Edith scowled and did not reply. She would not expect any man, not even Charles, to comprehend the answer to his question. Only a woman could understand what it meant to spend one's life a captive to one's clothing and then to be set free only to surrender to the captivity again.

She had no words of explanation. Few of the so-called Bloomer girls did. They were themselves ashamed of the vulnerability that had made them give up. It would remain for Elizabeth Cady Stanton to pronounce the epitaph for the Bloomer girl costume. "What incredible freedom I enjoyed for two years, like a captive set free from his ball and chain," she would write. But, she would add, in the end, "the cup of ridicule was greater than one can bear."

Charles realized that Edith was not going to answer his question. He suppressed his irritation. "In any case," he observed, "you look particularly comely tonight even if your gown was not designed by Mrs. Bloomer."

"You can't see my gown. My cloak covers it." Her silk-lined circular cloak of navy-blue cashmere with its narrow bayadere scarf did indeed conceal Edith's dinner gown. The deep, turned-down collar meeting the wide ribbon of her curved scoop of a bonnet where it was tied under her chin shadowed most of her face as well.

"I saw it before you put on your cloak. I remember it in detail," Charles assured her.

204

"In detail?" Edith was dubious. "I thought men noticed only the Bloomer costumes—and then just to jeer."

"In detail," Charles repeated firmly. "Your gown is of crinoline—a horsehair weave combined with linen. The color is robin's-egg blue, and it matches your eyes. The skirt is full with passementerie decorating the bottom and soutache braid running up the front to the waist. The sleeves are tight with ruffles at the wrist and shoulder. There is a jeweled and buckled band at the waist. The bodice is rounded and cut quite low with a deep V dip in the center."

He had noticed her breasts! Edith did not know whether to be flattered or insulted. "You have very keen powers of observation."

"Now, as to your jewelry—" But Charles did not go on. They had arrived at their destination. The coachman reined in the horses, and the footman leaped to open the door to the coach. Charles got out first and turned to help Edith from the carriage.

Inside, Edith excused herself before removing her cloak and went straight to the dressing room set aside for the female guests. Charles's words about her bodice had left her nervous. Now she studied the rising half-moons of her bosom and wondered if the décolletage was perhaps too revealing. Surreptitiously, she studied the two other women who had come in to apply powder before joining the general company. Their necklines were quite as deep as hers. Edith took a deep breath, tugged the bodice up a bit, watched in the mirror as it slid back down when she exhaled, and decided she would brazen it out. Bosoms were one thing women had that men didn't. Why be ashamed of them?

Charles was waiting for her at the foot of the stairs when she descended. He folded her arm in his and led her around the room, making introductions. Most of the names, Edith guessed, would be listed prominently in the first volume of *Who's Who*.

They had been among the last to arrive. Shortly thereafter, Mrs. Cornelia van Steadman, their hostess, had a word with her majordomo, and a few moments later dinner was announced.

Edith was led in by Charles but was seated across from him. The men on either side of her were investment bankers and neighbors of the van Steadmans and Charles Stockwell. They each delivered the requisite three pleasantries to Edith, surreptitiously admired the creaminess of the exposed upper half of her bosom, and then talked to each other across her as if she had been removed with the soup plates before the main course was served.

Their behavior was not worth becoming upset over, Edith thought. They were bores in any case. Even if she didn't understand their financial gobbledygook, she quite comprehended the narrowness of their conversation.

Charles smiled at her from across the table. Edith smiled back. A man and a gentleman he might be, but Charles was infinitely superior to these fellows. Perhaps they didn't always agree, and he had often made her angry, but he had never bored her. Maybe her father was right. Charles really might be a rare bird, and she should not be so quick to spurn him.

You are cold-blooded, Edith told herself. What of love? Even if he is superior to most of his disgraceful gender, what do you really feel for him? Assuming he is falling in love with you, are you falling in love with him? Beware, she cautioned herself. Love is a trap, and women its victims! Still, she declined the rich Viennese pastry dessert now being served. Her waist was slim enough for Charles to encircle it with his two hands, and with the issue of love still to be decided, she didn't want that to change. She sighed and listened to the conversation flowing around her.

"Niggers and micks," the man on Edith's left pronounced. "There's a balance to be maintained."

"But if slavery's allowed to spread to the new territories," countered the man on her right, "the balance will go to the South."

"What difference? They're agricultural. We're industrial. That's the only balance we have to be concerned about."

"But can that balance hold if we add on slave states? How long before the agricultural South gluts the cotton market and has to seek other revenues for its new territories? That's when they'll turn to weaving their own cloth instead of shipping the cotton to northern mills. And why not, with all that free nigger labor right there waiting to be used? I tell you, no matter how we cut the wages of the harps, we won't be able to compete. And there goes your precious balance."

"Our shipping industry will pick up the slack. Of course we'll have to drop the anti–slave trade laws to do that. But once that's accomplished, we'll supply the black labor for new southern industry—maybe even use some of it ourselves in place of the Irish—and things will even out again."

"That won't happen." The man on Edith's right was positive. "The South doesn't need slaves from Africa anymore. They can breed all they need themselves. The statistics on the breeding farms—"

"Statistics?" Horrified, Edith could not stop herself from speaking. "How can you speak of statistics?"

"Ma'am?" The man she had interrupted regarded her courteously, puzzled by the remark.

"These slaves you talk about are flesh-and-blood people!"

"Oh, yes, ma'am. And so are our Irish workers. But you see, we were speaking theoretically in terms of the maximum labor potential needed to maintain an equitable balance between northern industrial supremacy and southern agricultural production. Now in those terms—"

"And I was speaking in human terms." Edith cut in without attempting to hide the outrage in her voice. She ignored the warning look Charles shot her from across the table.

"As well you should, ma'am." The man on her right was tolerant and gallant. "The ladies should always take the softer view. But we men of commerce—"

"Never hesitate to shed blood in the interest of profit." Edith finished the sentence for him.

Cornelia van Steadman, their hostess, stepped into the awkward silence that followed the raising of Edith's voice. "Ah, politics," she said lightly and with good humor. "The playthings of the gentlemen. Is it not so, ladies? Well then, let us leave them to their toys, and to their brandy and cigars, and retire to the drawing room and our coffee and own more pressing concerns."

"How right you are, ma'am." The man on Edith's right wiped his brow with relief.

"Indeed, the ladies know us too well." The man on her left was equally good-natured.

"It is because we give them free rein with their playthings that misery prevails," Edith declared stubbornly.

"Edith . . ." Charles spoke softly, but with a pleading note in his voice.

"*I* would like some brandy." Once again Edith ignored him in favor of defiance. "And perhaps a cigar, too."

"My dear . . ." Cornelia van Steadman was smiling, but there was a plea in her eyes as well.

"Very well, then. I will join the ladies in the drawing room." Edith pushed back her chair and was on her feet before the servant in livery could reach her. "I do hope that we will discuss the issues of the day there, among ourselves. Women do discuss such things, you know. At least my friends and I do. But then we are suffragists." She could not help noticing how very red Charles's face had turned as Cornelia van Steadman linked arms with her and led her firmly from the room.

"I've embarrassed you," Edith acknowledged when the evening had dragged uncomfortably to its close and she and Charles were once again in the carriage and on their way to her father's house. "And I can't even say I'm sorry. I have pledged not to be silent in the face of inhumanity. And what those men were saying was inhumane."

"You might have been a touch more tactful," he reproached her.

"Tact is never an answer to the ills of the world. To remain silent is to collaborate."

"Out of consideration for our hostess, I mean. Good manners—"

"You're right, Charles," Edith snapped. "I don't have very good manners. I do care more about ending slavery than about hurting the feelings of my hostess. I'm sorry."

"Except that you really aren't sorry." Charles, too, could become angry. "What you really are is smug and righteous."

"That's true, too. I have been an embarrassment to you, and for that I truly am sorry. But you see, Charles, I can't change."

"Won't change, you mean."

"Won't change, then. You see, we're too different, you and I. Actually, we're from two very different worlds. My feelings are too deep to deny with silence. I will always be an embarrassment to you. Really, we should stop seeing each other."

"Is that your answer. To run away?"

"It seems wisest," Edith told him.

"Not to me. To me it seems cowardly." He grasped her by her upper arms and turned her toward him. It was the first time he had ever touched her with possessiveness. "What about our feelings for each other?" he demanded.

"I'm not sure those have been defined," Edith answered carefully.

"I love you." His normally ruddy face with its sandy mustache appeared dark, even sinister, in the dim light inside the coach.

The high corset felt suddenly very tight around the lower part of her bosom. Edith was quite breathless. She didn't know what to say.

"I love you," Charles repeated. "Do you love me, Edith?"

"I don't know." She blurted out the words. They were

true. In her mind, she didn't know. But the wild beating of her heart was conveying another message entirely.

"You don't know?" Charles kissed her then. It was a long, experienced, deep, and demanding kiss. "I want to marry you," he said when it was over. "I want to make love to you. I want us to have children."

Be careful! Edith's mind insisted faintly in counterpoint to the clamor of her heart. Be very careful. "Time," she gasped. "I have to have time to think."

"I do love you. You exasperate me at times, but I respect your views. I don't really care a fig that you put those burgher noses out of joint. In all arrogance I must tell you that I am Charles Stockwell of Riverview, and if you marry me, Edith, they will bend to you as my wife. As a Stockwell of Riverview, you will not have to conform to New York and Westchester society, you will be one of the elite who lead it. As my wife you will lead and they will follow, I promise you."

"Is it marriage you are proposing?" Edith found the wit to inquire. "Or a coronation?"

"Call it what you will. Be my wife. Be my queen." Charles reached for her to kiss her again.

"No. Wait." Edith pushed him away. "I must have time to think, to consider." If she did not stop his kisses, his caresses, she would dissolve. She would say yes to anything. Bliss would overwhelm all of her commitment. "Please," she said. "No more tonight."

"But you have not said if you will marry me."

"I will think on it."

"Then you are not saying no?"

"I am not saying no," Edith assured him. But when happiness suffused Charles's face and he reached for her again, she backed into the corner of the carriage. "Nor am I saying yes." She steeled herself against his disappointment. "I am only saying I am most flattered and that I will consider your offer."

To Edith's relief, the coach turned off from the Bowery and pulled up in front of her home. The footman held the door, and Charles helped her disembark. He saw her to the front door and contented himself with kissing only her hand. Edith's heart was still beating a wild tattoo as she peeked out from behind the wine damask curtains of the front parlor and watched his carriage make a half circle and start back toward the Bowery.

Nor had her pulses slowed very much as she prepared for bed. There was so much to think about, so much to consider. Her emotions were a whirlpool. Sternly, she cautioned herself against drowning in them. Discipline was required. She must consider his proposal calmly and rationally.

Marriage meant surrendering her independence. Love was all very well, but there were some very serious grievances to be redressed in the world, and if she were a wife . . . well, it would leave very little time for participation in the struggle. Perhaps, after all, she told herself, denying the warmth and tingling of her flesh, I would be more content with spinsterhood. It is lonely, but it does permit independence, and that suits me well.

Still, Charles's touch . . . his lips on hers . . . the communication of flesh to flesh . . . Some of the suffragists, Edith knew, believed in what they called "free love." She had herself given lip service to the idea without ever really giving deep thought to what it would entail. Was "free love," then, a solution? Should she and Charles become lovers without benefit of clergy? Should that be the compromise between marriage and spinsterhood?

What was the answer? She tossed and turned. What should she be? Wife? Spinster? Mistress? Edith fell asleep, her lips parted slightly as if to receive one more kiss.

26

HER EYES WERE closed, her freckled face turned up to his, her red hair fanned out over strong naked shoulders. There was little delicate about Kathleen, to Fitz's way of thinking. She was a large, healthy girl with firm flesh and the Irish will to claim the satisfaction due her youth. A feast, this colleen with her clothes off; a feast for any man. Why then, Fitz asked himself, was his mind less than enthusiastic even as his passion rose unrestrained?

Patrice. The answer popped unwanted into his mind even as he kissed Kathleen. The thought of Patrice leashed his pleasure even as his fingers danced over the spattering of freckles to the risen nipple of Kathleen's large bare breast. Patrice was the reason his thoughts were dragging behind his passion.

She had turned from him. Doubted his word and faulted him for the betrayal of a friend with an adultery he'd never committed. And then she'd gone off to be with this very man. Fitz felt it in his bones, Jack's attraction for Patrice. She'd not hesitate to come between the very man and wife she'd been so concerned about Fitz coming between. Unfinished business it was, Fitz could tell, but it hurt all the same that Patrice could so quickly forget the feelings between them that night before the phone rang.

So here he was with Kathleen, their tongues dueling lightly, their breathing growing harsh with anticipation. He, too, could be attracted to another, and why not? But why was his mind deviling him with memories of a petite figure and chestnut hair, delicate bones, arched hips, and a fluttering of lashes?

"Ahh!" Kathleen moaned slightly as the tip of Fitz's tongue flicked her nipple.

"Lovely." Fitz took it between his lips and savored the warm female taste of it.

Kathleen had never made love with anyone but Matt before. It was strangely titillating to lie naked in the arms of a man for whom she had no really deep feeling. The absence of love was in itself a kind of aphrodisiac to Kathleen. She was attracted to Fitz, but there was nothing like the emotional oneness that existed between her and Matt when they made love. Oddly, that left her more free to participate as an individual rather than to merge herself with Fitz. It left her free to notice things about herself in the act of making love that she had never dwelt on before. This built a different sort of heat, a self-contained heat, perhaps, and she was thrilled by it even as she felt some slight twinges of guilt.

She had nothing to feel guilty about, she reminded herself. Matt had been spending more and more time up in Montreal. Kathleen knew he was seeing Wendy. She was sure he was going to bed with her. And so it was over between them. She was as free to be with other men as Matt was to be with Wendy. There was no reason to feel guilty. Except—and Kathleen did not admit this to herself—that a little guilt made lovemaking with Fitz even more exciting.

The initiative had been hers. Kathleen was never one to lie around feeling sorry for herself, and she frankly missed the sex Matt and she had regularly before the breakup. She thought about Fitz and what he'd said about not rejecting her the next time. She was ready. She'd contrived to catch him alone in the parlor earlier that evening, and she'd made her availability known without much coyness. Now they were in Fitz's room, in his bed, and their caresses were uninhibited.

Kathleen's hand slid down from his chest over the ridges of muscle to his groin. His chest was hairier than

213

Matt's, and he was brawnier, too. Matt was slim with long, ropelike muscles and high-boned, aristocratic features. Fitz had more flesh, and his muscles were rounded. In sex she had joined with Matt; with Fitz there was a slight, trembling fear that she might be overwhelmed.

She fondled his erect penis and his testicles and felt herself opening to his touch. His hands were not as gentle as Matt's had been their first time. His mouth closed over hers with a thrusting kiss as he explored her with his fingers.

Kathleen's long, powerful legs locked above his hips. She clutched his buttocks and looked up at him, green eyes sparkling with anticipation. He slid a hand under her warm, generous, squirming bottom and entered her.

Kathleen cried out with pleasure. They moved together then, exploring, savoring. Locked, they kissed and caressed, experimented and discovered. Their passion mounted slowly but deeply.

"Now is it, then?" Fitz asked finally.

"Oh, yes. Please. Please, now!"

Her head spinning, Kathleen clutched at him and was rewarded with the warm flooding deep inside her. Responding for a long time, she let herself go with the dizzying joy of it. Only when it was all over did she remember with a pain so sharp it made her wince that the man lying over her was not Matt Stockwell.

27

HER FIRST NIGHT on St. Martin, Patrice insisted to Peter that they stay at a Philipsburg hotel near the Dutch jail where Jack was being held. They visited it the next morning. The building looked like a relic from the back lot of Warner Brothers after they sold off their Hollywood studios. It was a 1930s black-and-white concept of a tropical island jail, dirty gray stucco, broken and rusting drainpipes, a sepia-tone corrugated roof that surely leaked, and bars just wide-enough apart for a man to get his head stuck in looking out.

Inside, there were a few offices with eight holding pens to the rear of them. The prison area was separated by a barred door that had been left swinging open. Only four of the cells were occupied—three by drunks or potheads sleeping it off, the fourth by a blond prostitute awaiting a transportation voucher to another island. Sex was easily available on St. Martin, but outside competition was frowned upon.

Jack Houston was not in the jail.

"I received a call from the office of the lieutenant governor," Captain Drees, his voice sad and cynical and fatalistic all at the same time, told Patrice and Peter once greetings were out of the way. "They had been contacted by a deputy of the island council, who was acting on instructions from the Netherlands Antillean government. You should understand that this government is a sort of buffer between the various island councils and the colonial office in The Hague in Holland. Usually the island councils formulate policy, and the colonial office says either yes or no to it. We Dutch interfere with the councils as little as possible. We are aware that the Caribbean is volatile and that the aim of all its peoples is to be free of colonial rule and self-sufficient."

"Excuse me." Peter was impatient. "What has this to do with Mr. Houston?"

"The colonial office bypassed the island councils and issued an instruction to the Netherlands Antillean government to produce Mr. Houston before a judge so that bail might be set. Believe me when I tell you that this was an unprecedented intrusion."

215

"Still, bail is a civilized procedure." Patrice smoothed the wrinkles of her linen dress carefully.

"Perhaps. Murder is not a crime we have very much experience with here in Sint Maarten. In any case, bail was set and quickly provided via a letter of credit which was immediately honored—and I am still amazed by this—by the Central Bank of the Netherlands Antilles."

"Why are you amazed?" Patrice asked.

"I am amazed because the Central Bank is not really a bank at all. It is a watchdog agency over all of the Dutch Windward Island banks similar to your United States Federal Reserve Board. Mr. Houston walked out of the court in a matter of moments. However," Captain Drees added, "my concern at the moment is with what has happened since then."

"And what is that?" Peter glanced at his watch. He thought the captain unnecessarily long-winded.

"Mr. Houston has returned to the villa of his wife in St. Martin."

"What difference does that make?" Patrice asked.

"Dutch Sint Maarten and French St. Martin are very much alike." The cloud darkened over Captain Drees's round face as he explained. "We have our lieutenant governor appointed by The Hague, our Netherlands Antillean government dominated by Curaçao, and our island council, which is elected locally. Similarly, French St. Martin is a territory of the Department of Guadeloupe. There are ninety-four such departments making up the French nation—"

"All very interesting," Peter interrupted, "but—"

"It is more than interesting. It is pertinent," Captain Drees assured Peter.

Peter yawned. Patrice frowned at him and signaled clearly for Captain Drees to continue.

He complied. "But I will get to the heart of the matter. On a local level, the Dutch and French police forces and judiciaries have always cooperated to reduce crime on the island. This despite the fact that there is fierce competition between us when it comes to banking, which has in turn opened us to the ravages of the Caribbean drug trade. But there has never been interference where local crime is concerned from Paris or The Hague." Captain Drees's gray eyes regarded them balefully. "Until now."

Outside the window the sun had burned away the morning breezes. The air shimmered, a thermal threat. Captain Drees stood and turned on the ceiling fan. "Extradition," he told them, "has never before been a problem."

"Extradition!" Peter snorted. "The whole damn island is only thirty-five square miles!"

"Exactly. Fourteen Dutch, twenty-one French. Therefore, it has always been understood that if we catch a fugitive sought by the French, we simply hand him over to them, and vice versa. We have never become bogged down in international legalisms. And so, when I heard that after his release Jack Houston had gone back to the French side, I thought nothing of it. We have not had any real conflict with the French police on this island since World War Two, when fourteen members of the Marigot constabulary marched into Philipsburg with guns drawn, hauled down the flag of the Dutch government-in-exile, and replaced it with the banner of Vichy France. In the end, of course, our flag prevailed, and they were all magically transformed into Free French Gaullists. But I digress."

"And how," Peter said under his breath.

"Peter!" Patrice admonished him. It was important that they placate the police captain.

Peter sighed, folded his arms, and scowled.

"We sent Mr. Houston a message asking him to come in for interrogation," Captain Drees continued. "We received back a formal letter from his attorney informing us that he would not willingly recross the border—the unguarded border, I might mention—to submit to our jurisdiction. The letter advised us that we should have to extradite him."

"I see." Actually Patrice was gratified that Jack was so well represented.

"My opposite number in Marigot tells me that he has received instructions via Guadeloupe from Paris not to interfere with Mr. Houston's right to refuse to waive extradition. It seems that there has been no extradition treaty between French St. Martin and Dutch Sint Maarten since the early days on the island when the Dutch kept slaves after the French had freed theirs. Many fled Dutch bondage and took refuge on the French side. The French refused to return these escaped slaves. The Dutch therefore refused to return criminal fugitives to the French. Our more recent cooperation has never been formalized by law. Now it seems informal cooperation has broken down. It is very awkward for me and for the French chief constable as well. I have been forced to ask Curaçao to refer the matter to The Hague to find out how the extradition treaty which does exist between France and Holland may apply. And that is where matters now stand."

"Please." Peter looked pointedly at his wristwatch.

"Bear with me, Mr. Stockwell. I am neither a stupid man nor a naive one. The situation is extraordinary. Why should power structures in Europe want to put this murderer beyond the reach of law? The answer is that the Stockwell family, your family, has exerted a great deal of diplomatic influence. There has been pressure on both The Hague and Paris via former United States Secretary of State Zelig Meyerling. Unofficial congressional contacts traceable to New York Congressman Stockwell have both Curaçao and Guadeloupe biting their nails over the possibility of curtailed tourism. This is not the sort of atmosphere in which justice may best be served."

"You're a civil servant, and you take orders." Peter shrugged callously. "If you have a problem, take it up with your superiors. Why tell us about it?"

"Would you rather," Captain Drees inquired softly, "that I tell the Philipsburg stringer for the Associated Press?"

"Don't threaten us!" Peter snarled.

"If Mr. Houston does not come in willingly for interrogation, our local newspaper will want to know why the case is not proceeding.'' Captain Drees spread his hands placatingly. ''The editor is also the Associated Press stringer I mentioned. He will demand that I explain in detail.''

''You must not like your job very much,'' Peter growled.

''This is a murder involving high society, and it has attracted wide attention. If I don't pursue the case vigorously, the local council will drive me out of office.'' Captain Drees shrugged. ''I might just as well be fired by Curaçao or The Hague for doing my duty as by the council for not doing it. I stand to lose either way, and so must use what weapons I have at hand, such as the AP stringer. Believe me, your interests will be best served by persuading Mr. Houston to come in for interrogation. Otherwise, I assure you, it will not be the name of Houston, but the name of Stockwell, which will make headlines.''

Peter glowered. Still, Patrice knew that the threat impressed him. The Stockwell name would always be his first priority. Patrice's first priority, however, was Jack's welfare. If saving him meant that the family would be dragged over the front pages, then so be it.

''We will do what we can,'' she assured Captain Drees, and then changed the subject. ''Has Carrie Tyler been located?'' she asked.

''No. We would like very much to interrogate her as well. We think she may shed much light on what happened. But Mejnfrow Tyler vanished the night of the killing, and we have not been able to find her. If she should contact you—''

''Of course,'' Patrice agreed quickly before she had to promise anything.

''We think she may be very important to the case. There are blanks that only Carrie Tyler can fill in,'' Captain Drees stressed.

''You won't go to the papers yet?'' Peter inquired as they stood up to leave. As he'd brooded on the captain's threat, his impatience had changed to concern. Peter had more reasons than Patrice suspected for not wanting the media to focus on the case.

"Not yet. But I would like to see Mr. Houston as soon as possible." Captain Drees, shrewd enough to read his advantage in Peter's face, was not about to relax the pressure. He escorted them down the hallway from his office to the outside door. "As soon as possible," he repeated as they stepped under the hammer stroke of the blazing sun.

An hour later Patrice and Peter were driving up the dirt road to the Houstons' villa on the cliff overlooking Baie Rouge. The atmosphere was more relaxed on the French side of the island, less populated, less bustling, than in Dutch Philipsburg, Patrice observed. Still, she was tense with the anticipation of seeing Jack again.

Peter's mind was weighed down with other concerns. There was always the danger that Victor Grieg might have died before adequately covering the trail of the money he had come to St. Martin to launder. And any transfers of money—bribes—Grieg had not completed would hold up the project. The wheels would not turn without the grease. Peter had to know who had and who had not been paid off so that he might make adjustments in his construction schedule. And since Helmut van Huyck was in St. Martin—although he knew not where—it was urgent that Peter confer with him about some new arrangement to launder the money.

It took Peter three days to make contact with Helmut van Huyck. During that time his anxiety was increased by confirmation from New York that the municipal tax abatements that had to be in place before the project could begin had not yet been granted. Grease had been denied the most important wheels of all. Peter leaned hard on the French manager of a Stockwell Enterprises tax shelter in Marigot, and when the squeeze was passed along to more vulnerable investment houses handling more dubious operations, van Huyck's St. Martin business address was finally provided.

Peter went there without calling first. He did not want to give van Huyck any opportunity to avoid the meeting. The address he had been given was for a building sandwiched between two tourist restaurants on the main street of Marigot. The office was on the second floor. Ostensibly it was occupied by an insurance broker. It was surprisingly modest, a small reception room with only one door on its whitewashed back wall. The receptionist did not recognize the name van Huyck.

Peter believed her. He took out a business card. "If you'll be good enough to show this to your employer, I think he'll agree to see me," he insisted.

She shrugged and took in the card. A moment later she emerged and nodded. Peter carefully took the card back from her long, slender fingers as she stood aside for him to enter the office. She closed the door behind him.

The jovial expression Peter recalled from their first meeting was missing from Helmut van Huyck's sleekly pink face. The eyes under the delicately arched silver brows were disapproving. "We were not to meet again, Mr. Stockwell. I thought I made that clear."

"Things have changed. Your man Grieg is dead. I am hanging by my fingertips. Also, this is St. Martin, not New York."

"St. Martin indeed! All the more reason not to take risks. St. Martin swarms with financial gossip. It is second only to Switzerland as a foreign depository for U.S. currency. There are currently six hundred thirty-two million American dollars on deposit with St. Martin banks, and perhaps ten times that amount in U.S. currency passed through St. Martin over the last year. All this is money which for one reason or another people want to hide. They come here rather than Switzerland because St. Martin wisely does not have numbered bank accounts. It's very difficult to trace money in St. Martin. People, however, are something else. When a Stockwell of Stockwell Enterprises comes here, his presence I assure you does not go

221

unnoticed. Many eyes—many—notice whom he contacts. Such information fetches a price from, for instance, certain banks, or real estate speculators, or even government agencies focused on corruption.''

Peter shrugged. "I had no alternative. I had to come. The tax abatements are being held up.''

"Well, of course they are, my dear Mr. Stockwell. What did you expect? Death does, after all, slow things down.''

"I'm concerned that certain payments may not have been made. I'd like to be reassured that Grieg left no loose ends. I want to be sure there is no money trail which might compromise Stockwell Enterprises.''

"I share your concern.'' Van Huyck examined the perfect half-moons of his manicured fingernails. "But alas, I cannot reassure you.''

"That wasn't your attitude back in New York,'' Peter reminded him.

"Surely rebuking me serves no purpose, Mr. Stockwell. Try to be philosophical. Life is risk.''

"What do you mean?'' Peter half rose from his chair. "Grieg must have kept records. They should indicate where the danger is. If we move quickly, we can plug up the holes.''

Van Huyck regarded him with a faint, humorless smile. "That is logical,'' he granted. "Grieg did keep records. If we had them, we could indeed, as you put it, 'plug up the holes.' But Victor's records are gone.''

"Gone? Gone where?''

"We're not sure where. Of more concern is the hands into which they might ultimately fall.''

"My God.'' The full weight of the danger pressed in on Peter. "If somebody decided to go public!''

"Exactly.''

"But who took them in the first place?''

"There was only one person who knew about them, probably knew where Victor kept them, and who would have had the opportunity to take them.'' The tongue poking out van Huyck's sleek cheek was like a dagger point-

222

ing an accusation. "I am referring of course to his companion and your relative."

"Carrie? But why would she—"

"I don't know why. I only know that we are quite convinced the documents are in Carrie Tyler's possession. She may or may not know their value. We can't be sure. Either way, from our viewpoint, they are a ticking time bomb."

"But where is she?" Peter blurted out.

"Where indeed?" Van Huyck was eyeing him with a certain shrewdness. "I was hoping you might shed some light on her whereabouts, Mr. Stockwell. After all, you are related."

"But I haven't a clue."

"Not yourself, perhaps. Still, sooner or later she will surely contact some member of your family. She'll need money to live. Help. Whatever. When that happens, you would do well to communicate with me."

"If she does know anything, whoever she gets in touch with in the family might not tell me," Peter protested.

"You will have to keep a sharp eye out, then, Mr. Stockwell. Believe me, our security—mine and yours—is in the young lady's hands."

"She could be back in New York with her cousin Max and on her way to the federal district attorney by now." Badly shaken, Peter leaped to the worst-case scenario.

"No. She hasn't left the island. Of that I am sure. She is still on St. Martin. You must help us find her, Mr. Stockwell." Van Huyck's gaze was momentarily penetrating. "Our fate lies in the hands of Carrie Tyler."

28

CARRIE'S IMMEDIATE PROBLEM wasn't money. She had enough for meals and for the dingy room she now occupied on the docks of the harbor behind Marigot's main street. Tourists didn't come to this area very much at night. They congregated instead around the yacht basin at the other end of town, where the bright lights reflected off the water. Carrie was living in an area for commercial shipping, and its few bars, shrouded in night fog, were patronized by seamen and working-class, budget-minded locals, black and white. Still, its very dinginess was comforting to her. She was running out of cocaine, and she knew that this was a neighborhood where she would be able to replenish her stock.

The white powder was all that stood between Carrie and the screaming meemies. Only cocaine could blot out the picture of Victor's murder. Without the drug, the scene was sharp, unlike the blur of the flight that had followed after she'd witnessed his murder. Panic-stricken, Carrie had driven the rented Mercedes sports coupe at top speed back to La Samanna. Locking herself in the suite, she'd tried to think. But even after showering, she had not been able to stop perspiring. It was the ongoing sweat of fear. Fear had been her constant companion since the night of Victor's murder. First flight and then furtiveness had become her way of life. Only cocaine made it bearable, and now she was running low.

The night of the murder she had thought of Junot. She'd remembered how afraid Victor had seemed of his pig-eyed associate the last time he'd mentioned him. And with cause. Carrie's own fear had brought bile to her throat. And then there was "the man," the one she'd never met, the one whose arrival had seemed to congeal Victor's apprehension. Helmut van Huyck: that was the name. Now she was the one in danger. What should she do? She couldn't stay at La Samanna. They would find her, and then . . .

Carrie had remembered the papers Victor had locked in the strongbox in the hotel safe. She had looked in his suitcase. The receipt and the strongbox key had still been there. After snorting a line to clear her head, Carrie had dressed and retrieved the contents of the strongbox and gone back out to the Mercedes she'd left in the hotel parking lot.

The cocaine calmed her. She devised a plan. After driving the Mercedes to Philipsburg and leaving it there, she took a cab back to the French side of the island. She got out across from one of the quieter entrances to the yacht basin at Marigot. Then she walked to the harbor at the other end of town and found a dingy hotel fronting the docks. She took a room—small, bare, ugly—and locked the door behind her. She went to bed immediately and fell into an exhausted sleep.

Carrie's head ached the next morning, but she forced herself to concentrate on the papers she'd taken from the strongbox. They might be the only thing that could insure her safety—perhaps the only thing that could keep her alive.

She read them over twice. Much of what she read, she didn't comprehend. Even so, she wasn't stupid, and she understood enough. In effect, the papers were a second set of books that Victor had been keeping. What it added up to was that Victor Grieg had been commingling bribe money he was laundering for Stockwell Enterprises with funds he was laundering for Colombian drug wholesalers and the various United States officials necessary to their operation.

Victor had commingled the monies for a reason. It was a way of muddying up any trail he might leave while skimming the funds. From what Carrie could ascertain, Victor had skimmed a considerable amount. He had opened secret accounts for himself and reinvested the money he stole. It ran into millions of dollars, which he had reinvested through both French and Dutch banks and investment companies on the island. The bottom line was that he had stolen millions of dollars from his organized crime employers.

No wonder he'd been afraid. He had known they would not hesitate to kill him if they found out. And they would not hesitate to kill Carrie because of what she knew—not just of the murder, but of their activities. Yet if she could figure out what to do with them, the papers she had taken from La Samanna might be a shield against their killing her. They gave her a hold over them—Helmut van Huyck, Junot, whatever other organized crime figures were involved. The papers revealed too much about their operation. They couldn't risk their coming to light. They would kill her for them. But they would not kill her if they thought that doing so would result in the papers coming to light.

Carrie put the papers in a strongbox in the Banque des Antilles Françaises in Marigot. She mailed the key to a pseudonym care of General Delivery, Marigot Post Office. She did not pick up the letter. Instead, she mailed another letter to her cousin Max Tyler in New York. This one contained a brief note and a sealed envelope. Max was only to open the envelope, the note said, if something happened to her. Otherwise he was simply to keep it in a safe place until she returned to New York and retrieved it. Inside the envelope were instructions to pick up the letter waiting at Marigot General Delivery, which in turn provided the key to the strongbox with the incriminating papers. Max was one of the few people she trusted to follow her wishes.

That had been how many days ago? Carrie wasn't sure. Her fear had not abated. When she had taken the steps she took, she had thought it would give her time to sort things out in her mind and decide on a course of action.

But the time had slipped by without things becoming any clearer. The problem was that she hadn't really worked out how to be sure that the people involved knew she had the papers before they took action.

The cocaine did not seem to be helping her think things through—if it ever had. Even so, the thought of running out of the drug before she located a source of resupply panicked Carrie. And this panic had pushed her into taking the chance of picking up the sailor in the bar the night before.

The sailor was off a tanker from Venezuela. He had a long, drooping Latin American mustache, a salt-spray-toughened skin, and a smile that dazzled with one gold tooth. His dark eyes had been drifting to Carrie since he'd come into the bar. His glance dipped into the bodice of her dress and climbed the rungs of the bar stool to where the cotton sundress sculpted her bottom.

Wary, Carrie ignored him until just after he returned from the men's room. That was when she noticed the telltale white specks clinging to the long, limp mustache. When he caught her glance he wiped them self-consciously away with a sheepish grin. Still, it decided Carrie. He'd been snorting in the john. The smile she shot back at him was inviting.

An hour later they were in her room. The seaman was berthed on his ship, where Carrie wasn't allowed, so this was their only choice. His hands on her were hot and eager. He had been at sea for a while, and a blond *norteamericana* was an exotic treat for him. His hands moved up under her skirt with the first kiss.

Carrie backed deftly away. "Couldn't we—you know—" she inhaled sharply—"first?"

His hands were tightly clasping her breasts from behind as she snorted first one line and then the other. She could feel him hard and throbbing slightly against her buttocks. With the relaxation of the cocaine, Carrie also felt a surge of desire.

She forced herself not to give in to it too quickly. Sex was all very well, but it had not been her prime objective in luring the Latino up there. She reached behind her and stroked him through the rough cloth of his jeans. "How much coke am I worth?" she asked him.

"¿Señorita?"

"How much is this worth?" Carrie turned around. She kissed him with her tongue. She felt the muscles of his buttocks tense and thrust forward under her fingers.

"You want more cocaine?"

"They call it the champagne of drugs." Carrie unzipped his pants and sank to her knees in front of him. "How much champagne am I worth?" she inquired softly.

"How much do you want?"

"How much have you got?" Carrie shrugged her shoulders so that the top of her sundress fell away from her exquisitely molded breasts. Taking the swollen tip of his penis between her lips, she touched it briefly with her tongue. She released it with a kiss. "How much will you give me?"

"An ounce." The seaman shrugged. "Pure. Uncut."

"That will do nicely." Carrie sat back on her haunches and removed her panties, allowing the sailor a glimpse of glistening blond pubic hair. She settled on her knees again. "Very nicely indeed." She took him deeply in her mouth.

The coke would get her through. It would assuage the fear. Really, she had to force herself not to be so anxious. Her predicament really wasn't as horrible as it sometimes seemed. She had Victor's records. She had protected herself with the letter Max Tyler was holding.

Good old Max. He could be depended upon. Was that because he was gay? Carrie wondered. Did being gay make you more honorable and empathetic because everybody else treated you so badly? What was it like to be gay—a man with a man, doing it to a man? Carrie wondered, heady with cocaine. What did it feel like for Max Tyler?

Her passion mounting, Carrie sucked.

* * *

Patrice lay stretched out on a chaise longue on the patio of the villa, her skin darkened and glistening with tanning oil in a bikini covering not very much more firm and sensual flesh than the large bow that adorned it at one hip. By the sound of the motor starting in the driveway around the side of the building, she knew that Peter was leaving for his business appointment in Marigot. The servants had been given the day off to participate in Whit Monday, a combination saint's day and feast day celebrated by the native islanders. Therefore, Patrice and Jack were now alone in the villa.

The sun was quite strong on the point of the cliff where they lay. There was no shade here as there was down below where the beach was. There was none of the coolness provided by the surf. But Patrice wasn't comfortable wearing a bikini on a nude beach, and she wasn't comfortable with the idea of not wearing one. Perhaps it was because she felt so keyed up sexually since coming to St. Martin and being with Jack every day. God, how she wanted him! The last thing she needed was any more stimulation.

A few minutes after Peter left, Jack, shirtless in shorts and sandals, appeared on the patio. He carried two tall, frosted glasses, one in each hand. "Iced lemonade," he announced, handing one to Patrice. "Would you like something in it?" he suggested. "Rum? Vodka?"

"No, thanks. It's too hot for alcohol." Patrice took the lemonade gratefully and drank off half the glass.

"That's what I thought, too."

"That hits the spot," she declared.

"Yeah." Jack stretched out on the chaise beside hers. They were silent for a moment, and then he spoke. "There's something I've been wanting to say. . . ."

His tone made Patrice's heart skip a beat. She said nothing. She waited for him to continue.

"It's how grateful I am to you for coming to St. Martin."

"Oh." The last thing Patrice wanted was gratitude.

"I mean it. If ever anybody ever really needed a friend, I did."

The very last thing she wanted was to be his friend. "Peter came, too," she reminded him.

"Well, not to be ungrateful, but I suspect that Peter has his own reasons for coming. Still, I suppose I shouldn't talk like that. He is a Stockwell, and it was the Stockwells got me out of the hoosegow and provided me with the lawyer who makes it possible for me to stay out."

"Are you going to go into Philipsburg for interrogation the way Captain Drees wants?" Patrice asked.

"Yes. But only after my lawyer strikes a deal with him. I'll sit still for interrogation, but there has to be official acknowledgment that this doesn't constitute a waiver of extradition. Also, there's to be no grabbing of me for jumping bail or anything like that."

"And will Captain Drees buy that?"

"My lawyer says his superiors will see that he does. I believe him. He wouldn't take any chances that the captain might carry out his threat and leak the story to the AP stringer. The attorney may be representing me, but he's paid for by the Stockwells. He wouldn't risk their being embarrassed."

"You don't sound like you're overwhelmed with gratitude to the family," Patrice observed.

"Oh, I'm grateful to some of them. Holly, Max, Zelig. You. I think you all acted because you care about me. But Peter and all the others are only concerned about the Stockwell name. And as for my wife—" Jack rolled his eyes. "Well, she couldn't even bother coming here to lend support." He propped himself up on his elbows and regarded Patrice warmly. "Unlike you," he added. "You did come, and you are lending support. And I know how much reason you have to hate me, Patrice."

"Blood under the bridge." She waved away the hurt and rejection she'd never really stopped feeling.

"It means a lot to me. You expect it from someone you love, someone you're married to." Once again Jack ex-

230

pressed his bitter feelings toward Buffy. "You don't expect it from someone you've treated as shabbily as I've treated you."

"Well"—Patrice stretched under the heat of the tropical sun—"I guess it's because I'm just a born doormat."

"Don't talk about yourself like that." Jack grasped her arm impulsively. "If I'd had any sense—"

"Sense never has much to do with love," Patrice responded softly. "We all of us go with our feelings." She was very much aware of his continuing touch, his grip on her arm.

"Your skin's on fire," Jack said. "Maybe you should get out of the sun."

"I guess I should." Patrice stood up.

Jack also got to his feet, and they faced each other for an instant in the small space between the two chaises with only the sensually shimmering thermal air dividing them. Patrice caught her breath sharply. Her breasts swelled with the inhalation, overflowing the skimpy bikini top. Her hand fluttered to her hip and grasped the bow there like a lifeline.

"Patrice—" Jack said.

She swayed toward him. His chest was hard and burning with the fire of the sun. She turned her face up and half closed her eyes. Her lips parted.

"Are you sure, Patrice?" he asked, his voice husky with his own desire. "I've never been very good for you. It's never turned out well. Are you sure?"

"I'm sure." She pressed into him, clinging urgently, and brought his mouth down to hers. This time it would be different. This time she would vanquish Buffy. She would fight for Jack, and she would win.

She could feel the heat of his flesh. Lovemaking had always been good between them. The desire of their bodies, each for the other, had always been shameless. Yes. This time she would make her claim and not let go. "I'm sure," Patrice repeated when the kiss was over. "I'm very sure."

Jack picked her up. He carried her inside, upstairs to

the cool bedroom. He removed the bikini and quickly stripped himself naked. He made love to Patrice just the way she had envisioned it when she'd decided to come to St. Martin. Yes, this time she would not let Jack Houston go.

And it was only for the fraction of an instant, the flicker of an eyelash, that Patrice's mind skipped from the ecstasy she was experiencing to suddenly envision the face of Fitz Connely, the man to whom she had not made love.

BOOK FOUR

29

T HE CHILL WINDS of March persisted through midmonth at Riverview. Fitz Connely raised his dark, brooding face to them like the prow of a ship challenging the storm. He pitted himself against their force and bite, traipsing the woodlands of the estate with the fervor of one for whom even the indoors of a mansion could be a prison. He was burning off the energy stoked by the fire in his blood. During the weeks since Patrice had left for St. Martin, ambivalence increasingly ruled his flesh. He was a young man possessed by a passion that was unattainable. Fitz tramped the wilds of Riverview in a truculence of self-denial.

Amid bramble and oak, high reeds and bare, budding branches, slippery moss and peepings of grass, face pricked by wind and stark green pine needles, Fitz pondered the amorous opportunities of Riverview. Living in the same house with Buffy, their bedrooms on the same floor, he found her frequent innuendos like the breath of leprechauns steaming the air with sensual suggestion. Always it seemed, in his presence, there was material slipping away from a thigh, casual unbuttonings revealing the full curve of a breast. Her glance reduced him to a sex object fit only for satisfaction and disposal. Fitz turned away from Buffy with no regrets, ego triumphing easily over appetite. With Kathleen O'Lunney, however, the situation was different.

They already had made love. It had been enjoyable, and there was no cause to deny it. But without really analyzing his reluctance, Fitz went out of his way to avoid an encore. Indeed, he was so busy avoiding Kathleen that he did not really notice she wasn't really pursuing him.

In this dourest of moods, Fitz forced himself to focus on other concerns. If circumstance had made him a man of means, then he must see to the control of what was his. Observation had taught him that Halsey De Vilbiss could be trusted just far enough to manage the affairs of his inheritance for maximum profit. What Halsey could not be trusted to do was insure that the money was put to uses of which Fitz approved and not to uses that offended him. For this—and particularly in Patrice's absence—Fitz had to rely on himself.

In particular, he was concerned about the East Side waterfront development project in which Peter had involved Stockwell Enterprises. He was still too new to his wealth to look with equanimity upon the billion-dollar profit that was projected. Didn't the Stockwells already have a billion dollars—and then some? What was the purpose of such monetary overkill? Could another billion have any effect at all on the family of which Fitz was now a part? That question aside, Fitz was sure the project would adversely affect a lot of other people in the city of New York.

Some of them would be rendered homeless. With visions of his own homelessness fresh in his mind, with memories of the city shelters as meat grinders and human beings the meat, Fitz could not help but be concerned. He was not naive. Wealth could be quickly dissipated by sentimental Irish philanthropy, but he had been thrust into the role of the tycoon, and he was prepared to be hard-headed. He would not, however, be hard-hearted.

Peter Stockwell was cutting corners. That was obvious. He was doing what had to be done to get the project off the ground. All the board members—even those who didn't like him—seemed to feel he was just the man for the job. Hardheaded with the know-how for hardball, that was Peter. The board's attitude, however, smacked of something else to Fitz. It was the age-old practice of the powerful purposely cutting off knowledge of the more heinous deeds undertaken in their interest. It was an attitude anticipating a day that hopefully would never come. But if it ever did, the question would be, ''What did the board know, and when did it know it?'' And in all calculated innocence, they would be able to answer candidly that they knew nothing. They would not have to explain that their ignorance was the traditional ''don't look'' policy of the powerful.

As yet, Fitz's suspicions were vague. He didn't know enough about how things worked to comprehend the doing of the dirty. Real estate development on the giant scale was new to him. Nevertheless, Fitz thought about it. At the board meetings the business at hand seemed to involve only the moving around of large amounts of money. But the project had to involve something else, didn't it? It had to involve building. It had to involve construction.

Building . . . construction . . . And didn't that mean there had to be a contractor, then? Yes, a contractor and a lot of subcontractors. It was natural, then, that Fitz should think of Paddy Corcoran.

When Fitz had come out of federal prison, one jump ahead of the immigration authorities, he'd been forced to go underground. He'd been passed along from one safe house to another, more of a handicap to the movement than an asset, taking up lorry space needed for the arms they were smuggling to the IRA. Finally he'd ended up in New York with no prospect of being anything other than the burden he'd become.

235

"I'll not be an ongoing hindrance," Fitz had declared. "I'll be on my way."

Relieved as they'd been to see the back of him, comradeship and conscience had decreed that they give him what help they could. It wasn't much, but it was something. They had given him the name of a hiring boss on a construction gang who'd match him up with a nonexistent identity on a union list and put him to work as an unskilled laborer. The name of the firm had been Corcoran Construction, Inc.

Paddy Corcoran was the owner-boss. Needless to say, he and Fitz—whose job involved preparing building foundations but was really no more than being a ditch digger—did not move in the same circles. Indeed, Fitz had no expectation of ever meeting the big boss in person. He was flabbergasted the day the foreman called him over, gave him Paddy Corcoran's home address in the fancy town of Hewlett Bay Park on Long Island, and told him to be there at nine-thirty promptly that evening.

Paddy Corcoran, himself a wheel in the New York support system for the IRA, had received a tip that the Immigration Department was planning a sweep of the job site. "Some bloody informer"—in Paddy Corcoran's words—"had done a bit of whistle-blowing." There were six illegals working there, "good movement lads all," and much as he hated to, for their own sake Paddy Corcoran now had to fire them. He told Fitz not to show up for work the next morning. He gave him his pay and sweetened it with an extra hundred "for emergencies—in case the price of beer goes up, or the like" and sent him on his way. "Should things get really desperate, you can call me here, and I'll try to help."

Those had been his last words to Fitz. Things had indeed gotten desperate, but he'd never called Paddy Corcoran. The goodness of a good man is no reason to be leaning on him so hard he'll have cause to regret it. Such was the philosophy Fitz's father had passed on to him. And bad as things had gotten, Fitz had lived up to it.

But things weren't bad now. They were good. Fitz's

immigration problems had been paved over through the influence of the Stockwells and Zelig Meyerling. There would be no risk involved for Paddy Corcoran if Fitz called on him for help now. All Fitz wanted was information concerning the construction trade.

The contractor agreed to meet him in a Yorkville bar the following week. It was only after he hung up that it occurred to Fitz they'd made the date for St. Patrick's Day.

On the appointed day, Fitz took himself by train into New York. He left early in order to view the festivities. Because he'd mostly been on the run since coming to New York, he'd never seen the city's famous St. Patrick's Day parade before.

Every crowded car of the Hudson River Valley express had been commandeered by youth. Boys in their teens and giggling girls had drained their towns of beer before embarking to join the Irish conquest of the city. The gurgling from cans and bottles overwhelmed the click-clack of the train wheels on the rails.

"Up the Irish!" A spindly young lad with choirboy freckles thrust a bottle at Fitz.

"Thank you, no. I've given it up."

The boy stared at him suspiciously. The brogue was right; the sentiment was not.

"Are you Orange, then?" The green-uniformed majorette with the boy, fourteen-year-old thighs ajiggle with baby fat, was hostile.

"Are you not still young enough to be spanked for disrespect to your elders?" Fitz glowered.

"Perhaps he's an ulcer," another young girl with saucer-blue eyes suggested. "My uncle Brian suffered something fierce with an ulcer until he went off the sauce."

"You're a smart lass," Fitz told her gravely.

After that they let him alone. When the train arrived at Grand Central, Fitz saw that they were only the tip of the green iceberg. Early as it was, and the parade not yet started, Irish youth for a hundred miles around were already proclaiming their ethnic with the slosh of beer, the slug of the hard stuff, and the expulsion of emerald-green bile onto Manhattan pavements.

"Top o' the mornin'!" A wiry man with an olive complexion and limpid Spanish eyes tried to sell Fitz a shamrock.

Fitz thanked him kindly and kept going. He made his way up Forty-second Street to Fifth Avenue to a reviewing stand set up between the stone lions in front of the library. The crowd was particularly dense in that area. Fitz pushed farther up Fifth Avenue. The people were only slightly less jammed together toward uptown. At Fiftieth Street, in front of St. Patrick's Cathedral, it became extremely difficult to move. Fitz cut back east to Madison, walked uptown to Fifty-fifth, and then went back to Fifth. There he managed to wedge himself into a space behind one of the barricades. He stayed there until the parade, led by the Hibernian grand marshal, the Italian governor, and the Jewish mayor, started moving past him.

He remained through the entire march. It bore no resemblance to any of the celebrations of the good saint's day that he'd witnessed as a boy in Ireland. Indeed, Fitz was quite overwhelmed by the parade and not quite sure if he approved.

After the onlookers dispersed, Fitz ambled uptown, zigzagging east as he went. On Eighty-sixth Street between First and Second avenues, he found the Irish pub where he was to meet Paddy Corcoran. It was jammed, the ebullient crowd singing rebel songs and shouting out anti-British slogans. It reminded Fitz of places in Chicago he had frequented with his father before his death. He felt right at home.

Taking his time, he made his way to the bar. He ordered a large Coke. The bartender, a small, wizened man, stared briefly at Fitz with disbelief. Then he shrugged and served him the soft drink.

"Plumbing on the fritz is it?" Paddy Corcoran materialized out of the crowd. He was a large man with a face like a side of raw beef. He regarded Fitz sympathetically.

"Ulcer." Fitz stayed with Uncle Brian's ailment. If a story does the trick, why change it?

"Drown it," was the florid, beer-barrel-chested Corcoran's advice.

"Life threatening." Fitz smiled and sipped his Coke.

"Well now, you have to die of something, don't you? Sure and it might as well be something you enjoy."

"But isn't the pain too fierce for the enjoyment?"

"You're in a bad way, then, lad." The red-faced Corcoran drained his beer stein. "Let me stand you a"—he winced—"Coke, is it?—in honor of St. Paddy." The arm bringing the fist down onto the bar for service was a shillelagh of hard muscle and bone.

"Thank you."

Jammed into the bar face to face, they continued talking. Fitz bought the next round over Paddy Corcoran's protest. With the one after that, Paddy inquired in a deep, rumbling voice what line of work Fitz was in these days.

Now, there was a question. Fitz hesitated. Just what was his line of work? "Being rich," he answered finally. "That's my line of work these days. Being rich."

"Ah, now, and haven't I always wished I'd gone into that line myself?" answered Paddy Corcoran without blinking an eye. He washed down his tonsils with the contents of a stein the size of a growler.

Fitz grinned and bought him another beer. "And how's your construction business going, Mr. Corcoran?" he inquired.

"Well, now, I've done all right contracting as far as the money goes. It's the wear and tear on my immortal soul's the problem."

"Sure and doesn't temptation abrade the best of men, Mr. Corcoran?"

"Perhaps, lad. Perhaps. I'm not softheaded, nor unfond of the almighty dollar, mind, but sometimes I wonder. I really do. All I ever wanted was to build decent housing for people to live in and make a fair profit. But

239

you see, there's no way you can do that in the city of New York today. The real estate boys won't let you. And believe me, it's the speculators call the shots. They tell you what to build, and worse, they tell you how. You see, it's them that owns the land. If I could lay my hands on a decent-sized chunk, I'd put up high rises with sensible apartments people could afford the rent on, not condos for millionaires. But the land is never to be had, and so I've put away my dreams of building decent, affordable housing along with the tooth fairy.''

Fitz was more impressed by Paddy Corcoran's idealism than his disillusionment. Obviously Corcoran was a good man who wanted to do good things, and if Fitz's new wealth really did give him power—he filed this way in the back of his mind—then someday he would help Paddy Corcoran attain his objectives. ''Well, we all of us have to live in the real world, sir,'' was all, however, that he put into words now.

''And isn't that the truth, lad.'' Paddy Corcoran shrugged. ''Building is real enough all right. High steel. Pouring concrete. Electrical wiring. Plumbing. The works. I take on the main job and farm out bits and pieces of it to reliable subcontractors. That's how it's supposed to work, anyway.''

''Supposed to?'' Fitz repeated when Corcoran didn't continue.

''Oh, yes. You see, lad, that's not how the ball game is really played. If you want the contract these days, you sell out your dependable subs and take on who you're told to take on.''

''And that's more wear and tear on your immortal soul.'' Fitz thought about it a minute and then came to the point. ''Do you know anything about the big new development project slated for the East Side on the river?'' he asked.

''Do I know about it, now? Well, of course I do, lad. Not a major contractor in the city of New York doesn't want a piece of that one. Stockwell money behind it, you know, and that means power, and that means it will slide right through the red tape like a green-dollar-greased pig. Oh, I put in my bid early on that one, I did.''

''And what happened?''

''What always happens.'' Paddy Corcoran shrugged. ''Play along or don't play, Paddy, they tell me. Fall into line, don't you know, or fall through the bottom and the big one will go to another. Well, I'm not proud. I said I would. I told them I'd cut all their corners, but that wasn't enough. It was the beating human heart they'd have me cut as well. No John McCafferty for concrete with his fair price and honest measure. Instead, Paddy, they tell me, you'll be using Murphy Brothers with water in the brick and bumper jacks under the prices. Forget Petrocelli for plumbing and take Dawson with leaks in the pipes and sand in the solder. You'll be buying the lumber from Mendoza and double the price for the knotholes. All systems go, and quality control down the drain and the crooks all lined up. That's the big East Side job, lad. Vigorish skimmed from the top all the way. That's how the tallest buildings get built, you know. Taking the money from the top down.'' Paddy Corcoran chugalugged his beer, wiped the foam mustache from his wide mouth, and shook the bar with his fist's demand for another. ''I'm no Jesuit, lad, but in the end I had to turn my back on the big one. Not that they'll have any trouble finding other contractors to do the shoddy.''

''Who is the 'they,' Mr. Corcoran? Could you give me a hint?''

''Why, the powers that be, lad. The devil has many faces, don't you know. Even so, you never clearly see a one of them. It's the politicians, and the Wall Street boys, and the union bosses, and the mob. All of them, to be sure. Just who is calling the shots? you ask yourself while the dark night gooses the sun from its hiding place. But you never know. You get the message, but you never really know.''

''Might you be more specific, Mr. Corcoran?''

'' 'Paddy,' lad. Never 'Mr. Corcoran' after the third beer. 'Who?' you want to know. Well, as concerns the likes of me, nobody important, you may be sure. Messenger boys. It's very complicated, you see, and few involved are their own master. It's Stockwell money that's invested and the Stockwells who'll be reaping the profits, but you may be sure they'll not dirty their hands when it comes down to my level. All the dirty work will be handled for them.''

"By whom?'' Fitz persisted. "I don't just mean the construction. I mean, who handles the building code waivers and the matching funds and the like? Who greases the governmental skids for them?''

"The governmental skids is it? Well, now you're into mob talk, you know. Nothing moves on a construction project in the city of New York—not a brick put on a brick, not a hod carrier hired, not an on-site inspection form stamped—without a nod from the mob. Fact, lad. And doesn't it start at the beginning? It starts with government approval, the paperwork, moving the papers, shuffling them, hacking through the red tape. None of that happens without the mob tells the politicians and the civil servants it's all right for it to happen. The biggest mob operation in the city of New York isn't narcotics, laddie. It's real estate. Even the mighty Stockwells have to go to 'the man' tophat in hand.''

"I can guess that much, Paddy,'' Fitz told him. "What I want to know is, who is 'the man'?''

"You're not talking about down on my level now. You're looking higher. Much higher. Is that right?'' Paddy's voice was low in his stomach now, not to be overheard.

"Yes.''

"Then the name you want to know is Helmut van Huyck.'' Paddy Corcoran was too large a man to whisper. It came out hollow.

"He's the go-between for Stockwell Enterprises with the pols?'' Fitz asked carefully. "This van Huyck spreads the bribes around?''

"It's not that simple, lad. No dollar passes through van Huyck's hands, I'm sure. All the necessary vigorish

242

gets distributed somewhere abroad. The Caribbean, I think. This van Huyck has a hotshot accountant name of Grieg—"

"Grieg?" Fitz stared sharply at Paddy Corcoran. "Victor Grieg?"

"That's the fellow. Do you know him?"

"No. I never met him. All I know about him is he's dead."

"Well, small loss to humanity from what I've heard." Paddy Corcoran's generous nose sniffed disdainfully.

"Tell me about them," Fitz requested. "Tell me about this Helmut van Huyck and how he might fit in with the Stockwell project. Tell me about this Victor Grieg."

Paddy Corcoran told Fitz all he knew.

30

"HIGHLY IRREGULAR!" DAVID Lewis glared at Fitz Connely. The portraits of the various Stockwell ancestors on the oak-paneled walls of the boardroom lent weight to his disapproval. "No official standing!" His scowl circled the oval table. "We are not a quorum."

"Isn't there a majority present?" Fitz disagreed mildly.

"There is not!" David Lewis looked from Fitz to Max Tyler to Buffy and back to Fitz again. "A majority would be four members of the board as it is constituted." He spaced out the last four words syllable by syllable. "As it is constituted," he repeated in exactly the same fashion. "That is myself, Mrs. Houston, Peter Stockwell, Patrice O'Keefe, Mr. Tyler, and Mr. De Vilbiss. You are not a member of this board, Mr. Connely. You have never taken steps to replace Mr. De Vilbiss. Since he is in California and Peter and Patrice are in the Caribbean, there are only three official members of the board present. They are Mrs. Houston, Mr. Tyler, and myself. That is not a quorum."

"I do think, David, that you've made your point." Buffy stifled a yawn. "The question is, if we aren't the Stockwell board, then why are we gathered here?"

"Because Mr. Connely insisted. And when he called me, I was under the impression that Mr. De Vilbiss would be here with him for the conduct of what Mr. Connely characterized as 'very important board business.' Evidently I was misled."

"It was only after I called you that I learned Mr. De Vilbiss was in California on business. I'd no desire to mislead you. I only thought it a matter of some urgency for us to talk about what I've learned."

Max leaned forward. "And what have you learned?"

"It has to do with the East Side development project in which Stockwell Enterprises has involved itself."

For the first time David Lewis looked more interested than annoyed. "What about it?" he asked cautiously.

"Ah, well now, it's that Victor Grieg is involved in it," Fitz told him.

Buffy looked surprised, and Max's expression gave way to concern. "Victor Grieg?" The name did not quickly find its place in David Lewis's memory.

"The man they say my husband killed." Buffy enlightened him. Her hand shook as she lit a cigarette.

"The same man that Carrie went to St. Martin with," Max added.

"I don't understand." Reluctantly, David Lewis allowed himself to be drawn into the topic. "What has Victor Grieg to do with our project?"

"I am sure you will remember the two point two million dollars the board authorized Peter to spend for what he called 'R and D for all levels of government,' " Fitz replied. "We all do remember that, now, don't we?"

"We remember," Max Tyler assured Fitz. "But what does it have to do with Victor Grieg?"

"The money, it seems, was for the use of a gent name

244

of Helmut van Huyck in exchange for his services in securing cooperation from various functionaries."

"I don't think we have to hear this." David Lewis sensed peril. As senior member of the Stockwell board by many years, he knew two things well: some knowledge is power; some knowledge means danger.

"Oh, come on, David. In our heart of hearts, we all knew Peter didn't want the two million to buy bubble gum. Even if we don't want to know, we can't help being aware of how real estate development works in New York." There was rarely a spade that Buffy hesitated to call by its given name. "What about this Helmut van Huyck?" she asked Fitz.

"He's connected to the mob."

"Now I'm sure we shouldn't hear this." David Lewis grimaced as if he'd just sunk his teeth into a sour lemon.

"Actually," Fitz corrected himself, "Mr. van Huyck is very high up in the mob."

"I still don't see—"

"I'm beginning to." Buffy cut Max off. "Go on, Fitz."

"Victor Grieg was working for Helmut van Huyck." Fitz spelled it out. "What you might call a sort of money expert."

"You mean a financial adviser." It pained David Lewis when people deviated from accepted business designations.

"Well now, I don't actually think that is what I mean." Fitz stuck by his choice of words. "Unless 'financial adviser' is what you might call the party that launders money." Before David Lewis could interrupt him again, he went on to explain that the money Peter had passed on to Helmut van Huyck to insure local and federal government and union cooperation had actually been handled by Victor Grieg. "Took it to St. Martin, he did," Fitz summed up, "washed it clean, and saw that it found its way into the pertinent dummy bank accounts."

Unhappily, David Lewis pondered what he was hearing. "And this Victor Grieg is the man Jack killed."

"So they say. Still, we don't know that for sure, now,

245

do we? Mixed up with the mob as the unfortunate victim was. . . ."

"So that's why Peter was so eager to get to St. Martin," Max realized.

"You didn't think it was because he's so fond of Jack, darling, did you?" Buffy asked sarcastically.

"Nope," Max replied. "I never did think that. But I never figured anything like this, either. My God, think of what Peter may have gotten us into! Suppose the Stockwell money hasn't been laundered. Suppose the fingerprints of bribery are still on it."

"We have no real proof that Peter actually bribed anybody," David Lewis protested.

"Ah, well now, not directly, perhaps . . . but many a felon has found himself convicted on the bad appearance of things," Fitz observed. "And the appearance is that the untimely death of Victor Grieg is of concern to Peter and potential embarrassment to Stockwell Enterprises."

"Why are we mincing words like this?" Buffy was impatient. "I've been going over various Stockwell enterprises during the last few weeks—including the East River project—and in light of what Fitz has just told us, there's plenty of evidence of what Peter was up to. He went to this mobster van Huyck to get political cooperation. The money went to Victor Grieg. When Grieg was killed, Peter panicked. He wasn't concerned about Jack. He just had to get to St. Martin to make sure Grieg hadn't left any evidence of the mob tie-in with Stockwell Enterprises. That's his main concern now. And if it serves his purpose to throw Jack to the wolves, he'll do that, too."

"The thought had crossed my mind," Fitz agreed softly.

"Jack Houston is charged with murder!" David Lewis reminded them. "There must be good and sufficient evidence for the charge to have been brought. Peter isn't responsible for that."

"No." Buffy shrugged. "But I wouldn't put it past Peter to suppress evidence that might mitigate Jack's situation if it meant safeguarding his own interests."

"An unsavory business." David Lewis shook his head unhappily.

"And isn't that a fact, sir." Fitz was conciliatory. "But shouldn't the board be taking steps to extricate Stockwell Enterprises from the East Side project before we're in so deep we bury ourselves?"

"I would not dream of taking so precipitate a step without discussion by the full board."

"But there's no time for that."

"We have to protect ourselves, David," Buffy told him.

Although there was no love lost between David Lewis and Buffy, a grudging respect had grown up between them during the time they'd served together on the board. Her opinion carried weight. David Lewis looked from her to Fitz and then to Max Tyler. "What do you have to say about all this, Max?" he asked.

"We have to get out while we can." With a sigh, Max looked away from Fitz and addressed David Lewis. "It's no longer a question of whether or not the project's a good investment. Now it's a matter of protecting our ass."

"And Peter?" inquired David Lewis.

"One of us will have to fly to St. Martin immediately and let him know that we know what he's up to and that the board is holding him responsible for his actions from here on out," Max replied. "Including how they might affect Jack's case."

"I'd gladly go and stand by Jack," Fitz volunteered.

"You can't." There was a grudging but genuine concern in Max's voice. "Zelig may have gotten Immigration off your back, but you're still an illegal alien. If you went there, you might not be able to get back in the country."

"Well, I can't go," David Lewis declared. "I'm up to my ears putting together the Silicon Valley package for the Japanese."

"I'm busy, too," Max reflected. "Still, if there's no one else—"

"Never mind, Max." Buffy took them all by surprise. "I'll go."

"Will you, now?" Fitz smiled at her approvingly.

"Yes. Someone has to put the leash back on Peter. And there is the effect of all this on Jack. Well, don't look so surprised, you three. The son of a bitch *is* my husband."

A bit late with that, Fitz reflected. But all the same, to be fair, it surely did seem that Buffy was finally remembering her marital obligations.

31

TWO DAYS LATER Buffy was back in St. Martin. She had thought about calling ahead and decided against it. There was no point in telegraphing the punch to Peter. She took a cab from the Queen Juliana Airport to her villa and let herself in unannounced.

The sun over St. Martin was a topaz fireball in a melting cerulean sky. It had scattered tourists and locals alike from its path, sending them scurrying either toward the haven of air-conditioning or to the beaches, where, in the absence of any breeze, there was at least the relief of the surf. Buffy's servants, her husband, and Patrice had all taken refuge at Baie Rouge. Peter, however, was going over some papers in the living room of the villa, his stocky frame shirtless in rugby shorts, the cooling system straining at the maximum.

"What are you doing here?" was the greeting he blurted out to Buffy.

"It's my villa. Remember?"

"So it is." Peter shrugged. He really had forgotten that the place belonged to Buffy.

"Is everybody at the beach?" Buffy asked.

"Everybody but me," Peter confirmed.

"Good." Buffy sat down in the chill path of the air

conditioner. "I'm glad we have a chance to speak alone." Bluntly she told Peter that his machinations with the East Side project and his real reason for coming to St. Martin had surfaced.

"So you know." Peter wasn't at all fazed. "Well, so what? I didn't do anything that every other New York developer doesn't do. And you know damn well that when the profits began rolling in nobody on the board would have raised any questions about the ethics involved in setting things up."

"Maybe." Buffy blew a cloud of smoke and waved her cigarette holder through it for emphasis. "But right now questions have been raised. In short, Peter, I'm here for damage assessment. Both current and potential. But before you fill me in on that, there's something else I want to ask you. Does Jack know about your involvement with Victor Grieg?"

"No."

"You didn't think he had a right to know? That you had a duty to tell him?"

"It wouldn't have altered his situation."

"He's accused of murdering Victor Grieg, for God's sake!"

"More than that," Peter pointed out. "He doesn't deny it."

"Nevertheless, you should have informed him about your connection to Grieg. You shouldn't have let him believe you were here out of consideration for him."

"I don't think his mind is on why I'm here," Peter told Buffy insinuatingly.

"What's that supposed to mean?"

"I didn't come here alone."

Buffy thought that over. Patrice! Of course! But then she had only herself to blame. She'd given Patrice carte blanche before the little bitch left Riverview. With an effort, she hid her fury. "You really do have a nasty mind, Peter," she told him.

Peter smiled and made no reply. He knew when he'd drawn blood.

"Now suppose you bring me up to date on the situation," Buffy suggested. "Just what have you been up to since you came here?"

The board knew about van Huyck, so Peter saw no reason to hide his meeting with him in Marigot. What it added up to, he told Buffy, was that nobody knew how deep the trouble was because certain key documents belonging to Victor Grieg had been missing since his murder. "Van Huyck is convinced Carrie has them," he told her. "If he's right, then just how badly Stockwell Enterprises gets hurt by all this is in her hands."

"Carrie Tyler." Buffy was scornful. "*Cherchez la femme.*"

"Joke all you want, but finding Carrie has to be our number-one priority."

"*Your* number-one priority," Buffy couldn't resist telling Peter. "No matter what comes out, Stockwell Enterprises will survive. But I'm not so sure about you, Peter."

"Touché." Peter recognized that he was being paid back for his innuendo before. Buffy's putting the obvious into words made it no worse.

Buffy stood up. "I'm going for a swim," she told him. "I'll see you later, Peter."

She went up to her room and changed quickly into shorts and a halter. When she'd passed the entrance to Baie Rouge on her way up before, she'd noticed that the makeshift parking area was jammed. There was no point in taking a roadster. She'd probably not be able to park any closer to the secluded woodland entrance to the beach than her own driveway anyway. Buffy decided to walk the three-quarters of a mile down the cliffside to Baie Rouge.

When she emerged from the hidden woodland path onto the beach, she was covered with perspiration. She walked a little up the golden strand and bought a bottle of beer from the naked St. Martin couple ensconced in a lightly shaded niche of cedar and nameless bramble. She chatted with them as she drank it, mildly titillated by the woman's gleaming mahogany flesh and the younger man's long, arched penis. They knew her from before, and now they made jokes about her returning from New York just in time for the late March heat wave. Too hot, they assured her with wide, teasing smiles, even to make love.

Buffy was about to learn that they were wrong.

Not, however, about the heat, which was indeed relentless. Finishing her beer, she glanced up and down the shore. The ninety-degree-plus temperature had brought more people to Baie Rouge than usual, yet it was far from crowded, and the sunbathers were spaced apart with plenty of room for privacy. Scanning the scene as Buffy did now, she could easily see that just about all of them were taking advantage of the "clothes optional" policy that prevailed at Baie Rouge.

Laughing to herself, Buffy realized she must be very conspicuous in her shorts and halter. Taking them off now, she left them with the couple selling beer. Naked, Junoesque, she strolled to the shoreline and plunged into the surf.

It was delicious. Buffy swam for fifteen minutes. When she emerged, she was cool and refreshed. She strolled up the beach, a woman with a body that was perhaps no longer young but nevertheless superbly youthful. Her raven hair was a shining mantle splayed over her shoulders; droplets traced the voluptuous curves of her full breasts and ample hips and proud derriere; there was a small smile on her full lips. It was an acknowledgment of the appreciative glances of the men observing her as she moved from dune to valley to dune up the shoreline toward the least populated area of Baie Rouge.

Earlier that day Jack Houston and Patrice O'Keefe had walked far up the beach to find a small crater ringed by high dunes where they might sunbathe in private. Relatively new to the customs of Baie Rouge, Patrice was still somewhat skittish about displaying herself naked. They had come early and walked a fair distance. Settling on this

251

spot, she had relaxed, sure that they were secluded from other eyes even when they walked to the shoreline to swim.

They lay side by side on a beach blanket, face up, their limbs spread wide to the shimmering azure sky. Their bodies glistened with suntan lotion, Patrice's flesh deeply tanned under her auburn hair, Jack's bronzed. They had swum and dozed, lunched and swum again. Now, lazily erotic in the heat from the sun, they changed positions frequently and struck up a casual conversation to divert themselves.

"This could be heaven." Patrice sighed.

"It is heaven," Jack corrected her.

"It would be if—well, you know—if the whole damn mess wasn't hanging over us." Patrice bent one leg at the knee and angled it to catch the sun rays on her inner thigh more evenly.

"I know." Jack was reflective. "I keep asking myself, How did I get into this fix?"

"I don't understand that either."

"It all seemed to happen like one of those old-time silent movies where everything is speeded up beyond reality." Jack turned over on his stomach and rested his chin on his elbows the better to see Patrice's face as they talked. "I keep running the film over and over in my head, trying to slow it down so I can figure out how it happened, but it's no use."

Lord, he has a beautiful bottom! It wasn't the first time Patrice had noticed it. It might have been sculpted by Ghiberti working in bronze. Patrice's fingertips tingled with tactile memory. She straightened the leg she had bent, stretched it out, and then bent the other at the knee.

"It was an accident." Patrice tried to reassure Jack. "It was a fight. You were defending yourself. It got out of hand. You didn't mean to kill him. It was self-defense."

"That's what I keep telling myself." Jack lowered his face in his hands and rested his forehead on Patrice's bare thigh. His breath tickled her flesh as he spoke. "I mean, the last thing I remember is taking a very hard punch.

Like they say, I saw stars. I actually remember going down to my knees and telling myself, Oh, shit! now he's got me. I was waiting for the follow-up haymaker, see? In my gut I had myself labeled the loser.''

"You must have reacted without thinking." The sun on Patrice's belly was not calming her; it was having the opposite effect. "When you went down you just automatically grabbed for the lug wrench. You used it without thinking.''

"I guess so.'' Jack took a deep breath. His nostrils filled with the scent of Patrice's perfume. "It's just so frustrating not being able to remember.   I mean, one minute I was going down from a roundhouse right to the head, on my knees, not focusing, waiting for the clincher. And then the next thing I know I'm standing there with a tire iron at my feet and a dead man lying in front of me with his head bashed in.''

"And you really don't recall hitting him?'' Patrice stroked her troubled lover's tousled hair.

"Not at all. I don't even remember picking up the tire iron.'' Jack shifted so that his face was on a level with hers. His eyes, moving up and down her naked body, were considering. "All I remember is standing there with people coming at me and telling each other there had been a murder.''

Patrice sat up. Her breasts, large for her petite body, bounced with the movement. She bent both her knees double and hugged them to herself. Without her willing it, her thigh muscles were straining. The heat of the day, her proximity to Jack, their nudity—sensuality was flooding her body.

She looked up at him. Her tongue, unbidden, moistened her lips. Embarrassed, she lowered her eyes. That's when she saw, unmistakably, that Jack, too, had become aroused. Patrice caught her breath audibly.

Jack reacted to her gasp, taking her in his arms and kissing her. Patrice's breasts, slippery with lotion, flattened out against his hard chest. The raised nipples dug into his flesh. She felt his straining erection burn against her naked belly as they stretched out with their bodies arced to each other.

"Not here," Patrice managed to protest when the kiss was over. "Someone will see us."

"There's nobody around." Jack stroked her quivering body, intending to soothe her but only succeeding in making her tremble more.

"Let's go back to the house." Patrice touched him intimately and then snatched her hand away. "I'm not comfortable here."

"All right, darling." Jack took her in his arms and kissed her thoroughly, fully intending to pack up their things when the kiss was over and go back to the villa to make love.

Buffy, having reached the peak of the sand dune overlooking their blanket, let out a howl of rage.

Normally she was the most sophisticated of women. A rapierlike wit was her main weapon in situations that evoked her hostility. Competitive with other women by nature, she was an expert at decimating rivals with words. This occasion, however, was different. The sudden shock of stumbling on her husband and Patrice in such a blatantly erotic clinch made her react with uncharacteristic violence.

"Son of a *bitch*!" she howled, slipping and sliding and finally tumbling in her haste to descend the dune to their blanket. "Cheating bastard!" She landed on Jack with her knees in his kidneys, and her long, manicured, scarlet nails raked from behind the flesh of both his cheeks, drawing blood.

"Stop!" Patrice scrambled out from under them. "Leave him alone!"

Jack was making no attempt to strike back at Buffy. Blood trickling down both sides of his face, he was only trying to ward her off, to protect himself. "You've got no damn right—" The rest of what he might have said was lost in the flurry of her next assault.

"You marry me for my money and then knock over every young tramp in sight!" Fiery and sweating, Buffy

254

hurled punches and kicks at him. "And this one! Every time she crooks her little finger, there you are, my husband, with your pants off and your lust on high!" Diving low, she managed to sink her teeth in Jack's calf.

"You said you didn't care!" Patrice wailed. "Back at Riverview you as much as told me you were through with him." She had hold of Buffy's long blue-black hair, yanking hard until she stopped biting Jack and wheeled around.

"As if anything I said mattered." She grabbed Patrice's wrist and twisted, freeing her tresses. "For years you've been after Jack like the bitch in heat you are!" She slapped Patrice hard.

Patrice was smaller by a head, but she had a fierce temper. Head down, chin tucked in, her body coiled for action, she returned the slap.

Buffy, taken by surprise, responded with a kick. It knocked the wind out of Patrice, and then she lunged at Buffy.

"Enough." Jack tried to pull them apart. "Stop it before somebody really gets hurt."

"He's my husband!" Buffy panted, trying to attack Patrice. "You keep your hands off him!"

"It's me he loves! You could never give him what he needs!"

"Damn it! Stop it now! You've attracted attention. People are coming!"

It was true. From far down the beach other sunbathers were approaching, drawn first by the angry voices, then by the sight of the struggle between the two women. There was a chatter of philosophical French as they speculated on the role of the handsome American male in the drama.

"Haven't we had enough notoriety?" Jack pleaded.

It was actually hearing the approach of French voices, however, and not Jack's plea that finally made Buffy and Patrice give up. For a moment they glared their hatred at each other. Then Buffy wheeled and stalked off in the direction from which she had come. She walked tall and proud, her magnificent naked body flaunting its wounds like medals.

Behind her, Patrice and Jack wearily packed up their things and dressed for the return trip to the villa.

32

RIDICULOUS! PATRICE STARED into the mirror of the PLM St. Tropez hotel room she had moved into after the fight with Buffy. She had a black eye, a shiner! Two days and it showed no signs of fading. No wonder Jack hadn't driven the few miles up the road from the villa to the hotel on the outskirts of Marigot to see her. What man would want to make love to a woman who looked as if she'd just lost the decision to Marvin Hagler?

Still, Patrice admitted to herself, that really wasn't it. The reason was that Buffy had come back. She had reclaimed her rights to the marital bed, and Patrice could only hope that Jack had taken up residence in one of the other bedrooms of the villa.

If he wasn't comfortable joining her at the hotel, she could live with that. She didn't for a moment believe that sex was all they had going for them. She would be patient; she would wait.

It was, however, lonely. She missed not only Jack, but also Riverview and, guiltily, Fitz. She was all alone, without companionship. It was boring, too. She could only occupy herself admiring the rainbow colors of her shiner in the hotel room mirror for so long before ennui set in.

In this mood, grateful to have something to occupy herself with, Patrice abandoned the looking glass and settled down to peruse the next in the series of Seabury diaries. . . .

It was, Edith Seabury admitted to herself, a very unconventional understanding. Publicly, she and Charles Cabot Stockwell had announced their engagement. Privately, they had agreed that it would be a long engagement with no pressure to rush into marriage. The question of whether or not they would sleep together before they were married was up in the air.

Aroused beyond her expectations by Charles's increasingly fervent embraces, Edith read up on human sexuality. The literature of the day was not very illuminating. Summed up, it presented sex as an uncontrollable animal pressure upon men and an inescapable marital burden for women—a state of affairs evidently necessary to the propagation of the species. It explained neither Edith's own desire nor its accompanying fantasies.

Unenlightened, Edith drifted with her feelings. Charles was passionate, but very much a gentleman. It was not archaic in the year 1850 for him to respect her virtue. He restrained himself. Had he not, Edith did not know how far she might have gone.

As it was, they progressed from kisses to caresses to fondlings to greater intimacies. Knuckles rubbed raw by the whalebone supporting Edith's bodice, Charles established a precedent of toying with her bare breast. The thrill of his touch on her nipple coursed through Edith like wildfire. She let him guide her hand to the ridge bisecting his fawn-colored trousers. Once, eyes averted, she held him unencumbered in her fist inside the trousers. Once he reached under her skirts and petticoats and pantalets to touch her moist, unfolding womanhood. For the most part, however, they engaged in a clandestine fumbling through their clothing.

Very often they sublimated with the cold shower of conversation. Charles commiserated with the lack of artistic training available to Edith and with her being barred from the life classes male artists attended. She won him over to the understanding that women artists did not so much lack innate ability as they did the opportunity to develop themselves. ''From earliest childhood society conspires to point us in 'more feminine' directions,'' Edith proselytized. And Charles, not only because he was in love, but also because of his innate sense of fairness, came to share her view. More and more Edith appreciated how truly decent a man Charles Cabot Stockwell was, even if his attitudes were sometimes typical of his class and gender.

He had started out encouraging Edith's art and disapproving her social activism. Now she made Charles see that it was the limitations imposed on her as an artist that pushed her into greater and greater involvement in the causes of the day—particularly the suffragist campaign. But that wasn't the only reason or Edith's only cause. She neglected her artistic career because the need in other areas was so great.

In particular, the plight of the New York poor had claimed her sympathies. Along with other concerned women, she visited the slums regularly with the aim of helping the poor people trapped there. It was on one of these forays that Edith met a teenage prostitute named Letty.

''It's a sinful life.'' Edith had tried to reason with Letty. ''But worse than that, it's a short one. Sooner or later, with so many men, disease will claim you.''

''No argument, missus.'' Letty got through the hopeless days and tawdry nights with pragmatism. ''Die of the life later for sure, but live it now with food on the table at least.'' She liked Edith. At least this uptown lady didn't lecture her about the punishment awaiting her immortal soul.

Edith recognized that she wasn't making much headway in weaning Letty away from the life. Even so, there was something touching about the girl, about her bravery in always insisting on the positive side of her unhappy existence, that made Edith concerned for Letty's future in a truly personal rather than an abstract do-gooder fashion. She was genuinely anxious for her when Letty announced one day that she was pregnant.

"Do you know who the father is?" Edith asked hesitantly.

"Now given my profession, missus, how could I know a thing like that?"

"What will you do?"

"Have it. What else can I do?"

"Well"—Edith was appalled at herself even as she gave oblique voice to the thought—"I have heard that down here on the waterfront there are ways for women to . . ." She left the sentence unfinished, but the meaning was obvious.

"Oh, I could never do that. I'll go to hell for all the sinning got me in this fix, I know. But if I got rid of it, I'd burn for all eternity."

"I see." Later Edith thought about that. She had not herself been raised religiously. Still, she had a great reverence for life. Admittedly, looking at it as a relatively well-off young woman with no real understanding of what it meant to make her body available to a variety of men, she was sure that in Letty's position she would abort the pregnancy. She understood that the baby might well be the only thing in her whole life that Letty could look on as her own, could truly love, but even so—even so, the burden for an adolescent girl was too great. But she had no right to try to convince Letty to follow such a course.

The real horror to Edith was that Letty continued to ply her trade. The economics were such—and Letty made Edith understand this—that the young prostitute had no choice. She took pains to put on as little weight as possible and to hide what extra pounds there were and continued working into her sixth month.

One night Edith was awakened by a young boy with a message. Letty needed her. Please, could she come right away? Edith dressed and followed the boy down to the poor residential neighborhood behind the Federal Building and east of the docks. She arrived at her destination to find that Letty had already had a miscarriage.

Two of her fellow whores had seen her through the ordeal. They had been sympathetic and had disposed of the fetus, but finally they'd had to go back to work. Letty understood this. She was only glad that Edith had responded to her summons. At least there would be someone to share her tears over the loss of her baby.

Edith did more than that. She packed up Letty's meager belongings, had a coach summoned, and over her father's mild objections took the young girl back home with her. Letty would remain in their guest room until she had recovered from her ordeal.

Neither Charles nor her father, their friends nor their neighbors, gave Edith the most difficulty over this decision. It was the Seabury servants who were hardest to stare down. They recognized without asking that Letty "wasn't respectable." They were offended that they, who had worked their lives long to stay above the muck, should now have to wait on one who had immersed herself in it.

Troublesome as their attitude was, it gave Edith an idea. She was determined that she was not going to nurse Letty back to health only to return her to the life of a prostitute. Why could she not become a house servant? Surely it could not be such a difficult skill to master.

Edith spoke to her father about it. He pointed out that their household staff was full; there was no place for Letty to fit in; they had not even a bed in the servants' quarters for her. Besides, she could see for herself that the other servants wouldn't stand for it. And even if they would, surely Edith wouldn't suggest that they discharge one of their own loyal housemaids to create a place for Letty.

No, Edith wouldn't suggest that. For the moment she shelved the idea.

Letty recovered quickly. Quite soon she was no longer confined to bed. She was up and about, enjoying the freedom of the house although not yet ready for the out-of-doors.

She was in the parlor by herself one afternoon, waiting for Edith to return from an errand, when Charles came to call. He knew from Edith of Letty's background but was nevertheless courtly. He introduced himself and set about making himself agreeable to her while they waited together for Edith's arrival.

Letty was flattered at his attention, and relieved that his chatter made no demands on her. At the same time she was distracted by a nagging uneasiness.

It was a while before she recognized Charles as having been a customer at a brothel where she had once been employed. This recognition was an occasion, as far as Letty was concerned, for no more than a sigh of fatalism that granted the essential animal nature of man.

It had been a long time ago, more than a year, perhaps almost two, since she'd last seen Charles Stockwell. Letty had left the brothel shortly thereafter, and Charles had not been a customer of hers. But he had visited the place with frequency enough for Letty to remember him. If she had stayed, she was sure that sooner or later he would have chosen her for his evening's pleasure.

Obviously, he did not recognize her. He was behaving the perfect gentleman. And it wasn't just an act. He really was nice. Why, he might even be worthy of someone Letty valued as highly as she did Miss Seabury. Well then, there was no reason for her to let the cat out of the bag.

Later, when Edith and Charles were alone, she broached the subject of a position for Letty. "Might not there be something at Riverview?" she inquired hesitantly.

Charles considered it. "We're always hiring maids," he admitted. "It seems like every time I turn around one or another of them has gone off to get married and there's a new one. Of course I have nothing to do with that. My butler, Wilfred—more of a majordomo, really—takes care of it. And I should warn you that as far as the staff is concerned, he's an absolute tyrant. It goes without saying that he would never consider taking on Letty if he had the slightest hint of her background.''

''Need he know?''

''Well now, do I look to you like the sort of man who would lie to his butler?''

''You strike me as the sort of man who could be influenced by other considerations.'' Edith leaned in to him, her golden eyelashes fanning out over her cheeks, her lips parted invitingly.

Charles kissed her long and thoroughly. ''You're right,'' he said when the kiss was over. ''I have been influenced.''

Two weeks later, Letty went to work at Riverview as a kitchen maid.

It was approximately two months after the start of Letty's employment that Wilfred, the butler, asked Charles if he might speak with him.

''What is it, Wilfred?''

Wilfred carefully shut the door to the sitting room. ''A delicate matter, Mr. Stockwell,'' he murmured.

''Get on with it.''

''It concerns Chauncey, the footman, sir.''

''Yes? What about Chauncey?''

''And the new girl, Letty, sir.'' The way he pronounced the name was itself an insinuation.

Charles stared at Wilfred. ''Are you implying what I think you are?'' he asked finally.

''I'm afraid so, sir. There is—and I have no doubt about it—hanky-panky going on between them.''

''Hanky-panky.'' Charles resisted the impulse to smile. ''I see.''

''It has occurred to me that you might want to think about discharging the girl, sir.''

''All right, Wilfred. I will think about it.''

''Very good, sir.'' Wilfred bowed and glided from Charles's presence.

That evening Charles told Edith what Wilfred had told him. "Hanky-panky," he repeated. Obviously the business amused him.

"Are you going to discharge Letty?" Edith demanded. She was not amused.

"Not if you don't want me to. Even so, I can't have her playing the harlot at Riverview. It's too disruptive."

"Playing the harlot?" Edith echoed. "Did Berkley say that she'd been getting money from this footman?"

"Well, no. I only assumed . . ."

"Perhaps she's really attracted to this Chauncey."

"Well, even if that's so, Edith, I can't have her crawling into bed with him whenever Wilfred's back is turned."

"If it ever is," Edith reflected.

"I really can't allow it. Wilfred's authority with the staff would be undermined, for one thing. I can't be a party to that by allowing my footman and kitchen maid to misbehave."

"Misbehave?" Edith's glance was withering. "Is that what you call it?"

"Well, yes. How else could it be characterized?"

"And our embraces?" Edith asked. "Do we also misbehave?"

"I don't think I quite understand what you're driving at," Charles said carefully.

"Class, Charles. That's what I'm getting at. Our fondlings are permissible because we are people of substance. Theirs are not because they are servants. Well, I would submit to you that there is no logic to the idea that the blood of menials runs any less hot than our own."

"A good deal more hot if Wilfred is to be believed." Charles was trying to lighten the tone of the conversation.

"It's not a joke, Charles. It concerns Letty's future, her livelihood. Is she to be punished for passions no different from my own? And what of the footman? Does Chauncey escape with a scolding because he's a man while Letty faces discharge because she's a woman? Is his lust to be winked at while hers is condemned? Must it always be Eve to blame for tempting Adam? If that's so, Charles, then it bodes ill for us. Would you allow your own manly desires free rein and have me deny my own as unladylike? Truly, they are not unladylike. Truly, they are expressive of that which is most womanly in me."

Charles stared at her and said nothing for a long moment. Then he crossed to her and took her by the shoulders. His face very close to hers, his eyes conveyed his message before he spoke. "My God, how I love you," he said. "You are the most remarkable woman—indeed, person—I have ever known. Do you never dissemble? I think not." He embraced her and kissed her soundly. "Never deny your desires," he whispered in her ear. "Never restrain yourself. What you are is what I want. My God, how I want it!"

For a moment, Edith felt enveloped by his heat. She could only guess what feelings Letty might have for the footman, but of her own for Charles right then, there was no doubt. Nevertheless, she did restrain herself. Breathless, she pushed him away. "You won't discharge Letty, will you?" she asked.

"She will remain in my employ," Charles promised. "Nor shall I pry into her trysts with Chauncey. Only it would be wise if you urged upon her some discretion regarding Wilfred."

Edith assured him that she would have a talk with Letty.

Letty responded to the talk with assurances that she would be discreet. Loyal to Edith, grateful to Charles for employment, she went even further. To Chauncey's dismay, she ended their affair. It had never been love, only desire, and the experienced Letty knew with some accuracy the value of that. "Let a hansom pass by," was the lore of the streets. "There's always another." Even so, the next hansom was the last one Letty anticipated.

She was alone in the subpantry where both cooking utensils and cutlery were kept, intent on polishing the silver. She did not hear his footsteps when Wilfred entered. The butler came up behind her and put his hands lightly but firmly on her shoulders. Moist lips brushed the shell of her ear. "Time to step up in rank, my girl. There's more choice cuts than a footman," he offered.

"Unhand me, if you please, Mr. Wilfred."

"Just Wilfred, Letty." He ignored her request. "No formality." One of his hands slid down from her shoulder to cup her breast.

"You've no right." She squirmed to escape his fondlings.

"Careful, my girl. What's good for the footman should never be denied the one in charge."

"Well, denied it is!" Letty wrenched away from him, stood, and wheeled to face him. "And there's an end to it, Mr. Wilfred!"

"You'd best be more friendly, Letty, if you want to continue in service at Riverview."

"That's not for you to say. It's for Mr. Stockwell."

"He leaves such matters to me. I assure you that it wasn't he who discharged those female servants who were uncooperative in the past." Wilfred moved toward Letty with determination.

"They left to be married." This was what Letty had been told by Edith.

"They wish!" Wilfred had her backed into a corner of the pantry now. "I let them go because they were—umm—standoffish. Now don't you make that mistake, Letty. You haven't been standoffish with Chauncey. I've asked around, and you were no lily before you came to Riverview. A slut, that's what you were. So give us a kiss, and up with your skirts. Let's have no more playing coy, girl."

"Bastard!"

"There's no such thing as rape of a slut, you know." Wilfred grabbed her wrist and twisted it, forcing her to her knees.

Letty went with the pressure and turned it to her advantage. As she crumpled, she butted Wilfred in the groin with her head. He grunted and doubled over, releasing her. Letty scrambled to her feet and started for the door.

Wilfred seized her ankle and brought her down again. This time he was quick to fling himself over her. Both furious and aroused, he pinned her with his weight, reached under her skirts, and pulled her pantalets down around her ankles. He exposed himself then, randy and ready.

The sensation of her thighs being forced apart was the snapping point for Letty. It was as if she were being compelled to return to her life as a prostitute against her will. She had in the past made love to many men who revolted her. Wilfred, however, was one too many.

Her hand flailing behind her encountered the hilt of a paring knife on the hardwood pantry floor. It had fallen there during the struggle along with a handful of other utensils. Letty grabbed up the small knife and plunged the serrated blade into the fleshy part of Wilfred's shoulder.

It remained embedded there. Wilfred yelled and cursed. He released Letty so that he could pull the knife out.

She had not struck a mortal blow. Even so, Letty recognized that she was in serious trouble. She scrambled away from Wilfred, who was now examining the wound, and bolted the house. Within moments she was fleeing the grounds of Riverview as well.

Trudging and catching occasional rides from farmers, it took Letty almost two days to reach the Seabury house. It was late afternoon when she burst in on Edith Seabury painting in her fourth-floor studio. Hair askew and clothes coated with dust from her journey, Letty blurted out her story.

Edith was outraged. "I shall speak to Charles. That awful man must be discharged immediately."

"Not likely." Letty understood the Riverview pecking order. "I'll be content just not to go to jail for sticking a knife in Wilfred."

"Don't be silly, Letty. You had to defend yourself."

"I've been a strumpet." Letty stuck out her jaw. "That's the fact of it. The police are men, same as Wilfred.

For men there's no forcing of a strumpet, and no non-sense of her protecting herself, neither. If Wilfred signs a complaint, I'll go to jail all right."

"I'll speak to Charles. He won't let Wilfred sign a complaint."

"Why not?" Letty was bitter. "He's a man, too, isn't he? Gent and varlet, they're all the same when it comes to girls like me."

"You're wrong, Letty. Not Charles. Why, he'd never—"

"Oh, wouldn't he now?" Young as she was, Letty's harsh laugh was old and wise. "Well, I'm here to say he would, same as any man. Yes, missus, would and has."

Edith considered the implication and paled. "Has Charles tried to force himself on you since you went into service at Riverview?" she made herself ask Letty.

"Oh, no. I never meant to say that," Letty replied, already regretting her words.

"What did you mean to say, then? Don't hem and haw, Letty. Say it straight out."

"I knew him from before. Mr. Stockwell, I mean." Letty muttered.

"From before?" It took a moment for Edith to realize what she meant. "From before. You mean from when you were—?"

"It was when I worked in the brothel."

"I see." Edith went quite pale. "And did you—? I mean, did Charles and you—?"

"Oh, no, ma'am. We never. It was the other girls he went with."

"Girls." The plural was a second blow to Edith. "Were there a lot of them?"

"Not really, Miss Seabury. Mr. Stockwell was a regular, but not as regular as most regulars, you might say."

"A regular . . ." Edith did not know which was the stronger of the two emotions she was feeling: hurt or anger. "And does he still . . . ?" she wondered aloud.

"Oh, there's no way I'd know that, Miss Seabury." Letty regarded her unhappily. "I never should have said nothing," she said. "But listen, Miss Seabury, I know I'm the last one should be advising you, but listen anyway. Men is men, and that's a fact. The best of them can't change. And no matter he follows his you-know-what, Mr. Stockwell is still one of the nicest I've ever met. Don't you be foolish and spoil things with him just because he did what they all do."

Edith winced at the advice, and forced herself to consider Letty's plight. There was a principle involved here that was more important than her feelings. "I will speak to Charles," she repeated to Letty. "Wilfred will be discharged. You will be restored to your position. Charles will see to it that Wilfred prefers no charges against you."

"I'll settle for just that last," Letty told her. "You see, Miss Seabury, Wilfred will have his own story for Mr. Stockwell. And the way things work belowstairs, plus men being men, Wilfred's story is what Mr. Stockwell will believe."

"But if you leave Riverview, where will you go?"

"Back to where I've been, probably."

"That's awful!"

"Not so very." Letty was philosophical. "Comes right down to it, there's little difference between satisfying the likes of Wilfred to go on being a scullery maid and satisfying others who often as not are real gents. Except," Letty added with a grin, "that being a professional, you don't have to scrub floors."

The short, painful meeting that Edith later had with Charles confirmed Letty's cynicism. "Letty's version of the story," he told Edith, "is a complete contradiction of what Wilfred has told me. The knife wound she inflicted on him isn't serious, but it is painful, I am sure. He says that she took him to task for telling me about the business with Chauncey and claimed it cost her money because Chauncey had been paying for her favors. She then asked him to make up the money, offered him sex in exchange for it, and finally became violent when he would not allow himself to be seduced. Wilfred has of his own volition offered to forgo pressing charges against Letty in order to spare Riverview the notoriety. Under the circumstances, however, I cannot keep Letty in my employ.''

''You believe Wilfred's story?''

''I do.''

''And if he's lying and Letty is telling the truth?''

''I have never known Wilfred to lie to me. He has been in my employ for many years and has never given anything but satisfaction. Under his stewardship, Riverview runs like clockwork.''

''Evidently he runs you, too. Rarely have I seen such a clear case of the tyranny of servant over master.''

Charles ignored the remark. ''All I know about Letty,'' he pointed out, ''is that she has caused nothing but trouble since coming to Riverview and that she did for some time support herself through harlotry.''

''And all she knows about you,'' Edith shot back, ''is that you were a regular customer at a brothel in which she worked.''

Charles was taken by surprise. His face turned red. ''I don't deny it,'' he said finally. ''It's embarrassing that you should know. But you mustn't be hurt by the revelation. It has nothing really to do with us.''

''Wilfred stays on running Riverview. Letty goes back to being a prostitute. And I am to ignore your brothel visits,'' Edith summed up angrily.

''I no longer make brothel visits,'' Charles remonstrated quietly.

''But you did. I've always known you were a chauvinist. But until now I never understood to what extent you were an exploiter of women as well!''

''You are overreacting. Try to understand. I am thirty-two years old. I have been a healthy man. Surely you did not imagine that I have been restrained by vows of chastity since puberty.''

''I am twenty-three years old,'' Edith shot back. ''I have been a healthy young woman. Yet I do believe that chastity is indeed what you expect of me.''

"It's not the same thing. I am a male. You are a female. Our needs are different."

"And that explains why there are no brothels in New York for women."

"As a matter of fact," Charles agreed, "I believe it does."

"Well, I have news for you, Charles. Our needs are not so different as you think. Just as you think you're entitled to the release of sex with any young girl so poor and desperate as to sell it to you, I believe that I am entitled to indulge myself in like fashion—or as close to like fashion as a woman can come in our society. Do I make myself clear?"

"You do not! We are engaged. You're my fiancée. You were right before. I do take it for granted that my wife shall be unsullied on our wedding day."

"Take what you will for granted." Edith's voice went up the scale. "In any case, that wife will not be me. As of now, our engagement is broken."

"Don't act hastily, Edith. We're both angry. Don't sacrifice our happiness to suffragist theory. We love each other."

"I no longer know if that is so," Edith told him coldly.

"I love you. That hasn't changed."

"Well, my feelings have, Charles." Edith folded her arms. "I think you'd better leave now."

"Very well." Charles stood, picked up his hat and stick, and started for the door. He turned. "And shall I call again?" he inquired in a carefully measured voice.

"It would be better if you did not."

"I see." Charles opened the door. He turned to Edith again. He bowed. "Good-bye, Edith," he said.

"Good-bye, Charles," she replied as the door closed with what seemed to her like finality behind him. "Good-bye."

33

GETTING OUT OF his rental car in the bustling main street of Marigot, Peter all but collided with Patrice stepping into the gutter to avoid a sidewalk mud puddle left over from the morning's sunshower. She had hiked into Marigot from her hotel and was on her way to the produce market alongside the docks to handpick some fresh fruit. Each suppressing their dislike of the other, they walked through the town together.

Peter spent most of the time hoping that Patrice wouldn't ask questions about his business in Marigot. And he hoped that Buffy had not yet told her about Grieg. Whatever she knew or didn't know, he would have had to go through the bother of inventing answers and then of committing the lies to memory so as not to ensnare himself in them later. He had enough on his mind to worry about without that.

Now caution made Peter wait until Patrice was out of sight before crossing the street to enter the building that was his destination. This time the receptionist in the second-floor insurance office recognized him. Her smile lingered as she went into the inner office to announce his arrival. She came back immediately and motioned for Peter to enter.

Van Huyck was seated behind his scarred desk of St. Martin cedar. He was not alone. The man seated to one side of the desk was large and bull-like, but not flabby. Except for the fact that his eyes were very small and constantly shifting and that he had a vaguely French accent, he reminded Peter of the TV character Kojak. Van Huyck introduced him as Junot without specifying whether that was his first or last name. "Junot," van Huyck added meaningfully, "is one of us."

Peter wasn't comfortable with the man. There was an air about this Junot that reminded him too much of the violent side of van Huyck's services. What had started out as a simple business arrangement was quickly becoming a quicksand of criminal complications, and Peter felt as if he were being sucked down into it.

"There have been new developments as to that delicate matter we talked about last time." Peter was trying to tell van Huyck without coming out and saying it that it would be better if they spoke privately.

"No need to be oblique, Mr. Stockwell." The pink face beamed with a reassurance that Peter did not find reassuring. "Junot knows all there is to know about the Victor Grieg situation. Nothing you may say will be out of context for him."

"Maybe not. Even so, I don't think—"

"Don't think, Mr. Stockwell." A hint of impatience crept into van Huyck's voice. "Really, this is our area of expertise, not yours. Just tell us what you have come to tell, and we will put our experience and know-how to the service of weighing it. Isn't that right, Junot?"

"*Oui!*" Gallic as the assent was, falling from Junot's heavy lips the reply sounded guttural.

"There. You see? Now proceed, Mr. Stockwell."

Junot's bald head, bent to the cleaning of his fingernails with a penknife, caught the slattings of sunlight filtering through the bamboo blinds and distracted Peter for an instant. He turned his eyes from the gleaming, brutish knobbiness of Junot's skull and collected his thoughts. "The Stockwell board knows what we've been doing," he began. He went on to tell them in detail what Buffy had told him. "It seems," he summed up, "that the board is planning to pull the rug out from under me and withdraw from the East Side project. They are very concerned that Stockwell may be linked by the media with your organization."

272

"I do hope they understand that if Stockwell withdraws, our fee will be forfeit."

That was not, Peter knew, the board's main concern. They would write off the two point two million dollars if they had to in order to protect the Stockwell name. Even so, such a loss would surely not enhance his prestige with his fellow board members. "There will have to be a discussion of that," he told van Huyck. He wasn't about to agree to forfeiting the money without a fight.

"I think not." Van Huyck was equally determined.

"Excuse me." Junot's voice sounded even harsher speaking English than speaking French. "Could that discussion wait? I think the additional pressure from what Mr. Stockwell's just told us gives us more problems than what happens to the money."

"Junot is right," van Huyck agreed. "Let us postpone our differences, Mr. Stockwell. We all share one common danger right now. Myself and my people, you and your Stockwell Enterprises board. We must retrieve the incriminating documents that disappeared after the death of Victor Grieg. If those should surface, if the media should get hold of them, it would be far more serious for Stockwell Enterprises than anything they might be afraid of at present."

"I've made them aware of that. Even so, they don't share your assessment. They're sure they can survive any revelations—possibly by throwing me to the wolves," Peter added bitterly, recalling Buffy's attitude, "but they do know it's serious and will probably cooperate in avoiding publicity if they can."

"Any one of them might cooperate individually by telling us where Carrie Tyler is," van Huyck reminded Peter. "We have had the airports and the shipping lines watched, and we are sure that she is still on St. Martin. I cannot stress enough how important it is to all of us that she be found."

"And when she is?" Peter asked. "What then?"

Van Huyck looked at Junot, whose head came up slowly from his penknife. The bald man did not look back.

Nor did he look at Peter as he answered his question. "Just find her," he said to the peeling pastel wall. "I'll take it from there."

The chill Peter felt stayed with him after he left van Huyck's office. He went into a nearby cafe in quest of a daiquiri to dispel it. He ordered the drink straight up, winced at its sugariness at the same time that his stomach welcomed its warmth.

He was sorry he'd gone to see van Huyck. He was sorry he'd brought him up to date on the position the board was taking. He felt in his bones that at some point— the two point two million? the records Victor Grieg had kept? the finding of Carrie Tyler?—he was going to have to deal with Junot. Peter was used to playing hardball. Cheating, bribery, even stealing could be in his league. But Junot—and the violence that Peter sensed Junot represented—was not. He did not feel capable of coping with that.

That feeling overwhelmed him two drinks later as Junot came through the door of the cafe, spied him sitting there, waved casually, and made straight for his table. "Mind if I join you?" The small red eyes dared him to mind.

"No. Please do." Peter was sweating.

"*Merci.*" Junot sat down and ordered a drink. "I'm glad to run into you," he said. "We should get to know each other better. After all, we're both on the same side."

Peter nodded dumbly. He drained his third daiquiri. It had no effect. He signaled the waiter for another as Junot's words echoed inside his head:

On the same side . . .

34

PETER HAD BEEN dismissed from Patrice's mind as soon as she left him on the main street of Marigot. In culottes with a bright red cotton belt tied into a bow and a cotton shirt with a St. Martin sunburst on the front of it, her real reason for walking into Marigot had been envy. She had convinced herself that she wanted fresh fruit from the market on the docks, but actually she wanted to get away from the couples at the hotel pool. It seemed that honeymooners had discovered the small hotel this season, and the spectacle of them calf-eyed in bikinis, most of the young brides topless, stealing embraces and murmuring sensual insinuations, had made Patrice jealous. All by herself, she felt deprived in a milieu so lovingly populated two by two.

On the dock she went through the motions of judging the fruit that was for sale. She prodded it, eyed its color, and weighed it in her hand. With no place to go but back to the hotel, Patrice, using up time, was as picky as possible. She had bought only one mango and one persimmon when she looked across the wharf and saw something that made her stop and squint.

Against the assault of the St. Martin sun, Patrice had been wearing nonprescription sunglasses. Now she took them off and fumbled in her bag for her regular eyeglasses. She put them on quickly and squinted into the glare.

Yes! It was Carrie! She was hurrying across the dock with a long brown paper bag from which protruded the end of a loaf of French bread. In her other hand she carried a wedge-shaped package of waxed paper in which was wrapped the fresh cheese she had just bought. Her head was down, and a flowered bandanna covered her bright apricot hair, but there could be no doubt about it.

Patrice hurried to intercept her. They came face to face just outside the entrance to a small, run-down residence hotel—the kind frequented not by tourists, but by locals. Carrie went pale when she saw Patrice. She looked awful, hollows under her eyes and skin stretched tight across her cheekbones.

"Carrie, where on earth have you—" Patrice started to greet her.

"Shh! Not here." Carrie grabbed Patrice by the arm and drew her into the entrance to the hotel. Silently she led her up the narrow stairway to her room. Only when the door was closed and bolted behind them did she seem to relax a little.

"What is going on, Carrie?" Patrice demanded then. "Why are you acting like this?"

"I'm in trouble."

"Trouble? Is that why you disappeared?"

"Yes." Carrie put the bread and cheese away. She was breathing very quickly, and she looked frightened.

"Are you in some kind of danger?" Patrice asked slowly.

"Yes." Carrie sat down on the edge of the sagging bed. "If they find me," she said, weighing her words, "they'll kill me."

"Who is 'they,' Carrie?"

"The same people who killed Victor."

"But . . ." Patrice stared at her, bewildered. "Jack killed Victor."

"No. I know from the newspapers that's what everybody thinks, but it's not true. Jack was fighting with him, but he didn't kill him."

Patrice felt her body tense. If Jack was innocent, then he would be free to leave Buffy and . . . "How can you know that, Carrie?" she asked carefully.

"I saw what happened. I guess I was the only one who did."

"If you saw what happened, why didn't you come forward? Jack's facing a murder charge. He could go to jail. For life, even. Why didn't you come forward?"

"I know. I wanted to. But I didn't dare, Patrice. Once they knew where I was . . ."

"Tell me what you saw," Patrice demanded. "Take your time. Tell it just the way it happened."

"There was a sort of fight—nothing much, really—at the party between Victor and Jack. Jack was pretty drunk. After the to-do, he left. We left—Victor and I—about a half hour later. We ran into Jack in the parking lot. He'd had a flat and was changing the tire. As soon as he saw us, he started up again. I guess he'd drunk too much for it to have worn off. Anyway, he and Victor started slugging it out. I ran back in the house to get someone to break it up. I found the countess de Guillemaine—she was our hostess—and she came back out with me and brought some of her servants to stop the fight. I was very upset, and I guess when we ran back out I was pretty much in front of them. Coming back to the car where they were fighting, I saw Victor really smash Jack with a punch to the head. Jack went down to his knees and sort of collapsed forward. A man stepped out of the shadows to one side of Victor. He snatched up the tire iron where it had been leaning against the side of the car. He smashed it over Victor's head and tossed it in front of where Jack was sort of rocking on his knees. It was horrible. The blood was gushing from Victor's skull as he went down. I screamed, and the murderer saw me and started for me. By then the rest were close behind, and he left. Then I ran away, and I've been running ever since."

"You knew the man who murdered Victor," Patrice realized. "Is that it?"

"Yes."

"And he knows you?"

"Yes."

"Who was it, Carrie?"

Carrie weighed the question for a long moment before she answered. "Junot," she said. "It was Junot."

Patrice looked at her blankly. "Who is Junot?"

Carrie explained to Patrice that Junot, like Victor, worked for the mob. She told Patrice how Victor had told her before his death of being afraid of Junot. And how after Victor's death she had taken the papers that he had left in the La Samanna safe-deposit box. Finally she recounted what she had learned from them. "Victor was stealing from the mob," Carrie concluded. "He was mixing up all kinds of money and skimming. He sensed that Junot had been sent to check up on him by his boss, a man named van Huyck. He was afraid of Junot. He was right. I've thought about it a lot. There's only one way it could have happened. Junot must have told van Huyck that Victor was stealing from the mob, and van Huyck must have told Junot to kill him, and then Junot saw his opportunity and he did it."

"How did you get mixed up in all this?" Patrice asked. "What were you doing with this Victor Grieg?"

"We'd been sleeping together back in New York," Carrie revealed frankly. "I talked him into taking me to St. Martin with him."

"Did you know he was mixed up with the kind of people who would kill him?"

"I knew he was connected to the mob. Yes."

"How did you ever get involved with such a man?"

"Peter Stockwell introduced us." Carrie smiled slightly—a wry, sad smile. "Victor was laundering some money for Peter."

"Peter!" Things were beginning to fall into place for Patrice. No wonder Peter had been so anxious to get to St. Martin. Patrice had never believed he was interested in helping Jack, but she hadn't been able to figure out what his real purpose was. Now she knew. He was making sure that Victor Grieg's death didn't reveal any connection between the mob and Stockwell Enterprises. Peter was scrambling to cover his tracks.

"Would you show me Victor's papers, the ones you took from the La Samanna safe?" she asked Carrie.

"I don't have them. I was afraid to keep them here with me. I put them in a strongbox in the Banque des Antilles Françaises."

"Is that here in Marigot?"

"Yes."

"Can we get them out?"

"I mailed the key to General Delivery under a phony name. First we'd have to go to the post office, then to the bank." The idea obviously made Carrie afraid.

"Listen, Carrie, I'm here with you now," Patrice reassured her. "I want to look at the papers. Then I want you and me to take them by taxi to Philipsburg. There's a police captain there named Drees who may be the last honest cop in the whole world. He's fuming right now because he thinks that Stockwell money bought a murderer immunity from prosecution on an extradition technicality. But I think if you tell him your story and we show him the papers to back it up, he'll see that Jack's innocent and arrest the real murderer, this Junot."

"I'm really scared," Carrie told Patrice.

"I know, honey. But you can't hide out in this hotel room forever. Sooner or later you have to come out. If you don't take some action, these people will find you and kill you. And if you do it now, I'll be right beside you every step of the way."

Finally Carrie agreed. With Patrice in the lead, the two young women slipped out of the hotel and went to the post office. Carrie retrieved the key, and then they went to the bank, where she took Victor's records from the strongbox. They were walking toward the yacht basin at the other end of town where the taxi stand was located when Patrice saw Peter exit from a cafe and start walking in the same direction on the other side of the street. He was with a tall, heavyset bald man.

Peter saw Patrice at the same moment, but he didn't notice Carrie. He waved but made no move to cross the street to walk with them. Patrice was relieved.

Then Patrice saw the man with Peter look casually over at them, too. Suddenly his glance wasn't casual anymore. His small eyes vanished into the slits of their lids as he focused on Carrie. Grabbing Peter by the elbow, he propelled him quickly toward them.

Patrice's instinct was to grab Carrie's arm and start running. But it was early afternoon and the streets were filled with tourists shopping. In this crowd they wouldn't get very far. Patrice was still trying to gather her wits in order to react to a danger she sensed more than identified when Peter and his companion were upon them.

Carrie took one look at the man with Peter and clutched at Patrice as if she were about to faint. "It's him!" she moaned. "Junot!"

"Be careful!" Peter's voice was fearful, although he didn't really understand all the implications of the situation. "He's got a gun."

As if to prove that Peter's words were true, Junot, under cover of a newspaper he was carrying, jabbed the revolver into Patrice's ribs just above her belt. At the same time he contrived to reveal the weapon to Carrie. "We're all going to walk back across the street," Junot told them. "We're going into that building there." He pointed to the entrance to the building where van Huyck's office was.

The three of them did exactly as Junot wanted. They crossed the street, entered the building, and went up the stairs. The receptionist, unaware of the gun, went to tell van Huyck that his two morning visitors were back with two young ladies.

Waiting for her to return, Carrie whispered to Patrice, "They're going to kill us," she said, her voice breaking. "When they find out they've got Victor's papers back, they'll kill us."

Patrice did not reply. Heart pounding, as frightened as she had ever been, she was certain that Carrie was right.

35

"WE BELONG TOGETHER." Matt Stockwell stood in the path, blocking Kathleen O'Lunney's way. The long muscles of his thin, wiry frame were tensed, as if knotted by unhappiness. "We can't just turn away from each other. We have to talk it out."

Kathleen had been taken by surprise. At first she thought their meeting accidental, a chance springtime encounter on the greening woodland trails of Riverview. As Matt continued speaking, however, she realized she was wrong. He had contrived to intercept her.

"I had to see you," he told her. "I've been miserable. I miss you so damn much, Kathleen."

For an instant Kathleen was reminded of a print she'd had of Picasso's Don Quixote. Matt, too, at this moment, had a woeful countenance. "I'm willing to talk," she told him, pushing down the hope that she felt welling up inside her. Nothing had changed. Well—she was honest with herself—that wasn't true. She had gone to bed with a man other than Matt. That was a change.

"We belong together," Matt repeated. "What's come between us can be worked out. I promise you." His soft brown eyes were adoring on Kathleen's open, freckled face. His hands ached to stroke her bright, silky red ponytail, to take her in his arms, to feel her soft, generous, pliant body against his own.

"Wendy?" Kathleen asked, determined not to let herself be carried away.

"I'll stop seeing her completely, if that's what it takes to get you back."

"And your son? Bruce?"

"That will be hard," Matt admitted. "He's only seven, Kathleen, still a little boy, really. It's going to be hard to explain to him why I won't be coming up to Montreal anymore."

"I don't expect you to give up your son for me." Kathleen was appalled at the idea. "It's only his mother I don't want you involved with. I'd have no objection to Bruce coming down here and staying with you—us."

"Wendy—or rather her father—would never go along with that." Matt sighed. "That hasn't changed."

"It's her way of holding on to you. She uses Bruce. Oh, what's the point?" Kathleen was frustrated. "We've been all through this before. Wendy wants you back, so she arranges things so you have to go to Montreal, where—after your son's in bed—she can be alone with you."

"That's true," Matt admitted.

Kathleen stared at him. "What did you say?"

"I said it's true. Wendy does contrive to be alone with me when I'm in Montreal. I didn't realize it before, but she is still in love with me. She's told me so. You were right about that, Kathleen. But I'm not in love with her, and that's the truth."

"Then why do you make love to her?" Kathleen demanded, the wound of what she'd seen when she'd walked in on them as fresh now as the night it happened.

"I don't."

Kathleen reminded Matt of what she had seen.

"I told you the truth about that," he insisted. "It was pain and nostalgia, and we got caught up in the moment. That was all."

"And when you go to Montreal and spend all that time with Wendy? Do you expect me to believe you don't make love to her?"

"I don't." Matt took Kathleen by both arms and looked into her eyes. "Listen," he said. "I want you to know the truth." He was earnest, and his honesty was writ plain on his angular face. "Wendy wanted us to go to bed. I

282

was tempted. I won't lie about that. I came very close. But in the end I couldn't do it. I kept seeing your face. It was you I wanted, only you, and I didn't want that between us. So I didn't go to bed with Wendy. Please, Kathleen, you've got to believe me.''

''I believe you.'' Kathleen looked into Matt's decent, pleading face and burst into tears.

''What is it?'' Now he did take her in his arms. ''What is it, darling? Don't cry. Tell me.''

''I can't.'' Kathleen was overwhelmed by sobs again.

''Of course you can. I love you. You can tell me anything.''

''Not this.'' She could not stop crying.

''I love you, Kathleen. Every Irish freckle of you. Now come on. What are you crying about?'' He patted her cheeks with his handkerchief and handed it to her to blow her nose. ''Tell me.''

Kathleen looked at him from reddened eyes. Her mind was whirling. Should she be honest with Matt? Would it spoil things between them forever if she was? Crazily, her mind shot back to an old movie she had watched in her college dorm over a year ago.

Unable to sleep, Kathleen had wandered into the common lounge. There was one other girl there who had turned on the TV set and then fallen asleep in front of it. Idly, Kathleen had plopped down on the couch and watched the late night film.

She never did catch the name of the movie. It must have been about half over when she started watching it. It starred Elliott Gould and Brenda Vaccaro. Brenda Vaccaro had intuited that Elliott Gould, her husband in the film, was having an affair. They were in bed together when, very gently, she confided her suspicion to him. When he denied it, she said, Look, we're man and wife, but we're good friends, too; you can tell me anything; I won't blame you; I won't get angry; I'll understand— words to that effect. She was sweet, sympathetic, concerned, and in the end she lulled her husband into confessing that he was indeed having an affair. As he did

283

this, suddenly—unexpectedly—the screen was filled with the picture of a Japanese kamikaze diving straight for the deck of an American battleship and bursting into flames with a tremendous explosion.

At the time, Kathleen giggled. It was funny. And in this scene from what had been a decidedly B movie, there was a cynical germ of truth: Confession of infidelity is self-destructive; the facts of unfaithfulness always overwhelm understanding.

But that had been a movie, and this was real life. This was her and Matt. This was the man she loved, the man who loved her, the man who still wanted to marry her. They had been estranged, and whatever their life together was going to be, she could not start it by hiding the truth from him. Voice shaky, her red head bowed, Kathleen told Matt that she had gone to bed with Fitz Connely.

Matt heard Kathleen out and looked at her as if from a daze. He had been faithful to Kathleen, had turned Wendy away, had hurt her in doing so, he knew. Even though they were estranged, he had not wanted to spoil his special relationship with Kathleen by casually making love to someone else.

Obviously that was not the way she had felt. Fitz Connely! It hurt. A picture twisted like a snake in Matt's mind, a lewd picture. The hurt filled his eyes, crowding out any signs of forgiveness, as he looked at Kathleen.

"It didn't mean anything," Kathleen said miserably. But it was no use. Still Matt's eyes showed only hurt and anger and no forgiveness.

And hidden in their depths, she knew, was the reflection of a kamikaze plane bursting into flames.

36

Patrice watched van Huyck study Victor Grieg's secret records, the papers Junot had taken from Carrie. What would they tell van Huyck had to be done? Would they dictate more deaths? And why? To cover up the murder of Victor Grieg? To conceal Victor's double cross of van Huyck's clients? Or to protect against the exposure of those clients and the services rendered to them by van Huyck? Either way the victims would be just as dead. Would she be one of those victims? Patrice shivered. Her fingers tried to make a cat's cradle of the bow at her waist and failed. Would she be murdered?

Beside her, Carrie was sobbing softly with fear. On Patrice's other side, Peter's thuggish face was worried and watchful. Behind them, Junot had positioned himself on a wicker couch. He was out of Patrice's sight, but she could sense the gun with which he was still covering them.

Van Huyck looked up. He drummed his fingertips softly on the pocked cedar desktop. The sound was like the padding of furry paws. Finally he got to his feet. "I'll be right back." The words were addressed over their heads to Junot.

He left the door slightly ajar as he exited the office. Patrice could hear van Huyck murmuring to the receptionist that he and his visitors would be leaving soon and that since there really wasn't any pressing business, she might as well take the rest of the day off. The woman thanked him, and Patrice heard the sounds of her gathering up her things to leave as van Huyck came back into the inner office and closed the door behind him.

Although he had closed it quietly, there was a finality to the sound. Patrice's throat became very dry. If van Huyck had decided to have Junot kill them, naturally he wouldn't want any witnesses around. That was why he'd sent the receptionist home.

Van Huyck sat back down behind his desk. He looked from one to the other of them. "These papers are quite incriminating," he told them. His eyes went to Carrie, who was still crying, and then back to Patrice. "What did you intend doing with them?" he asked.

"We were taking them to Captain Drees, the head of the Philipsburg police."

"The Philipsburg police." Van Huyck made a steeple of his fingers and looked at Peter until Peter looked up and met his glance. "In the hands of the police, these papers could hang us all," van Huyck told him. "Do you understand me, Mr. Stockwell? If this Captain Drees were to pass these records along to the police in New York, you would personally be implicated, Stockwell Enterprises would be implicated, and half the political appointments of the mayor would be at risk. Not to mention certain key state and federal officials."

"Would Captain Drees pass them along?" Peter asked carefully. "I mean, why should he?"

"Why?" Van Huyck's laugh was as unpleasant as the snarl of a trapped hyena. "Because yours was not the only money being laundered by Victor Grieg. He was also channeling funds for the Colombia-Miami-New York drug loop. He commingled the funds in order to skim them, Mr. Stockwell. To steal from us, to put it baldly. This Captain Drees would pass the data in these records on to New York because it spells out in money terms just how large and regular shipments of cocaine are smuggled into the city."

Peter lowered his eyes and emitted a shaky sigh. It wasn't just that he was more concerned now than he had been. It was also, Patrice noted, that he was more obviously frightened.

Van Huyck turned back to Patrice. "Why were you so eager to pass these papers along to Captain Drees?" he asked.

"I thought that if he saw them, he'd be more likely to believe Carrie's story."

"Story?"

'Patrice, don't!' Carrie was terrified. Behind her she could sense Junot coming to attention like a snake poising to strike.

Patrice hesitated.

"Please." The word van Huyck uttered was a request, the tone a command.

Her mind raced. Had Junot not seen Carrie that night? Was there anything to be gained by withholding the information or by lying? Patrice could not see that there was. "Carrie saw who really killed Victor Grieg," she said. "The documents provided the motive. Our purpose was to get the police to drop the charges against Jack Houston."

"*Merde!*" In back of Patrice, Junot was on his feet. Patrice's stomach lurched. Junot hadn't seen her!

Van Huyck nodded to Junot. There was a certain reassurance in the nod. He opened the center drawer of the desk and took out a rather large pistol—a Luger, Patrice thought, or perhaps a Magnum; she really didn't know enough about guns to be sure. "I will see to our guests' good behavior," he told Junot. "But we're going to have to move them. Go and fetch the van and pull it up in front of the building. Then come up and let me know you're back, and you and I will bring them down."

"As you say." Before leaving, Junot stuck his own pistol back in the belt to his pants and buttoned his jacket over it.

Van Huyck waited half a minute and then began to speak very rapidly. All the time he was talking, the large pistol lay on the desk only an inch or so from his grasp. "Reasonable people should be able to reach a reasonable arrangement," he said. "I keep these papers. They represent a lot of money to me—money that would be lost if the information they contain were to come out. You three keep your mouths shut about them. Remember, they are very compromising to you personally, Mr. Stockwell, and to Stockwell Enterprises as well. If the whistle is blown on my organization, it will most certainly be blown on you and yours as well. Is that understood?"

"But what about this Junot?" Peter wanted to know.

"Why?" Carrie asked half-hysterically. "Why would you let us go? Why wouldn't you just kill us the way you had Victor killed?"

"What about Jack?" Patrice asked. "Do you expect us to keep quiet about his being framed?"

"Now listen carefully. We haven't much time." Van Huyck addressed their concerns. "I do not pretend to humanitarianism. The reason you won't be killed is that if three members of the wealthy and world-famous Stockwell family were to turn up dead on this little island, it would focus a spotlight on St. Martin the heat of which would melt every profitable venture in which my people are engaged. Your murders would create many more problems than they would solve. Even so, I will reconsider if you balk at the arrangement I'm proposing."

"And just what is the arrangement?" Peter wanted to know.

"Junot—in the parlance of your great American mystery writer, Dashiell Hammett—takes the fall. He is, as the genre has it, our patsy. He takes the rap, and Jack Houston is off the hook."

"That sounds satisfactory to me." Peter sounded quite relieved.

"And all the criminal evidence gets buried," Patrice observed.

"That is correct." Van Huyck's fingers slid toward the gun on the desk.

"But Jack goes free." Carrie was pleading with Patrice not to upset the delicate balance.

"All right," Patrice capitulated. She had no choice. The

important thing was to stay alive. "Junot is armed," she remembered. "He's not just going to toddle along to the police station. How—"

"Leave that to me," van Huyck told her. "Just go on acting like you're our prisoners, mine and his. Act frightened."

"That won't be hard," Patrice told him. "I'm a long way from over being terrified yet."

Junot was really not gone very long. They heard him entering the outer office, and then he appeared. "The van's right out front," he told van Huyck. "We had best move them out fast before the police start giving us a rough time for parking illegally."

"Right." Van Huyck got up and came out from around his desk with the large pistol in his hand. "Junot and I are escorting you downstairs and into the van parked in front," he told them. "Just remember that we both have guns on you. Now we'll go down the stairs in this order. The two ladies first. Then Junot. Then Mr. Stockwell, and I will bring up the rear. Let me caution you again. Don't make any false moves."

They proceeded as van Huyck said. Patrice, Carrie, and Peter climbed into the back of the van. Van Huyck got in behind them and leveled his gun at them. "You drive," he instructed Junot.

Junot closed the rear doors of the van. He walked around to the front and got in the driver's seat. He turned his head around and peered in the back. "Where to?" he asked van Huyck.

"The salt marshes this side of Philipsburg," van Huyck told him. "We'll dump them there."

Carrie began to sob. Patrice couldn't tell whether it was an act or not. Still, it seemed like a good idea if they wanted to lull Junot. She squeezed out a few terrified tears herself. Even Peter managed a panicky sob for his life.

After about fifteen minutes, Junot slowed down. "Salt marshes coming up," he announced. "Less risk of anybody seeing if you do it in the truck, and then we dump the bodies."

"Good idea." Van Huyck stood and motioned with the gun for the three of them to get up against the rear doors of the van. He backed toward the front and leaned against the driver's seat as if to steady himself in order to take better aim. Patrice shredded her bow. Then, almost casually, van Huyck turned and pressed the muzzle of the large handgun to Junot's right temple.

"What are you doing?" Junot hit the brake, but he was coming around a curve and couldn't take his eyes off the road.

There was a loud click as van Huyck released the safety on the gun. "Junot," he said, "you do exactly as I say, or you're a dead man. Very slowly, no more than twenty miles an hour, and very easy on the curves so my finger doesn't slip and pull the trigger, you drive this van into Philipsburg and to the municipal police station and jail."

"I don't understand."

"It's simple." Van Huyck chuckled. "You see, Junot, you're taking the fall for the murder of Victor Grieg." He repeated the phrase, savoring it. "You're taking the fall."

Patrice remembered to start breathing again.

37

A FEW DAYS later, Patrice and Jack were seated across from each other with tall rum drinks at a small table belonging to the snack bar behind the PLM St. Tropez Hotel pool.

"You put yourself in real danger for me," Jack said. "You could have been hurt. You could have gotten yourself killed."

"Not a chance." Patrice was flippant even as her milk-chocolate eyes adored him. "I cut my teeth on Nancy Drew reprints. There was never a doubt in my mind that the good guys would win out over the baddies."

"You proved I didn't kill Victor Grieg when even I myself thought I was guilty." There was wonderment in Jack's voice.

"You were drunk," Patrice reminded him. "You were out of it. After he hit you and you went down, you didn't really know what happened."

"That's true." Jack grimaced. "I was all too ready to believe the worst of myself. That's what being married to Buffy has done to me, I guess."

"What's going to happen now?" Patrice asked, trying to appear casual.

She meant between him and Buffy, but Jack's answer addressed his more immediate concerns. "My hotshot lawyer says that if I waive extradition and come in and make out a deposition, Captain Drees will drop the charges against me. He's satisfied that this Junot character is the murderer, and Carrie has said she'll testify that she saw him kill Grieg."

"I know." Remembering the agreement with van Huyck, and all that was being shoved back under the rug in the interests of not embarrassing Peter Stockwell or Stockwell Enterprises, Patrice felt a sharp twinge of guilt. In real life the baddies didn't lose; they made a deal. "Carrie's really scared to face Junot," she told Jack. "But she's standing up to her fear because she feels responsible for getting you into the mess in the first place. She says if she hadn't been high, she wouldn't have deliberately tried to see if she could entice you away from Buffy. She's sorry about the trouble she caused between you."

Patrice's words had been carefully thought out in advance. What she was saying about Carrie was true, but it was most important to Patrice how Jack reacted. After all, Carrie's coming between Jack and Buffy had really been no more than a transitory flirtation. Her own affair with Jack was ongoing and rooted in a mutual history and—Patrice could only hope—a mutual love. How Jack felt

291

about what came between him and Buffy, about what might threaten their marriage, was of key concern to Patrice.

"If it hadn't been that, it would have been something else." Jack's response, accompanied by a fatalistic shrug, was all that Patrice wanted it to be. "I don't have to tell you, Patrice, that our marriage has been under a strain for some time. Buffy's jealous suspicions have been driving me crazy. They've driven me away from her." He looked steadily toward Patrice. "They've driven me toward you," he told her.

"Oh, darling!"

"I want you, Patrice." His voice was husky—hungry.

"Oh, Jack, I want you, too."

"Now." He signaled the snack bar waiter for a check. His eyes, however, remained on Patrice, filled with desire.

"We'll go up to my room." Patrice's heart was pounding. Her flesh felt liquefied with its own heat. She had not been so consumed with eagerness to have sex since that night at Riverview with Fitz Connely. Fitz Connely! Why had she thought of him? Why now, when Jack was hers, when all the signs were that his marriage to Buffy was really over, when his wanting her was as tangible and urgent as his hand on her warm, naked hip as he led her back to the hotel, to her room, to the bed awaiting them?

What she had always wanted was coming true. Jack and Buffy would divorce. She and Jack would marry. The man Patrice had longed for would finally be hers. She and Jack would live happily ever after. Wouldn't they?

BOOK FIVE

38

RIVERVIEW AWAITED. LOOSE ends, emotional and corporate, had been left dangling. There were deeds undone and deeds regretted. Relationships were in limbo, futures uncertain. "Sure and isn't it just what the Eyetalians say?" Kevin O'Lunney remarked to Ulbricht, the head gardener of the estate. "The opera is never over until the fat lady sings."

If Kevin was optimistic, however, others were not. Holly Meyerling in particular was aware of the sour notes in the libretto. She said as much to her husband, Zelig, when he returned from Washington to spend one of his increasingly rare weekends at Riverview. Patting her golden hair to perfect sleekness with a characteristically delicate movement of her slender hand, Holly remarked that "Everything's in a dreadful mess."

"Just like the National Security Council." Zelig's mind was still on Washington, his answer typically cynical.

"A good part of the mess isn't even here at Riverview," Holly mused. "It's on St. Martin, far, far away."

"Again like the mess in Washington, which is also frequently not in Washington at all."

"But the anguish is here at Riverview."

"You're ahead of me there," Zelig told her. "The anguish hasn't quite reached the White House yet, but it will."

"Matt is unhappy all the time. He can't seem to resolve the situation in Montreal with his son. He and Kathleen are washed up, and they're both miserable about it."

"If they're miserable, why don't they work out their differences and reach some kind of accord?" Zelig asked.

"Like Iran and Iraq?" Holly raised one eyebrow, a gesture that although meant to be sarcastic never failed to melt Zelig's heart.

"Yes. Well, you're right. Detente is an art, not a formula."

"Uncle David is fuming. It seems that Peter's real estate scheme has come a cropper and the family is going to swallow a substantial loss. And Fitz . . ." Holly sighed. "The way he mopes around."

"Why is that?" Zelig asked. "After all, the young man has just inherited a sizable fortune."

"I'm not sure. But I think it just might have something to do with Patrice. I think they might have been involved. Or getting involved. Or about to get involved. Something like that."

"The exactitude of a diplomatist's wife." Zelig smiled. "I'm proud of you."

"But Patrice has this thing for Jack." Again Holly sighed.

"Who is married to Buffy, who was once approached by somebody close to Ollie about financing arms to the contras, but declined on the grounds that the Sandinistas were sexier."

"Now you're being silly," Holly chided him.

"Sorry. It's the Washington syndrome. You can't always tell where policy leaves off and silliness begins. Forget it. What about Jack? Does he reciprocate Patrice's 'thing'?"

"As far as I know he's always been hopelessly hooked on Buffy. Which is like being in love with destabilized uranium."

"Too technical," Zelig judged. "You'll never sell the daytime serial rights using jargon like that."

"As slippery in love as an eel in flight. How's that?"

"A well-mixed metaphor. Eels don't fly. Even slippery ones. Still, it will do for Buffy." Zelig refilled Holly's martini glass and then poured a second one for himself. "How," he wondered, "will it all turn out?"

"Well, we'll know soon. With the charges against Jack dropped, they'll all be coming home to Riverview."

"When will they be here?" Zelig sipped and nodded approval of the second martini. The ice in the shaker hadn't melted. The cocktail hadn't gone watery.

"Tuesday," Holly told him. "They should all be arriving home on Tuesday."

39

ON MONDAY AFTERNOON Jack went back to Buffy's villa to pick up his clothes. It was a warm, wet day, tropically soggy. The dew on the frangipani overwhelmed its delicate perfume with a rain-gutter aroma. The air promised rain but defaulted, providing only a pervasive St. Martin steaminess. As he packed his things, sweat was imposed on Jack from outside himself.

"You're making a puddle on my hand-woven Peruvian throw rug."

Startled, Jack looked up to find his wife standing in the doorway to the bedroom they had once shared. She was wearing a knee-length, loose-knit, black net beach throw over an extreme, deep-slash, black silk bikini. There were droplets on her long, tanned legs as if she had only recently come out of the water. She must have had a dip in the swimming pool, Jack thought, although as a rule she preferred the ocean. "Sorry." His apology was curt. "It's the humidity."

"Try one of these." Buffy was holding two very tall, narrow glasses peaked with frost and slices of lime. Ice tinkled as she moved to hand one to Jack. The rippling net accentuated the full, womanly curves of her body with the movement. She smiled tentatively under the broad-brimmed white beach hat covering her tightly drawn-back hair. Despite the revealing bikini, she looked more chic than sexy.

"Thanks." Jack took the drink. It was the first time he had seen Buffy since the scene on the beach. She looked— well, as appealing as she always had. He tasted the drink. It was tangy, sweet and sour, cold, and intoxicating. "Delicious," he exclaimed. "That really hits the spot."

"Don't sound so surprised, darling."

"I guess I am." Jack was honest. "To tell the truth, I wasn't expecting even small kindnesses from you."

"With your tongue hanging out from the heat like a thirsty cocker spaniel? You know I've always had a soft spot for dumb animals."

Jack's grin was a grimace. "That," he said, "is more like it."

"Well, my bitchiness always was my most attractive quality to you." Buffy sat on the edge of their bed and watched him fold garments into a suitcase. "Are you leaving tomorrow with the others?" she asked after a moment's silence.

"Yes."

"And so back to Riverview with the fair Patrice."

"No," Jack corrected her. "Back to New York, but not to Riverview. My days at Riverview are over. And Patrice, of course, has her apartment in New York."

"Then you'll be moving in there, I suppose." Buffy

296

spoke down into the narrow mouth of the tall, frosted glass.

"Nothing's been decided yet."

"Nothing? I would have thought everything." Buffy looked up. Her violet eyes, lambent with just a hint of pleading, held his for a moment. Then the long lashes fell and screened them. "Or is it just the fate of our marriage that's been decided?"

"I would have thought that was decided when you walked out on me and refused to come back even when you learned I was facing a murder charge."

"Dear Patrice." Buffy was momentarily bitter. "She does report in full detail, doesn't she?"

"Your attitude was hardly a secret, Buffy. Don't blame Patrice."

"But I did come back, didn't I? And I brought the information that laid the groundwork for the charges against you being dismissed. I came to tell you about Peter and the gangsters he was involved with. I wanted you to be aware of all the factors involved in your situation. I did come back to St. Martin for your sake, Jack."

Jack balled a pair of socks. Then he unrolled them, turned each one right side out, and reballed them. "I'm grateful, Buffy," he said finally. "I mean that sincerely. I really am grateful."

"I don't want your gratitude, Jack." The violet eyes regarded him steadily.

"Then what do you want?"

"To be twenty years younger." Buffy sighed. It was a moment of naked candor. She had exposed herself in a way that she rarely did, in a way that was very painful for her. "To be Patrice's age." Her smile was wry. "When I was thirty," she said, "you never would have looked at another woman."

"Damn it, Buffy, that was never it." Jack flung the balled socks into the suitcase so hard that they bounced out again. "I never went looking for a younger woman. You were all the woman I ever wanted. And when it

297

comes right down to it, I was faithful to you a lot more than you were faithful to me.''

''But not completely faithful.''

''No. Not completely faithful. When you hurt me, I hurt back.''

''And just how did I hurt you so that you felt compelled to hurt back with Carrie?'' demanded Buffy.

''I explained that the night it happened. You didn't believe me then. I don't imagine you'll believe me now.''

''And on the beach with Patrice? Did I only imagine I saw that, too?''

''Apples and oranges, Buffy.'' Jack picked up the socks and laid them in the suitcase more gently. ''You left me. Patrice and I did become involved. That day on the beach I had no idea you were even back in St. Martin. But in any case, at that point I didn't owe you fidelity. And from what I've heard, you weren't exactly practicing it yourself back at Riverview.''

''Riverview? What do you mean?''

''Fitz Connely. That's what I mean. He was seen coming out of your room in the middle of the night.''

''By Patrice,'' Buffy guessed. ''Well, when she compiles a dossier, she doesn't leave out anything, does she? Imagine, lurking about the halls in the middle of the night checking up on me! Is that the kind of woman you want, Jack? Think, my boy. If I were you, I'd be very careful.''

''I'm not your 'boy,' '' Jack replied coldly. ''And Patrice doesn't go 'lurking about halls.' She's not sneaky. It was purely by accident that she saw Fitz coming out of your room.''

''And if I told you that nothing happened between myself and Fitz, would you believe me?''

''No.''

''But you expect me to believe you about Carrie when I saw you both with my own two eyes.''

''What's the point of this, Buffy?'' Jack asked. ''What I believe. What you believe. We don't either of us trust the other, and with good reason. We just plain aren't into fidelity. If it hadn't been that night with Carrie, it would

298

have been something else—someone else—that pushed us apart.''

"Then it's hopeless?" Buffy asked in a very small voice.

"We just don't have anything going for us."

"Love?" There was no mistaking the plea in the violet eyes now.

Damn her! Inside, Jack could feel himself starting to weaken. Love! That was his word, not hers. Buffy almost never used it. Her inability to say the word "love" had always been one of the great frustrations of their marriage for Jack. She would call him "stud," scream with rapture during their lovemaking, sigh to him in its aftermath that he was the best and she would die without him. Sex was important to Buffy, and she left him with no doubts that he fulfilled her completely. But love? That was Jack's department.

"You mean sex," he corrected her now, harshly.

"It is good between us." Buffy found it hard to make a distinction. "You can't deny that."

"No. I can't deny that."

"I've never stopped wanting you." It was unusual for Buffy to state it so directly. Usually she relied on seductive hints, innuendo, perfume, body language. "Right up to this very moment, I've never stopped wanting you."

"Damn it, Buffy!"

"Have you stopped wanting me, Jack? If you have, just tell me. I haven't got much left in the way of pride, but I have enough to leave if you really don't desire me anymore. Age diminishes a woman in many ways, but it doesn't rob her of all her pride. Not all. Just tell me you feel no desire for me and I'll go."

Jack's silence was tortured, but it was his answer.

"Darling." Buffy made no move save to let her hands drop to her sides. Under the black net her full breasts rose and fell quickly, straining against the skimpy black silk bikini top.

I'm going to regret this, Jack thought even as he felt his groin stir. "Lust isn't love," he said hoarsely.

"Of course not, darling." She stood, waiting. The inner muscles of her sleek thighs tensed slightly.

"If I want you for the moment, that doesn't promise one damn thing for tomorrow."

"I know." Slowly her arms bent, moved up, out, spread wide to receive him. "At my age, today is enough."

"You bitch!" Jack took one long step, and she was in his arms. "You do it to me every time. Every goddamn time!"

His lips were hungry on her mouth. He was hard against her bare belly under the net, above the brief triangular top of her bikini bottoms. The muscles of his chest flattened her breasts and squeezed the air from her lungs even as her nipples rose. "Are you hot, darling?" she asked when the kiss was over. Her long nails dug through the material of his lightweight slacks and into the toughness of his straining buttocks. "Are you very hot?"

"Very. You're doing it to me again. You know you can, and you do." As he spoke, Jack pulled the black net throw from her body. He removed the bikini top. His hands moved eagerly over her breasts, caressing the flesh, squeezing them, thumbing the quivering, erect nipples. "And I can't turn away. I want you too damn much." He peeled off his shirt. There was a sheen of perspiration on his muscular upper body. His naked chest crushed her breasts. "It's my weakness and your strength." He pulled the string at her lower hip, and the bikini bottoms fell to the rug. His hand moved between her thighs and found her moist and open, welcoming, waiting. "But it's only lust, Buffy. Just that. Lust." He pushed the open suitcase off the bed and laid her down, then kicked off his sandals and removed his slacks and underpants. "Just lust."

"Just lust," Buffy echoed, staring at him—so big, so hard, so ready. "We turn each other on, darling. That hasn't changed." Her voice was breathless, eager, impatient.

He was on top of her then, bending her body in half, opening her to the fullest.

300

Buffy rose to meet him. She received him with a passion that had never been feigned. Lust? Love? Weren't they one and the same?

Later they sprawled exhausted side by side on the bed. Buffy felt fulfilled. Nothing had been decided, but she couldn't help it. That was how she felt: fulfilled.

Jack's feelings were more ambivalent. Their lovemaking had been terrific. It always was between them. But it hadn't changed anything. They could always complete (yes, that was the word—complete) each other in bed, but they would always destroy each other in every other aspect of their relationship.

"Thank you, darling." Buffy snuggled up to him, moist and warm, satisfied and still desiring.

"Don't thank me. Sex is always easy. It's living together that's impossible."

"I know." Buffy sighed voluptuously.

"This only means you can still make me want you. It doesn't change anything else."

"I know." Her hand came to rest lightly on his thigh.

"It was just sex, not a commitment."

"Of course, darling." Her head on his chest, Buffy's tongue peeped out and licked his right nipple.

"It doesn't really mean one damn thing."

"If you say so." Buffy's mouth moved down from his chest to his belly to his groin.

"Just a one-time incident." Jack's penis moved.

"A one-time incident," Buffy repeated, her voice muffled as her mouth found its target. "But if once is good, twice is better." She enveloped him.

Jack did not argue the point.

40

LATER THAT SAME day, at twilight, Patrice sat propped up in the large double bed at the hotel and leafed through a magazine. Jack was late returning from the villa, but she wasn't really concerned. Her attitude was one of anticipation rather than worry.

She was wearing a lime silk spaghetti strap nightgown that clung to the soft curves of her body. The color complemented her chestnut hair, and the style accentuated the curves of her petite figure. Frequently, she had discovered, Jack liked to make love before they went out to dinner.

When at last she heard his key in the door, she arranged herself on the bed in an outlandishly seductive pose reminiscent of precensorship Mae West. "Hello, big boy," she greeted him. "Is that a pistol in your pocket, or are you just paying me a compliment?" She ruined the effect, however, with a giggle. "Damn it!" she said. "I never could come on like a siren with a straight face."

Jack was not smiling back. Patrice looked at him questioningly. Obviously something was wrong.

"Where are your suitcases?" she asked slowly. "Where are the clothes you went to get?"

"I'm sorry, Patrice. I'm so damn sorry."

"Sorry? What are you sorry about?"

"I won't be flying back to New York with you." There was real shame in Jack's voice.

"Buffy!" Patrice realized. "You saw Buffy at the villa."

Jack nodded.

She stared at him. The color drained from her cheeks.

The guilt of his answering look was unmistakable. "The two of you made love." It was not a guess.

"Yes." Jack took a deep breath. "I really am sorry."

"She wiggled, and you turned to jelly." Patrice was trying to be angry. That would be the healthy response—anger. But it wasn't what she felt. What she felt was futility. And with it came a sort of perspective. Her love for Jack was obsessive. Jack was weak. And it was inevitable that Buffy would lure him back. Better now than later.

"It's not that simple," Jack was replying even as he wondered to himself how much truth there was in Patrice's accusation.

"You saw her. You made love. And now you're staying here on St. Martin with her. That's about it, isn't it? Sounds pretty simple to me."

"I really didn't want to hurt you, Patrice."

"Funny how you never want to hurt me and you always do."

"I feel lousy about this."

Again Patrice tried to summon up anger. Instead she found herself responding with a curiously compelling honesty. "It's not your fault," she told him. "I asked for it. I knew what to expect. I wouldn't face it, but inside I knew. The fact is, it's my problem. I became addicted to you, and I just gave in to the addiction every chance I got. I chased you just as avariciously as a junkie chases a fix. But I'll tell you something, Jack. At long last I think I've OD'ed. But I'll live through it. And from here on in, that old Jack Houston monkey is off my back."

"I'm sorry, Patrice. I don't know what else to say."

"Good-bye. That's what else to say, Jack."

"Good-bye, Patrice." He paused awkwardly in the half-open doorway, wanting to say again how sorry he was, then deciding it was pointless. "Good-bye." The door closed behind him.

"Good-bye, Jack," Patrice echoed. "And"—suddenly there was a strong, sure flare-up of the anger she had thought wanting—"good riddance!"

41

PATRICE SAT IN first class with Peter and Carrie and pretended to read a magazine. She didn't feel like talking. She felt numb inside. The phrase "no pain, no gain" kept echoing in her mind. Did it work the other way, too? she wondered. No pain, no loss?

Truly, she didn't feel that she had lost anything. Her obsession for Jack was gone, but that was like having a bad tooth pulled. Your tongue kept returning to the space where the tooth had been, but that didn't compare with the ache when it had been there.

Lousy analogy. Patrice smiled wryly to herself. It hadn't been all ache with Jack. Would she have fought so hard to have him, she wondered, if he hadn't been Buffy's in the first place? Love was one helluva lot more complicated than a toothache.

"How about it, Patrice? Another martini?" Carrie interrupted her musing.

"No, thanks. I'm fine." Truly she had barely tasted the first cocktail the steward had brought her.

"I'll have another." Peter's tone was morose. He was not usually a drinker. It interfered with his concentration, and in business concentration was everything. But business had not gone well, so Peter was allowing himself some rare liquid solace before he reached New York and had to face the board of Stockwell Enterprises. The financial loss would be extensive, balanced only by the retention of the good name of Stockwell. David Lewis would not write off the investment lightly. Peter shuddered and drank off his second martini at a gulp. He signaled the steward for another refill.

Waiting for the drink, he reflected that Patrice was on the board. It wouldn't hurt to ingratiate himself with her. He would certainly need all the backing he could get. And if not backing, then perhaps he could at least neutralize her so that she didn't line up with such poised-to-pounce critics as Max Tyler. Yes, it wouldn't hurt to exercise some charm on Patrice.

Of course Peter exercising charm was somewhat like a haddock demonstrating tricks on a bicycle. He had neither the experience nor the talent. With his very first attempt, he fell on his flippers.

"Jack Houston is a cad," he announced, pushing his thuggish face forward to be sure he had Patrice's attention. Everything about Peter was prematurely yuppie except for his choice of words; they had a tendency toward the mid-Victorian.

"What?" Patrice was startled.

"I said Jack Houston is a cad. The way he ditched you is unforgivable."

Carrie closed her eyes. It was too painful. Peter rendered sympathy with the same complete lack of finesse he brought to the act of lovemaking.

Patrice laughed harshly. "Thank you for your support, Peter." She raised the magazine in front of her face, effectively shutting off further conversation. Shrewdness, she must remember in future when dealing with Peter on the board, was a crippled skill when unaccompanied by sensitivity.

Sensitivity . . . The word made Patrice think of Fitz Connely. He did have that quality. Fitz was a sensitive man, but was he a discriminating one? Could he have been telling the truth when he'd said that nothing had happened between him and Buffy the night Patrice had seen him coming from her room? Certainly he had intuited her interest in Jack. But even while she had been obsessing on Jack, she had been genuinely attracted to Fitz. He had been attracted to her, too. He had made that obvious. Fitz Connely. Had she, Patrice wondered, burned her bridges behind her?

"I don't see how Jack can prefer Buffy." If there had been any doubt, Peter now clinched his utter lack of sensitivity. "She has no morals at all, just crude sex appeal."

So that's what I lack, Patrice thought, sex appeal. How shrewd, Peter. Hit it right on the nailhead. You sure do know how to comfort a cousin in need. "I'm going to read now, Peter," she said calmly. "So no more commiserations, please."

Patrice laid aside her magazine and fished the last volume of the Seabury diaries from her carry-on bag. She propped it up to block off any further conversation from Peter. Focusing her attention, Patrice began to read. . . .

The year 1853 in New York City was highlighted by the Crystal Palace Exposition, the first world's fair to be held in the United States. As an artist, twenty-six-year-old Edith Seabury had looked forward to viewing the much heralded aesthetic works of the exhibition. Not hesitating to use her father's influence with his friend Horace Greeley, one of the event's major organizers, Edith was among the elite group present at the opening ceremonies.

"Charles Stockwell will be there," her father advised her. "He's one of the major backers recruited by Horace."

"Of what interest can that possibly be to me, Father? Any relationship that may have existed between the master of Riverview and myself has been over for two years."

"Two unmarried years," Linus Seabury muttered.

"What did you say, Father?"

"Nothing. Nothing at all."

"Well, I did hear you, Father. And you may as well resign yourself. Marriage is not a matter of any urgency to me. And if it were, Charles Stockwell is no longer among those I would consider for a husband."

Nevertheless, when Edith spied Charles among the luminaries on the platform during the brief opening speeches before the doors of the Crystal Palace were opened to the crowd, she regarded him with some curiosity. He looked older. At thirty-five there were already flecks of gray in his long sideburns and in his flowing blond mustache. The first time she met him he had seemed dashing and arrogant in his uniform, a soldier back from the wars with a sparkle in his eye to turn the head of the most committed suffragist. Now he looked more composed, more thoughtful, and, somehow, kinder. There was a pinched look between his eyes as if he had been reading too intensely by candlelight.

Standing just below the speaker's platform, Edith was really quite close to him. At first, among the small group surrounding Greeley making last-minute adjustments to the opening day schedule, he did not see Edith. When he did, he caught the full impact of her eyes regarding him. His handsome, slender, ruddy face registered surprise, then pleasure, and finally a certain confusion.

Immediately when their eyes met, Edith turned away. She felt caught out in a rudeness. Had he interpreted her glance as encouragement? She hoped not. She didn't want to offer any false hopes after all this time. She was committed to the single life, dedicated to the uplifting of the downtrodden. Her painting, the equality of women, the abolition of slavery—these were the subject matters that claimed her concentration. She had no time for frivolity, none to waste on men. There was no room in Edith's long-term schedule for the likes of Charles Cabot Stockwell.

Her ruminations ceased as a light, early springtime drizzle began to fall. Bumbershoots and parasols clashed in the crowd's haste to raise them. The speeches were hastily concluded, and the Crystal Palace was opened to those waiting. The shuffling crowd repacked itself more tightly as it moved to enter.

From the first, the aesthetics inside the octagon-shaped main building were disappointing to Edith. The "cultural exhibits" provided by the almost five thousand exhibitors, half from twenty-three foreign countries, half from the United States itself, added up to all glitter and little substance. The pretensions to art were only a facade for the peddling of exports. English woolens, French wines, and Viennese gewgaws held center stage while the few works of classic Belgian weaving, Oriental silk screening, and Scandinavian furniture design were relegated to the shadowy recesses of the hall. Even those few paintings and sculptures worthy of note were obscured by the general vulgarity of the exhibit as a whole.

Edith thought to herself that she really shouldn't be surprised. From the first, the exhibition had been ill conceived. It had been inspired by the British Crystal Palace Exhibition of 1851, but the imitative spirit of the New York project had been bound to keep it from surpassing the successful Hyde Park project. Even the main building had been modeled after the famous London structure of the same name. However, local New York architects of what Edith privately defined as "the Gingerbread School" had added to the basic octagon a Greek cross superstructure, a centered round dome, and tall, jarring Moorish minarets. The result had turned the central focus of the thirteen-acre Reservoir Square over which the exhibition sprawled into a stylistic hodgepodge that just as surely as it caught the eye repelled it.

The Crystal Palace was made of glass and iron. A block north, three hundred fifty feet high, stood the Latting Observatory. It was constructed of iron and wood. Both these main edifices of the exhibition suffered from the same fatal flaw. Their roofs leaked. That flaw was brought home to Edith and the crowd around her now as the spring drizzle outside the Crystal Palace turned to driving rain. Drops turned into rivulets and accumulated at the edges of the dome and the mitering of the eaves supporting the minarets. Soon the accumulation was pouring into the great hall in a dozen locations, drenching some of them with the force of a waterfall.

Many exhibits were ruined before they could be adequately covered. The clothing of most of those in attendance was soaked to the skin. From Horace Greeley on down, those charged with responsibility for the exhibition were overwhelmed by the rainstorm. Most of their early efforts to counter its effects were in vain.

Edith sought shelter from the badly leaking roof under the overhang of a Greek confectioner's stand. She was standing there trying to decide if the deluge outside was abating when she felt a tentative hand on her elbow. She turned and found herself looking up into the lean face of Charles Stockwell.

"Hello, Edith." His greeting was not as tentative as his quick touch had been.

"Hello, Charles."

"How are you?"

"I'm fine. And you?"

"Fine." There was a long silence. "And your father," Charles asked finally. "How is he?"

"He's fine."

"Please convey my regards to him."

"I will." The pressure of the crowd was pressing them together in a way that made the lack of intimacy in their conversation even more difficult. Now it was Edith who floundered for something to say. "Father said that you are one of the backers of the exposition," she recalled at last.

"Yes, I am."

"Have you invested heavily?" Edith's question took note of the rain pouring down from the ceiling.

"Only moderately. Still, I fear my judgment was faulty."

"I fear it was."

Charles winced. "You think it is a perfect catastrophe, then?"

"Nothing is perfect."

"Well, I take little solace from that." Charles looked up and then back down at Edith again. "The roof can be fixed."

"Of course. The concept, however, cannot. It's too late. The exhibit is a triumph of shoddy merchandising over good taste."

Charles smiled. "If that is true, then I shall surely recoup my investment. The general public always prefers bad taste."

"You are mistaken. And I do not believe you will reap any great profit."

"Undoubtedly, I am mistaken and you are right. No wise man would challenge the judgment of a beautiful woman." Charles attempted a compliment.

"And I thought we had done with banalities," Edith reacted coldly.

"I am destroyed."

"You are not. You are merely prey to the glibness of your gender."

"Not at all," Charles protested. "I meant it. You are beautiful."

"If you have nothing serious to say, then perhaps it would be better if we didn't speak at all."

"You wish me to speak seriously?" Charles took a deep breath. "Very well, then, I shall. I have missed you, Edith. I have missed you very much."

"I think it would be better if—"

"Not a day goes by that I don't long for your company."

"—we did not discuss—"

"I still love you, Edith."

Outside, the rain was tapering off. Inside, the leaks had subsided to a dribbling. The crowd was moving to leave. A path was clearing between the exit and the confectioner's stand where Edith and Charles stood.

"You have no right to speak to me in this way." Edith's protest was not as forceful as she wished it to be.

"I had to seize the opportunity."

"You have not the right." Edith gathered her skirts. "I must go."

"Wait. Just tell me that it will be all right for me to call upon you at your father's house."

"No," Edith replied. "It will most certainly not be all right. You may not call." She moved away with her golden-blond head held high. "Good-bye." She did not turn around as she bade Charles farewell.

A few days later Edith made one of her small compromises between commitment to the movement and her art. An important abolitionist rally was being held in the park across from City Hall. But Edith was on the crest of the wave carrying her to completion of a painting of the Brooklyn harbor front as viewed from the Manhattan side of the river and afraid that if she interrupted herself, the lost momentum—the ongoing inspiration, as it were— could never be regained. She chose to miss the meeting and go on painting.

She was particularly sorry to pass up the chance to hear once again the keynote speaker, a black woman born into slavery in Ulster County, New York. The woman had only escaped that condition some time after New York State abolished adult slavery in 1827. Her owner, however, had continued to enslave her in defiance of the law until an abolitionist bought her and set her free. By that time the son to whom she had given birth had been illegally sold south by her master. The early years of her freedom had been devoted to a prolonged but ultimately successful court battle to have her child returned to her.

When she was born, the black woman had been given the name Isabella. When she was set free, she had added the name of her liberator, Van Wagener. But she had become famous under quite a different name, one she claimed to have received from God. That name was Sojourner Truth.

Sojourner Truth could neither read nor write. But she could talk. "My God, how that woman can speak!" was the judgment of famous abolitionist orator William Lloyd Garrison. Sojourner Truth herself explained her talent by opening each of her addresses with the same phrase: "Children, I talk to God, and God talks to me!"

To Edith she was, quite simply, a heroine. New York City, Edith believed, should count itself blessed that this illiterate woman had chosen to settle there despite the unpleasantness that followed her arrival. The "unpleasantness" involved charges of sexual involvement with a self-styled religious prophet. Despite her illiteracy, Sojourner Truth brought and won a slander suit, thereby becoming the first black person in American history to win such an action against a white.

Since that time she had devoted herself to spreading the word regarding slavery and women. The word in both cases was "freedom." To Sojourner Truth it was "the Word of the Lord."

Still, Edith convinced herself to pass up the meeting and finish the painting. She had not quite accomplished this when, later in the day, her poet friend Susan Talley— recently arrived from Philadelphia to settle permanently in New York—burst in on her in a state of agitation. "There's been trouble!" she announced, out of breath. "But Sojourner Truth was magnificent, Edith. You should have been there. She put her hands on her hips and stuck out her chin and called on God to forgive her oppressors and to shield her from the rocks and tomatoes and rotten eggs they were throwing."

"What happened?" Edith put down her brush. "Calm down, Susan. Now tell me from the beginning."

"Well, it started out peacefully enough. There was a goodly crowd, and it almost filled City Hall Park. But behind the speaker's platform, on the steps of the City Hall itself, these hoodlums began to congregate. The police just stood there and watched them with their arms folded. Every so often this man would come out of City Hall and move among the rabble as if he were telling them what to do."

"He probably was." Edith nodded. "Not much happens in New York without the City Hall gang's orders." The "City Hall gang" was the common description given to the mixture of businessmen, hoodlums, and ward bosses who controlled the choice of candidates and thereby filled the offices of the municipal government.

"Yes," Susan agreed. "Anyway, they didn't really do

anything until Sojourner Truth started to speak. She was comparing the situation of black women slaves in the South to female immigrant servants in the North when the crowd of rowdies suddenly broke from the steps of the City Hall—almost as if someone had given an order—and attacked us. The people on the outskirts—most of them women—got the worst of it, I think. Where the crowd was thinnest, you see, the hooligans were using clubs. Where it was tight-packed, they threw things instead of trying to force their way through.'' Susan shuddered. ''What I still don't understand is why,'' she said. ''Why should they be so opposed to a decent, God-fearing woman like Sojourner Truth?''

''What Sojourner says represents a handy target for the people holding power to maintain their control. If the workingmen of New York, the immigrant Irish and Germans on the bottom of the heap, can be made to look at blacks and women as a threat to their own status—to their livelihood—then their misery can be turned into hate toward a black woman like Sojourner Truth. That way their dissatisfactions are defused. The powder keg blows up at blacks and women instead of at those who hold down their wages and exploit them.'' Edith had been carried away. Now, however, she remembered to be concerned about those involved in the riot. ''Was there a great deal of violence?'' she wanted to know. ''Was anybody seriously hurt?''

''Many were injured. How seriously, I don't know,'' Susan told her.

''Sojourner Truth? Did she make her escape without injury?''

''I don't know. The violence toward her was still mounting when I myself managed to get away.''

''Then we must go to her.'' Edith stood up. ''We must go to her home directly and make sure that she has not come to harm.''

''Very well, Edith.''

Edith put on a light spring coat, and the two young women left the Seabury house, walking uptown past an immigrant shanty town to a modest residential district populated exclusively by free blacks. They turned in at the house shared by a black family with Sojourner Truth and her children.

To their relief, Edith and Susan found the former slave woman sitting in her parlor, unharmed, holding council with some of her followers. " 'Whites only' is for the sick," proclaimed the tall, solidly built but not fat luminary of the abolitionist movement. "Sojourner is never better. I ain't plannin' to be nothin' but a visitor."

She noted the two arrivals and nodded to them. "Glad you has got away unhurt, Miz Talley," she told Susan. "Movement rightly does need its poets. And how you keepin', Sister Edith? Stayin' out of harm's way today, I reckon."

"I was worried for you." Edith ignored the gentle gibe at her absence from the meeting. "I'm glad you're all right."

"Obliged for your concern, but they can't do damage to ole Sojourner. 'Cause ain't I a woman?" A quick twinkle came and left her eyes as Sojourner Truth paraphrased her own already famous speech to the recent National Women's Rights Convention. "Did have help, though," she added. "And from a man at that. Took the blows meant for me on himself, he did. That's what we be talkin' about just now."

"He was evidently hurt," added one of the other women. "We were told he was taken away in the infirmary wagon."

"Infirmary. Hospital." Sojourner Truth shrugged. "Be saying I can't go see how he is because it for white folks only. But I say I don't want to use it, only to visit."

"They won't let you in." Edith was blunt. "Not unless you go with a white person."

"Nothin' makes less sense than evil." Sojourner Truth sighed. "But how come they pass me if I go with a white?"

"They'll think you're a servant. They won't pay any attention to you."

314

"Pay me no mind. Well now, that always has been their mistake." Sojourner Truth's smile fell on Edith like a beacon. "Could you use a lady's maid now, Sister Edith? I'd be obliged for the position."

As the other women laughed, Edith smiled and agreed. "Hired," she said. "But I would caution you to assume a humility proper to your ends."

"Oh, I be humble all right. Talk the talk and bend the back. For an hour, maybe two. Longer than that, ole Sojourner like to bust out with a potion of the good Lord's truth for all the sinners to hear."

"We'll make it a short visit." Edith laughed.

It was only when she was on her way to the infirmary with Sojourner Truth that Edith thought to inquire as to the identity of the man they were going to visit. When she was told that it was none other than Charles Stockwell and that Sojourner Truth knew him more than casually, her reaction was quite mixed. Her first concern was instinctive. How badly hurt was he? Soon, however, she began wondering what he was doing at an abolitionist rally. Edith could not reconcile his presence at the rally with the opinions he held and which had caused her to turn away from him three years ago. Why had he intervened in Sojourner Truth's behalf? That Charles was brave, Edith took for granted, but he had also always believed that the so-called rabble-rousers were asking for trouble and deserved what they got. And would he not take for granted that Edith's visit signified a change in her attitude toward him? Did she really object to his coming to such a conclusion? Was his hospitalization under these circumstances perhaps not reason enough for her attitude to soften?

The questions were unresolved when Edith—the cannily servile Sojourner Truth in her wake—was admitted to the private hospital room that Charles's status accorded him. His face lit up when Edith entered the room. The

315

expression turned to respect when he recognized Sojourner Truth. "I am honored." His greeting was sincere.

"Had to come and say I'm obliged for your helpin' me and to see for myself just how bad hurt you be," Sojourner Truth told him.

"Not too bad." Charles's smile turned to a grimace as he shifted in the bed. "Two broken ribs, they tell me. The doctor set them, and now there's nothing to do but lie still and wait."

"And don't scratch," the black woman told him. "That was the hardest for me when the slave master broke my ribs some years back. Not scratchin'."

"I won't scratch," Charles promised. He turned his attention to Edith. "It was very nice of you to come," he said.

"She had to." Sojourner Truth chuckled. "I needed missy coattails to get in."

"Even so. I do appreciate it."

"You two be acquainted," Sojourner Truth realized.

"Yes," Edith confessed. "We were once engaged."

"Once?" The abolitionist leader snorted. "You sayin' you let a good man like this get away from you?"

"All too eagerly." Charles sensed an ally. "But maybe Edith was right. I was a pretty rigid fellow back then."

"You were a racist and a misogynist," Edith confirmed.

" 'Misogynist,' " Sojourner Truth repeated. "Too big a word to be much use. You really a woman hater?" she asked Charles.

"No, I never was." Charles laughed. "But even so I've changed. If only I could have the chance to prove it."

"Now I do owe him that," Sojourner Truth told Edith. "No way I can pay it, though. Only you can, Sister Edith. How say? Will you take up my debt?"

"How have you changed?" Edith asked Charles.

"Put his money where his mouth say it was," Sojourner Truth answered for Charles. "Miz Stowe tell you that."

"Harriet Beecher Stowe? What does she—"

316

"Mr. Stockwell here was one of them put up the money to get her antislavery book out when the slave owners leaned on the book publishers to hold it down."

"*Uncle Tom's Cabin?*" Edith regarded Charles with surprise. "You put up money to have *Uncle Tom's Cabin* published?"

"I was only one of those who financed private publication and distribution. We felt that it was an important book—a book that had to be read as widely as possible."

"*You* felt that way?" Edith was not over her astonishment. "But you weren't an abolitionist."

"Mrs. Stowe's book turned me into one. The evil is too great. Her words have washed away any argument for gradualism as regards the ending of slavery."

"There now, Sister Edith. He is rightly one with us. We be women and hard. We be women and soft. Some of the soft now for my friend here. How say?"

"I don't know what Mr. Stockwell wants of me." Edith had softened, but she was still cautious.

"Permission to call on you when I am released from the hospital." Charles was quick to take advantage of the opportunity that had opened up to him.

"Very well." Edith was not as reluctant as her tone might have indicated. "You have my permission to call."

"Well now"—Sojourner Truth beamed—"and ain't you a woman?"

It was three weeks before Charles paid his first call. By prearrangement he came for afternoon tea. Edith had it served in the parlor and sat across the small table from him with her hands folded in her lap as primly as if they had never spent long evenings of intimate and rapturous fondlings together.

"And so, Charles, you *have* come out for abolition." Edith had made inquiries and knew that Charles had become active with the movement. She offered him a scone.

"I have announced my sentiments publicly, yes." He

balanced his teacup and saucer agilely on his knee and accepted the small biscuit.

"And you do not view the abolition of the slave system merely as a means to obtain more cheap labor for your foundries?" Edith asked, shrewdly recalling their earlier conversations. "Strawberry preserves?" she offered, holding out the jam pot to him.

"Yes, please." His balancing act became more complex as he spread the jam on the scone, but Charles, bred a gentleman, carried it off without much difficulty. "I am as pragmatic as the next businessman," he said, "but my conviction in this matter is sincere and not self-serving. I hope you will believe that."

Edith studied him for a moment. "Yes," she said finally. "I do believe that you have changed in some respects. Of others, however, I'm not so sure."

Charles finished chewing his jam-spread scone, washed it down with a swallow of tea, and only then replied. "To what do you allude?" he asked.

"To the suffragist movement. To equality for women in all fields of endeavor. To a single standard as regards morality."

"It is true." Charles spread his hands to indicate his frankness. "I have not finalized my views on this subject as yet. I see it still as a matter of differences as much as of equality. Mother Nature—"

"Oh, Charles!" Edith burst out laughing, and her stiffness left her. "Mother Nature indeed! You just want all the jam for yourself, and what is more, you want a woman to provide it for you."

Charles looked down at the tea table, and his face turned red. He had indeed in his nervousness polished off all the scones and jam. "But men and women really are different." His effort at recovery was weak. "And the difference may well dictate differing standards of behavior."

"What you mean is freedom for men to womanize and chains to bind women to virtue."

"But women don't—"

"But they do, Charles. You can't have forgotten." Argumentation pushed Edith into a brazen honesty. "You can't believe my desire was feigned and only yours ordained. You can't believe I was merely submitting to your caresses, your masculine demands."

"Still, we never—" Charles was aroused at the memories Edith's words summoned up, but confused as well.

"If not for all that nonsense of you being a gentleman and a proper marriage in our future, we might have," Edith told him frankly. "There was many a night you stopped when I would have been content to continue to a natural conclusion."

Charles stared at her. "It's almost as if you were saying that if we hadn't been engaged, we could have . . ." His eyes asked the question raised by his unfinished sentence.

"Well, perhaps that's true," Edith told him softly. "I was very attracted to you, Charles."

"Was?"

"Am," she admitted. "Am attracted. And I was—am—aroused by you."

Charles was never clumsy. He stepped very carefully around the tea table. He took the cup and saucer from Edith's lap and set it to one side. He raised her to her feet and drew her away from the table, kissing her with a passion too long held dormant.

Edith's body responded to his embrace. She melted into him. Finally the kiss ended and she pushed breathlessly away. "You see," she said. "Women can easily be as shameless as men. It is still afternoon, the light not yet faded from the sky, and I am as unrestrained in my passion as you are."

"Are you really?"

"How can you doubt me?" Edith took his hand and pressed it to her breast.

"Then marry me."

"But why bother?" Edith asked. "We can have each other without it and still keep our freedom."

"I want more than lovemaking. And I want more than freedom."

"That," Edith told him, "is what worries me. My body I would give freely. The 'more' I'm not so sure about."

Charles thought a moment. "You want equality with men," he said finally. "Isn't that right?"

"Yes."

"Then deal with my marriage proposal as a man would. Regard it as a business proposition."

"Now that's an interesting idea." Edith laughed and snuggled in his arms. "Just how do I do that?"

"Negotiate."

"Negotiate?"

"I want your hand in marriage—"

"Just my hand?"

"Be serious." Charles scowled at her. "Of course not just your hand. I want this"—he touched her—"and this"—he squeezed—"and of course this."

"Mmm. Of course that."

"Now what do you want in exchange?" Charles demanded.

"My oneness. To be myself. Not to submerge who I am in marriage. To be free to fight for what I believe in as an individual regardless of what my husband thinks or how it affects him. It's a lot to ask of any man, I know. But it is what I want."

"Then you shall have it." He kissed her. "Just say you'll marry me, and it shall be as you want." He kissed her again. "Say that you'll marry me."

"I'll marry you," Edith said, not without misgivings, but not without real joy as well.

Once the question of marriage was settled, events proceeded with a logic of their own. A date was agreed upon, announcements were printed, distant relatives were notified, a Unitarian minister was located who would agree to alter the ceremony in keeping with Edith's suffragist principles, schedules were shifted and reshifted, and

320

Charles and Edith were kept bewilderingly busy. There was no time for embraces, kisses, caresses. Lovemaking would have to wait until after the wedding. Despite all Edith's principles, conventionality had caught them in its trap.

"This prewedding experience," Edith summed up, "is the best argument I have yet encountered for free love."

They were at Riverview for the day, their first time away from the nuptial pressures in the city. Charles had wanted Edith to come out and see her new home so that any alterations she might desire could be effected before they returned from their honeymoon abroad. Edith, however, was viewing her domain-to-be with something other than a wifely eye.

She squeezed Charles's hand and smiled a calculating smile as she surveyed the ornately paneled formal dining room with its huge black marble fireplace. "Ah, the dinners we shall give here for your illustrious Hudson Valley friends," she declared.

"You have plans to entertain the local gentry?" Charles was surprised.

"Of course. What better way to raise money for the abolitionist cause?"

"I fear many of them will not be in sympathy."

"Then I shall change their minds, my dear. There are many opportunities for the persuasive powers of a clever hostess."

Charles remembered the dinner party at Cornelia van Steadman's Manhattan town house, where Edith had snarled her righteousness at male pragmatism and alienated most of those present. He raised an eyebrow.

"You are not the only one who has changed, Charles," she assured him. "I will astound you with my newly mastered tact and womanly charms. I have learned cunning and mastered restraint. I have come to understand what it means to catch more fools with honey than with vinegar."

"That's 'flies,' " Charles remonstrated mildly.

"If you say so, Charles." Edith followed him into the vast ballroom. "If you say so."

She looked at the glittering crystal chandeliers designed to hold over one thousand candles and craned her neck at the twenty-four-foot ceiling from which they were suspended. "Marvelous!" She clapped her hands. "I shall suggest to the ladies in Seneca Falls that the next Women's Rights Convention be held here at Riverview."

"Once we are married," Charles realized, "the Hudson River Valley will never be the same."

They passed through the ceremonial living room with its Louis XVI furniture, walls covered with imported watered silk, and windows framed by heavy, salmon-colored velvet drapes and entered the main sitting room. Edith, whose artist's eye favored simplicity, subtle colors, and clean lines, found the provincial American colonial style here more to her taste. The pillows were perhaps too plump and the upholstery too floral, but at least the maple furniture was functional and comfortable, and the organdy curtains permitted the sunlight to splash into the room with an energizing vibrancy that the more formal chambers lacked. "And here is where my suffragist group shall meet weekly," she announced.

"Shall I be husband to hordes of dedicated women, then?" Charles worried.

"Not at all. You shall husband only me. But I shall make Riverview utilitarian. Do you mind?"

"I don't think I mind," Charles told her. "Just so long as our bedroom is for us alone."

They went back into the living room and passed through the large French doors to a balcony overlooking the Hudson. Edith caught her breath at the vista of sculptured gardens and lush wildlands beyond. "Is this all Riverview?" she exclaimed.

"As far as the eye can see and beyond."

"What's that?" She pointed.

"It's called a gazebo." Charles smiled at her wide eyes. "And what use will you make of that, my darling?" he asked.

322

"It will be a safe house for escaped slaves in transit to Canada," she told him with absolute seriousness.

They went back inside. Edith insisted on examining the attic above the third floor of the manor house. "Yes," she said, brushing a loose blond curl out of her eyes. "This will convert nicely into a studio where I can paint. Could a skylight be cut there, do you think?" She pointed.

"If that's what you want." Charles led her back down to the floor below. "This room, however," he told her, "I have plans for myself."

Edith looked at him inquiringly.

"A nursery," he told her. "I'm hoping you'll find time between your art and your commitments to abolitionism and suffrage to have children with me."

The words brought Edith to a halt. She looked at him gravely. It was the first time the subject had seriously come up. She thought a moment. "Well," she said finally, noncommittally, "you never know."

"I know." Charles took her firmly by the wrist and turned her to him. "I want us to have children, Edith."

"We'll see."

"This is not a principle of the movement to be debated, Edith. This is between you and me only."

"I'm not sure that's so. There may well be important principles involved as regards childbirth." Suddenly, unexpectedly, Edith relaxed and smiled. Her tone became conciliatory. "Well, girl children to carry on the fight, certainly," she told Charles in the spirit of compromise. "But about boys, I'm not so sure."

"I am," Charles said.

And although history would put its stamp of approval on those causes for which Edith would never cease to fight, in this one matter, Charles prevailed.

42

Peter Stockwell was not a young man to admit failure easily, but to his mother he was forced to admit that the redevelopment project was now a total loss. Peter's mother had, over many years of being married to the ineffectual Jonathan, mastered the technique of being supportive without being overly sympathetic. Too much sympathy when poured over masculine failure was like too much syrup on a pancake: it turned the recipient soggy with self-pity. "It happens," she told her son. "There will be another day."

"I'm not so sure."

They were seated in the east wing parlor of Riverview. Outside, the flowers were budding, the leaves polishing their green. The air was balmy, spring seeking summer. Their drinks were tall and cool and nonalcoholic. Their lack of potency did not cheer Peter. He was morose—a quality reminiscent of his father.

A Stockwell genetic trait, Ellen thought. Dominant in her husband, Peter's father, but merely recessive in her son. With Jonathan it determined failure, while with Peter it merely reflected it. Still, it was irksome to see him so sullen and beaten. "You were betrayed by your associate." Shifting the blame had always helped to bolster Jonathan's ego.

"I entered into the arrangement without taking sufficient precautions." Peter was not his father; he did not so easily let himself off the hook. "It's not the two point two million, Mother. Stockwell can easily afford that. It's having to scrap a project that promised billions in profits, a project that would have put me right up there with Trump and Helmsley and Zeckendorf. Not just Stockwell Enterprises, me personally. It's having to eat crow with the board. It's knowing they don't trust my judgment anymore. You see, I was on my way to gaining control of that board, Mother. That's the most important thing I've blown."

"David Lewis has always exercised a sort of control." Ellen thought out loud. "But David is not getting any younger."

"That's true. I was his natural successor before this happened." Peter's sullenness made him look even more like a thwarted hit man.

"Well, who else is there?" Ellen tried to keep the conversation on a practical tack. "If not you, who? Let us appraise the competition."

"What's the point?"

"Max Tyler, Buffy, Patrice, and Halsey."

"I'm not so sure about Halsey." Despite his mood, Peter allowed himself to be drawn into speculating about his possible rivals. "I have a hunch the new boy may ease him out and take over for himself. You know, Mother, Fitz was really the one who tattled on me to the board. Stockwell Enterprises may yet find itself in the hands of the Irish peasantry."

"Not all at once." Ellen was realistic. "Maybe someday, but at first he'll have to go slow. He may have won this round, but you can't tell if he has real staying power. Meanwhile, what about Buffy? I loathe her personally, but I can't deny she's shrewd. It would be just like her to capitalize on your mistake."

"I don't think so. Not just now. She isn't even planning to come back to New York right away." Peter's snort was derogatory. "She's too busy with her second honeymoon."

"Love conquers all." His mother was equally cynical. In her personal experience love had not only not conquered anything, it had completely eluded her. At age fifty-four she had no illusions that the future would be

325

any different. "What about Max Tyler, then?" she asked. "Taking the long view, does he represent any real threat to control of the board?"

"That gender bender!" Peter rolled his eyes. "Gay pride or no gay pride, the corporate world isn't ready for Max. One appearance by him at the Century Club as president of the board and the bottom would drop out of Stockwell preferred."

"Patrice, then?"

"She's the one to watch all right," Peter granted. "Those frilly bows of hers are strictly for appearance. She's got the head for business, and she's got the instinct for the fast track. Plus she's bitter over losing Jack to his wife. I get the feeling her eye is on the target and she won't be distracted by men anymore. Little Patrice is the one who'll see I don't pick myself up, dust myself off, and start all over again."

"Mm-hmm." Ellen shifted position on her armchair. "Well, despite her present frame of mind," she said, "we do know Patrice's weakness. She has a history of turning herself into a victim of love. And you know what I've always taught you, Peter. Play to the other person's vulnerability."

"Patrice?" Peter hooted. "Don't be ridiculous, Mother."

"I'm not being ridiculous. You're a very attractive young man. She is only a couple of years older than you are. If you can't lick them, Peter, join them."

"We're first cousins."

"So were the Romanoffs. That didn't stop them from merging their interests in marriage and taking over Europe."

"Marriage? Not a chance. Patrice detests me."

"Hate is only the other side of the coin of love."

Peter stared at his mother. He had a flash of rare insight. Ellen might have a good instinct for business—for the cutting edge, for which throats to go for and when—but when it came to love, she had neither instinct, nor experience, nor even much in the way of common sense.

326

All she had was banalities. The other side of the coin of love indeed. "Patrice is out as far as that's concerned," he told her flatly.

"Well, if you're going to just turn up your nose at my advice—" Ellen's feelings were hurt.

"I'm not. It's good advice. It just won't apply to Patrice. But it does contain within it the seeds of how I might undercut Max."

"Max?" His mother stared at him. "Peter, you're not—?"

"No." He laughed his humorless laugh, the one that always seemed to escape his lips without a smile. "I'm not. But it just occurred to me that Max represents all of the Tyler interests. That's where his vulnerability is. The way to capitalize on it is to fragmentize those interests."

"I don't think I'm following you."

"Carrie Tyler, Mother. I'm talking about Carrie Tyler. She has a large share of the estate, and Max handles it for her."

"I see." Ellen thought about it. An early robin chirped in the sculpted shrubbery at the base of the mansion. It was the only sound in the still air outside. "And do you think she would be receptive to your attentions?"

"Sometimes you can sound really old-fashioned, Mother."

"Perhaps. But my meaning is clear."

"Well then, the answer is yes. Carrie has already thrown herself at me once. She's—" hot for my body, Peter was going to say, but didn't. "Crazy about me," he said instead.

43

"I GUESS I'LL always be crazy about you." Wendy MacTavish's eyes were large and luminous looking up at Matt from the bed.

What am I doing here? Why am I doing this? Just to get even? Matt didn't like himself very much as he realized what a large part of the truth that was. He'd been hurt, and now he was going to hurt back. And he was using Wendy to do it. It was a lousy way to treat the woman he'd once lived with, once loved, had a child with, but he couldn't stop himself.

All through the drive up, he'd told himself he was only coming to Montreal to see his son. But it wasn't Bruce who was on his mind as first the thruway and then the Northway sped by. It was Kathleen. It was as if a hot branding iron were searing the pictures inside his head: Kathleen and Fitz in bed together, naked, making love. He couldn't let go of the image. It turned his knuckles white on the steering wheel; his furious hands strangled the gearshift.

"She did it to get even with me," he muttered to himself, "and I didn't do anything for her to get even about. She thought I made love to Wendy, and so she punished me. But I didn't! Damn her, I didn't." His lip curling back unconsciously, he decided without really deciding, made up his mind without thinking about it, that if the opportunity came up again, he would make love to Wendy.

Where the hell did nobility get you, anyway? He'd turned Wendy down once because of his feelings for Kathleen. And all the time she'd been going to bed with

Fitz. How many times? Matt wondered. She hadn't said. How many times had they made love? Were they still lovers? The thought gnawed at him, and it blinded him. A part of him knew he was being childish, petty, vindictive. There was no quid quo pro in love. Revenge could never even things out. And revenge on whom? How would Kathleen even know he'd made love to Wendy? And how fair was this to Wendy? Not fair at all. Matt didn't even want to think about that.

"Come here." Wendy held out her arms to him.

He went to her, took her in his arms, and kissed her. The rage inside him fired a sort of passion. Was he making love to Wendy or punishing Kathleen? He slipped between the sheets. Her body arced to his. He caressed her, as she did him.

"I want you," Wendy moaned. "It's been so long. I want you so much." She reached for him. "What's the matter?" Her voice indicated her surprise at finding him unaroused.

"It'll be all right. Give me a minute," Matt mumbled.

"Of course, darling. Relax. You've had a long drive. You're tired. Let me give you a back rub like I used to."

Matt turned over on his belly. Wendy straddled him and kneaded the tired muscles of his back. Her touch was loving. She had no way of knowing that it wasn't having the desired effect. Matt felt chilled, quite specifically cold; his groin was icy, his penis limp. You win, Kathleen! His teeth drew blood from his upper lip.

Before his failure could be once again revealed, there was a knock at the door. It was Matt's hotel room, so he put on a robe and answered it while Wendy went in the bathroom. But it was Wendy that the young woman at the door wanted to see. She looked very grave.

Wendy came out. The young woman crossed to meet her and took both of Wendy's hands in hers. "It's your father," she said. "He's had a heart attack. A bad one."

The blood left Wendy's face. Her eyes were searching. "He—he's not—?"

"I'm sorry." The young woman swallowed hard. "He is, Wendy. He's gone."

"No!" Wendy crumpled to the edge of the bed. "Oh, God, no!" Tears ran down her pale cheeks. "No!"

44

FITZ CONNELY LEVELED his eyes at Paddy Corcoran over the "suds in your eyes, lads" head on the beer that Paddy was drinking. "Don't say no until you hear the whole of the proposition."

The floor was covered with sawdust, and there was a saltwater breeze coming through the door of the old-fashioned Rockaway Irishtown pub where Corcoran had told Fitz he'd be able to meet him if it was that-all urgent as Fitz said it was. Corcoran had business in the Rockaways, a delicate matter of deciding the type of housing the city might underwrite for its seaside town and for the welfare cases it had been dumping there for more than twenty years. The issue was a hot potato with the community split between putting up badly needed low-cost units for the homeless poor and erecting middle-class housing that might upgrade the badly deteriorating area and reverse the slumward drift. There was little profit either way, and Corcoran was alone among the major contractors in his willingness to take on the project.

Paddy Corcoran had grown up in the area, up at the Far Rockaway end of the peninsula on a block between St. Mary's Church and St. Joseph's Hospital. "That was forty years ago," he'd explained to Fitz. "I was taught by the nuns, and my hands are still swollen from the smack of their ruler. The Rockaways were a garden to grow in then, and I owe the area whatever help to come back to its own that it's in my power to give."

His piece said, Paddy Corcoran blew the suds from his beer, scowled at the Coke Fitz was drinking, and drank off half the beaded amber in the old-fashioned tankard on the scarred wooden table before him. They were seated in the back of the pub where the sawdust was thickest and the light too dim to tell tales of how many drinks a man had. Setting down the tankard, Paddy asked Fitz bluntly what he'd wanted to see him about.

"The Stockwell East Side development project," Fitz told him. "Would you still be interested in taking it on?"

"Thanks no, lad. I had a bellyful of that one."

"Don't say no. Not until you hear the whole of the proposition." Fitz said it then. "It's a whole new deal I'm talking about."

"There's only one deal on the island of Manhattan. The mob writes the ticket, and City Hall stamps it."

"This will be different, Paddy. I promise you."

"You promise me?" To Paddy Corcoran Fitz was only a man who had once been a laborer on one of his jobs and was now on the run from the Immigration Department. "And just who are you to be promising me anything?"

"I'm the man whose line of work is being rich." Fitz reminded him of their last conversation.

"I am glad for your fortune, lad. Still, like the feller says, there's rich and there's rich."

"Very rich."

Paddy Corcoran looked up sharply at Fitz's tone. "Bragging is it?" he asked.

"Fact is what it is. A large part of the Stockwell estate has fallen into my lap."

"Has it now." Paddy Corcoran whistled low. "And how would such a thing come about for a lad like yourself?"

"Wrong side of the blanket and right side of the ledger."

"Well, congratulations, then." Paddy Corcoran raised his tankard high. "All drink to bastardy."

"Blood is blood." Fitz drained his Coke. "I'm more or less on the board of directors of Stockwell Enterprises," he told Paddy Corcoran with a grin.

"More? Or less?"

"Well, there's a feller represents me. Halsey De Vilbiss. But he's my man."

"Takes his orders from you, does he?" Corcoran inquired idly.

"Balks, but I'm breaking him to the saddle. A handy feller no more to be trusted than the distance you might throw a feather. Still, he knows a lot, and money making money is what he knows best. I can replace him if I want. With myself if I've a mind. But so far that's not necessary. He's backed the wrong horse on the board, you see, and so Mr. Halsey De Vilbiss is all too grateful to shelter in my paddock for the time being."

"There's a reason you're telling me all this, I suppose."

"I just want you to know that no matter who acts for me, I am my own man. And I can pull strings as far as Stockwell Enterprises is concerned."

"You're telling me then that these strings are tied to the big East Side project," Paddy Corcoran noted carefully. "But the word around town is that for one reason or another that operation is on the shelf."

"True. But perhaps only temporarily. It can be moved off the shelf for the right man with the right plan."

"And what is it happened to the original plan?"

"It self-destructed, you might say."

"I see." Paddy Corcoran hoisted his shillelagh of a fist, and the barman up front drew another tankard of froth-topped beer and brought it to him. "So what is there left, then?" he asked Fitz after he'd drawn off the head with an inward breath.

"There's the land," Fitz told him softly, his eyes glittering. "There's the land left, Paddy, and Stockwell Enterprises is wondering what to do with it now. I got their

agreement to give me sixty days to come up with a sub-
stitute plan before they are forced to sell it and do little
better than break even with inflation on their investment."

"The land." Paddy Corcoran smiled.

"It's what you said a developer needed in Manhattan
to put up decent housing for ordinary people at a livable
profit."

"Now I did say that, didn't I?" His broad middle finger, splayed by more than one misplacement of hammer
to nail, traced a speculative pattern on the tabletop. "Sixty
days for a plan, you say?"

"That's right."

"Forty-eight acres on the East River," Paddy Corcoran
remembered. "Matching funds for landfill. Or," he
thought to ask, "was that only available to the original
developers?"

"Stockwell Enterprises will still stand behind the project, Paddy. Our New York City lawyers employ Albany
lawyers and Washington lawyers to see to it we get all
the government funding the law allows."

"It's them that worries me, the lawyers. Ventriloquist
dummies for business is all I've ever found them to be.
And business says build tall and small and thin between.
Call it a condo and sell, don't rent."

"Not this time, Paddy," Fitz assured him. "This time
we scale down. We build less but broader. No hotel. No
office building. Strictly rental housing from low to lower
middle and no higher."

"You're dreaming, lad."

"Oh, yes. That I am. But I've got me some muscle to
make the dreams come true." Fitz grinned. "Twelve-inch
concrete floors, Paddy." He whispered it to him the way
a streetwalker murmurs to a prospective customer.
"Plumbing by the code. Your own subcontractors with
nobody looking over your shoulder when you pick them."

"Ah, lad, I'm too old for such erections." Paddy Corcoran smiled back wickedly, the double entendre all too

deliberate. "But what about the mob?" he asked. "How will they let such a fairy tale come to pass?"

"This one time they've agreed to keep their hands off."

"Now how would they ever agree to a thing like that?"

"It was a case," Fitz told him, "of us and them having each other by the short hairs. Certain organization people didn't go to jail, and the Stockwell name is left smelling clean as the dew on the heather at dawn."

"And the politicians? Will they sit still for what you're proposing?"

"They have no choice. Some have been paid off." Fitz shrugged. "It's a less than perfect world, and when was it ever different?"

"That's the truth of it."

"And those that haven't—well, Paddy, you might say there's incriminating paperwork on them which inclines them to be charitable."

"You're serious, then. But what about later? What about the rents?"

"Stipulated to an income-cost-of-living formula and no more."

"And Stockwell Enterprises will agree to this?" Paddy Corcoran was still disbelieving.

Fitz smiled mysteriously. "I've persuaded them to take the long view."

"Meaning what?"

"Meaning less immediate profits, but spread out over a longer period."

"In today's money market?" Paddy Corcoran narrowed his eyes over the emptied tankard. "Why would they do a thing like that?"

"Someone leaned on them."

"Someone? What someone?"

"Why, the man who'll do the building, of course."

"The man who'll—" Paddy Corcoran sat back in his chair and looked at the dark young man facing him. "Me," he realized. "You mean me. You're saying I leaned on them."

"I'm very much afraid you did, Paddy."

"You're a black Irishman and a pirate."

Fitz nodded. "A bad lot all around."

"And just how did I lean on them?" Paddy Corcoran wanted to know. "Just how did the likes of me lean on the almighty likes of Stockwell Enterprises?"

"You knew things, Paddy. Things about someone named van Huyck and someone else named Victor Grieg. But you promised to be very discreet if—"

"If I got to build this project and got to build it my way." This time Paddy Corcoran pounded on the table for another beer. "Well, I'll be damned."

"You'll be blessed," Fitz contradicted him.

"You've made me a blackmailer." Paddy Corcoran's expression was ferociously pleased. "I'll do it, but that's the truth of it. You've turned me into an extortionist."

"It's only business, Paddy. Only business as usual, New York City style."

"Well, for the short time you've been here, you've certainly learned fast. Business is it? Well, I can only hope for you, lad, that you're half as successful in love."

"Ah, Paddy, it's hoping in vain you are." Fitz sighed. "Business is easy, but love is something else again. I've no talent for it at all."

And although his meeting with Paddy Corcoran had gone successfully, Fitz Connely left feeling sad and depressed and unable to stop himself from thinking about Patrice.

45

PATRICE SAT IN the cool dimness of the posh Beekman Place cocktail lounge and sipped at a negroni as she waited for her brother Matt. Before she'd arrived, strolling from Saks Fifth Avenue to the East Side, the premature summer heat wilting the bow of the light gray blouse she was wearing with her dotted silk-cotton skirt, Patrice had fantasized a taller drink than the negroni she was now drinking, one sour and beading over ice. The calendar said May, but the thermometer said August-in-New-York, and you could have cut the air with a knife if you weren't too squeamish about what was exposed.

Once inside the watering hole, however, aggressive air-conditioning had prompted Patrice to slip her jacket back on over her shirt and to opt for the negroni—alcoholically potent with eye-opening bitters—over fizz and lemon and ice. It was tingling through her smoothly, and she was just considering ordering another when Matt entered the bar. She half stood and gestured, mouthing his name until he saw her and waved back and told the maître d' he'd located his party. He started toward her with that loose-jointed, awkward gait that had always made Patrice feel protective and tender toward him.

"Hi." Matt enveloped her small hands with his long, callused fingers.

"Hi, stranger." Patrice stood to be kissed.

"Waiting long?" Matt folded his angular frame and squeezed in beside her on the banquette.

"Long enough to have one of these"—Patrice held up her empty cocktail glass—"and to be ready for a second."

336

"I'll order a double to stay even with you."

"Sure. Drown your sorrows." Patrice signaled the waiter. "It's the only way to cope with our Stockwell legacy—star-crossed in love from puberty to menopause."

"I don't think the score's quite in yet on male menopause," Matt responded when the waiter had taken their drink order and departed.

"Whatever, then. Set your own boundaries on amorous misery."

"Set my own boundaries? I can't even figure out my own feelings." Matt scowled. "If 'Know thyself' was the best the ancient Greeks had to offer, then it's tragedy tonight and every night for yours truly."

"It's bad enough mixing metaphors without mixing Sondheim with the classics." Patrice lifted the negroni the waiter set in front of her. "And feeling sorry for yourself will get you absolutely nowhere. Take it from one who knows."

"Still carrying the torch for Jack, sis?" Matt's tone was not unsympathetic.

"I'm not sure," Patrice answered honestly. "I'm miserable, but I don't know that I'm still carrying the torch. I actually may have learned my lesson. The next time Jack snaps his fingers I think I'll be smart enough not to come running."

"Well, that's progress."

"I guess so. But it's a long way from happiness."

"You're a very attractive woman, sis. There are other men. You'll connect with one of them." Matt squeezed her hand.

"Actually, I almost did." Patrice sighed. "It was just before my lemming leap to St. Martin. Things were moving right along. Romance at the boiling point and all that. Then one night I saw my new guy coming out of Buffy's room. I flipped out. We had words. That was just before I left. And since I've come back, Fitz hasn't really shown much interest."

"Fitz Connely!" Matt went pale with anger under his usual leathery tan.

"Yes. He seems awfully damn busy these days. Or maybe he's just lost interest." Patrice stopped talking as she noticed the expression on her brother's face.

Matt couldn't suppress his fury. "All I know is that your Irish rover covers a lot of ground. While you and Buffy were in St. Martin, he was making it with Kathleen."

"Are you saying that he and Kathleen—? But how could you know that?"

"Kathleen told me. That's how."

"She told you they made love? She and Fitz?"

"You've got it."

"Oh." Was that the reason for Fitz's seeming lack of interest in her? Was he involved with Kathleen? Patrice signaled the waiter for another negroni. "Well, I guess he's entitled to like them young."

"Young and freckled." Matt nodded to the waiter that he, too, was ready for a refill.

"I suppose it's better for my ego than losing out to Buffy," Patrice decided. "Young and freckled, that is. As opposed to mature and irresistible."

"I'm glad one of us still has an ego left."

"Poor Matt. Are you going to get together with Wendy again, then?" Patrice wondered if the child Matt and Wendy had parented together would push him in that direction.

"No." His answer was firm.

"You're still in love with Kathleen."

Matt's silence confirmed it.

Patrice had known her brother all his life. She felt his pain now as keenly as her own. "You really wanted her to marry you. Her rejecting you must really hurt."

"She didn't reject me." Matt's features hardened. "I rejected her."

"Well, if she and Fitz are lovers—"

"I don't really know if they still are," Matt admitted.

Patrice pulled the ribbon of her blouse, and the bow came undone. "Well, if it's over, if Kathleen had an affair with Fitz and now it's in the past, if that's the case, and she's not rejecting you, then why do you want to reject her?'' Patrice retied the bow.

''I trusted her.''

''But didn't it happen after you broke up with her?'' Patrice asked.

''No. Yes. I mean, she broke up with me, but I figured it was just a hassle and we'd make it up. I never figured she'd jump into bed with the first guy who came along.''

And Fitz, Patrice realized, very probably had been the first man who came along. It wasn't hard to see what must have happened. Kathleen had been bitter at Matt, angry at his ongoing involvement with Wendy, probably a little sexually frustrated, and then along came Fitz. Was it really so different from her own reactions when she'd almost gone to bed with Fitz herself? Patrice sighed. ''Maybe it was just the one time,'' she suggested to her brother.

''Maybe.'' Matt shrugged. ''What difference would that make?''

''Well, it shouldn't earn her a scarlet letter.'' Now Patrice was starting to get angry.

''You don't understand, sis.'' Matt drained his drink. ''The thing of it is that Kathleen was a virgin before . . .'' His voice trailed off.

''Before Fitz?'' Patrice misunderstood.

''No.'' Matt's voice was very low. ''Before me.''

''I don't believe this!'' Patrice twisted the bow savagely. ''Are you for real, Matt? Or are you some kind of lord of the manor decreeing chastity belts in the sixteenth century? You—what's the word? deflowered, that's it— you deflowered Kathleen. Presumably she did not find the experience unpleasant. Then, after you two had split up, she repeated the pleasurable act with someone else. And now you're making that your reason for not getting back together with her? What are you, running for ayatollah of the Hudson River Valley?''

Matt looked at his sister in surprise. ''What are you so mad about?''

''You, you dumbhead. You and your nauseating morality. You're right, though. You shouldn't forgive Kathleen. For her sake you shouldn't. You shouldn't get back together with her. She hasn't done anything to deserve a fate like that.''

''You think I overreacted, huh?''

''Overreacted? Oh, no. You're just making man's last stand for the double standard is all.'' None too steadily, Patrice lurched to her feet. ''I'm leaving, little brother. Pay the check. That's man's role, isn't it?''

''Hey! Where are you going?'' Matt called after her.

''To a nunnery, little brother,'' Patrice called back. ''I am getting me to a nunnery and inviting Kathleen to join me so we can organize all the good sisters against assholes like you!''

46

KATHLEEN PINED FOR Matt, but she was honest with herself, too. If that relationship was truly never to be, there would be some other man to fill her needs. She wasn't a woman to wither on the vine.

She had sinned. She was Catholic. She felt guilty. She repented. And if forgiveness from Matt was denied her, redemption was not.

''Marriage on the back burner is it?'' Her father, Kevin O'Lunney, stood four square behind her. ''Well now, isn't it just like the almighty Stockwells to botch their chance to improve the strain.''

He slid on his back under the Rolls-Royce Silver Cloud. Kathleen was perched on a tool cabinet handing him various wrenches and taking them back as he requested. She was wearing a tattered pair of jeans, her red hair was tied back in a careless knot, and there was a streak of motor oil demarcating the freckles on her cheek.

Kathleen didn't answer her father. She was grateful for his support. But she didn't want to talk about the ending of her marriage plans or of her relationship with Matt. It was too fresh a scab to be picked at. She didn't even want to think about Matt Stockwell.

And then, as she was determinedly not thinking about him, she looked up and her green eyes were filled with the sight of him. Matt was standing in the open garage doorway with the verdant summer backdrop of the Riverview estate silhouetting him like the hero back from the wars in some Hollywood Technicolor epic from the heyday of the silver screen. Lean in the work clothes he always wore around his horse farm, Matt stood there awkwardly, his angular face nervous with the fear of rejection as he stared back at Kathleen.

"A number-four washer," Kevin O'Lunney requested from under the Rolls.

Matt opened his mouth, but no words came out. Nor could Kathleen find any words to greet him.

"It's a number-four washer I'm asking you for, Kathleen," Kevin repeated with mild irritation from where he was wedged behind the muffler of the limousine.

Automatically, not taking her eyes off Matt, Kathleen fished out a washer and reached under the chassis to hand it to her father. "What are you doing here?" Her tongue addressed Matt with no prompting from her mind.

"I had to see you."

"Why?"

"I met my sister Patrice for cocktails yesterday afternoon," he blurted out.

"This is a number three," Kevin called out, irritated. "I said a number four, Kathleen."

"Sorry." She took the washer from the hand poking at her ankle and replaced it with another. "Your sister Patrice?" She was bewildered by Matt's words.

"We talked about things. About us. You and me. Pa-

341

trice could see I was unhappy, and of course she knew why.''

''And isn't this a number five, Kathleen?''

''I can't tell them apart. Here. Take the tray.'' Kathleen handed her father the tray of screws, nuts, and washers.

''Who would that be you're talking with?''

''It's Matt, Dad. Matt Stockwell.''

''Matt Stockwell is it?'' Kevin laid the tray of screws down beside the oil pan and cocked his head to listen.

''So you had drinks with your sister, and you talked about us.'' Kathleen strained to keep her voice even, to keep it from betraying the hurt she still felt, the hurt Matt had inflicted when he'd rejected her. ''Is that what you came to tell me?''

''Patrice thinks I'm behaving like a prig. She thinks I'm unreasonable. Chauvinist, too.''

''Patrice loves you for a brother, but sees you as a man. Still, there was a time I could have lived with the chauvinist. It's the property-holder judge rejected me, and he's the one I don't think I ever could have over me as a husband.''

''Are you still involved with Fitz Connely?'' Matt couldn't stop himself from asking.

''I was never involved with him. We made love the one time, and that was it.''

There are some things, Kevin O'Lunney thought to himself under the Rolls-Royce, that a daughter's father would rather not know.

Matt took a deep breath. ''The hell with it,'' he said. ''Let's put it behind us, Kathleen.''

''Are you forgiving me now?''

''Well, yes—''

''And if it had happened twice instead of only the once?'' Kathleen asked.

Matt frowned. ''I want to put it behind us.''

''Or three times? What do you suppose if it had happened three times? Or more?''

''All I want to do is forget it happened at all. I want us to get married.''

342

"And if there had been more than the one man, then you wouldn't want us to get married?" Kathleen's green eyes were unrelenting.

"Why are you saying these things, Kathleen?" Matt was truly bewildered as well as hurt.

"Haven't I had time to think, Matt? Didn't you give me time when you walked away from me? And what could I think but that what I did wasn't so terrible. It wasn't anything men don't do all the time. It wasn't anything you haven't done yourself. A one-night stand and no regrets. That's all it was. But you acted as if I should run right on down to the train station and throw myself under the wheels of the Moscow express."

"I never—"

"That's just how you *acted*, Matt. Your eyes gave me back a fallen woman. And let me tell you something: I won't be anybody's fallen woman. I won't be forgiven. Do you understand me? I won't be forgiven and marched to the altar."

"Hell!" Matt burst out. "I don't forgive you! I can't forgive you! Yeah, I know it's chauvinist, and I know I don't have the right. I can't help it. Your going to bed with Fitz Connely hurts. It did then, it does now, and it probably always will."

"Is that what you came here for, then? To tell me that?"

"In a way. I came to tell you I want us to get married. But I don't think we should start out with any lies between us. No matter how harsh or unfair, we should start out with the truth."

"The truth?" Kathleen faced him, hands on hips and freckled chin jutting. "Well then, what about Wendy MacTavish? What about your trips to Montreal? Do you expect me to marry you and sit home and play wife while you go north down Memory Lane twice a month or more?"

"That's over. Completely over."

"Over?" Kathleen was taken aback by his absolute tone. "What are you saying to me now? What about Bruce? What about your son?"

"Wendy and I have worked out a schedule. Bruce will be spending a lot of time at the farm here with me—with us, I hope."

"And his mother won't be with him?" Kathleen was dubious.

"That's right. Wendy will be in Montreal. Anything the two of us have to decide about Bruce we can do by mail, or over the phone. I don't expect we'll have to see each other at all."

"What about Wendy's father, then? Wasn't he the one so sick he couldn't be upset by his grandson coming down here to see you?"

"Wendy's father had another heart attack, Kathleen. This one was too much. He died."

"Oh." Kathleen was taken aback. "Well, I'm sorry for Wendy's trouble." Despite her mixed feelings about Wendy MacTavish, Kathleen was sincere.

"There are no more obstacles to our getting married," Matt told her. "I love you, and I'll always cherish you. What do you say? Do you love me, Kathleen? Will you marry me?"

"I do love you."

"Oh, baby. . . ." Matt took a step toward her.

"But I shouldn't marry you." Kathleen held up her hand to keep him away. "Honest as you are about your righteous, jealous feelings, I'd be crazy to marry you." She lowered the hand. "But I will." She held out her arms to him. "I will marry you, Matt. Crazy or not, I love you and I'll marry you."

Under the Rolls-Royce, Kevin O'Lunney stopped holding his breath. Glory be! he thought. And then—I suppose I'll have to rent a monkey suit now so's to stand up with the Stockwell toffs and give the bride away. Well, rented or not, chauffeur's daughter or not, it's too good for them she is, and that's a fact!

344

47

THE WEDDING TOOK place at summer's end. The marriage was performed at Manhattan's renowned Gotham Memorial Church—sometimes known as "the Stockwell church" because its Italianate marbled majesty had been endowed in perpetuity by Jonathan Braithwaite Stockwell, the father of Governor Stockwell. Officiating was the Reverend Malcolm Darrow Cabot, "the Stockwell minister," who sustained the souls of New York Protestant high society by relieving them of charitable contributions at every opportunity.

By Stockwell standards it was a modest ceremony. Of course certain luminaries had to be invited, and of course Stockwell prestige dictated that they should attend. Thus Wall Street and Washington rubbed elbows while the incumbents of City Hall and the Statehouse pretended to an amiability above politics, and the UN representatives of Great Britain and Argentina put the width of the cathedral between them and tried not to think of the Falkland Islands. A Metropolitan Opera soprano sang "O Promise Me," a string quartet on loan from the Boston Symphony played Mendelssohn, and Ravi Shankar rendered a tone poem on his sitar especially written for the occasion.

Zelig Meyerling, greeting cabinet members for the family, looked as if he had been born to a cutaway. The groom himself, however, looked uncomfortable in his formal attire. And Kevin O'Lunney, feeling like a gooney bird squeezed into a penguin suit, huddled to one side with Berkley and Gustav Ulbricht, the gardener, as well as the other Riverview servants until it was time for him to escort the bride down the aisle.

Kevin was even more uncomfortable after the ceremony was over. That was when he climbed into the back—the back, mind you!—of a chauffeured limousine for the ride back to Riverview, where the wedding reception was being held. He found himself sharing the car with James Stockwell, who had flown in for his son's wedding from Europe, where he now lived. During the years between the death of Governor Matthew Adams Stockwell and James Stockwell's retirement, Kevin had served as James's personal chauffeur. And now James sensed Kevin's discomfiture. He put his hand on Kevin's shoulder and squeezed it. "I could not be more delighted in my daughter-in-law," he told Kevin sincerely. "My son is a very lucky young man."

The "harrumph" of James's brother Jonathan, who was also sharing the limousine with them, was an acknowledgment of defeat. The Stockwell marriage to a chauffeur's daughter was now a fait accompli. He would simply have to live with it.

There had—with more hope than faith—been a place saved in the limousine for another member of the family. But David Lewis had not come to the wedding, and he would not come to the reception. As far as he was concerned, this was not an occasion for the burying of grudges. He had not forgiven Matt for running away to Canada to avoid the draft, and he never would.

Otherwise, the Stockwell clan was generally delighted with the marriage. Holly Meyerling thought Kathleen a fine, intelligent young woman, and Zelig's snobberies were as always reserved for his intellectual and political—not social—inferiors. Michael Stockwell, the congressman, regarded his brother Matt's marriage into the working class as a positive step in his own democratic image; it might one day translate into votes. And while Peter Stockwell was really rather disinterested in the nuptials, his mother, Ellen, was secretly pleased to have a new family member whose origins might be considered even

346

more lowly than her own. The Tylers—Max, Diana, Carrie, and her twin, Beth, who was also one of those who had flown in for the wedding—all liked Kathleen and Matt and approved the match. And Patrice had of course gladly given her brother her blessing along with a sisterly lecture regarding his tendency toward chauvinism. Jack and Buffy hadn't come to the wedding, but they had sent a lavish gift of imported, signed-in-the-stone Limoges china. Fitz had attended the ceremony, but, Patrice was glad to note, he had positioned himself discreetly in the rear of the church. Later, at Riverview, Matt had been civil to Fitz on the receiving line, but not overly friendly.

Because of the more than two hundred limousines that had lined the parkway from Manhattan to Riverview, the receiving line had been late getting started. Matt whispered to Kathleen that his stomach was growling as the guests filed past them to bestow their good wishes and then passed on into the main-floor ballroom where—under Berkley's tyranny—the caterers had set up groaning boards of hors d'oeuvres and a cocktail bar. In addition, perhaps twenty waiters in livery circulated among the guests with trays of beluga caviar and bite-sized hot provender as well as a variety of cocktails. Later a full eight-course dinner would be served in the upstairs ballroom.

On the verandah a forty-piece orchestra played for those who wished to dance. Patrice took her drink outside and watched the dancers. She felt confidently attractive in her ankle-length, off-the-shoulder, peach-colored satin jacquard with its pearlized embroidery bow at one hip, but—disconcertingly—nobody asked her to dance. She removed her eyeglasses and patted down her wavy chestnut hair.

"It won't help." Carrie materialized beside her, leggy in sky-blue taffeta, jiggly in a sparse-cut bodice sans bra. "It's the curse of feminism. Now it's the men who are the sex objects, and don't they just love it."

"I don't agree with that even a little bit."

"Yes, well, I'm probably just bitter. All the goddamn loving couples around us." Carrie's sweeping gesture took in the bride and groom, who had just come on the dance floor to a tarantara of trumpets. "And a dearth of unattached men. Have you noticed?"

"Well, yes," Patrice confessed. "I have."

"Oh, hell! Not enough of a dearth." Carrie had spied Peter Stockwell, looking like a hastily recruited, hastily garbed professional pallbearer, heading toward them.

"Ladies." Peter's teeth overwhelmed his smile of greeting. "Would you like to dance?"

"Awkward." Carrie deliberately misunderstood. "Six feet tripping all over each other, chins fighting for a shoulder to rest on."

"Will you excuse us, Patrice?" As if solving the problem Carrie had posed, Peter led her firmly to the dance floor, leaving Patrice behind and laughing at the moue Carrie made at her behind Peter's back.

On the dance floor, Peter was masterful, which was not the same thing, Carrie could have told him, as being a good dancer. "You know," he murmured in her ear, his words unconsciously picking up the beat of the rumba they were dancing, "I think about that—umm—interlude of ours a lot."

"Interlude?" Carrie drew a blank.

"The time we made love. You know."

"Oh. Yes."

"It was great. Really great."

"Great," Carrie echoed, sliding her thigh into his groin as the only way to keep her ankle from being crunched under his foot.

"We really were in sync."

"Like Laurel and Hardy," Carrie murmured.

"What?"

"Nothing." She became aware that Peter's hand had slid slyly down under cover of responding to the music and his fingers were digging into the taffeta covering her left buttock.

"You really turned me on." Peter consciously expanded his chest against her bobbling bodice. "You still do."

Carrie considered. She had not made love to anybody since the sailor in Marigot. It was the longest period of time she had gone without sex since her early adolescence. Ever since she'd come back to New York she'd been feeling libidinous in a free-floating way, but she somehow hadn't done anything about it.

Of course Peter was a nerd. But he was a man. He was a terrible lover, but there were ways of improving his performance. It might even be looked upon as a challenge. His hot breath in her ear actually aroused her. His words, however, did not.

"You know, we'd make quite a team," he was murmuring. "I don't just mean in bed."

"What do you mean?" Carrie asked.

"Well, are you absolutely satisfied with how Max is handling your portfolio?"

"I never thought about it."

"Would you be willing to discuss it?" Peter's tongue flicked her lobe as if by accident as he spoke softly into her ear.

"Discuss it?"

"Yes. Like right now." They were at a corner of the mansion, half-concealed by the bushes. He was grinding against her, belly to belly, the music forgotten.

Despite herself, Carrie's breathing quickened. "Where?"

"We could go upstairs to my room." His hairy knuckles pressed hard against the bare rising half-moon of her breast.

"All right."

"We could—you know." He started to lead her back inside the mansion. "And then we could take a look at your holdings."

"My holdings," Carrie repeated.

"Sure. I'm not being conceited when I say I'm an expert in that department. Why, I'm almost as good at finance as I am at making love."

That brought Carrie up short. The memory of the last time she'd made love to Peter came flooding back to her.

349

And now, she realized, he was trying to use what he considered his sexual irresistibility as a means of driving a wedge between her and Max for his own financial purposes. Incredible! "That"—she disengaged herself from the arm he had around her waist—"is what I'm afraid of." She turned and started to walk away.

"Hey? What's the matter?"

"I changed my mind."

"But what about—you know."

"My portfolio wouldn't be worth it to you, Peter. Believe me."

"What do you mean?"

Carrie paused in her flight and beckoned him to her. "Lean down," she purred, "so I can whisper to you."

Peter obliged.

"I've got herpes," she murmured in his ear.

His jaw dropped. He watched Carrie as she walked away from him. He was still standing there watching a moment later as she rejoined Patrice.

"Hi," Patrice greeted her. "What happened to Peter?"

"He made me an offer I could refuse."

"A sexual offer?" Patrice was surprised. "Meaning no insult, but that's not like you, Carrie."

"Well," Carrie replied, "it suddenly seemed to me that even being alone without a man might be better than settling for Peter."

Patrice smiled. "You are growing up."

"Maturing," Carrie agreed ruefully. "Getting older."

"Older but wiser," Patrice assured her. "Older but wiser, Carrie."

Time moves on, the irresistible tide, the current that can buoy one up or drown one but, in either case, inexorably carries one along. Patrice, too, was older. But am I any wiser? she wondered. And if I am, what has that to do, after all, with happiness? When did wisdom ever make anybody happy?

Carrie had gone in pursuit of a waiter with a tray of cocktails. Patrice was standing, momentarily, alone among the wedding celebrants. The light touch of the hand on

350

her bare shoulder was electric even before she turned to confirm who it was. When she did, her hand fumbled for the bow at her hip in the same way that an infant on waking gropes for the fuzzy blanket that is its security.

"Hello, Fitz."

"Top o' the nuptial day to you, Patrice."

"How are you?" There was no more real security in banality than in the bow, but Patrice asked the question anyway. She tilted her head and forced herself to look up directly into his dark, expressive face.

The deep-set eyes looked back at her seriously, the mischievous pirate who usually lurked in their depths evidently on shore leave. "I am well, but lonely, don't you know."

"Surely that's by choice." Patrice tried to be flip, but the tremor in her voice tripped her up. "There's no reason you should lack for company, Fitz, particularly female company."

"You mean because I'm such a shallow fellow with such superficial charm?" His reaction was harsh.

It took Patrice by surprise. "I didn't mean—"

"I think you did." He glowered at her. "You've not made any secret of the kind of feller you believe Fitz Connely to be."

"I don't spend a whole lot of time thinking about you at all," Patrice retorted, feeling unjustly attacked.

"Yes, you do." His eyes held hers. "There may be no flattery in your opinion of me, but you do think of me, and there's the fact of it."

"I don't think it's a good idea to ruin my brother's wedding day by standing here and having an argument when I don't even understand what it is we're arguing about." Patrice drew herself up with a petite dignity, gathered the peach satin folds of her jacquard skirt, and started to move away.

"You've a point there." Fitz spoke quickly to keep her from leaving. "A time for dancing is it?" In his formal clothes, his obeisance was slightly comic. "Will you do me the honor, ma'am?"

"All right," Patrice relented, taking the arm he offered and allowing him to lead her to the dance floor.

They danced in silence for a while. The orchestra, catering to the older Stockwells and their hallowed guests, leaned toward slow fox trots from the forties, the big-band repertoire without the big-band pizzazz. Responding to the rhythms, however, Patrice felt the tension leave her.

Her head, with its crown of silky red-brown hair, nestled comfortably in the crook of Fitz's wide shoulder. The curves of her small, compact body adapted themselves easily to the rough-hewn muscle and bone of his lanky frame as they moved together. Indeed, dancing with Fitz felt as if she had come home. There was a lulling comfort in the gentle sway and warmth in his arms.

When the set was over, she looked up at him inquiringly. He smiled at her and ran his fingers through his dark, curly hair. Like Patrice, he didn't want to relinquish the closeness of the dance, but— "It's the lads' break." He stated the obvious. "They've stopped playing."

"I'm thirsty." Patrice found a ploy. "Could we have a drink?"

Fitz grinned, approving her use of the plural. "I'll fetch you some of the champagne punch, and myself a whiskey-soda without the whiskey and meet you by the rose trellis. It'll be cooler drinking in the garden."

She was waiting for him when he brought the drinks. She sipped hers and smiled at him tentatively. He smiled back.

"About before," Fitz started to say. "I'm sorry I was so—"

"I wanted to tell you that I approve—"

They had both started to speak at the same time, and both stopped. Patrice laughed. "You first," she said.

"No, you."

"All right. I just wanted to tell you that I think it's wonderful how you've salvaged the river project and turned it into something so very worthwhile."

352

"Well, I am grateful for your support and your vote to allow Paddy Corcoran to go ahead, too."

"You really are having an effect on the board. It's remarkable, considering how short a time . . ."

"And haven't I had an expert to guide me?"

"Halsey De Vilbiss? Well, I've been on the board with Halsey since my father retired, and I've never seen any evidence that he might be interested in building anything useful, or in pursuing any project where he couldn't see an angle to maximize profit for himself. Halsey is just an older and more experienced version of Peter. That's all."

"That isn't all there is to the man at all," Fitz disagreed. "Peter was handed it on the sterling platter. Halsey had to scramble to find the foot in the door to claim a share. Peter may be just as greedy, but it's a long way he has to go before he'll see as clear as Halsey."

"How can you say that? Halsey was Peter's staunchest backer on the East Side development."

"And with nothing to lose, why wouldn't he be? Peter backed him when De Vilbiss wanted to hire his company, that Productivity Insights outfit, to squeeze more work out of the employees. Quid pro quo is it? Sure it cost Halsey nothing to give the nod to Peter's real estate machinations."

"I don't care what you say. I don't trust Halsey De Vilbiss." Patrice was blunt. "I never will."

"Oh, well now, if we're talking about trust, that's a different matter. You don't trust him. Sarah Stockwell Tyler didn't trust him. And I surely don't trust him. Nor did I ever say I did. But I'll use him, same as she did."

"Then you're not going to fire Halsey? You're not going to replace him on the board yourself?" Patrice was disappointed.

"Oh, no. He's very useful to me, he is."

"Because he knows so much about how Stockwell Enterprises operates?"

"Well, that, and also because he keeps everybody else on the board so busy keeping tabs on him they'll have little time to devote to me."

"Well, of all the—!" Patrice sat back on the white-scrolled wrought-iron garden bench and laughed. "But why are you telling me? I'm on the board, too," she reminded him. "Now I'll know to watch you instead of Halsey."

"Well now, anything that will get your attention suits my purpose," he told her softly, and by the teasing warmth in his eyes she knew he was no longer discussing business.

"One more woman's attention." Patrice was blushing in spite of herself. "With all you've gathered, why should that matter to you one way or the other?"

"You're doing it again. What you did when I first came up to you before. Putting me down. Labeling me the trifler and never serious at all."

"Well, I don't know about 'at all.' I only know as concerns myself."

"You think I'm not serious about you, then?" Fitz scowled ferociously.

"You haven't exactly gone out of your way to see me since I came back from St. Martin."

"True. But if there was to be any seeking out, shouldn't it have been you doing the seeking? Considering what you said before you left, I mean."

"Because I saw you coming out of Buffy's room? I don't think I said anything out of line. It was a natural conclusion."

"It was an incorrect conclusion. And didn't I tell you that? And didn't you not believe me and run off to the lady's husband?"

"That's all over," Patrice was quick to tell him. "It really is. And as far as Buffy—well, the truth is I was jealous."

"Jealous is it?" Fitz looked pleased. "Well, there was no need. I told you the truth. Nothing happened."

"Oh? But you aren't always so innocent, Fitz. What about Carrie? What about Kathleen?"

"You've a reason for asking, have you?" Fitz regarded her from eyes that had narrowed.

354

"No." Patrice's blush deepened. "No reason. No right. No excuse. I'm sorry, Fitz. It really is none of my business."

"Well then, just so long as you see that, I'll tell you. Carrie was a fling and without importance. You must have had a fling in your life, Patrice—a meaningless fling?"

"Yes."

"And Kathleen was a mistake. A bad mistake trying to get the taste of you turning away from me out of my mouth. A mistake I regret, and so does she, and one best forgot by all concerned."

"Of course." Patrice felt embarrassed for having mentioned it. After all, it was Kathleen's wedding day.

"It was you I was hungering for, but you were in St. Martin."

"Oh, Fitz!" Patrice was shaken by the intensity of feeling she saw in his eyes.

"But the way it was left, you'd no appetite for me."

"That's not true. I was confused. I didn't know what I wanted."

"That was then. And now?" He held her shoulders firmly but gently and turned her to him. "Do you know what you want now?"

"Yes." Her face told him all he needed to know.

"Well then—" He kissed her.

It was a long kiss. Patrice gave herself up to it completely. And when it was over, still clinging to him, she put what she wanted into words. "I want us to go to Holly's studio over the library now," she said. "We left something undone there. I think we should finish it."

Fitz nodded. He drew her to her feet. Side by side, quickly, they walked toward the north tower of Riverview.

"Hey, Patrice!" Holly saw them walking away and called to her. "Don't go too far. They'll be serving the wedding dinner soon."

"We won't go far," Patrice called back. "We're only going to the library. We'll be right here. Right here at Riverview."

Right here at Riverview, Patrice thought. Right here where it began for all of us—Matt and Kathleen, Holly and Zelig, Jack and Buffy, Peter and his mother, and Uncle David and Max Tyler and Carrie Tyler and—yes—and for Fitz and me, too. Right here at Riverview.

Smiling to herself, she thought of Edith Seabury Stockwell and Charles Stockwell. She thought of Sarah Stockwell Tyler and Governor Matthew Adams Stockwell and all the other Stockwells of Riverview who had gone before. She thought of all the Stockwells past and the Stockwells present of Riverview-on-the-Hudson. She followed Fitz into the library and up the circular lighthouse staircase.

And, fumbling to undo the ubiquitous bow at her hip, Patrice thought of the Stockwells of Riverview yet to come.